CASTLE MAGIC

A CAYNHAM CASTLE COLLECTION

MORGAN BRICE

CASTLE MAGIC
A CAYNHAM CASTLE COLLECTION

eBook ISBN: 978-1-64795-077-4
Paperback ISBN: 978-1-64795-078-1

FOREWORD

I've been very fortunate to be one of the authors in the Caynham Castle series (idea developed by Nancy Northcott and Jeanne Adams) about a fictitious English castle on the Welsh border and its wonderfully quirky town. Together with several other authors, we have published five collections with stories that return to the town and castle for various holidays.

I've written three novellas under my Morgan Brice pen name and two under my Gail Z. Martin name, depending on which series the characters came from. Four of the stories are MM romance, and one is MF romance. This collection includes all four of the MM novellas.

Since this is a multi-author shared world, many of the places and people mentioned were created by others, and the Intellectual Property listing gives credit to the creators. My novellas are reprinted with permission and have reverted from their original publications.

Crewel Fate appeared in *Christmas at Caynham Castle* and features characters from my Deadly Curiosities series written as Gail Z. Martin.

Secrets and Ciphers appeared in *Trick or Treat at Caynham Castle*, featuring characters from my Morgan Brice series Treasure Trail.

Memories and Malice appeared in *Ring in the New at Caynham Castle*, featuring characters from my Morgan Brice Badlands series.

Fae-ted Mates appeared in *Love and Valentines at Caynham Castle* with characters from my Morgan Brice Kings of the Mountain series.

You don't have to be familiar with the origin series to enjoy these novellas since they stand alone. And if you discover new favorite characters, please check out the rest of their home series!

CREWEL FATE
A DEADLY CURIOSITIES NOVELLA

By Gail Z. Martin

CHAPTER ONE
TEAG

I f I'd realized how cute you are when you're excited, I'd have started planning trips like this ages ago," Anthony Benton said, sliding his hand to give Teag's thigh a squeeze. The rumble of the train along the tracks jostled their seats as the English countryside flashed by outside the windows.

"It's my first international trip, and we're in the UK, and we're going to a castle." Teag Logan grinned from ear to ear. "*And*, we're engaged." He couldn't help waggling the fingers on his left hand, where the platinum band with the embedded baguette diamond sparkled as it caught the light, just like the matching ring on Anthony's hand. "Best birthday presents *ever*."

Anthony chuckled, a deep, rich sound that made Teag happy inside. He and Anthony had been a couple for several years, but the proposal had happened just a few months ago, at the birthday party Anthony had thrown for Teag. The party itself—with all their close friends—and the trip to a castle for Christmas would have been amazing enough as a present, but having Anthony pop the question put Teag over the moon.

"I hope you like the castle. Friends of my parents stayed there, and when they talked about the place, I just knew it would be perfect for you," Anthony replied. "And the best part? It's not supposed to be very haunted. So you can really take time off from your *other* job."

Teag reached over and twined his fingers with Anthony's. Anthony was a lawyer in his family's law firm, and he had the blond, broad-shouldered, prep school boy-next-door looks to match. His family was old Charleston money, and Bentons had been living in the tony South of Broad neighborhood since before the Civil War. Teag, on the other hand, came from a solidly suburban middle-class background. His dark hair with its asymmetrical haircut gave him a bit of a skater boy vibe, although he had been close to finishing his Ph.D. in History before a summer job changed his life.

"I'm ready for a break from anything haunted or cursed," Teag swore. He leaned in and whispered confidentially, "And the only thing going bump in the night should be us."

Teag's day job was Assistant Store Manager for Trifles and Folly, an antiques and curio shop in historic, haunted Charleston, South Carolina. The shop had been in business over three hundred years, almost from the founding of the city itself, and had a reputation for fine estate jewelry, silver tea sets, and vintage decorative items. But Trifles and Folly had a secret—and so did Teag. The store's real mission was to get cursed and haunted objects out of the wrong hands and save the world from supernatural threats. Teag's Weaver magic—being able to weave spells into cloth—earned him a place among a small group of allies who kept Charleston—and the world—safe from monsters, dark magic, vengeful ghosts, and much worse.

"I didn't think you'd mind that I skipped booking any ghost tours," Anthony replied. "You'd feel like you were working, and the tour guides would probably be miffed if you banished their source of income."

"I'm totally up for a ghost-free vacation," Teag swore. "Bring on the roasted chestnuts, figgy pudding, hot tea, and partridges in pear trees!"

Despite the overnight flight and early morning, Teag felt as bouncy as a kid on Christmas morning. Anthony had been to Europe several times with his family growing up, but Teag's family's idea of a big vacation involved Disney World or a national park. He'd used his passport for a couple of long weekends in the Caribbean and longed to see the places in person that he had studied in college and grad school, but the circumstances had never seemed right. Until now.

"I'm already thinking that vacations might make the best anniversary presents," Anthony teased. "If I'd have realized you had a touch of wanderlust, I'd have done this before now."

Teag shrugged. "It's not exactly wanderlust as much as I've read so much about certain places—like London—in novels or studied them with my classes that it's exciting to see them for real."

"It makes you happy. That's enough for me." Anthony leaned over to brush a kiss against Teag's temple.

The three-hour train ride to Caynham-on-Ledwyche passed quickly. When he and Anthony weren't comparing thoughts about the things they wanted to see at the castle and in the nearby village, they were people-watching as their fellow travelers made their way to the commissary car for tea, snacks, or sandwiches. Teag could have sworn that even the cold box lunch tasted better because it was part of the adventure.

After the bustle of Heathrow, the clamor of the Tube, and the clatter of Paddington Station, the small platform at Caynham-on-Ledwyche felt quiet and unhurried. Teag hoped that was a sign for the rest of the vacation.

"As soon as we have the luggage, we'll get a cab to the castle," Anthony said, heading toward where the porters were unloading the bags. They each had a medium bag, a small roller bag, and a backpack, and although Teag had gone on longer vacations with less luggage, the cold of a Shropshire winter meant packing heavier clothing as well as bringing a warm coat, hat, scarf, and gloves.

A cab pulled up to meet them as they came to the curb with their luggage. "Caynham Castle," Anthony replied to the driver's question as he loaded the bags into the back.

"You've come at a nice time of year," the man said. He wore a brown tweed cap and a tan canvas jacket, and Teag guessed the man was in his sixties. "Lots to do around here at Christmas. You fellows going to stay for the Ball?"

"We're not sure yet," Teag replied. He and Anthony had talked about the Frost and Flame Ball, which would be just a few days before Christmas. While it sounded like it would be a wonderful event, neither of them were quite sure how open the rest of the guests might be to a same-sex couple joining in on the dance floor.

"Better make up your mind soon," the cabbie advised, stowing the last of their luggage. He climbed into the cab, and they took off with a rumble. Teag figured the vintage cab had to be at least forty years old. "I hear they're almost sold out." He adjusted the visor against the angle of the sun. "My name's Henry, by the way."

"I'm Teag, and this is my fiancé, Anthony." Teag tried not to let a hint of challenge seep into his voice. He could have just stuck to names and left out their relationship. In some situations, that would be the wise thing to do, although he and Anthony had been out and proud all their adult lives. But the new, shiny ring and the excitement of the proposal were too hard to resist. Teag found himself bracing for Henry's reaction.

"Well, congratulations," Henry replied without missing a beat. "If you decide to come back for your honeymoon, ask about one of those tower suites. I hear they're really fancy."

Teag had already pored over the castle's website and had decided to check out the suites if they enjoyed staying at the castle.

"What's your recommendation on things to do around here?" Anthony clasped hands with Teag. Both men looked out the side windows as they drove through town. Teag decided he'd never get used to being on the "wrong" side of the road and tried to stop wincing every time a car passed.

"Well, now. There's the Boar and Knight Pub, which is as fine a place as any you'll find anywhere in Shropshire, I wager," Henry replied. "Good place for a pint or two, and their Shepherd's Pie is tasty. Although, mind your wallet if you decide to play a round of darts with the locals."

"I'll definitely steer clear," Anthony replied with a laugh. He elbowed Teag and shot him a look that Teag interpreted without a problem. *Just because I'm good at throwing knives doesn't mean I'd take on the town's hustlers at darts.*

"If you're looking for a nice bite at tea time, there's the tea shop up at the Castle. It's very good. But the Ewe & Ply—that's a wool shop—has a lovely tea room too. It's worth checking out both," Henry added with a wink. "Can't have too many scones, I always say."

"Oh, wow." Teag couldn't help himself as they drove past the half-timbered shops that looked like something out of a Dickens novel, interspersed with other stores built from brick and stone. The cut-stone parish church stood out, with its bell tower and stained glass windows, anchoring the village for over five hundred years.

"Back in Charleston, we think something's old if it's over three hundred years," Teag murmured. "But a lot of the 'new' stuff here is already older than that!"

"Aye, we often joke that we have furniture layin' about that's older than most of your cities," Henry teased. "All in good fun, of course."

"I can't help feeling like everything should have a velvet rope around it and 'Do Not Touch' signs," Teag confided.

"Now where would be the fun in that?" Henry said with a laugh. "Over at the Boar and Knight, they've been serving up pints to thirsty folks since 1415. Yer lookin' at one of the last two thatch-roofed buildings in the town."

"Oh look, Teag," Anthony chimed in. "Right next to the pub is an antique shop. We can stop by tomorrow."

"I'm on holiday." Teag shook his head. "Not talking shop, remember?"

"If you like old stuff, we've got it," Henry said. "In fact, someone just discovered several needlepoint samplers tucked away in a closet that were done by one of the daughters of the family who owns the castle back in the day. Gave them back so they could be on display. You never know what might be lurking in a drawer or the back of a shelf!"

That is very true, Teag thought, but not in the way Henry thought. In Teag's experience, those tucked away oddities tended to be bad mojo and bad luck.

The town square sat right in front of an old stone bridge across Ledwyche Brook. A tall fir tree adorned with electric lights and baubles stood proudly in the center of the square. Ribbons and evergreen cuttings graced the lampposts, and all the shops they had passed seemed to have gotten the holiday spirit because their windows were bedecked with electric candles or light strings, bunting in red, green, and white, dangling snowflakes and candy canes.

"Now look sharp, boys," Henry said as the car turned from the main road onto the driveway. "We're almost to the castle."

Teag caught his breath as the outer walls came into view. The tall buff-colored stone walls rose high, originally built for defense. Henry drove through the first gate, and both Teag and Anthony murmured when the main castle came into view.

"It's beautiful." Teag took in the thick walls, mullioned windows, and stately towers. "Just like in all the stories."

"Wait 'til you get a chance to explore," Henry told them. "I've brought the missus up here a few times over the years for birthdays and such. Down in the garden, there's what they call a 'folly'—it's a right nice place to sneak a snog," he advised with a wink. "Not to mention the conservatory, which might warm you up a bit with how hot they keep it for those exotic plants and all."

Henry pulled into the car park to the right of the castle. Up ahead, Teag saw where a bridge crossed a dry moat and led through a narrow gateway into the inner bailey.

"I can't go closer—not safe for cars," he told them. "But if you give the front desk a ring to let them know you're here, they'll send out a man with a golf cart to take you and your luggage in." Henry got out and helped pull their bags out of the back.

"Now this is real important," Henry said with a serious expression. "If you two want to make a proper go of things, you need to find the original gargoyle. The legend says that if you kiss in front of the original gargoyle—not just any old one, mind you—that you will find and keep your true love." He gave them a broad wink. "Me, I don't like to take chances, so I say, kiss in front of every gargoyle you see. Better safe than sorry!"

They waved goodbye as Henry drove off, and moments later, a white golf cart headed their way, driven by a teenager wearing a bellman's jacket and hat.

"Welcome to the Castle," the boy said. Teag figured he was probably seventeen, eighteen at the most. "Let me get your bags."

Teag and Anthony helped, and before long they were headed for the check-in office, with the two of them riding in the back seat.

"I'm Patrick," the young man said. "Bellman, cart driver, unplugger of drains, and stomper of spiders—not that we ever need that sort of thing," he added quickly. "But I'm sort of the jack-of-all-trades around here, so if you need something, just give a yell, and it'll probably be me they send."

"Are you from the village?" Teag tried to remember how involved the Mortimer family—the owners of the castle—were with the actually day-to-day-operations.

"Aye. My mum's the manager of the gift shop, has been for thirty years," Patrick said proudly. "She got me a job here because she was afraid clearing tables down at the pub would be a bad influence to my impressionable youth." He turned so they could catch his dramatic eye roll.

"Your mom sounds like a smart woman." Teag laughed.

"She does all right," Patrick agreed. "And Priscilla Donovan, at the front desk, will take good care of you. Keep your eyes sharp, and you might get a glimpse of the earl, Sir Edward Mortimer. He's a busy bloke, what with the castle and a few other businesses and that new microbrewery of his in town. Here's a tip—if you go down to the brewery and you see a fellow behind the counter wearing an apron that says 'Earl,' he's the real deal. But you don't have to bow or nothin'. Not anymore."

"Microbrewery?"

Anthony's ears certainly pricked up at that, Teag thought.

"They say it's pretty good. Not that I'd know myself or nothing, if my mom were to ask," Patrick added.

"I'll stay here with the cart, while you gents check in." Patrick pointed toward the main lobby. "Then come back out, and I'll drive you to your room. We're a bit spread out if you didn't notice."

"I think the room I reserved is on the wall of the inner bailey." Anthony turned to try to orient himself from the map. "Dower apartment area. Second floor."

"Your second floor, or our second floor?" Patrick asked. "There's a difference, you know. You count the ground floor as one, and we don't."

"Um, yours?" Anthony replied, sounding unsure.

"Go get your key, and I'll make sure you get to the right place," Patrick promised.

Teag and Anthony walked into the reception area, and Teag couldn't help swiveling his head from side to side to take in the Mortimer family coat of arms, several flags, and some crossed swords, as well as the rough stone walls and dark wooden check-in counter. Evergreen swags hung from the counter and adorned the doorways. Sparkling electric twinkle lights wrapped around the large fir wreath that hung over the mantle of a huge fireplace, and instrumental Christmas music played in the background.

Anthony stepped up to talk with the vivacious woman behind the desk, whose brown ponytail swished back and forth with every movement. Teag guessed she was Priscilla, and she looked like she could handle any complications that might arise. He really hoped that none did, but already Patrick, Henry, and Priscilla made him feel like they had friends here.

"Priscilla said we should try the tea room for lunch, and then we have a number of places to eat for dinner, including the pub and the microbrewery," Anthony told him.

"This place is wonderful." Teag leaned over to give Anthony a peck on the cheek. "Thank you so much for planning all this."

Anthony's big smile warmed Teag's heart. "I was hoping you'd love it."

"I love *you*. Everything else is icing on the cake."

Patrick took one look at the room number, and then they headed off in the golf cart toward the bridge. "Out here where the gift shop, tea room, and front desk is, that was the outer bailey," Patrick called over his shoulder like a tour guide. "Across the moat and through the gate is the inner bailey, and there's even a private garden near the keep. When the castle got attacked, all the people would fall back to the walled yard, and if things got real bad, to the keep. Like in Lord of the Rings. Only, without orcs."

"And did it get attacked?" Anthony asked.

Patrick nodded vigorously. "Oh, yeah. Back during the War of the Roses and all. Lots more than just that. Goes all the way back to 1282, so you know it's seen some stories in its time."

Teag wondered what his best friend, Cassidy Kincaide, would make of that. She was a psychometric, which meant her magic could read the history of objects by touching them. Museums could give her the willies, and her abilities had unlocked the secrets of more than one historic home back in Charleston. For once, he was glad his gift was unlikely to trigger unless Caynham had haunted tapestries hanging around.

"You'll want to make sure you see the decorations in the Great Hall and the folly," Patrick told them as he trundled their bags into the elevator. "The chapel's nice, too. And of course, everything in town is done up. But if you're going to the Frost and Flame Ball, that's where it'll really be fancy. That big tent in the outer bailey is part of all that."

"We haven't made up our minds yet," Teag said. "But it sounds nice."

"If you decide to go, Priscilla can fix you up with tickets," Patrick assured him. "If there are any left."

Teag and Anthony thanked Patrick and watched him drive away in the cart. Their suite had a bedroom and a living room. The comfortable furnishings were an elegant melding of style and practicality. While Teag doubted that any of the guest rooms were outfitted with valuable antiques, he knew from his work at Trifles and Folly that the eclectic assembly of pieces in their suite spanned several eras. Some were good reproductions, while others were much older. It gave the suite a lived-in feel, with the continuity of pieces being re-used and added to over generations.

"What do you think?" Anthony asked, with an anxious glance, as if he were afraid Teag might be disappointed.

"I think it's perfect." Teag walked up to him and set his hands on Anthony's hips, pulling him in for a kiss. "You're perfect. Everything is perfect."

Just then, Anthony's stomach rumbled loudly. "Lunch would really be perfect," Anthony deadpanned.

Teag gave a wicked glance toward the plump, down comforter on the thick mattress of the four-poster bed. "And I'm thinking that bed is going to be perfect for all kinds of things once we go eat and find our way around."

"Mm. I like the sound of that." Anthony turned in for another kiss, but he couldn't deny his rumbling stomach. "Come on." He tugged Teag by the wrist. "Let's go eat and do some exploring."

The castle's Lady Neville Tea Room was close by, and Teag followed Anthony inside. Monogrammed china cups and saucers sat ready atop white tablecloths. A front counter case held a delectable array of treats, and the chalkboard overhead listed enough varieties of tea to make Teag's head spin.

"Is it too late for high tea?" Teag asked.

"You're just in time," the efficient woman in a taupe twinset replied. "I'm Helen. Follow me." She led them to a table for two in the corner, where they had a good view of the rest of the tea room.

"I hope you're hungry because our high tea is more than a snack," she advised. "First, you pick your tea—one pot per person, so you can each have a different flavor." She placed a sheet of paper in front of them, listing all the teas Teag had seen on the chalkboard.

"First, there are four varieties of tea sandwiches—cucumber, egg salad, cheese and pickle, and smoked salmon. After that, there are the sweets—apricot scones with clotted cream, lemon tarts, macaroons, strawberry jam cake, and the like. Then if you're still hungry, there's a slice of layer cake. We have three varieties—changes each day. Today it's blackberry and coconut cake, chocolate biscuit cake, and a Battenberg cake. Can't really go wrong with any of them," she added.

"It all looks so good." Teag figured they would have to come back several times to try all the specialties. He and Anthony debated over the tea selection, finally choosing a Darjeeling and an Earl Gray.

"I always thought afternoon tea was a little nibble between meals—like a few cookies," Anthony confessed. "We may need to eat a later dinner."

Their early departure and the hours on the train made them more hungry than they had realized, and they made short work of the small sandwiches, slowing only as they came to the end of the sweets.

"I really want the blackberry and coconut cake, but I also want to see what a Battenberg cake tastes like," Teag said. "I've seen those people on the baking show make them, and I'm curious."

"Then let's get one of each," Anthony replied. "They're included, and we don't have to finish them."

"We can walk it all off when we go exploring," Teag agreed with a grin.

When they finally finished, Teag thought he might never need to eat again. They thanked the hostess, assured her they would return, and then headed out to walk the perimeter of the castle walls before checking out the Great Hall.

"Keep an eye out," the hostess said. "You might see our ghost, although she usually only re-enacts her tragic fall from the tower during the summer."

"I knew there had to be one," Anthony said with a chuckle. Teag just groaned.

The cool air helped to settle their food, and when the wind picked up, Teag felt it nip his nose and bite his cheeks. He was glad for the warm gloves, hat, and scarf, things he rarely needed back in Charleston.

"Look how thick the walls are," Anthony remarked. "The oldest buildings back home are like that, too. Built to last."

Teag and Anthony chatted as they walked around the outer bailey and then crossed the bridge back to the inner bailey. Teag eyed the castle architecture and pointed out things he remembered studying when he had been working on his history degree.

"Keeping up with one of the old houses in Charleston is an expensive proposition," Anthony said. "I can't imagine what it's like trying to do the upkeep on a castle, but the Mortimers have done it up nicely."

Without warning, Teag pulled Anthony in for a kiss. He grinned at Anthony's surprise. "Technically, that's a grotesque." He pointed up toward the roof's edge, where a squat stone figure glowered down at them, so ugly it was cute. "If it's a waterspout, it's a gargoyle. If it's just decoration, it's a grotesque. I'm not taking any chances on which one is original." He tapped Anthony on the nose.

When they finally reached the Great Hall, Teag welcomed the

warmth. Everything was done up for Christmas, with evergreen boughs, red ribbons, fairy lights, and gold bells. A huge fir tree nearly reached the ceiling, and Teag could only imagine how much more decorating would happen before the night of the ball.

"It said on the website that the mother of the current earl took that hand-blown glass tree topper down into the air raid shelters during World War II," Teag added. "She said she wasn't going to let the Nazis ruin Christmas!"

"It's pretty fantastic." Anthony slipped an arm around Teag. "Look at that ceiling!"

Teag craned his neck. "It's called 'hammerbeam,' and it's an English Gothic style of open timber roof truss," he said. "See the kind of stuff I remember from my classes?"

Hand-cut beams arched downward at intervals, while still others formed arches along the flat of the timber ceiling, embellished at the corners with intricate woodcutting. It reminded Teag of the ceiling of the great hall in the Harry Potter movies.

"I wish they could really make candles float in the air," Teag said with a sigh. "But I guess twinkle lights are almost as good." He took in a deep breath. "I love the smell of a real Christmas tree."

"And the fireplace looks big enough to roast a boar—or maybe an ox." Anthony nodded toward the huge opening in the stone wall with its carved firebox and ornate mantle. "I could stand up inside and not hit my head. And I bet that if I spread my arms wide, I still wouldn't touch on either side."

"Come on," Teag said. "There's more to see in the solar and conservatory." He led Anthony by the hand out of the Great Hall through an archway into two adjoining glass-enclosed rooms. Christmas lights twinkled in the now-dry central fountain and wrapped around the potted shrubs. Poinsettias, icicles, ribbons, and tinsel turned the greenhouse rooms into a wonderland.

Anthony hauled Teag in for a kiss under a ball of mistletoe tied with a red velvet ribbon. "Turnabout's fair play," he said.

"This is so beautiful," Teag gushed when they headed back through the main hall. "And there are a few of the other rooms open for display if we go this way." He led them toward Bride's Tower, where two sitting rooms on the third floor were decorated and furnished as the castle would have looked during the 1920s. From the colors, fabrics, and scale of the furniture, it was clear that one room was meant for women and the other for men.

"So this would have been the way it locked right around World War I," Anthony mused, reading a sign near the door. "Their *Downton Abbey* period."

"I love that show. So elegant. And the old miniseries we watched of Brideshead Revisited? If I could have tailored suits like those, I might not mind giving up my jeans," Teag gushed.

"Maybe we'll have to throw a Gatsby party for Halloween next year if the spooks give you the night off," Anthony teased. "Just thinking of you turned out like that is giving me all kinds of naughty ideas." He leaned against Teag, brushing his groin against Teag's leg to let him know exactly what kind of thoughts were going through his mind.

"I like the way you think," Teag purred.

The more masculine of the two rooms had dark wood wainscoting and upholstery in rich emerald and sapphire hues. Brass fittings and etched glass shades accentuated the wall sconces and table lamps. Leather-bound books filled the shelves, along with display cases of watches, silver cigar boxes, monogrammed flasks, and a taxidermied lion that was likely a trophy from safari in Africa. It was easy to imagine well-off men sitting down with cigars and good Scotch to discuss the news of the day or play a few hands of cards.

"This is so far beyond 'man cave' I'm not sure what to call it," Anthony remarked. "But I guess it's not that different from what some of the big plantation houses had. For as nice as this is, I'm glad things have changed. I like our friends, and I'd hate to have to split everyone up instead of being able to all hang out together."

The ladies' sitting room had high-backed upholstered couches and wing chairs arranged in conversation groupings, with side tables to hold drinks. The furniture was roped off for display only, and glass covered the bookshelves, protecting both the books and an assortment of family personal items and trinkets from around the world.

Teag felt a pull toward a framed piece of hand-embroidered fabric.

It was a sampler, the kind done by young women learning to practice various stitching and designs, common at the time. But as soon as Teag saw it, he felt traces of the maker's magic, old, faint, and still potent.

"What's wrong?" Anthony laid a hand on Teag's shoulder. "You've got that look."

Teag managed a smile. "Nothing bad. It's just that whoever did that embroidery had my kind of gift. Weaver magic."

"You can pick up on that, after all these years?" A note next to the frame said that the needlepoint had been done by Lillian Mortimer in 1916.

"Uh-huh," Teag replied, distracted as he read the rest of the note-card. "So Lillian was one of two daughters to the Mortimer family who lived in the castle around the time of the First World War. She and her older sister, Mabel, would have been in their late teens or early twenties when the war started. It ran longer over here—the war. In the States, we think of it as just 1918, but it started in 1914 in Europe." He couldn't help being a history nerd, and thankfully, Anthony shared his interest.

"From what we've watched on the History Channel, that war pretty much broke the aristocracy, didn't it?" Anthony replied. "The death toll was so high—wiped out most of an entire generation of men. I can't even begin to imagine what it must have been like."

Teag shivered, although the room was warm. Lillian's needlework held both power and emotions. Now that Teag's gift had tuned in, he could sense sadness, grief, loneliness, and anxiety that made his heart pound.

"Teag? Hey!"

Anthony's voice brought him out of his thoughts, and Teag stepped back. "I'm okay. I just could pick up some feelings from the magic Lillian used. I don't think she was very happy."

"It must have felt like the world had gone mad during the war. I don't imagine most people were happy," Anthony replied.

Lillian's magic had brought Teag's ability to the forefront. As he walked around the room with Anthony, he gently probed other objects like a needlepoint pillow and a small tapestry near the fireplace. None of them held any magic of their own.

But when he came to the display case with a gold and pearl hair comb, an ivory fan, and a black, enameled cigarette holder, Teag recoiled as he glimpsed a gray, transparent figure near the case.

"More magic?" Anthony asked in a whisper, glancing around to make sure they were alone.

Teag shook his head. "No. There's a spirit attached to those pieces, I'm sure of it. Maybe not the one they told us about at the tea room, but it's definitely a ghost. And she's not friendly."

CHAPTER TWO
ANTHONY

Anthony and Teag agreed to set the issue of the haunted hair comb aside for now and walk down to the village while there was plenty of daylight left. Heading across the inner bailey from Bride's Tower, they had another look at the huge Christmas tree and all its gleaming decorations.

"I want to check out the chapel, too." Teag pointed to a round structure a little farther away. "I've heard it has some very pretty decorations—and maybe the original gargoyle!"

"How do you know where all the gargoyles are?" Anthony enjoyed this playful side of Teag that he got to see all too rarely.

"Well, there's a cheat sheet on one of the travel sites," Teag admitted. "Although visitors are encouraged to hunt on their own first, and then use the sheet to find the carvings that are more challenging."

"But you already looked?"

"Of course! We don't want to miss any!" Teag looked aghast.

Anthony gave his hand a squeeze. "Want to check out the gift shop? We can head into town from there."

"Welcome to the Castle Shop," a woman called out as Teag and Anthony entered the store. She had short blond hair, and when she turned around, Anthony could see the resemblance between Patrick, their golf cart bellboy, and his mother. Her name tag read "Marianne."

"Patrick told us to stop in," Teag said. "He saved us from having to haul our luggage all the way from the parking lot."

Marianne laughed. "He loves that silly cart! I'm glad he helped you get settled. Please, have a look around. And if you're heading into town, I can hold your purchases until you get back."

The small shop smelled of locally-made goat milk soaps, the castle's own brand of tea, and a clove and orange potpourri that simmered near the register. Most of the items either had the likeness of Caynham Castle or the monogram of the Mortimer family. Teag picked out an ornament of the castle and a few other small gifts for friends back home.

"I'll just put these behind the register with your name on them until you get back," Marianne said after she rang them up. "If we're closed, no worries. Just stop by in the morning."

They thanked her and headed out. Anthony pulled his cap down over his ears. "It must be true what they say about Southerners having thin blood. I don't know how anyone lives with the cold here!"

"You know we aren't to the worst of the winter yet," Teag joked. "And I heard we're supposed to get a dusting of snow for Christmas."

Anthony glared. "That stuff is pretty on Christmas cards and in holiday movies, but not for real."

"Grinch."

"Scrooge."

They both laughed, and Anthony took Teag's hand as they headed out of the castle area and down toward the village square. It had been a long time since he'd felt this light-hearted, and he decided they needed to make vacationing a priority.

"The whole place looks like a movie set," Teag said in awe. Between the half-timbered buildings—what Americans often called "Tudor" style—and the old brick or stone buildings, the village seemed too picturesque to be real.

"You know, most people think that about Charleston," Anthony pointed out. "Or did you forget about the busloads of tourists who come to oooh and ahh over our architecture and all the 'old' buildings?"

"I guess you're right—this is just home for the people who are from here," Teag conceded. The square was in fine holiday form with another big tree, twinkle lights wrapped around lampposts, and ribbon-bedecked evergreen swags everywhere they looked.

Knights Road was the main street in Caynham-on-Ledwyche, and Anthony couldn't wait to check out the shops they had seen on their way in. "It's really great that all the stores are local," he said. "No big chains. Helps keep the feel of a place. Once the chains come in, everything's all the same."

"From what I saw in the comments on the tourist rating sites, the Mortimers—at least the more recent ones—have done a lot to support the local economy," Teag replied. "A lot of the items in the castle gift shop were by local companies or artists. And I'm sure the castle itself is a huge draw."

"There's the antique shop," Anthony said. "Do you want to go in?" He left that up to Teag, not only because the store might seem too much like the shop he worked in back home, but because he didn't know if Teag wanted to risk finding more items with a hint of haunt.

"Yeah, actually. If you don't mind. I'd like to find out more about Mabel Mortimer and why her ghost is so pissed off," Teag replied. "Just in case there's trouble."

"Curiouser and Curiouser Antiques" was the name emblazoned in gold lettering on the store window. A bell tinkled as they opened the door. Anthony and Teag stepped into a shop filled nearly to the rafters with dark wooden shelves laden with curios and antiques. Bone china, porcelain figurines, mantle clocks, and silver tea sets vied for space beside Wedgewood vases, cut crystal bowls, and vintage kitchenware.

"Hello there! Come on in and have yourselves a look around." An older man with a fringe of white hair waved at them from behind the counter, setting aside his cup of coffee and newspaper.

"Are you the owner?" Teag asked.

"Oh, no. I'm Mr. Porter, one of the staff," the man replied, chuckling. "What can I help you find?"

Anthony couldn't help looking at the fascinating mishmash of items. A large, taxidermied bear stood next to a tall mahogany coat rack. Behind that were several pieces of furniture that looked like they came from India's Colonial period, next to a brass telescope and an ornate Victorian floor lamp with a fringed shade.

"I couldn't resist coming in," Teag confided. "I work in an antique shop in Charleston, back in the States."

"Ah. Busman's holiday, is it? Can't quite get away from the job," Mr. Porter said with a laugh. "I know the feeling. Antiques get in your blood, they certainly do." He shook his head. "It's a wonder, really, how you can feel like you've seen into the past when you handle an old object. These pieces have seen a lot of living."

From the way Teag's eyes narrowed in thought, Anthony guessed his fiancé was thinking Mr. Porter might have a bit of psychic sensitivity himself.

"I heard someone say that a few pieces of needlework were found that were done by Lillian Mortimer and given back to the Castle," Teag said. "I'm always fascinated when things find their way home. Do you know the story of how that happened?"

"Well, now. That's quite a tale. Both Lillian and her sister, Mabel, were born just before the turn of the last century. Mabel, the older sister, was the serious one. Lillian, from what I've heard, was more of a free spirit. They clashed, as sisters do. Or maybe a bit more."

Mr. Porter perched on the stool behind the counter as Teag and Anthony drew closer. No one else was in the shop, and Anthony wondered if the older man welcomed a chance for conversation. Passing gossip about people long dead seemed harmless enough.

"When the Great War broke out, the earl and countess volunteered to help with the war effort, so they were gone for long periods. That left Mabel in charge of the castle, and—at least to her mind, Lillian." He laughed. "I don't think Lillian saw it that way. Anyhow, right before the war, Lillian had taken up with a young man from a wealthy family, Bertram Granville."

Mr. Porter peered over his spectacles at Teag and Anthony and clarified since they were clearly not local. "The Granvilles are landed gentry, with a country house a distance from town. The earl's family, the Mortimers that own Caynham Castle, are titled nobility. It's been Granvilles and Mortimers in these parts since long, long ago. Anyhow, Bertram Granville went away to the war, and like many of the young men, didn't come back."

"What happened?" Teag asked, leaning forward.

"Lillian didn't take the news well, as you can imagine. I guess today, they'd call it a nervous breakdown," Mr. Porter replied. "She turned to her needlepoint—it became something of an obsession—and didn't often leave the castle. Unfortunately, she died young of Consumption—Tuberculosis. Mabel eventually married and produced an heir. But…"

"What?" Anthony couldn't help being drawn into the story.

Mr. Porter shook his head. "Somewhere along the line, Mabel and Lillian had a big falling out. Mabel stayed bitter, even after Lillian's death. While she was alive, none of Lillian's needlework was permitted to be on display—a pity, because Lillian did fine work. No one knows what came between the sisters—or at least, if they knew, they didn't tell." He shrugged. "That's all I know of the tale."

"It's very interesting," Teag said. "Thank you for sharing it with us." He purchased a few vintage photographs and postcards of the castle and the village. Anthony avoided touching anything, wary from all the tales he'd heard from Teag and Cassidy of objects that carried bad mojo.

"Make sure you grab a pint at the earl's brewery," Mr. Porter said. "It's very good."

They promised to do so, which to Anthony's mind was no hard-ship. Next, they wandered into the Ewe & Ply yarn shop, which also carried some lovely scarves, shawls, capes, and other pieces made by the owner. Anthony felt Teag relax almost as soon as they stepped in the door.

"Can you feel that?" Teag asked quietly.

"Feel what?"

"Whoever's done the knitting definitely has my kind of magic—whether they know it or not. It's very comforting. Serene. I can't imagine how they can keep pieces in stock. I just want to wrap myself in them like a giant hug."

"Then pick a scarf or whatever you'd like," Anthony said. "Consider it a late birthday present."

Teag chose a blue scarf for himself and insisted on buying a green one for Anthony. The owner wasn't in, so Teag passed along his compliments. They stuck their heads into the tea room. It was as cottage kitchen comfy as Lady Neville's Tea Room back at the castle was formal, with mismatched china, tablecloths, and chairs. The walls were covered with a mix of old photos of the area, vintage prints of sheep and spinning wheels, and work by local artists.

"We're definitely coming back here," Teag said. "Those cakes look delicious."

Anthony groaned. "How can you even look at food? I'm still stuffed!"

Teag shot him a look. "It's always good to have a plan. That way, I can look forward to my meal, and then I can enjoy it twice."

Seeing Teag so relaxed warmed Anthony's heart. Back in Charleston, they often kept a hectic pace between Anthony's responsibilities at the law firm and Teag's job, not just with Trifles and Folly, but his *other* job with the Alliance, helping keep the world safe from supernatural threats. It had been too long since they had just taken a day to wander and see the sights.

Back outside, Teag slipped his arm through Anthony's. Anthony tensed, but only for a second. Caynham-on-Ledwyche seemed tolerant enough, but old habits died hard. Charleston had gotten a lot better than it used to be, but two men hand-in-hand on a busy street would still draw unwanted attention. As if he sensed Anthony's discomfort, Teag withdrew his arm, and Anthony immediately felt a loss.

"It's okay," Anthony told him. "I like walking arm in arm. I'm proud of us."

Teag gave him a hug and instead snagged Anthony's pinkie finger with his own. "I know. I am, too. But it's a small town. And we're a long way from home."

Anthony let it go, and Teag walked close beside him, shoulders bumping. He felt chagrined at his reaction. Their coming out experiences had been very different, and sometimes, it showed. Teag had come out in middle school, and his family had been supportive.

Anthony hadn't come out until law school, and while it hadn't cost him his position with the family firm, he was well aware there had been family members and clients who hadn't been happy about it.

"Hey, quit thinking so hard." Teag jostled his elbow. "Vacation, remember? And we're *engaged*! I'm going to keep saying that over and over to myself until it really sinks in," he added with a grin, waggling his fingers on the left hand.

"Sorry. You're right. And look—there's a bookstore!"

Caynham-on-Ledwyche was picture-perfect, Anthony thought. Decked out for the holidays, every store glistened with tinsel, lights, red bows, and accents of gold and silver.

"Oh, and there's a hotel in town, as well as the rooms at the castle," Teag pointed out.

Anthony nodded. "I saw that when I made reservations. It's a lovely place, and the restaurant is very good. But I thought you'd rather be in a real castle."

"You totally understand my inner geek," Teag replied, but the look in his eyes was worth every penny of the cost of the room.

"And I love your inner geek, as well as your outer one," Anthony assured him. "Just remember when you're in the bookstore—we have to be able to fly home, so whatever you buy needs to fit in the luggage."

Cadwell's was a charmingly old-world bookstore with bookshelves packed full from floor to ceiling and extra volumes spilling over onto tables and into corners. New books were in the front of the store, and the used books stretched in a warren of connected rooms and repurposed closets.

"I could get lost in here and stay for a year," Teag whispered in awe. "And there's an upstairs and a downstairs!"

"Can I help you find anything?"

Both Teag and Anthony jumped at the voice. They turned to find a short, bald fellow in a plaid shirt, sweater vest, and corduroy pants.

"You're—" Teag started.

"Ptolemy Cadwell, proprietor. At your service," the man replied. "Now, what kind of books are you looking for?"

"Weaving," Anthony said.

"Magic," Teag answered at the same instant.

Cadwell's eyebrows rose. "Well. That's an interesting mixture. I happen to have both. Follow me."

"I thought you were on vacation," Anthony whispered as they hurried to keep up with Cadwell. The stacks seemed to go on forever, and Anthony marveled that the store managed to pack so much into the space.

"I am. But you never know what you'll find in a place like this," Teag replied.

Anthony had to agree. There was something fanciful about Cadwell's and its odd proprietor that made him think anything might be possible—like meeting a troll or a unicorn around the corner or walking through an armoire or a grandfather clock into another world.

"Here you go," Cadwell said. "Weaving is here." He thrust out his left arm to indicate a section of shelves. "And magic would be over here." He bustled away, leaving Anthony to hope he could find his way back.

"Just let me know if you need anything else," Cadwell said when he had led Teag to the books on magic. "I'll be up front."

"What are you looking for?" Anthony asked, keeping his voice low.

"Nothing in particular," Teag replied. "Mostly making sure there isn't anything dangerous. Habit," he said with a shrug.

In the end, Teag selected a slim volume on the history of the Pendle Hill witch trials and a thin book on needlework. If Cadwell thought it a strange combination, he didn't say so, packing them up with a smile and adding a flyer to come back after Christmas for the January book sale.

"So no cursed grimoires, I presume?" Anthony asked as they strolled back toward the pub.

"Fortunately, not," Teag replied. "But I am interested now in finding out a little more about needlework. I think there's something still going on between the Mortimer sisters, and Lillian's embroidery is the key."

Anthony couldn't bring himself to be put out at Teag finding a potential ghost problem. It was too much a part of who Teag was, and Anthony wouldn't change that for anything. "All right. I'll be your sidekick," Anthony said once they got settled at a table at the Boar and Knight. "Just tell me what to do, and try not to get us thrown in the dungeon."

Teag peered over his menu. "I really don't think they do that anymore. Wait. Does the castle *have* a dungeon? Is it on the tour?"

Anthony smacked his palm to his forehead. "Me and my big mouth," he grumbled, but he grinned as he did it. "There's no dungeon on the castle map, but if you ask Priscilla at the desk real nicely, maybe she'll tell you whether there's one on the tour."

Teag leaned in. "Maybe we could pretend our room is a dungeon. The *other* kind."

"You're incorrigible," Anthony sighed, but he couldn't deny that his face reddened, and his pants tented at the mental imagery. Neither of them were really into that scene, but a little fantasy role-play certainly added spice.

The Boar and Knight was one of the oldest buildings other than the castle, and Anthony marveled that it had been in continual use as a pub since the early Middle Ages. A sign with the names of every proprietor going back over six hundred years graced one wall. The pub looked its age. A fireplace across from the bar was blackened with the soot of ages. The dark wood of the tables, chair rail, and bar was worn from use, and the plank floor showed the toll of centuries of foot traffic.

"The food must be good if they've been around since the Crusades," Teag said as he looked in one direction and then the next to see everything in the pub's cozy rooms.

"I suspect the ale is good, too," Anthony replied. Teag went for Shepherd's Pie, while Anthony chose Bangers and Mash, and they each got a pint of the pub's signature brew.

Anthony loved the way Teag's eyes lit up at the old pub and how excited he was to dig into his food and sample the ale. Anthony had been over to the UK several times, both for business and with his family, but seeing everything fresh through Teag's eyes made all the difference, and he felt himself fall, impossibly, even more in love than before.

The pub was fairly small, and the tables were closer together than in modern restaurants, so it was impossible not to overhear conversations.

"…when Old Man Granville dies, that's the last of the lot," a man at the next table said to his companion. Both were men who looked to be in their late sixties. The speaker had a shock of white hair that poked out at all angles, while the other man had a monk's fringe of gray hair around a bald pate. "There's no one to inherit his country house or the land with it."

"How'd he manage to end up without heirs?" the other man replied.

"Dunno. Guess it wouldn't be too hard with a run of bad luck. All you'd need is a generation or two without many kids, and then toss in accidents or sickness. It's a shame. There've been Granvilles in these parts since the War of the Roses. I always heard tell that's when the Granville family got their land from the king. Same time as the Mortimers got the castle."

"So, what now? Everything Old Man Granville owns reverts to the Crown? Next thing you know, the land'll get sold off, and we'll have flats going up, you mark my word."

Anthony couldn't help listening, caught up in the mini-drama of a stranger's tale. Other patrons argued about soccer scores, cricket, or the latest political news. When Teag tapped him on the arm, Anthony realized he had been lost in thought.

"Tuppence for your thoughts," Teag asked with a grin. "I'd have offered a penny, but when in Rome…"

"I'll tell you later," Anthony replied, well aware that others could hear them as clearly as he heard the people at the next tables.

By the time they finished their food, polished off the ale, and paid their tab, night had fallen. Twinkle lights festooned the trees near the walkways, wrapped around light posts, and sparkled in shop windows. The big fir tree in the town square glowed.

"It's so pretty," Teag said with a sigh as they strolled back toward the castle. "Now, what was the big secret back in the pub?"

Anthony shook his head. "No secret. I just didn't want the old men at the next table to know I'd been eavesdropping. They were talking about a local family—the Granvilles, well-to-do, I'm sure—

who might lose their lands because there aren't any heirs after the patriarch dies."

"That happened to a lot of landed gentry over the years," Teag replied. "It's really more of a surprise that a family like the Mortimers were able to hang onto their castle and make a go of it. The upkeep alone has bankrupted plenty of nobles, and two World Wars went hard on descendants. It's a shame—that's the way history gets lost."

When they reached the inner bailey of Caynham Castle, Anthony looked to Teag. "So do we go up to the room and call it a night, or did you want to go back to the sitting rooms?"

Teag took his hand and gave it a squeeze. "I have all kinds of ideas for when we go back to the room, none of which involve calling it a night," he said with a lascivious smile. "But I'm worried about the ghost I thought I sensed. It might be a good time to catch Priscilla and see if she knows anything if she's not busy."

They headed to the front desk. Anthony figured Priscilla would be gone by now, but she was still there, albeit looking a bit less perky than she had earlier.

"Hello, gentlemen. Problem with your room?" she asked.

"Oh no," Teag assured her. "Everything with the room is great. But I had an odd question I was hoping you could answer. Has anyone reported anything strange happening in the ladies' salon, over in Bride's Tower?"

"Strange, like…"

"Odd cold spots, things suddenly falling off shelves, people feeling a push when no one's around, that sort of strange," Teag replied with his most winning smile.

Anthony loved watching his boy work. *He'd have been a natural at swaying a jury if he'd gone into law,* Anthony thought. Teag had a way of setting people at ease and getting them to talk to him, regardless of age or status.

"A ghost, you mean. One that isn't Lady Alice's daughter."

"More like Mabel Mortimer," Teag said. "And very unhappy."

Priscilla gave Teag a measured glance and then looked at Anthony. He thought they might be about to get tossed out on their ear for wasting her time.

"You're Teag Logan, from Charleston? Mr. Sorren said you'd be coming here. And that if you asked for help with something, to do whatever we could."

"You know Sorren?" Anthony's eyes widened.

Teag's best friend and boss, Cassidy Kincaide, owned Trifles and Folly. Sorren was her business partner—and a nearly 600-year-old vampire who had founded the store back when Charleston was first chartered. Anthony knew Sorren had dealings in Europe with the Alliance—the coalition of mortals and immortals who used Trifles and Folly—and other stores like it—as a cover for dealing with haunted and cursed objects and occasionally saving the world. He just hadn't expected to stumble over a connection on their trip.

"He's an old friend of the earl and the earl's family, the Mortimers," Patricia said. "I'm a Mortimer cousin. The castle is really a family affair. And as for ghosts, I'm not sure we'd want the other guests to overhear, but yes, there have been some…disturbances…lately in the ladies' salon. That's kind of what you folks do, isn't it? Handle that sort of thing?"

"Actually, I'm a lawyer," Anthony said. "But that's totally Teag's area."

"I might be able to help, so no one gets hurt," Teag said. The registration area was empty, and Teag figured everyone was at dinner or at the castle restaurant's bar.

Priscilla glanced around again and relaxed when she didn't see anyone nearby. "We never had any problems in there before," she said. "Family items like Mabel's hair comb rotate on and off display. But we'd never had anything from Lillian before. She died young and tragically, poor thing," Priscilla confided.

"So this is the first time you've had something from both sisters on display together?" Teag asked. Anthony could practically see the wheels turning in his fiancé's head as Teag formed a theory.

"Yes. There are a number of items belonging to Mabel in our archive storage," Priscilla said. "She lived into her nineties, so it's been less than thirty years since she passed away, and she was born and died in the castle."

"What about Lillian's personal belongings? What happened to them?" Teag asked.

Priscilla shook her head and shrugged. "No idea. She died in 1920. A century is a long time to keep track of things. And since she had Tuberculosis, the family might have gotten rid of her things, for fear of catching it."

"But the needlepoint pieces, they just found their way back to the family, right?" Teag was definitely on the trail of something, but Anthony wasn't sure yet exactly what.

Priscilla nodded. "Yes. She'd given some as gifts, and the families gave or loaned them back to the castle for display. They're scattered about in several of the rooms."

"And the salon is the only place where there are pieces from both sisters together?"

"Yes, but there are other items Mabel owned elsewhere." Priscilla hesitated. "I'm glad you said something. Odd things have happened to me in that sitting room, but I'd convinced myself it was my imagination. We'd heard a few guests mention that they thought it was very cold in the room, or that they had the feeling someone was watching them. And then the day before yesterday, a guest was walking through and tripped, right by Mabel's display case. The guest thought she caught her foot on something, and she wasn't hurt, thank goodness, but now I wonder what really happened."

Teag chewed on his lip; Anthony knew it was a sure sign he was working out a puzzle.

"If Mabel's strong enough to hurt people, then we need to do something. Just putting her items back into storage won't be enough, because her spirit is attached to them, and she's riled up now. It might be as simple as saying a banishment ritual over Mabel's grave," Teag suggested. "Do you know where she's buried?"

Priscilla nodded. "Yes. In the family crypt. I can make arrangements to give you a private tour tomorrow if you'd like. And if, during the tour, you happen to recite some strange poems or prayers, I won't tell anyone," she added with a broad wink.

Teag grinned. "I think that tour would be a lovely addition. Thank you very much."

They agreed to meet Priscilla at ten the next morning and said goodnight. As they walked back to the inner bailey where the dower apartments were located, Teag reached out and took Anthony's arm. This time, Anthony didn't flinch.

"Look at those stars," Teag marveled, staring into the sky. The cold, clear night made for perfect viewing, even if their breath misted in the chill. "This is absolutely perfect. And so are you."

"Even if the castle does have a ghost problem after all?" Anthony asked.

Teag ducked in to press a quick kiss to his lips. "You know, that makes it even better, somehow. Thank you for being so patient about me finding a 'job' on vacation."

Anthony shrugged. "If Mabel is hurting people, something needs to be done, and you know what to do. We'll go to the crypt tomorrow, you'll say the banishment, and we can go on with our vacation. It's like doing a good deed."

"Hmm…since I've done a good deed, does that mean I can do some naughty deeds now?" Teag teased in a voice that went right to Anthony's groin. The heat in Teag's eyes left absolutely no room for misinterpretation.

"I think that could be arranged," Anthony replied, in a tone made husky by more than just the cold air.

Once they were in the elevator, Teag pushed Anthony against the wall, slipping a hand between them to cup his package. "You're filling out your briefs, Counselor."

"I plead totally guilty," Anthony replied. "But since I'm sure there are cameras in these elevators, let's save the rest for our room, and then maybe I can make you plead—I mean, beg."

Teag gave him a quick kiss on the lips and turned to wink at the camera in the corner. "Sounds like my kind of plea bargain."

CHAPTER THREE

TEAG

The next morning, Priscilla met them after breakfast, and they headed outside the castle walls to the Mortimer family crypt.

"This isn't all of the family," she told them as they trekked along a gravel path. "Some of the older burials are in the crypt beneath St. Peter's church in the village. But Mabel and Lillian are recent enough, relatively speaking, to be in the 'new' crypt."

The crypt looked like a small church without a steeple, made from the same Silurian limestone as the castle's walls. "Mortimer" was engraved on the lintel.

"The crypt is only for the earl's direct descendants," Priscilla told them. "The rest of the newer folks would be laid to rest in the churchyard."

"Do you know where Mabel was placed in here?" Teag asked as they entered the family mausoleum. The stone held a chill. Light filtered down from windows around the eaves. A stained glass rose window over the engraved bronze front doors bathed the interior in warm shades of blue, crimson, and gold, the colors of the Mortimer family crest.

Priscilla nodded. "I looked it up before we came. She should be over here." Her heels clicked on the marble floor as she led them toward the corner and pointed to a square stone marking Mabel's niche, engraved with her name and dates.

Teag pulled out a bundle of sage and an abalone shell. "I'm going to burn some sage to purify and say the banishment rite Father Anne taught me. Sometimes, that's enough."

What he didn't say was that often, it wasn't. Teag hated dragging Anthony into a ghost problem on their vacation, but if Mabel's spirit had turned vengeful, having her loose in the castle with a holiday ball just days away could lead to catastrophe.

"I'm just going to stroll around outside," Priscilla replied as if she hadn't heard him. "When you've paid your respects, just come to the door." With that, she headed outside.

"Score one for plausible deniability," Anthony said. "What can I do to help?"

Teag used a lighter to catch the tip of the bundle on fire and let the flames settle to a glow as the smoke rose. "Watch my back. If I'm concentrating on the words of the rite, I'm not paying attention to what's around me."

"You've got it." Anthony palmed the iron fireplace poker they had borrowed from their room in case Mabel showed up, and he had a salt shaker in his coat pocket from breakfast. Salt and iron disrupted ghosts and made them vanish—at least temporarily. That meant Anthony could buy time for Teag if Mabel decided to throw a hissy fit.

Teag laid down a thin line of salt in front of Mabel's drawer—more insurance, in case she showed up. Then he walked clockwise around the small open area in the center of the crypt with the sage, letting the smoke fill the air.

"Mabel Mortimer. You have departed this life, and it is time to move on. By all that you hold holy, by the saints and apostles, and in the name of the Father, Son, and Holy Ghost, leave this place and trouble their house no more."

Teag's voice echoed in the stone room. He tensed, waiting for a cold gust of wind, or the grip of invisible dead hands, or maybe a glowing orb diving for his head. Nothing happened.

"Do you think she heard you?" Anthony asked.

"Dunno. The banishment isn't like an exorcism, and I'm not a priest."

"Obviously," Anthony smirked.

"What I meant," Teag replied, rolling his eyes, "is that it's more like a sternly worded request to leave, but it's not the same as picking her up by the scruff of the neck and throwing her out."

"Have you ever seen it work?"

"Sometimes. Mostly when spirits don't realize they're dead and that they've become a nuisance. If Mabel has more of an agenda or some serious unfinished business, she might not take the hint." He blew out the sage, closed the abalone shell around it, and tucked the shell and the salt shaker back in his pocket.

"I guess we'll find out." Anthony stepped closer and ran a hand down Teag's spine, ending at the small of his back. "Have I ever told you how sexy you are when you do your ghostbuster thing?"

"Really?" A grin tugged at the corner of Teag's mouth. "Sort of like how sexy you are all dressed up for court when you do your Atticus Finch thing?"

"Yeah," Anthony replied. "The day's still young. Why don't we head back to the room before lunch? We have plenty of time."

"I like the way you think," Teag replied with a saucy wink.

They headed to the door and found Priscilla on the steps of the crypt with her phone against her ear. Her expression was distraught. She ended the call as they reached her and looked up.

"We've got go to back. A guest was injured in the ladies' sitting room by something that 'seemed to fly off the shelf,'" Priscilla said. "I don't think Mabel is ready to give up."

Teag swore under his breath. A glance at Anthony told him his fiancé was on the same page without needing to confer. "All right. Lock up here, and we'll go back with you. I'm sorry this didn't work. Thank you for giving it a try."

An old ring of keys jangled in Priscilla's hand. Teag and Anthony helped to close the heavy doors and the lock *clunked* into place. "I appreciate you taking time out of your vacation to help. I feel guilty asking."

"We couldn't just ignore the problem when people are getting hurt," Anthony said, and Teag's heart warmed. It had taken a lot for Anthony to fully embrace his "side gig," and at one time, Teag had feared that Anthony might leave him if he ever discovered the truth. Instead, Anthony had held on tighter than ever, and Teag felt so thankful.

"Let's go find out more about what happened. Then I think the next step is to go see the rooms that used to be Mabel's and Lillian's," Teag replied.

Priscilla pocketed the keys, and they walked back at a brisk pace. "We know where Mabel's room was, but we've never been sure about Lillian's. Mabel's is on the fifth floor of Bride's Tower. She moved there during the First World War because it seemed safer and never left."

"Maybe Lillian's room was somewhere nearby," Anthony suggested.

"I just wish you had more of Lillian's possessions than just the few needlework pieces," Teag said, thinking out loud. "There's something driving this, and I don't think we'll get rid of the ghosts until we figure it out."

Teag was relieved not to see an ambulance when they reached the tower. Still, he could see several castle employees hovering around a woman seated on a chair who was holding an ice pack to her head.

"I'm going to have to deal with this and fill out paperwork," Priscilla said, turning to Teag and Anthony. "How about you two go over to the tea room and have a bite, and I'll catch up to you when I'm done here. On me." She pulled two vouchers out of her pocket.

Teag thanked her and watched her walk toward the injured woman, not envying the clean up she was going to need to do. Fortunately, the guest didn't look badly hurt, but Teag knew that for vengeful ghosts, it was only a matter of time before problems escalated. They stopped by their room just long enough to return the fireplace poker, then headed to the tea shop.

"Back again?" Helen, the lady in the tea shop, greeted them. "You're early for lunch."

"We just stopped by for tea," Teag replied. "And maybe two of those scones…with the apricot preserves and clotted cream?"

"We've got those fresh right out of the oven," Helen said. "Let me get you seated."

She led them to a different table, affording them a slightly new perspective on the tea room. "Have you had a chance to explore the village?" Helen asked as they got settled.

"We've walked up and down Knight Street," Anthony replied. "But I'm sure there's more to see."

"Not really," Helen replied with a laugh. "Well, a little. You'll want to go to the earl's brewery, because it's very nice, and the beer is good. I'd say that even if he wasn't the earl or my boss. If you haven't walked to the folly down by the river, it's worth the hike, especially the way it's done up now for the holidays. The gardens aren't blooming, of course, but the trees and shrubs give it good bones. And there's a second pub, over by the grocery store, if you feel the need."

She bustled off to get their order. Teag unfolded his linen napkin and set it in his lap. "Well—there's still lots to do, apparently."

"I'd like to go to the folly," Anthony replied. "It looked interesting on the website, and I bet it looks great with the Christmas decorations." He paused. "Have you thought any more about whether you want to go to the ball?"

"If I lose my shoe, will you chase after me at the stroke of twelve and carry me off?"

"I already know your name and where you're staying. I can find you and bring you your shoe."

"That's it. Ruin all the romance," Teag fake-pouted. Something about Caynham Castle brought out a whimsical side he hadn't indulged in a long time. Grad school had taken a toll, and it seemed like he and Cassidy often went from one supernatural crisis to another. But here at the castle, they could play. Teag knew he didn't have to prove anything to Anthony. His fiancé was well aware of Teag's martial arts ability, and he'd seen Teag in a fight. That sense of security made Teag feel safe being flirty and silly, and he appreciated that Anthony was willing to play along.

"Come back to the room with me, and I'll romance you." Anthony bumped his knee against Teag's under the table, and the look in his eyes made Teag's cock fill, and his stomach do a little flip. They had broken in the new room very enthusiastically the previous night, and Teag was hoping for a repeat tonight.

"I'll hold you to that," Teag teased.

"Oh, there'll be a lot of holding. Count on it." Anthony's sexy wink meant Teag needed to surreptitiously adjust himself.

"Here you go!" Helen interrupted, bearing a tray with tea, scones, and all the fixings. "Enjoy!

The scent of the English Breakfast tea filled the air, mixing with the smell of the scones. Teag realized he was more hungry than he had thought. Still, he couldn't resist teasing Anthony a bit more, as he took a bite of his scone and very obviously licked the remnants of the clotted cream off his lips.

"You're killing me," Anthony whispered.

"You know how much I love cream," Teag replied, not even trying to look innocent.

Anthony groaned. "You're going to be like this all day, aren't you?"

"Uh-huh. And you love it."

They took their time, knowing Priscilla would need a chance to deal with the guest situation. She arrived just as they finished their pot of tea, looking frazzled.

"You look like you need the tea more than we do," Teag said. "Do you have time for a cup?"

Priscilla shook her head. "I'm afraid not. Did you give Helen the vouchers? I can get you into the fifth floor of Bride's Tower if we go now."

Teag handed over the vouchers and thanked Helen, promising they would be back. Then he and Anthony followed Priscilla back to the inner bailey. She had walked over in just a tweed jacket and scarf, without a coat. Looking at her made Teag shiver and burrow down into his heavy jacket.

"The upper levels of Bride's Tower aren't usually open to guests," Priscilla said. "It's where we keep items that aren't on display. The family had apartments there, during both World Wars, but they haven't stayed there in years."

"What about Mabel?" Teag asked.

"She was the last to leave Bride's Tower," Priscilla said. "I guess she was just comfortable there. Or maybe she felt like the manor house wasn't really her home. She died in her room, in her sleep. I was just a kid, but I remember thinking it would have been creepy to be all alone in Bride's Tower at night."

Priscilla unlocked the door at the base of the thick-walled tower and flipped on the lights. They followed her inside. "The stairs are this way," she said. "That's another reason why we didn't use this for guests for a long time. It only had an elevator put in after Mabel's death."

"Mabel navigated the stairs all those years?" Anthony asked.

Priscilla shrugged. "She was pretty spry for her age, until the very end."

The stone stairs were in good condition, but Teag wouldn't have wanted to run them, certainly not when he was in his eighties.

"We use the first floor for the brides' and grooms' rooms and other wedding preparations," Priscilla said as they climbed. "The second floor is the Honeymoon Suite. You've been to the sitting rooms on the third floor. The fourth floor houses the archives and storage for off-rotation items. Those floors are climate controlled. The fifth floor is exactly as it was when Mabel died. We haven't needed the space, so nothing's been done with it."

When they reached the fifth floor, Priscilla turned on the hall light. The scuffed paint and old light fixtures made it clear that the area hadn't been modernized. Framed prints hung on the walls to the right. A large tapestry hung against the left wall, starting midway down the corridor.

"This was Mabel's room." Priscilla opened the first door on the left. Dust motes floated in the air as she turned on the light. Sheets covered the remaining pieces of furniture, but everything personal had been removed, including anything on the walls. The space had a cold, impersonal feel to Teag, more like a dormitory than a home.

"What was Mable like?" Teag asked.

"I never met her," Priscilla replied. "But even her picture frightened me when I was a kid. I remember family members talking about her. They didn't really like Mabel. Not that she did anything mean to them.

She just wasn't a warm person. I remember this picture of her in a black dress, with a severe look on her face. People didn't talk about her much, and what they said was polite...but I don't think anyone was comfortable around her. I got the impression she was very judgmental and more strict than necessary."

That squared with what they had learned from Mr. Porter at the antique shop. "Can we look in the other rooms? One of them probably belonged to Lillian if the sisters came to the tower during the war."

"Sure," Priscilla agreed. "But anything that belonged to her would be long gone."

They walked back into the hallway, and Teag turned his attention to the tapestry. "It's a scene from Mallory's *Le Morte d'Arthur*," he said, recognizing the depiction. "Interesting choice. Arthur's betrayal by Mordred. If it's not a reproduction...and I don't think it is...the piece probably dates to the late sixteen hundreds."

He looked to Priscilla. "Rather odd that it's just been left in an abandoned hallway, isn't it?"

"It's how Mabel wanted it," Priscilla replied. "She was rather odd herself. Other than wanting to be buried in the family crypt, the only other stipulation of her will was that she wanted the tapestry to remain where it was. I honestly think that people just forgot about it after she passed."

Teag moved closer to the tapestry. The workmanship of the piece was excellent, and given its age and the fact that it had been hanging in a dusty hallway, it remained in relatively good shape. But as he drew nearer, the Weaver magic danced in his mind's eye like threads of flame.

"What are you seeing?" Anthony asked.

"Someone stitched magic into the tapestry." Teag moved slowly from one side of the piece to the other, close but not touching. "The stitches are much, much newer. Less than a century, I'd guess. And it's not just magic..." he concentrated, focusing his gift on the places where he envisioned the bespelled threads.

"Whoever added the threads to this didn't just work their magic into the stitches. They left behind a piece of their soul." He turned to face Anthony and Priscilla, wide-eyed.

"How is that even possible?" Priscilla asked.

"I don't know," Teag admitted. "I imagine there are ways to do that, but I'm not sure why anyone would want to." He turned back to the tapestry and frowned, then reached out and grabbed hold of one side, lifting it away from the wall. The Weaver magic of the added threads tingled through his arm.

"There's a door under here," he said to the others. "I think we just found Lillian's room."

THEY LEFT THE TAPESTRY HANGING, so as not to damage it, and slipped behind. Teag tried the door. "Locked."

"Let me." Priscilla shuffled to change places. She withdrew a bulging keyring from her pocket and found the key she was looking for. "This is supposed to be the master key."

Teag held his breath while she tried the key and exhaled when the knob turned and the door opened.

"Wow," Anthony said, summing up what they all felt, from their gobsmacked expressions.

Other than a thick coating of dust, the room looked like its owner had walked out and never returned. Enough light came from the window for them to see. The faded bedspread was pulled up neatly on the bed, with a book propped open on the nightstand. On the desk lay paper and writing pens. A partially open armoire revealed clothing on hangers. But what caught Teag's attention was the full-sized loom in one corner and the many embroidery hoops with half-finished pieces of needlework scattered on every surface.

"Everything looks like Lillian just wandered off," Anthony said. "So why is there a big trunk in the middle of the room? She was very sick at the end, wasn't she? She wouldn't have been packing for a trip."

Priscilla walked over to the trunk and opened it. Inside were piles of needlework pieces of all sizes—tablecloths and runners, doilies and antimacassars, handkerchiefs and scarves. Nothing was neatly folded;

instead, it looked as if someone had just dumped the pieces in and shut the lid.

In the corridor, a door slammed, then another, and another, but not the door to Lillian's room.

"Uh-oh," Teag murmured. "Someone just woke up."

The air in the bedroom grew suddenly cold. Teag reached for the salt shaker in his pocket, wishing he had his iron knife. Anthony and Priscilla took a step back, away from the trunk.

Gray mist rose and took the form of a young woman. She had long dark hair and a heart-shaped face. Her long nightdress hung from a thin body.

"Help me."

As quickly as the ghost appeared, she vanished, and so did the sudden chill. Teag, Anthony, and Priscilla exchanged wide-eyed looks.

"Did you see that?" Priscilla whispered.

"Yeah. I think we all did," Anthony replied.

"I'm betting that's Lillian," Teag said. "And the temper tantrum in the hallway might be Mabel."

"She wanted the tapestry left in place," Anthony said. "Why would she want to hide Lillian's room? It's almost like she wanted to—"

"Erase her from history," Priscilla finished. "I think that's exactly what she wanted. But why?"

Teag ran a hand through his hair. "I know you don't know us very well, other than Sorren vouching for us. And I know it's a lot to ask. But I think if we could stay in the room for a while, go through what's here, we might find out what happened and why Mabel's ghost suddenly got violent."

"What are you thinking?" Anthony asked.

Teag gestured toward the loom and the unfinished needlework scattered about. "I think I might be able to read Lillian's Weaver magic from her pieces. There's so much—it's almost like it became an obsession. Did Mabel lock her up? Why would she do that? Maybe there's a journal or something..." He turned to meet Priscilla's gaze. "I think this is the heart of the haunting. If we can solve this, we might be able to make the sitting rooms safe again."

Priscilla swallowed hard, then nodded. "Okay. Seems like you're our best shot. What do you need from me?"

"Salt," Teag replied. "A canister from the kitchen. I'll put a line of it down by the door. It'll keep Mabel from bothering us. An iron fireplace poker, just in case. We took ours back to the room," he said. "And please let your security guards know not to arrest us if anyone notices we're up here."

"I'll do all that, and bring you some cold drinks and wet wipes as well," Priscilla said. "Thank you. I really appreciate all you're doing."

"We're happy to help," Anthony replied, and the genuine smile assuaged some of Teag's guilt for dragging them into a case. "Teag's good with this kind of thing. He'll get to the bottom of it."

Priscilla left, and Bride's Tower seemed eerily quiet. "You could go do something fun," Teag said as he walked around the room, mentally cataloging all the needlepoint pieces and trying to figure out where to start.

"I came here to be with my fiancé. And that's exactly what I'm going to do," Anthony said. "How about this? Since I can't pick up any clues from the embroidery, why don't you focus on that, and I'll search the room for anything else—diaries, journals, letters, that kind of thing."

"I love you so much," Teag replied.

"Because I'm going to help you search the room?"

"Because you're taking this in stride and not making me feel awful about it."

Anthony moved closer and turned Teag's chin so their eyes met. "We're helping people, making sure no one gets hurt, and solving a mystery. Some people pay extra to get a mystery package at a hotel, you know. So think of it as a bonus."

Teag decided to start with the least complete embroidery on the assumption they might be the last pieces Lillian created. The needlework was finely crafted, with careful, regular stitches. Teag could feel traces of Lillian's native Weaver magic—untrained, but still strong. In the pieces where she had stitched in a nearly-invisible set of symbols with white thread, Teag could sense the presence of a wisp of something more powerful and feared it was a breath of Lillian's soul.

The echoes of power were fainter in the least finished works. Those were also the pieces that were flecked with rust-colored stains Teag feared were blood. He remembered how Lillian died and wondered if she had stitched until the very end.

"It's odd," Teag remarked as Anthony started at one corner and devoted himself to thoroughly searching the room. "The pieces that Lillian did before the war were all kinds of designs—samplers, flowers, still lifes. But all her later pieces have an archery theme. Arrows, bows, quivers, bowmen, targets. There must be a reason she chose those images, but I don't understand."

"How about the pieces in the trunk?" Anthony asked as he moved slowly from searching in, around, behind, and under one piece of furniture to the next.

"I'm working on those now," Teag replied. "I can almost feel Lillian fading from one piece to another. She must have worked obsessively to create all these."

"If she was shut away in her room, there might not have been many other distractions," Anthony replied. "Poor woman. First she gets her heart broken, then she dies young from TB. And it doesn't sound like her sister was very supportive."

"I don't get it. What was Mabel's deal? Lillian got dealt a shitty hand, and Mabel stood to inherit everything. Why all the drama?" Teag handled the pieces in the trunk carefully, pausing with each one to take in the design, type of stitches used, and the expertise, as well as sensing the magic.

"None of the pieces in the trunk have the soul-threads," Teag said after a while. "Just the ones laying about in the room—and the tapestry. I was right about the variety in the designs—but there aren't any arrows or archers. There's so much life and energy in her early pieces. The colors are bright, and I think a lot of the designs were original. And then it all changes."

"Is there any way to put a date to the shift?" Anthony leaned into the armoire, carefully going through pockets, drawers, and nooks. Dust lay like snow flurries across his shoulders and in his hair.

"Not all of her pieces have a date stitched in, but I haven't found anything with soul threads or the archer theme before 1917," Teag replied.

"Then we need to figure out what happened in 1917 that changed everything."

Priscilla returned with the salt, a bag full of bottled water, and the fireplace poker. "If you find anything you need to examine closely, there's a small meeting room you can use near the front desk. Just bring whatever it is down, and I'll get you set up," she offered.

Once Teag had gone through the needlework, he felt exhausted and knew he needed to set the stitchery aside for a while, so he joined Anthony in searching the room. As Anthony moved to check the desk, Teag went to the bookshelves.

"I haven't found anything odd so far," Anthony said. "Let's hope there's more on this side of the room."

Lillian's taste ran to mystery and romance, with a mix of classics, some yellowed with age. Several of the books were accounts by botanists and explorers, and Teag wondered whether Lillian used their descriptions for inspiration in creating her designs. He was all the way down to the bottom row when a dark leather book caught his eye. Teag pulled it from the shelf and let out a low whistle.

"Well look at that. I found a grimoire, after all." He held the book up for Anthony to see.

"Seriously?" Anthony looked puzzled. "What would Lillian want with a book on magic?"

Teag sat down and started to page through the old book carefully. "It doesn't actually come right out and say that it's a grimoire—or about magic. It's almost written in language like a prayer book. Not unusual, back in the day, to try to protect the owners of such dangerous books."

"Do you think she knew what it was?"

Teag frowned as he found some of the symbols Lillian had used in her hidden stitching. "Maybe not," he mused. "She was young and rather sheltered. Magic wasn't exactly a common topic, and there was no internet to look things up easily. Maybe she really did think it was a prayer book, and, I don't know—she was trying to ask for divine help?"

He noted the symbols that looked familiar. "She used several of the same markings. According to this, they were for protection, memory, finding lost things. That's a rather unusual focus, don't you think?"

Nothing else on the bookshelves looked out of the ordinary. Teag even pulled a few volumes at random to see if Lillian had put false covers over more controversial books, but to no avail. The desk, likewise, held no secrets. But when Anthony checked under the bed, he found a locked suitcase, and when he shook it, the sounds from inside were definitely more paper than clothing.

"I doubt anyone has the key," Anthony observed.

"If you didn't find it in Lillian's things, then I doubt it, too." Teag found a bobby pin, straightened it out, and jimmied open the lock.

"Should I be worried that you know how to pick a lock?" Anthony asked.

"Can I plead the Fifth?"

"Only on TV. That's not how it actually works."

Teag shrugged. "We get a lot of old locked boxes at Trifles and Folly. Someone needed to know how to open them."

"Uh-huh," Anthony responded skeptically but didn't push. Teag figured his fiancé could figure out that handling haunts and monsters sometimes required a bit of breaking and entering.

Teag opened the suitcase reverently as if they were entering a tomb. He and Anthony both let out a breath when the contents were revealed. Inside were yellowed envelopes with faded postmarks, thin leather-bound notebooks, sketchpads, and small keepsakes that must have been dear to Lillian's heart.

Outside in the hallway, doors opened, then slammed shut. "I don't think Mabel wanted us to find this," Anthony observed, gripping the fireplace poker.

The temperature dropped, and Teag felt the hair rise on the back of his neck. They turned to see Lillian's ghost take shape once more. A ghostly finger traced letters in the thick dust on the dresser. "*Save Archer,*" it read.

"Who is Archer?" Teag asked the spirit. "What do the arrows and bows mean?"

Lillian's ghost had the pale, fragile appearance that went with

Consumption, but determination blazed in her eyes. She pointed toward the writing in the dust and then vanished.

A woman's furious shriek echoed in the empty hallway, and a tremor passed through Bride's Tower, rattling glass and making the cobwebs sway.

"I think we'd better get out of here," Teag said. "I can come back later and remove the soul-threads to let Lillian rest in peace. For now, let's figure out what was so important in this suitcase."

"How are we going to get out? There's a pissed off ghost in the hallway!" Anthony's eyes were wide. He'd been up against vengeful ghosts before, and Anthony was right to be cautious, Teag knew. But he was determined that Mabel Mortimer was not going to keep them trapped like she did Lillian.

"We stay close together. I'll take the suitcase, and I'll fan the salt out ahead of us. You come right behind me with the poker, so you can jab and slash if Mabel gets handsy," Teag told him. He grabbed the case and made sure the salt canister was open, then moved to the door.

"Ready?" he asked.

"Not really, but we're going anyhow," Anthony replied.

Teag sloshed salt into the corridor ahead of them, spreading it wide across the hallway. He stepped out and heard the grains crunch beneath his feet. "Go!" he yelled to Anthony, who was right behind him.

The temperature in the hall was colder than outside, enough that they could see their breath. The doors opened and shut, the overhead lights flickered wildly, and Mabel screamed in fury as a ghostly shadow chased them toward the stairs, clawed hands grasping to catch hold.

Anthony swung the iron poker, keeping the ghost at bay as Teag kept up the spray of salt. The salt limited where Mabel could go, and if they kept to the center of the hallway, they could elude her grasp.

"Do you think she'll go down the steps?" Anthony yelled, jabbing at the ghost when she slipped along the wall at the very edge of the salt. She vanished, only to reappear in another location.

"No idea. I just want to get out of here."

They thundered down the stairs, and Mabel's shrieks reverberated in the stairwell, but she did not follow. Neither man felt like taking chances, and they ran as fast as they could down the steps and then outside, where they gasped for breath until their lungs ached from the cold.

"Look!" Anthony said, pointing to a window at the top of Bride's Tower. Just for a moment, Teag thought he saw the shadowy form of a woman with upswept hair, and then the apparition vanished.

"Let's go find Priscilla," Teag huffed. "And set up in that meeting room. Maybe we can also get some lunch. I think we've earned it."

CHAPTER FOUR

ANTHONY

W hen they dragged themselves into the reception area covered in dust and flushed from outrunning Mabel's ghost, Anthony knew they probably looked like madmen. Teag clutched the old suitcase like a drowning man with a life preserver, and he had a white-knuckled grip on the salt canister. Anthony had the presence of mind to lower the fireplace poker before heading into public areas to avoid scaring anyone.

Priscilla ushered them into a meeting room before their appearance could raise eyebrows in the lobby and promised to be back with hot tea and sandwiches. When she returned, Teag and Anthony had spread the contents of Lillian's suitcase across one half of the large table.

"What's all this?" Priscilla set down the tray of food at the other end.

"Something Mable really didn't want us to see," Teag replied. He brushed dust out of his hair, but Anthony knew they would never be rid of it until they showered. "If it's all right with you, I figured we'd hole up in here and read."

"Did you figure out any more about her needlework and the… magic?" Priscilla looked curious, not fearful.

Teag nodded. "Yes. I found the book she took the spells from, and

I'm sure I can undo them and set her soul free. But first, I think we need to figure out what's got Mabel riled up before someone else gets hurt."

"All right," Priscilla replied. "I have to be up front, but if you need anything, just let me know. Lunch and dinner are on me. You're doing us a great service." She cleared her throat. "When you've got everything figured out, at some point, we need to brief the earl."

"Understood. Do you have any idea how he'll take it?" Teag asked.

She shrugged. "He knows Mr. Sorren, doesn't he? I imagine he'll deal with it just fine." With that, she headed back to her post.

They settled down to eat and found a pot of hot Earl Gray tea, a variety of tea sandwiches, a box of scones and tarts, and a slab of cake for each of them. "I'm going to be so spoiled by the time we get home." Teag polished off the last of his cake. "Is there a tea room in Charleston? If not, we should start one. This food is too good to give up!"

"I'm sure we can find one," Anthony replied. "But I agree—aside from being chased by screaming ghosts, this is all a pretty great adventure."

Teag smiled at him, and Anthony felt his insides turn to jelly with the emotions in Teag's eyes. Love, gratitude, and acceptance. Figuring out a century-old mystery wasn't the worst way to spend part of their vacation, and Anthony had plenty of plans for their time after they stopped the ghost problem.

"Divide and conquer," Teag said once they had finished their lunch and washed their hands to avoid leaving marks on any of the old documents. "Do you want letters or journals?"

"Letters," Anthony replied. "And if I get finished first, I can help with the journals that are left."

"I've got a hunch that what we want is from 1916 forward," Teag said. "Let's start with that."

They each took a stack of papers and sat across the table from each other, engrossed in their reading. Anthony squinted to make out the neat cursive script in faded ink.

"I feel like a peeping Tom," Anthony said. "These are love letters written to Lillian from Bertram—Bertie Granville. Why is that name familiar?"

Teag looked up from the journal he was reading. "It's the name that guy in the pub mentioned, and Mr. Porter in the bookstore. Landed gentry, country manor outside of town."

Anthony nodded. "Okay. I knew I'd heard it from somewhere. It looks like Mr. Porter had the story right. Bertie and Lillian were very much in love. He even wrote out a proposal and signed it." He couldn't help tearing up a bit. "But I guess he never came home from the war."

Teag went back to reading through Lillian's journals, and the squinch between his eyebrows told Anthony his fiancé was fully immersed in what he was doing. Anthony hadn't been completely kidding about feeling like a voyeur reading the old love letters. He knew that people in past generations were just regular folks who loved and laughed and cried, but it was one thing to try to imagine an elderly couple as being young and in love, and entirely another to read the intimate endearments between two lovers from a prior generation.

An hour passed in silence as they worked their way through the letters and diaries. Teag's sudden outburst made Anthony startle.

"Holy shit!"

Anthony looked up. Teag was staring at the journal as if it had bit him. "What?"

"It's all here. In TMI detail," he added, his cheeks coloring a bit. "Bertie didn't just propose to Lillian. They had a 'last night on earth' lovemaking session before he got sent off to war. She, uh, noted all the details," he added, looking adorably flustered.

"And?" Anthony nudged, having a feeling where this might be going.

"The war was going full tilt, and not well for the Triple Entente—Great Britain, France, and Russia," Teag said. "So Bertie got rushed through training and sent off to the front in short order. He died almost as soon as he was deployed in the Battle of the Somme," Teag said. "Of course, there was a lag between when Bertie died and when his family was notified, and a few days more before Lillian heard. A couple of months. Long enough for Lillian to realize she was pregnant. She sent Bertie a letter, but it sounds like it didn't reach him until it was too late."

"That poor woman couldn't catch a break." Anthony felt fresh grief for a loss suffered more than a century ago.

"Mabel was furious." Teag flipped journal pages to keep up with the story. "The earl and Countess were off helping the war effort, so Mabel was in charge, like the man at the antique store told us. And Mabel couldn't stand the thought of the family reputation being sullied by an out-of-wedlock pregnancy."

"But they were engaged," Anthony protested. "Didn't Lillian tell her that?"

"Lillian says in her journal that Bertie got a hero's funeral, and she didn't want to 'besmirch' his name." Teag sighed. "So she kept quiet."

"So what about the baby?"

"Here's where I think Lillian has more of a reason to haunt Mabel than the other way around. Lillian had a difficult birth. By the time she was really coherent, Mabel had given the baby to a cousin who had suffered a miscarriage to raise as their own."

"But the baby wasn't really a Mortimer," Anthony protested. "He's a Granville. Oh, shit."

Teag and Anthony's gazes locked. "He's the heir to the Granville estate—or at least, his descendant is," Teag breathed. "That's what the men at the pub were talking about, how Old Man Granville was the last of his family and when he died, the estate would revert to the Crown. Remember?"

"Wow. What else does it say?" Anthony prompted.

"Obviously, Lillian didn't take it well, that Mabel gave away her baby, which was all she had left of Bertie. She had a 'bout of hysteria'— a nervous breakdown. That just made Mabel more angry because she didn't want anyone saying the Mortimers were 'weak minded.' So she locked Lillian up."

"She sounds like a real peach," Anthony growled.

"But Lillian wasn't as weak as Mable thought," Teag went on, and Anthony felt like he'd been dropped into a soap opera. "Before she gave birth, she'd begged the midwife to have the child baptized and make sure there was a certificate. And there is—for Archer Mortimer Granville," he said, with a gleam of triumph in his eyes. "Mabel never found out."

"But the cousins still took him, right?"

Teag nodded. "Yeah. Lillian never saw him again. Her later journals are really bleak. She got depressed—no big surprise. She said her loom and her needle were her only companions, and she wove or sewed until she was too exhausted to sit up."

"All those 'archer' designs," Anthony supplied.

"Yeah. That strain probably broke her health, and then when a TB epidemic came through, she was vulnerable. She was twenty-two when she died."

"Jesus," Anthony murmured. "While Mabel lived into her nineties, inherited everything, and had a husband and family. That's just all kinds of wrong." He thought for a moment. "But no one's reported seeing either of the sisters' ghosts until now."

"I think that somehow, Lilian knows about the Granville estate. And she wants her son's descendants to have their rightful inheritance."

Anthony drummed his fingers on the table. "I'm a lawyer, not a barrister. All I know about English law I learned from watching BBC crime dramas. So how do we do right by Lillian and Archer?"

Teag's eyes were alight, and it was clear he enjoyed playing ghost detective. "First, I think we need to figure out which 'cousins' took Archer and then try to find out who his direct descendants are."

"I think there was a Mortimer family tree on the website," Anthony said.

"Let me run back for my tablet, and we can look it up—assuming we've got wifi in here," Teag replied. He left and came back quickly, flushed from running in the cold air.

"I kept the tablet inside my coat, so it shouldn't be too cold to boot up," he said. Anthony pulled his chair closer, and Teag turned on the tablet, crossing his fingers until they found a signal. A few clicks got them to the right page on the website.

"So we have to go back to who would have been the earl during World War I—Mabel and Lillian's father," Anthony murmured, thinking aloud.

"Okay. That's here," Teag pointed to the family tree. "Earl Charles

Mortimer is the grandfather of the current earl. Charles had a brother and a sister. The brother had three children. The sister had four."

"All right," Anthony replied. "Charles's brother and sister would have been Mabel and Lillian's uncle and aunt. So baby Archer was given to one of their children—someone who would have been Mabel and Lillian's cousins. So which of those cousins had a male child in 1917?"

Teag did his best to enlarge the small writing. "Charles's sister's son, Elliott, had three children. A daughter, Elizabeth; a son, Reginald who died as a baby. And look—there's a third 'son' named Archibald."

"Archibald. Archer," Anthony said quietly, meeting Teag's gaze. "Do you think it's the same child?"

Teag squinted to see the birth and death dates. "Let me do a little math. We know when Lillian and Bertie spent their night of passion together. So nine months from then should have been…yeah. It's gotta be Archibald. The similarity in the names might be a coincidence."

"Or perhaps Mabel mentioned the Archer name, and they did their own twist on it."

"Maybe." Teag leaned closer, trying to see better. "The type gets fuzzy when you blow it up too much. If Archer was born in 1917, he's probably dead by now. So let's look at his descendants. Okay, he would have been just the right age to end up serving in WWII. So that explains why his kids weren't born until after 1945. And he's got three —a son in 1945, a daughter in 1946, and another son in 1947. The oldest son died four years ago, and the daughter died in her forties. But the youngest son…" He trailed off, then raised his head, triumphant.

"Shit. He could still be alive," Teag said, with a look on his face as if he'd just discovered King Tut's tomb. "The youngest one, Theodore, would be seventy-two. This says he had two children, Ben and Helena, who are probably in their late forties, and they had children whose names aren't listed, probably for privacy reasons."

"Want to bet Priscilla could fill in the blanks?" Anthony asked with a grin.

"I bet she could!" Teag headed toward the lobby, where Priscilla was just finishing up with a guest. She saw him in the doorway to the meeting room, and he gestured for her to come over.

"We need to pick your brain for a moment," Teag said, bringing her over to the tablet. "You said you were a Mortimer cousin. How much do you know about the family tree?"

Priscilla grinned. "I'm a total genealogy nerd."

Anthony held out a chair for her. "Sit down. We've got a story to tell you."

"AND THAT, my lord, is how you ended up with a ghost in the sitting room and the lost heir to the Granville estate as your extended cousin," Teag recapped, sitting back in his chair and waiting for the earl's reaction. Priscilla stood nearby and seemed to be making a real effort to keep from bouncing on her toes in excitement.

"That's quite a tale," the earl said. "And please, call me Ward."

"All the documents are right here," Teag replied. "The signed proposal from Bertie Granville to Lillian, his letters to her, her diaries—and the baptismal certificate."

"And these were all under a bed in a room people forgot about up in Bride's Tower?" the earl said, looking a bit gobsmacked at the revelation.

"Yes, my lord, er, Ward," Teag replied. "We just found the room and the suitcase earlier today and brought them here to read through."

"Well, that's a very interesting turn of events," the earl replied. "I've known Hollister Granville all my life—he was a friend of my father's—and he's been most distressed about the lack of an heir. It wasn't for lack of trying—he had three children and outlived them all. No grandchildren. I think he'll be relieved, finding there is a blood heir to his estate. And if he accepts the evidence you've found—and I think he will—he can acknowledge Theodore Mortimer as actually being Theodore Granville," the earl said, shaking his head as if it was all too much to take in.

"Hollister doesn't just dislike the idea of having his manor and estate all revert to the Crown; he hates to see the family name disappear and all its history with it," he added.

"Now it doesn't have to," Anthony responded, and part of him couldn't believe he was talking to a real, live earl.

"I'll have to ring up my barrister, and he'll need to look everything over, authenticate it, of course," the earl said, "so that when Hollister Granville turns in documents to acknowledge Theodore and leave him the Granville estate, there's no trouble. And I guess that means I'd better call 'cousin' Theodore as well and let him know he's the descendant of Lillian's love child." He shook his head. "Theodore never did care much for Mabel. There'll be no living with him if he ends up foxing her plans to keep Lillian's child a secret." His tone was resigned, but his smile suggested otherwise.

"Is there time?" Teag asked, then looked chagrined. "I mean, we overheard some of the locals down at the Boar and Knight talking, and they sounded like Mr. Granville wasn't long for this world."

The earl let out a roar of laughter. "Oh, I'll have to tell Hollister. He'll get a kick out of that. Hollister Granville might be close to one hundred years old, but I assure you—the reports of his death are greatly exaggerated."

"What about the ghosts?" Priscilla asked. "And why did Mabel fuss at both of you in the bedroom and not at me when I was in the hallway?"

Anthony shrugged. "You're a Mortimer. She might have respected the family connection. We were strangers, about to reveal what she thought was a shameful secret."

The earl cleared his throat. "Yes, well. About that. A good bit has changed since those days. It sounds to me like Lillian and Bertie were very much in love and married in all but technicality." He leaned forward conspiratorially. "Not to speak ill of the dead, but just between us—I never liked Mabel, either."

"It might be as simple as having you go up to the fifth floor of Bride's Tower and telling Mabel that the jig is up," Teag replied. "That you know the secret and don't care—and that Lillian's son will get his due."

"You think it could be that easy?" the earl asked.

Teag nodded. "Sometimes, it is. These ghosts are aware. They've been here all this time without causing problems. Lillian 'woke up' because, in her mind, Archer was about to lose his inheritance. And Mabel became active to protect the family name. Unfinished business is a powerful tether for spirits. But now that the matter is settled, they can both move on—and hopefully, find peace."

"I do hope when it's all said and done, that more of Lillian's handiwork can be displayed somehow," Anthony said wistfully. "The pieces are beautiful, and it's a shame they've been hidden away for so long."

"I think that can be arranged," the earl replied.

"You know, Uncle, when the dust settles, and everything is official with Theodore and the Granvilles, this would make for marvelous publicity," Priscilla said. "Interest is still high in the Great War, with the centennial so recent. And the story has it all—a tragic love affair, a secret baby, all set against the backdrop of world war, and then redemption. The BBC might even want to make it into a miniseries," she added with a wink.

"Saints preserve us," the earl said with a shudder, but Anthony didn't get the feeling he really objected to the idea.

CHAPTER FIVE

TEAG

I still can't believe you already had tickets to the ball—and shipped our tuxes!" Teag sipped from a flute of Champagne as the music played. He and Anthony had stepped off to the side after dancing to several of their favorite songs.

The Great Hall looked even more spectacular than when they had seen it earlier in the week. Acrylic sculptures around the edge of the room had the look of ice and the glow of flames. Icicles and silver tinsel hung from the ceiling, evergreen boughs with crimson ribbon and gold bells adorned every window, and the tables all had matching artisan-created centerpieces. The lights and decorations on the huge fir tree just made the whole scene even more festive.

"I loved the Christmas Market-style stalls under the grand marquee in the outer bailey," Anthony replied. "And the hot chocolate!" The big event tent offered a variety of local crafts for last-minute shoppers, as well as delicious "small plate" servings of holiday fare. The serving tables in the Great Hall matched the look of the market stalls.

"I was blown away by the ice rink in the moat! I guess it's too cold for alligators here, right?" Teag remarked, taking in the whole glistening scene. Mistletoe balls hung everywhere, and he and Anthony had discretely kissed more than once as they danced. They were both pleasantly surprised when no one seemed to think that two men dancing together was anything out of the ordinary.

"At this point, I think anything is possible," Anthony replied. "Especially after you dragged me on a find-the-gargoyle kissing tour."

"We've done all of them but one," Teag said. "I think it's the real one. We couldn't get into where it is today, but we can later on. I am not going to miss out!"

"The folly was just as pretty as you promised. Even if I did freeze my…nether parts…off getting there." The open-air folly, located close to the river, stood exposed to the sharp winds, but the visit was completely worth it for the opulent and fanciful lights and decorations and the chance to see the castle's famous statue.

"The folly gave the solarium and conservatory a run for its money with decorations," Teag agreed. "That's where the desserts will be served, so we'll get another look. Whoever handled the decor did a fantastic job."

"You clean up well, did I ever mention that?" Anthony reached out to adjust Teag's bow tie and ran a proprietary hand down his arm.

"You're not too shabby yourself, Counselor," Teag said with a grin.

Anthony leaned closer. "I've wanted to peel you out of that tux since you put it on. That's going to be the highlight of the evening."

"Mm," Teag murmured. "I totally agree."

They finished their drinks and headed back to the dance floor. The slow song was one of Teag's favorites, and he leaned into his fiancé, enjoying the scent of his cologne and shampoo, and something else that was uniquely Anthony. He loved the way they fit together and how close Anthony held him.

Anthony rested his cheek against Teag's head and tightened his grip on Teag's hand. "What are you thinking?"

Teag nestled closer. Anthony was just enough larger and more solid that Teag always felt sheltered in his arms. "Just that this has been the best vacation ever."

"We still have a few days left, plus Christmas—and no more ghosts," Anthony pointed out. The earl had gone up to have a chat with Mabel and Lillian, and since then, no trace of ghostly activity had been spotted. Just in case, Priscilla didn't plan to re-open the sitting rooms until after the holiday.

"I'm glad I could set Lillian free. It wasn't as hard to neutralize the soul threads as I'd been afraid it might be," Teag replied quietly enough no one else would hear. "And I'm sure she's happy that her son—or at least his descendant—looks likely to get his due."

It would take a while for the earl and Hollister Granville to have the letters and birth certificate authenticated, but Priscilla had given Teag and Anthony an update, saying that Hollister was very willing to accept Theodore Mortimer as the long-lost son of Bertie and Lillian and make him the Granville heir.

"I'd think it certainly helped that Hollister had saved that box full of Bertie's correspondence from the war. Finding an unopened letter from Lillian telling Bertie she was expecting a baby kind of ties it up with a bow when you put it together with what we found," Anthony said.

They swayed to the music, and Teag swore the Champagne bubbles had gone to his head because the feelings in his heart made him giddy. He was here, in a beautiful castle, with the love of his life, dancing the night away. Teag couldn't imagine being any happier.

When they finally slipped away from the ball, not long before midnight, the crisp air felt good after the warmth of the ballroom, and the clear winter night had a velvet canopy of stars.

"The perfect end to a perfect evening," Teag sighed.

Anthony laughed. "Not yet. Or did you forget about the naked part?"

Teag gave him a wink. "Of course not. That's what makes it perfect!"

They hurried, hand-in-hand, across the open space to the wing where their room was located, happy for the relative warmth of the elevator. Inside, Teag pushed Anthony against the back of the car, fitting against him like on the dance floor, stealing a heated kiss.

"That's just to get you warm," Teag teased, stepping back with a grin.

"Oh, I'm plenty warm." Anthony reached down and discreetly shifted himself in his tuxedo pants. "I've been 'warm' all night watching the way that tux fits your shoulders, and those pants cling to your ass. I'm glad you clean up, but now I'm ready to get you dirty."

"I like the sound of that."

Anthony led the way to their room, and Teag enjoyed the view. The modern cut of the tux pants accentuated Anthony's muscular ass and strong thighs in the same way the jacket showed off his shoulders and V-shape to its best advantage. He was glad the room wasn't further away because walking was becoming difficult with a raging hard-on.

Anthony opened the door and yanked Teag inside, then closed and locked the door and pinned Teag against the wall. He cupped Teag's face, leaning in for a kiss that was hungry and hot. His tongue slipped across Teag's lips, and Teag opened to him with a breathy moan. Teag grabbed Anthony's jacket and pulled him even closer, then straddled Anthony's thigh and ground against him, making it clear just how ready he was.

"Too many clothes," Anthony gasped when he came up for air. His blue eyes were dark with lust, and his lips already kiss swollen from Teag's stubble.

"Then let me fix that," Teag replied, never losing eye contact. He reached forward and untied Anthony's bow tie, tossing it onto a nearby chair. He eased off the jacket, which quickly joined the tie, then rucked up Anthony's starched shirt, pulling it loose from his pants. Anthony's belt disappeared with a flourish, and Teag opened his fly, sinking to his knees, fully clothed.

"God, you're beautiful."

Teag didn't reply. He wrapped one hand around the base of Anthony's hard cock and licked the head, tasting the salty pre-come, then took him deep, bobbing and licking until he felt the quiver in Anthony's legs and heard him moan. Anthony's fingers combed through Teag's hair, tugging gently.

Teag pulled off with a wet "*pop*" and looked up through his lashes, well aware of what the sight did to Anthony. "I don't think we're naked enough yet."

"Not by half," Anthony agreed. He pulled Teag to his feet and made short work of his bow tie, then took his time unbuttoning the stiff shirt, letting his fingers slide down Teag's chest with every movement.

"Cuff links," Teag managed to remember when the front was unbuttoned. The onyx and silver set had been a Christmas gift from Anthony the previous year. Teag worked them off quickly, setting them in a bowl on a table by the door. Anthony was already stripping off his shirt, and his cuff links clinked into the bowl with Teag's.

They toed off their shoes and sent their socks flying. Anthony stepped out of his pants and boxer-briefs as Teag hurried to shuck off his own pants and underwear. Finally, they were both naked, and Anthony pulled Teag to him, wrapping his arms around him and reaching down to grab his ass. The hair on Anthony's chest scraped against Teag's smooth skin, making Teag's breath hitch and his cock leak.

"What do you want?" Anthony's voice was a husky drawl that went right to Teag's dick.

Teag moved to rub their erections together. "Obvious, isn't it?"

Anthony nipped his way down Teag's neck. "I meant, *how* do you want it?"

They liked to switch, although Anthony probably bottomed a little more often. In the years they'd been together, there had been plenty of time to try new things, but sometimes, basic was better.

"Long and slow. You, in me. Please."

"Anything you want, baby."

Teag gave Anthony a kiss, lightly nipping his lower lip. He slipped out of Anthony's arms and arranged himself on the bed, laying back, legs bent at the knee and spread wide, giving his lover a good view. Teag reached down and gave himself a tug, fully aware that Anthony's gaze followed his every move.

"I want to eat you up." Anthony's growl made Teag shiver. Anthony crawled onto the bed, stalking toward him, the look in his eyes predatory. He grabbed the lube from the nightstand and tossed it onto the bed, then he leaned down to kiss Teag's mouth, slowly working his way down Teag's throat, to his collarbone, then lower.

Anthony licked and sucked first on one dark nipple and then the other until they pebbled, and he blew lightly over them, making Teag shiver.

"Yes. This. Want you so much," Teag groaned. He could feel the sticky trail of Anthony's leaking cock on his belly, teasing him as it bobbed with every movement.

Teag slid his hands into Anthony's blond hair. It wasn't as long as his own, but there was enough to get a good grip, and he loved to see his usually impeccable lover looking disheveled and knowing it was because of him.

Anthony was as good as his word, leaving each nipple with a kiss and a gentle tug of teeth, and then moving on, licking, kissing, and nipping his way down Teag's belly to the trail of dark hair that led to his groin.

"Please." Teag's voice hid none of his raw emotions. He loved the openness they had between them, with no posturing, no pretending. He'd never let himself be vulnerable with a lover before Anthony, not like this, with no secrets between them.

"I'll take care of you, sweetheart. We're just getting started." Anthony moved to trace the tip of his tongue down the crease where leg met thigh, first on the right, then the left. He left Teag's rigid cock untouched and nosed lower, taking Teag's sac into his mouth, rolling it on his tongue. Teag arched up, and Anthony's broad hands took firm hold of his hips, lifting him so he could lick down the taint to the tight furl below.

"Jesus. Anthony, please."

Anthony drew a swipe across the sensitive skin with the flat of his tongue, then came back with the tip to tease at the rim. Teag shuddered and jerked at the sensation as Anthony lapped and poked with his tongue, alternating strokes until Teag could feel his balls draw up.

"I want to come with you in me," Teag begged. "Please."

Anthony reached for the lube and slicked up his fingers, then pressed one against Teag's pucker and pushed it slowly inside. "Taking my time, like you asked me to. Gonna make this good for you."

"I'm not going to last."

"Then I'll have to keep it up until you're ready to go again."

"Fuck."

"We'll get to that part." Anthony worked a second finger inside, turned them to hit Teag's sweet spot, and took Teag's cock in his mouth, down the root, burying his nose in the tangle of dark hair at the base.

"God, Anthony!" Teag arched, throwing his head back and tightening his hands in Anthony's hair as his release tore through him. Anthony swallowed it all, and the movement of his throat and tongue against Teag's sensitive cock drew a whimper.

Anthony pulled back, then swirled his tongue around the head of Teag's cock and drew the tip through his slit, getting every drop. Teag's heart hammered, and a light sheen of sweat covered his body as he lay panting and sated.

Anthony leaned over him and bent down for a kiss. Teag could taste himself on Anthony's lips, and damn if that wasn't hot enough to make his spent cock twitch.

"Let me in," he murmured against Teag's lips.

"Christ, yes!"

Anthony slid his hands to get a good hold on Teag's hips and lifted him to get the angle just right, then pressed the head of his stiff cock against Teag's hole and slid inside, one slow inch at a time. Teag tried to push forward, but Anthony held him off, chuckling.

"You wanted slow."

"You're gonna kill me!"

"You'll die happy."

When Anthony was fully seated, he hesitated, letting Teag adjust to the fullness, and then began a long, slow slide all the way out, and a fast rush back in.

"More," Teag begged.

"Gonna give you what you need. Hush." He kept up the slow, deep thrusts until Teag was panting and clutching at the sheets, and his dick had begun to fill again. Anthony shifted to make sure he hit Teag's spot, and Teag cried out, lost in the sensation. He reached between them to wrap his hand around Teag's stiffening cock and give it a few pulls, still keeping up the rhythm with his hips.

Just when Teag didn't think he could take the slow pleasuring any longer, Anthony slipped his hands behind Teag's shoulders and sat back on his heels, drawing Teag up to face him, straddling his lap.

Teag groaned as the position drove Anthony's cock deeper inside. Anthony leaned forward to kiss his throat and chest.

"Move for me, baby. Make it feel good for you, and I'm damn sure it'll feel fine for me."

Teag knew how much Anthony liked to watch him get lost in the sensation, fully admitting to his voyeuristic streak. Still buzzed from the intensity of his first orgasm, Teag draped his arms over Anthony's shoulders, getting his legs under him so he could lift enough to fuck himself on Anthony's cock.

"That's it. So damn sexy. So hot. I love to watch you," Anthony urged in a low, deep voice that went right to Teag's balls. "Ride me. Get yourself off. Take all of me." He slid his hand between them and gripped Teag's cock, making a channel for him to fuck.

Teag rolled his hips, satisfied when that drew a moan from Anthony. He rose and plunged down, and Anthony bucked up to meet him, again and again. Teag loved that he could put that look on Anthony's face, pupils blown, face flushed, hair sweaty and askew—in short, utterly fucked out.

One last undulation, which drove Anthony's cock against his spot and threatened to send Teag over the edge. Anthony was close, and he grabbed Teag's hips again, taking charge and chasing his release. He thrust hard once, twice, and then cried out Teag's name as he spent, filling Teag's channel as it tightened around him, and Teag came, shaking and gasping for air.

Teag fell onto him, resting his head on Anthony's shoulder. They were both a sticky mess. Teag could still pick up a hint of Anthony's cologne, mingled with the smell of sweat and come. He fluttered his tongue over the throbbing pulse in Anthony's neck and relished the shiver it sent through his lover's body.

"I love you," Anthony murmured with his face buried in Teag's hair. "Will you marry me?"

"Pretty sure you already asked, and I already said yes," Teag said, blowing in his ear.

"Good. 'Cuz I'm never letting you go."

"If we don't get a shower, we're going to stick like this, and you won't be able to."

Anthony responded with a smack to Teag's ass, just enough to sting. "Come on. Let's get cleaned up." Teag reluctantly crawled off of Anthony's lap and took his hand as they walked to the bathroom. The hot shower felt amazing, and Teag thought he might fall asleep standing up.

"Let me." Anthony worked up a lather between his palms, and then slid his soapy hands all over Teag's body, washing away the remnants of their lovemaking. He slid a slick hand over Teag's cock and balls, and then down his crack, managing to get a twitch of acknowledgment. Then he washed Teag's hair and turned him gently to rinse, making sure none of the soap got in his eyes.

"Your turn." Teag offered, though he could barely keep his eyes open.

"Next time," Anthony said. "Let me wash up quickly, and let's go to sleep. We can pick up again in the morning if you want."

Teag slipped his hand down Anthony's chest. "Oh, I want. I definitely want."

They toweled off and practically fell into bed. Teag retrieved the lube and put it back on the nightstand, then snuggled against Anthony, front to back. Teag wrapped an arm around Anthony, drawing him close.

"How about tomorrow we go to that tea shop in town and then try out the earl's brewery for dinner?" Anthony murmured. "And in between, we can come back here and *relax*." His emphasis left no doubt as to the type of relaxation he had in mind.

"Mm. Sounds like a plan. And I saw some comfy couches in the main lobby, near that huge fireplace. Looked like the perfect place to curl up with a sexy man, a hot drink, and a good book."

"We can do that too. Anything you want. Always." Anthony sounded barely awake.

Teag leaned forward and kissed Anthony's bare shoulder. "I love you too."

"SHOULDN'T we be waiting with the luggage for our driver?" Anthony protested as Teag dragged him by the wrist toward the castle's chapel.

"Shh. We have time. And with all the holiday events, this is the first chance we've had to get inside."

Teag opened the door to the Caynham family chapel. It was still decorated for the holidays, since today, the day after Christmas, was Boxing Day and part of the holiday festivities.

They had spent the last few days exploring the town, sprawled on the comfortable lobby couches in front of a roaring fire, or attending the Christmas Eve service at St. Peter's in the village and then the bell-ringing event at the castle. Christmas Day had been perfect, with just a dusting of snow. Teag and Anthony had agreed to leave their presents back home and traded small wrapped boxes with pictures of the gifts inside instead.

Anthony gave Teag a custom-designed, protective silver amulet with the help of some of their Charleston friends who were in the know about such things. Teag gave Anthony a vintage watch, knowing it was a kind Anthony really liked to collect. Of course, he had made sure it had no negative juju or bad magic attached.

"Up here." Teag tugged Anthony toward a stairway in the back of the chapel.

"Where are you taking me?"

"You'll see."

They emerged in a room with a dark wooden bench around the walls, and heavy ropes that hung from holes in the ceiling, each ending in a loop.

"What the hell? Are those...nooses?" Anthony asked, wide-eyed.

"Of course not. They're bell ropes. This is the ringing room," Teag explained. "The bell ringers hang onto those loops, because the bells are very heavy, and when they start swinging back and forth, it can lift the ringers off their feet." He glanced up. "That's why there's a ceiling, so they don't get pulled up into the bell tower."

"I hope they have earplugs," Anthony replied. Teag agreed, remembering how loud the peal of the bells had been at a distance.

"That's not why we're here. Look!" Teag pointed upward toward the stone molding around the top of the room, just below the ceiling. Carved gargoyles, ugly little faces that looked like gnomes or imps, looked down from every corner.

"I'm certain that's the original one," Teag said excitedly. "I brought you up here to kiss where he can see us. "If you kiss where the gargoyle can see, your true love you've found and will forever be."

Anthony reached out and drew Teag into his arms. "I like the sound of 'forever.'"

"So do I. I'm all in, you know that, don't you?"

Anthony nodded. "I know. And so am I. You're it for me."

Teag reached up to cup Anthony's face and drew them together in a long, satisfying kiss. When they finally stepped apart, they were both breathing hard.

"Did it work?" Anthony asked.

Teag looked up at the gargoyle, but the carving looked unchanged. "I'm going to believe it did," Teag said, giving the squat imp a wink. "That's my story, and I'm sticking to it."

Anthony pulled him close and kissed him again. "Just in case he wasn't looking the first time," he told Teag with a grin.

They headed downstairs and back to the front desk. Patrick and his golf cart had already brought down their luggage, and they had enjoyed a final full English breakfast at the castle restaurant earlier that morning. Now it was time to catch the cab to Heathrow and the flight back home. Teag knew he was going to miss Caynham Castle.

"We can reserve the honeymoon suite once we pick a wedding date, right?" he asked Anthony, suddenly needing to know that they weren't taking leave of this very special place forever.

"Absolutely," Anthony promised. "And if it isn't available exactly on the date we want, I'm all for planning a trip around when it is." He leaned down to whisper in Teag's ear. "I think you might just have an in with the earl for un-haunting his castle."

To their surprise, Priscilla was waiting for them. "Sorry to see you go. I hope you enjoyed your stay." Both men hurried to assure her that they loved the castle, the ball, and the village.

"Just let me know when you decide on your honeymoon dates,"

she told them. "We'll take good care of you." Priscilla held out a small, wrapped box. "This is from the earl, a token of his thanks for figuring out the haunting and doing right by Lillian."

"I'm just glad Mabel and Lillian's ghosts were willing to listen when he went to talk to them," Teag replied. The earl had taken Teag's advice and gone up to the fifth floor to tell Mabel it was time to move on and assure Lillian that her son's descendants were acknowledged and restored to the Granville family.

"I think he was sort of hoping he'd catch a glimpse of the ghosts," Priscilla confided. "But I guess they didn't want to show themselves. Anyhow—there hasn't been a hint of anything strange happening in the sitting room since then. Although we did move Mabel's hair comb to another location, just to put more distance between it and any of Lillian's needlework."

"Probably a good idea," Teag replied.

Teag and Anthony worked together to open the box while Priscilla watched them with a smile. Inside was an embroidered handkerchief, and Teag recognized it immediately as one of Lillian's early pieces when she was happy and in love.

"Wow. This is really amazing," Teag said, completely surprised by the gift. Anthony nodded, slipping an arm around him. "Please let the earl know how much this means to us." He silently vowed to write a thank-you note on the best stationery he could find, once they returned to Charleston.

"He thought it was a fitting reminder of your visit," Priscilla said with an impish grin, and Teag wondered if she'd had something to do with that. "And you can tell him yourself when you return to Caynham Castle."

They thanked Priscilla again, both for the gift and for all her help. Teag and Anthony headed out to the parking lot, where their cab was waiting with their luggage already loaded. To their delight, Henry was once again their driver.

"Did your holiday go well?" Henry asked.

Teag turned in his seat so he could see the castle as they drove away. "Very well," he assured their driver.

"It was full of surprises," Anthony added. "But they were all wonderful."

"I hope that means you'll be coming back," Henry replied. "A place like that can get under your skin, you know, if it calls to you."

"Oh, we'll be back, that's for sure," Teag told him. He met Anthony's gaze and took his hand, giving it a squeeze. "The sooner, the better."

SECRETS AND CIPHERS
A TREASURE TRAIL NOVELLA

By Morgan Brice

CHAPTER ONE

BEN

So when you said 'castle,' you really meant—holy shit! That's a friggin' castle!" Ben Nolan's eyes went wide as the hired car pulled into the parking area at Caynham Castle.

Erik Mitchell laughed. "What did you think I meant?"

Ben shook his head, still staring at the large stone building partially hidden within the inner bailey walls. "I thought you meant like Biltmore. Or San Simeon out in California. You know—a big, fancy house built by a gazillionaire. But this is an actual castle!"

"Parts of it date back to the eleven hundreds," Erik replied, nudging Ben to get him to open his door so their driver could retrieve their luggage. "The fortifications were meant to withstand warfare. It's been continually inhabited by the Mortimer family for nine hundred years."

"Wait until I tell my sister-in-law. She thinks it's extra special that she lives in the same house her grandparents built."

Erik paid the driver, and then he and Ben stepped to the side of the lot, awaiting the golf cart that would take them closer to the entrance. Caynham Castle had been converted to a hotel back in the 1930s, combining history, fine food, exceptional comfort, and aristocratic flair for those who yearned for a memorable destination.

"For the U.S., that's an accomplishment," Erik said with a shrug. "Different places, different times."

"And you're friends with the guy who owns it? The duke?"

"Earl," Erik replied distractedly, checking his text messages to ensure that they were in the right place to catch their ride.

"Oh, earl. My bad." Ben rolled his eyes.

"And I'd say we're more friendly colleagues than drinking buddies," Erik answered. "He was the patron of the task force I served on around a fraud investigation in a major museum. We hit it off. He's very down-to-earth. You'll like him."

"Are you on his Christmas card list?"

Erik gave him a weird look. "What?"

"You heard me."

"I get a holiday card from my mailman too. It's a polite fiction. Doesn't make us besties."

"So you *do* get a card from the earl?" Ben pressed.

Erik sighed and gave him a look of fond exasperation. "Yes. Are you happy now? It's a very fancy card with foil stamping and laser die-cuts, and the signature is printed on the card. In case you were keeping track."

"My dad always got a Christmas card from Earl Denning, the guy who ran the lawnmower repair shop near our house in Newark," Ben said. "Not quite the same thing."

Erik laid a hand on Ben's shoulder as if he could guess what was bothering him. "Relax. I never thought you'd feel uncomfortable. I just wanted to spoil you a little." He gave Ben a coaxing look that usually melted any hesitation.

"I've been to fancy places, just not quite this fancy," Ben admitted, wondering if any of the clothing he had brought with him would be suitable. *Well, at least there's the tux Erik had me get for Jaxon's big gala. But I don't think I can wear that all week.*

"Think of it as a museum," Erik cajoled. "And remember what I told you about the food and the cake at the castle tea shop."

Ben smiled, forcing his insecurities to the back of his mind. Erik had planned this trip to give them both some much-needed time off together, and Ben didn't want to dim that glow.

"I'm looking forward to all of it," he assured Erik. "The castle part just took me by surprise."

"Because I totally tricked you into coming to a castle by telling you we were coming to a castle," Erik said, but Ben could see his partner's worried frown had eased.

"Yeah. You're sneaky like that," Ben teased.

A golf cart pulled up with a driver who looked like he was probably still in high school. "Hi! I'm Patrick, and this is my humble carriage. Climb in, and I'll get you up to the front desk and settled into your room."

Ben tried to lend a hand with the bags, but the young man waved him off. "Nah, I've got it. My mum would be after me if I let a guest do the heavy lifting," he added with a laugh. "She works at the gift shop, so she always finds out."

Erik reached out and gripped Ben's hand in the back seat of the golf cart as they headed up a sloped drive and through the second set of fortified walls.

"Do you ever get used to working in a real castle?" Ben asked, resigned to having the same gobsmacked expression they always laughed at tourists for in New York City.

"I don't think about it, to tell you the truth," Patrick replied. "'Course, we've got castles all over the place here. They're everywhere, so no one pays attention." He chuckled. "Not so much where you're from, I take it?"

"Not really," Ben admitted. "I thought they were only in movies."

"Go on and find out your room number, and I'll take care of moving you in," Patrick promised. "The faster you get settled, the sooner you can start having fun on holiday."

Ben followed Erik into the check-in area. Dark wood paneling, rough stone walls, crossed swords, and heraldic banners just reinforced Ben's feeling that he was at a theme park. A tissue paper ghost peeked around a mirror, one of the portraits had a mask added over the face, and a pumpkin filled with flowers sat on the counter next to a dish of candy.

"Erik Mitchell. So good to see you again. It's been too long."

Ben's head came up to see a young woman with brown hair caught up in a neat tail shake Erik's hand. Her warm smile made it clear this wasn't their first meeting.

"Far too long," Erik agreed, returning a smile of the same wattage. He pulled Ben close to him, slipping an arm around his waist. "Priscilla Donovan, this is my partner, Ben Nolan. Ben, this is Priscilla. She was the earl's assistant when we worked on the task force together."

Priscilla grinned and shook Ben's hand. "He's my cousin, so it wasn't as impressive as it sounds." She turned her attention back to Erik. "And Claire's taken over that role—I'm head of reception now, a move into Hotel Operations. I see you're finally taking him up on his offer to visit."

"Seemed like a good time to do it," Erik replied. "I don't know if you heard, but I left the Coalition. Got out of the business. Now I run an antique shop in Cape May, New Jersey."

Priscilla nodded. "He mentioned it. I'm glad you've settled into something that makes you happy."

She handed them their room keys. "You're in one of the Dower Apartments, second floor," Priscilla told them. "Just follow Patrick—he knows the way."

Patrick kept up a casual monologue as he drove them to their room. "If you're hungry, you might want to stop by the castle tea shop. Cold sandwiches, mini quiches, all kinds of little cakes and tarts, and tea, as if you couldn't guess. That should tide you over until dinner. The food in our dining room is excellent. Lots to choose from, and it's all amazing. If you go into town, there's the Boar and Knight—good ale, better-than-most pub food. There's another tea shop in town—it's very good, but I think ours is better," he added loyally. "Have a look around. You'll be spoilt for choice!"

Ben wasn't sure what to expect from the room and found himself once again taken aback at the large suite filled with antiques and a huge four-poster bed with a mattress that seemed impossibly far off the floor.

"Wow. Fit for a king and all that." He wondered whether the bed was as comfortable as it looked.

"We've got elbow room and privacy." Erik pronounced the last word in the British style. "And I have lots of ideas on what to do with both," he added with a roguish wiggle of his eyebrows.

Ben pulled Erik closer and kissed him soundly, adding a squeeze of his ass for good measure. He might be a duck out of water, a Jersey boy far from home, but he was with Erik, and Ben trusted his partner to take care of them.

"I take it you like the hotel?" Erik teased when he came up for air.

"Very much," Ben replied, stealing another kiss. "And I like you in the hotel. Later on, I'm pretty sure I'm going to like you in that monstrosity of a bed."

"Only pretty sure?"

Ben took Erik's hand and placed the palm against Ben's half-hard cock. "Very sure."

At that moment, Ben's stomach growled. "But first…food," he said.

They headed back to the main entrance while Erik explained the difference in how floors were numbered, in case Ben ever had to find his way to the room by himself.

"So our second floor is their first floor?"

"Uh-huh. Don't bother with the 'why.' As long as you remember that, you'll be able to find the right room." Erik looked chagrined. "I learned it the hard way on my first trip over."

The Fall day was crisp, although the wind that rustled through dry leaves promised rain before the night was through. Erik led him out into the large walled courtyard, and Ben turned in a slow circle, taking in the huge stone building.

"This was built to keep the earl's family and his servants safe in case of attack," Erik told him. "Probably the villagers too. We're in the 'inner bailey,' which is the fallback area closest to the keep, that tower over there," he added, pointing. "The Keep was the last redoubt when the outer walls were breached. The inner bailey was supposed to slow down or hold off attackers who managed to get through the first walls —the outer bailey."

Erik kept up the narrative as they walked back down the long driveway, past the gift shop and tea shop they had seen near the entrance as if being at a real medieval castle was a normal, everyday occurrence.

"How do you know all this stuff?" Ben asked. "I mean, I read *Lord of the Rings* and *Harry Potter*, but I don't remember those kinds of details."

Erik grinned. "I studied a lot of art history, and that included some architecture appreciation classes. And I worked with the art authentication and fraud detection folks for almost a decade. Some of that involved museums, but a lot of it meant examining pieces in private collections to make sure they weren't stolen, misappropriated, or forgeries."

Before they crossed through the gateway, Erik grabbed Ben and pulled him in for a kiss. Ben belatedly kissed back, a little off balance. "What—?"

Erik grinned and pointed up to an ugly little stone gremlin on the corner of the wall. "There's a legend about the castle that if you kiss in front of the original gargoyle, your love will last forever. So I figured we'd play it safe and do it for all of them."

Ben's heart warmed at the sentiment beneath the surprise smooch. "How do we know where they are?"

Erik leaned in conspiratorially. "Teag gave me a map."

Teag Logan and his fiancé Anthony Benton had come to the castle at Christmas and ended up solving a century-old mystery. It didn't surprise Ben to find out Teag had primed Erik with plenty of touristy pointers and suggestions.

The castle sat higher than the village, and from that vantage point, Ben looked out over rolling hills, wooded places, and green fields beyond the edge of town. After a brisk walk, they crossed Ledwyche Brook on a stone bridge with antique ironwork lamps spaced evenly across its span and found themselves in the cobblestone market square.

Ben felt like he was walking onto a movie set as he and Erik strolled into Caynham-on-Ledwyche. The town looked picture-perfect, a mix of buildings from every century except their own. Between the half-timbered buildings—what Americans often called "Tudor" style—and the old brick or stone buildings, the village seemed too picturesque to be real. Knights Road was the main street through town, with local shops and restaurants on either side and not a big international chain to be seen.

He wasn't sure how a gay couple would be received here in a small village so far from London, so he took his cues from Erik and smiled when his partner reached out for his hand.

"Relax. I wouldn't have brought you here if we couldn't be ourselves," Erik told him. "Come on, let's do a little exploring."

Ben turned his attention back to their surroundings. "It's nice to not see the same stores as we've got back home," Ben said. "There used to be neighborhoods in Newark like that when I was a kid, but it's almost all gone to the chains now. Same stuff everywhere. That's one of the things I like about Cape May—there are so many locally-owned, one-of-a-kind places." He gave Erik's hand a squeeze. "Like Trinkets."

When Erik stepped away from his high-profile job stopping fraud, he sold his condo in Atlanta and moved sight-unseen to Cape May, New Jersey, after spotting an ad for an antique shop that was for sale. The high-end shop sold well to tourists during the season, and the cheeky blog that Erik created, *Treasure Trail*, brought in business the rest of the year with its mix of advice for collectors, interesting stories about notable items, and unique pieces for sale. Given Erik's background, buyers never needed to worry about the provenance of anything they purchased from the store.

"Teag said that the Mortimers have made it a point to boost the local economy, and keeping the mom-and-pop stores healthy certainly gives the town a more authentic feel," Erik replied. "I'm sure that helps with tourism."

Cape May, New Jersey, was a tourist town, so both men knew what it was like to be the "locals" catering to out-of-towners. Ben had taken over running his aunt and uncle's vacation rental business when they retired, after a stint as first a Newark undercover cop and later a private investigator. Both previous jobs left him feeling jaded and burned out, soured on humanity.

Erik came to Cape May raw from finding his long-time boyfriend cheating on him and newly recovered from a nearly fatal gunshot wound when a sting operation went wrong. Neither man had been looking to find love, but a mistake with a dating app introduced them, and after surviving a run-in with former mobsters and dangerous ghosts, Erik and Ben decided they made a good team.

"Let's check out the antique store," Erik suggested, pointing to a shop across the street. Ben let Erik tug him by the hand, and his grin put the lie to his beleaguered protests. *Curiouser and Curiouser* was written in gold lettering across the shop window. "I bet their antiques are older than ours."

Ben rolled his eyes. "The chairs in our room at the hotel are probably older than our country."

Bells tinkled as Erik pushed the door open, and Ben followed him inside. The store smelled of silver polish, old books, and freshly brewed tea, and the space was filled nearly to the rafters with dark wooden shelves laden with curios and antiques.

"Hello," an older man with a fringe of white hair greeted them from behind the counter. "I'm Mr. Porter. Happy to answer any questions. Have a look around."

Ben had gained at least a passing appreciation for antiques from time spent with Erik. He didn't always understand why ratty-looking objects sometimes drew high prices while much more attractive pieces were less valuable, although he knew age and who they had belonged to influenced the price. His own taste tended to be guided more by what caught his eye or what reminded him of something he'd seen in a movie more than the price or the story behind it.

He looked from side to side, taking in the crowded but well-dusted collection of items from across the United Kingdom and its many one-time colonies. China tea sets made up a much larger portion of the display than he recalled seeing at Trinkets, probably not a surprise given the British obsession with the beverage.

At Trinkets, Ben often glimpsed items that looked like something his grandmother or another older relative had owned. Nothing here looked as familiar, although Ben saw some knickknacks that would make nice accent pieces in some of his company's rental properties.

Out of the corner of his eye, Ben saw Erik make a beeline to an object in a glass case. Curious, he turned to follow.

"Excuse me," Erik called out to Mr. Porter. "Could I please get a closer look at this coin?"

The man gave Erik a searching look, taking his measure, and Ben figured he was trying to decide whether they meant to steal something.

He must have decided they looked trustworthy because he came over and unlocked the case with a key from a ring on his belt.

Erik pulled a jeweler's loupe from inside his jacket and held the coin under the light. "Fascinating," he murmured, turning the coin this way and that and then looking up with the kind of excitement in his eyes that Ben felt about finding a rare, limited-edition action figure of a favorite superhero.

"This is an authentic thirteenth-century Knights Templar coin," Erik said. "Do you know how it came to be here?"

Mr. Porter put the coin back in the case and locked it, then motioned for Erik and Ben to follow him up front. He perched on a stool behind the register and took a sip from his tea.

"There are lots of stories in these parts about the Templars back in the day and about a 'lost' Templar treasure," he told them.

"Many people have gone looking over the years, and if anyone ever found something, they sure stayed quiet about it. Treasure or no treasure, it's a fact that the Templars passed through this area, and I guess some people hung onto a few of the coins they spent. That particular one came from the estate of a man who passed away last year. He had a lot of little odds and ends, things he'd picked up over the years. That's all I know about it."

They thanked Mr. Porter and headed back outside. Most of the store windows sported fall decorations—colored leaves made from silk, resin pumpkins, baskets full of wax versions of bunches of grapes and apples. Some shop doors had wreaths made of grapevines or evergreen boughs studded with nuts and apples, and a few had ribbon wreaths in warm orange, gold, and brown.

"The earl runs a brewery," Erik mentioned as they strolled along, window shopping. "Teag said it was pretty good."

"We'll have to try it out," Ben replied. He wasn't a beer connoisseur, but he enjoyed trying new brews, especially when they were locally made or small batch.

They passed a yarn shop whose window was filled with beautiful hand-knitted scarves and sweaters, all in the rich colors of autumn. It shared the building with a quaint tea shop.

"I want to try both tea shops," he said, and Erik turned to him with a look of surprise.

"I'm fine with that. But you're not much of a tea drinker."

Ben shrugged. "I can take or leave the tea, but I want to try all those little cakes. Saw that in a movie one time and thought they looked good. Always wanted to find out for myself."

"We're going to be here long enough to try everything—and go back again to our favorites," Erik promised. "We're also invited to the gala, and we'll be here for the big bonfire. I'm looking forward to both of those."

Ben squeezed his hand. "Thank you for planning all this. I think I'm just a little punchy from the overnight flight and the time change. I liked the train—quite a bit nicer than what I was used to in Newark."

Erik looked off into the distance and sighed. "There were parts of the travel that I used to do that I enjoyed. I loved seeing new places, so I'd add on a day or two to explore. Places I went frequently—London, Rome, Antwerp, Paris, Berlin—I had favorite cafés and restaurants, little bookstores, hotels, that made me feel at home."

He smiled at Ben; an expression so full of a mixture of emotions Ben didn't know what to make of it. "Of course, after I got pressured into doing more with Interpol and agencies like that, chasing money laundering and smuggling, it got too dangerous to wander around by myself anymore. I stopped trying to ditch the bodyguards after I almost got kidnapped in Lisbon. After that, I couldn't even leave the hotel. Travel was a lot less fun. And then there was the whole getting shot part."

"Kidnapped—is this a regular thing for you?" Every time Ben thought he had heard all of Erik's stories, something new came to light. He had gotten snatched on the first case they worked together and almost didn't survive.

Erik shrugged as if it wasn't a big deal, but Ben saw the way his eyes narrowed and his mouth tightened, suggesting that the truth was more than he wanted to admit.

"There was a messy divorce between people with large bank accounts and long pedigrees. They'd already had the art collection appraised, but then rumors went around that some of the pieces were fakes or had been misappropriated during the Second World War. So they brought me in. If I proved the pieces in question weren't real or had to be returned to their rightful owners, it would have brought down the value of the collection substantially," Erik replied.

"So one night, when I was coming out of a lovely little bistro— alone—I got jumped. Three muscle-bound men in black ski masks had a white panel van, just like in the movies. Except a lot scarier."

Ben eyed his partner warily. He'd seen the scar from the wound that ended that chapter of Erik's life. They had compared scars since Ben had a few of his own. He also knew that Erik had training in Krav Maga and Systema, two badass mixed martial arts disciplines, so it would take real professionals to get the drop on him. Ben's heart sped up as he realized once again that he might never have met Erik if the attempt had been carried out.

"What happened?" Ben had been in tight spots before when he worked undercover. He knew how things could go bad, fast, even though he also had martial arts training.

"My boss put a tail on me," Erik replied. "Without telling me. Between the two of us, we fought them off. They got away—and I didn't get kidnapped."

"After all that, and you still want to travel?" Ben had been up and down the East Coast, out to Vegas once or twice, and had gone to a big concert in Chicago. But like a lot of people who grew up near enough to New York City to claim it as their backyard, Ben didn't need to go far to find just about anything he wanted. That, along with the expense and difficulty getting time off, had made travel a "someday" kind of thing—until his career crashed and burned, and he found himself starting over. Now, everything seemed possible.

"I'm not going to let those criminals take the beauty of the world away from me—from us," Erik said, turning to meet Ben's gaze. "There is so much to see, so much I want to show you. I always dreamed of having someone to see it with." The warmth in his eyes promised all kinds of naughty things once they were alone.

"I'd like that." Ben pushed himself past his fear of being out of his league. Erik wanted him. That was enough.

They made an interesting pair. Ben was an inch over six feet tall, and his dark hair—cut in a fade—highlighted his bright green eyes. Black geometric tattoos wound around his upper arms and one side of his chest, along with the phrase *Non timebo mala* above the bullet scars that almost cost him his life. At age thirty-three, Ben was two years younger than his partner, but between what he had seen and experienced as a Newark cop and then a private investigator, he felt older than his years.

In contrast, Erik stood three inches shorter, with blond hair, sapphire blue eyes, and scruff that gained a reddish cast if he didn't shave. Where Ben had a muscular build, honed by working out and the demands of his former jobs, Erik had more of a runner's build, strong and sinewy, whipcord strong.

"Hey, there's the church Anthony said we shouldn't miss. He said the stained glass was beautiful, and the interior was worth a stop." Erik's enthusiasm was infectious, and Ben once again let himself be directed into St. Paul's Anglican Church. The cut-stone walls and high tower looked solid, built to stand forever. A glance at the date on the cornerstone told Ben it was more than seven hundred years old.

Ben had been raised Catholic, although he lapsed long ago. Erik grew up Episcopalian—American Anglican—but hadn't attended in years. Ben's catechism came back to him as they stepped into the hush of the church's interior. Rows of time-worn wooden pews stretched toward the chancel, which held elaborately carved gothic-style choir stalls made of dark wood, overshadowed by an equally fancy wooden canopy to amplify sound.

The wooden pulpit was covered with fancy carvings, a raised octagonal booth with its own canopy. Arched stained glass windows along the walls gave the interior an otherworldly glow in hues of red, green, and blue, while a rose window above the apse shone down with magnificent colors. St. Paul's smelled of candle smoke and incense, and Ben found himself feeling like he was ten years old and about to be scolded by his grandmother for fidgeting.

"Wow," he breathed. St. Paul's reminded him of a miniature version of the Cathedral Basilica of the Sacred Heart in Newark, where he'd attended a cousin's wedding. He had focused his attention on the architecture and embellishments to ease the sting of knowing that he would never be welcome to wed his own true love within those walls.

"Look at this!" Erik's voice took on an awed tone. He headed straight for what Ben thought at first was a massive painting. Close up, he realized it was a mosaic made of thousands of small glass tiles.

"This is astounding," Erik breathed, eyes wide.

"Ah, you noticed one of our masterpieces."

The voice startled both men, and they turned to find a man in a black cassock behind them. "Forgive me for surprising you. I am Father Andrews."

"You have an original by Stefano Pozzi," Erik said, and while Ben had no idea who that was, it obviously was a big deal since Erik looked like he had found the Holy Grail.

Father Andrews raised an eyebrow. "Well done. That's hardly a household name."

"Art authentication is something of a specialty," Erik admitted. He turned to Ben. "Pozzi created the mosaic of Raphael's Transfiguration in St. Peter's Basilica in the Vatican. To find one of his works here is remarkable."

"The Mortimer family have a history of being generous patrons," Father Andrews said. "The story that's been passed down is that Pozzi was persuaded to do this mural after he finished the Transfiguration by the earl at that time who went to Rome to convince him."

He gave Erik an appraising look. "You said that your specialty is art authentication. Are you Erik Mitchell?"

This time, it was Erik who looked surprised. "Yes. I am. How did you—"

Father Andrews chuckled. "Nothing mystical, I assure you. The earl came by as he is wont to do, and mentioned he had a friend visiting who was an art expert and let me know that he vouched for you if you wanted to see some of the special collections. We have some unusual relics, as well as historical items."

Ben saw Erik melt at the offer. He smiled. "Go. Geek out. I'm going to wander around if that's okay?" he added with a glance at the priest, who nodded.

"Thank you," Erik replied, giving him a quick kiss. Ben watched him walk away deep in nerdy discussion with Father Andrews and was glad to see his partner look so happy. Ben didn't need to know all of the history of a piece of art to appreciate its beauty. He had always been moved more by the scene in a painting, the soaring vision of the cathedral architects, and the magnificent music than by the words of the person in the pulpit.

St. Paul's was fancier than Ben expected to find in a small country town, even one as prosperous as Caynham-on-Ledwyche. He liked looking at pretty things, and while he didn't have Erik's expertise to know the history of a piece and the biography of the artist, he could appreciate it just for its beauty.

Ben drifted, enjoying the peaceful atmosphere of the church. He could see Erik and Father Andrews on the other side of the nave, gesturing excitedly as they talked. Erik would fill him in later, even if it was the Cliff Notes version, which suited Ben just fine.

The church was empty other than the three of them, at least as far as Ben could see. So when Ben caught a glimpse of movement out of the corner of his eye, he couldn't help being curious.

He glanced over his shoulder at Erik, but his partner didn't look like he'd be ready to leave soon, so Ben followed his penchant for investigating and went looking for the person he'd seen. Ben headed down a transept and caught another glimpse of someone at the end of the corridor. The man went around a corner before Ben got a close look, but his odd apparel sparked a half-remembered memory. Ben followed him, but when he reached the corridor only seconds later, the man was gone.

Not a man. A ghost.

Seeing ghosts was nothing new to Ben. He'd glimpsed them all his life. Ben had kept that ability a closely guarded secret while he was a cop, although it occasionally proved useful during his short stint as a detective. His ability had played an important role in the last "case" he and Erik had solved, the life-or-death situation that had brought them together. To Ben's relief, Erik accepted his sightings without question. Then again, Erik could read impressions from objects by touching them, so just seeing some spooks wasn't a big deal.

Ben hurried to the next corridor but saw no one in either direction.

Although he could see ghosts, he had no special power to summon them. He wondered who the spirit had been and why they showed up now. The odd outfit jarred a memory, but it slipped away when Ben tried to remember. He walked back toward the main sanctuary, annoyed that he couldn't pin down what had seemed familiar about the specter.

"Ben! We wondered where you'd gone." Erik waved him over to where he stood with Father Andrews.

"I was exploring," Ben replied. Erik gave him a look that said he suspected there was more to the story, but thankfully, he was willing to wait for an answer.

"The good father here has been telling me about the fascinating history of St. Paul's," Erik told him. "Including some very interesting legends about the Knights Templar in the area."

Ben caught his breath as he realized why the ghost's odd clothing seemed familiar. He had seen something very similar back when *Assassin's Creed* was his obsession. "Oh? Like what?" Ben managed, hoping he sounded nonchalant and knowing from Erik's glance that he didn't.

"I'll fill you in over dinner," Erik replied, with a look that Ben interpreted to mean he had news to share. Erik turned back to the priest. "I would truly appreciate an opportunity to have a look at the relics that the church has, as well as the crypt. I did some work for the Vatican Museums, and I'm always interested in seeing variations on those themes."

Father Andrews smiled. "I think that can be arranged, especially since you're a friend of the earl. We don't often get someone with your experience visiting…it's a joy to be able to share information with someone who can appreciate the nuances." He and Erik exchanged contact information and made arrangements to meet again the next day.

Ben's stomach rumbled loudly, and Erik grinned. "We ought to get some food."

"There's plenty to choose from, and it's all good," Father Andrews assured them. "Enjoy exploring!"

CHAPTER TWO

ERIK

Y ou think it was the ghost of a Templar?" Erik asked as he and
Ben got comfortable at a table in the Boar and Knight.

"Pretty sure," Ben replied. "I recognized the tunic, although
it took me a moment since I never expected to meet one of those guys
for real!"

"Did he seem to be aware of you, or was he a repeater?" Erik asked.
He had seen a few ghosts in his time as well. Some spirits retained a
sense of who they had been and were sentient, able to control their
actions. "Repeaters" were like snippets of a faded movie, more of an
impression in time and space than a spirit capable of thought.

Ben considered for a moment. "He didn't say anything, but I had
the oddest feeling that he wanted to be followed like he was leading
me somewhere."

"When we go back tomorrow, show me where you saw him. Father
Andrews may know something about him as well." Erik paused, and
then he reached out and took Ben's hand, looking contrite. "I'm sorry
—I should have asked you before I committed us to go see the relics
tomorrow. That's not fair to you. I can call and cancel."

Ben shook his head. "I'm actually looking forward to it. Being with you is like having a behind-the-scenes pass. We haven't been in town a whole day, and you've already got backstage access at the castle and the church."

"Sorry that we don't have cool badges," Erik joked.

When the server came, they asked for recommendations on food and ale. Erik ordered the pork pie with a dark stout. Ben got the fish and chips with a craft brown ale from the earl's brewery.

"I went totally tourist and got fish and chips," Ben said with a chagrined smile. "But it's what I've always read about."

Erik leaned in. "This is your vacation and your first time to the UK. There's nothing wrong with being a tourist. Everyone does tourist stuff on their first trip. That's what's great about getting to come back— you've done the bucket list stuff, and you can try new things. I just want you to have fun."

"I'm here with you. No one's trying to kill either of us. It's all good," Ben assured him. "And by the way, this pub is seriously cool. I didn't think places like this were real."

Erik chuckled. "Next time, we'll have to go to Nottingham. You know—Robin Hood, Prince John—*that* Nottingham. There's a pub there that has been open since 1187. Which would make it almost three hundred years older than this place."

The Boar and Knight was one of the oldest buildings in town other than the castle. It had been in continual use as a pub since the early Middle Ages, and it looked its age. Its thatched roof was one of only a few remaining in all of Caynham-on-Ledwyche. A sign with the names of every proprietor going back over six hundred years graced one wall. The fireplace across from the bar was blackened with the soot of ages. The dark wood of the tables, chair rail, and bar was worn from use, and the plank floor showed the toll of centuries of foot traffic.

"That's hard to wrap my mind around," Ben confessed. "Back home, we slap a historical plaque on anything that's over a hundred years old."

"Wait until we go to Rome," Erik said. "The ruins there make all this look like the 'new' stuff."

The server brought their order, and both men tucked in with gusto, realizing how hungry they were. Erik was used to adapting to the time difference, but Ben wasn't and probably felt as if he'd missed a meal or two.

"It gets easier with practice," Erik said after they'd been eating for a while.

"What does?"

"The jet lag. There are tricks to keep it from messing with you."

"We lost about five hours, so today's going to feel short, right—except for the part where we tried to sleep on a plane?" Ben asked.

Erik nodded. "Going east isn't too bad. You just have to remember that your body thinks it's earlier than the local time says it is. That can make it hard to get to sleep, but you adjust. Going west hurts. Everyone else is having a lovely afternoon, and you are falling asleep on your feet."

"I remember a little of that from flying to Vegas and back," Ben replied. "I hope me being a travel virgin won't cramp your style."

Erik felt a blush rise at the word "virgin" as all kinds of inappropriate thoughts jammed his mind. He and Ben were in their mid-thirties, long past being virginal when they met. And yet they had found positions, techniques, and toys that were new to one or both of them, giving them some "first times" together.

"Are you saying I get to pop your passport cherry?" Erik murmured in a low voice no one else could hear.

A flash of lust in Ben's eyes told him their minds were running in the same sexy direction. "I like the sound of that."

"Something to look forward to when we get back to the room," Erik promised.

After the first few bites, they slowed down to enjoy the food and atmosphere. Both Ben and Erik eyed the pub's decorations. In addition to the framed photograph of the queen that hung to one side of the wall by the register, a fascinating variety of old maps, painted landscapes, botanical prints, and odd sketches of hunting dogs adorned the walls. Shelves held antique tankards, pewter pitchers, and old tin plates.

"Is that helmet real, do you think?" Ben asked with a nod toward a nook behind Erik that held an eclectic array of items.

Erik spotted the piece as soon as he turned. The crusader great helm looked old, but without handling it and testing the metal, Erik couldn't know for certain. Their server passed by just then, and Erik flagged him down.

"Excuse me, but do you know anything about that helm on the shelf?" Erik asked.

"The what?" The young man asked, puzzled.

"The helmet from *Assassin's Creed*," Ben spoke up.

"Oh, the bucket," the man said. "Been here long as anyone knows. The story is that some poor bloke from the town ran off to London and joined up with the Knights Templar. They shipped him off to the Crusades. He got run through in battle, and as he was dying, he made his friend promise to bring his helmet back to his hometown, so at least something of his got to come home."

The server shrugged. "Can't swear that's true or not, but it's what I've heard all my life. Mr. Clive, the proprietor, might know more." With that, he hustled off to fetch another round of drinks.

Ben looked at Erik and raised an eyebrow. "Well?"

"Maybe," Erik replied. "I doubt they'll let me examine it and send it off to the British Museum for analysis, but sometimes it's more fun not to know for sure."

"Isn't that sort of a strange way to look at it, coming from you?" Ben asked.

Erik leaned back in his chair. "Not really. Authenticity and value don't matter unless you need to sell something or insure it. Or pay estate taxes. So if your great aunt wants to claim that the Picasso sketch in her living room is the real thing, there's no harm done."

"Which is why so many people on that Roadshow program are surprised when their treasure turns out to be a knock-off," Ben supplied.

Erik nodded. "Yep. The story gets passed down through the family about the teacup that once belonged to Betsy Ross, and someone inherits it and decides to cash in, only to find out it's a hundred years too recent. But sometimes, it goes the other way, and turns out to be a lot more than they expected."

"That's the third Templar connection today," Ben said, savoring the last of his second pint. "Is that normal for here?"

Erik knew his partner meant the United Kingdom. "Yes, and no. England is a relatively small country with a big history. The Templars were a force for centuries. They moved all over the world. When you think about it that way, there were a lot of people over a long time coming and going. So it's not as weird as you might think."

Still, the same question had occurred to him before Ben mentioned it, and despite Erik's very rational explanation, his answer didn't lie settled in his mind. Erik had learned to rely on his "intuition" during investigations, and it had saved his life more than once. Sometimes, he got flashes of images from the past when he handled certain objects. Other times, he had hunches that worked out too consistently to be sheer luck.

"You think there's more to it, don't you?" Ben asked, and Erik reminded himself that it was tough to fool a cop—even a former one.

"Maybe. Not sure yet," Erik admitted. "But…we're on vacation, not working a case. So I can leave it be if you want."

Ben shook his head. "Why not poke around a little? Anyone can do the stuff on the travel sites and in the brochures. This could be a cool story to tell our friends when we go home. Lead on, Sherlock."

"I was probably closer to The Saint than Sherlock Holmes," Erik replied with a laugh. "But I'm flattered."

Ben grinned. "And here I was going to offer to let you cuff me and carry out a *very thorough* search," he said in a low voice.

"That can be arranged." Erik felt Ben's innuendo go right to his cock. He hoped that between the jet lag and the pints that they would be awake enough to make good on the promise by the time they got back to the castle.

They paid their tab and headed outside. Night had fallen, and the fog rolled in, blurring details and forming halos around the street lamps.

"When we come back tomorrow, I'd like to go through that bookstore." Ben glanced at a now-closed shop on the other side of the street.

Cadwell's looked like an old-time kind of place, and Erik imagined shelves that stretched from floor to ceiling, crammed with all sorts of hard-to-find books. "Could be dangerous," Erik warned. "We might never come back out."

Erik didn't care that Ben's taste in books tended toward thrillers, superheroes, or science fiction, while he generally liked fantasy, history, or biography. What mattered most was that they could be content spending a quiet evening together reading. Erik's last boyfriend hadn't been much of a reader, and from what little Ben had said about his previous, unlamented partner, their tastes had clashed on things like Ben's love of superheroes and anime.

"Oh, I imagine we'd find our way out eventually." Ben chuckled. "We just need to remember that whatever we buy needs to either fit in our luggage or get shipped back."

As they crossed the stone bridge, they came upon a handful of boys, probably around ten years old, playing pirate. Erik guessed they might have purchased the bandanas, eye patches, and plastic sabers from Poundland. He and Ben hung back for a moment, not wanting to disturb their fun.

"Looks like the castle may be in danger from some scurvy sailors," Ben commented with a grin. "My cousin and I used to play like that for hours when I came up to Cape May to visit over the summer."

"I didn't always have a bunch of friends to act out the battles with, but I spent a lot of time reading *Treasure Island* and anything like it I could get my hands on," Erik replied.

Something caught his eye as the boys swashbuckled from one side of the bridge to another.

"I need to see something." Erik walked toward the boys as Ben rushed to follow.

"We'll get out of your way, sorry," the tallest of the group said as the game came to a halt.

Erik shook his head. "Oh, no worries. You looked like you were having fun. But I wonder, might I see that sword up close, please?" He nodded toward the metal weapon one of the other lads held.

"You're not going to tell my mum, are you?" The boy asked. "She'll take it away. She always says I'll put my eye out."

Erik barely heard him as he weighed the old blade across the flat of his palms. Its edges were dull, and the steel had tarnished, but Erik recognized what he was holding immediately. "Where did you get this?" He kept his tone light so the boy didn't think he was being accused of anything.

"Found it in a hole in the ground. I didn't steal it or anything."

"No, no—I didn't think you had," Erik hurried to reassure him. He handed the sword back to its young owner, then reached into his pocket and pulled out pen and paper. "Would you draw me a pirate map of where you found it? My friend and I are on an adventure of our own."

The boys traded wary glances, and then the tallest one—obviously their leader—shrugged. "Up to you, Rory."

Rory tucked the sword under his arm to take the paper and pen. "There's nothing else to find there," he said as he drew a map and marked a spot with an "X." "I went back, but the hole closed in."

"That's okay. Half the fun is following the map, right?" Erik replied with a conspiratorial smile. He thanked Rory for the drawing and wished them well in their battle on the high seas. Their friendly scuffle resumed once he and Ben were past.

"What was all that about?" Ben asked.

"I wanted to find out why a fifth-grader was playing with an authentic fourteenth-century sword," Erik replied.

"He had a real sword?" Ben looked back over his shoulder.

"Don't worry—it wasn't sharp enough to cut butter, although it would hurt to get smacked with it," Erik said.

"You believe him? About the hole in the ground?"

"King Arthur got Excalibur from a tart in a lake." Erik grinned. He knew Ben would get the Monty Python reference. "Seriously, though, I doubt that boy took it down off the wall over the mantle at home. So I lean toward believing him. And I definitely want to get a look at the place he found it."

When they got back to the castle, it still seemed too early to go back to their room. "Tomorrow, let's explore some of the castle," Erik suggested, eager to make sure Ben had a good time. "There are a couple of rooms that have been restored with family heirlooms and furnished to be period-authentic. And there's a private chapel, a garden folly, and plenty of gargoyles. I can make dinner reservations for the dining room, and we could have lunch at the tea room."

Ben leaned in and kissed his cheek. "That all sounds wonderful, but we don't have to try so hard. I want to see all of that, but we can take our time, go slowly, enjoy ourselves."

"I want you to have fun," Erik said.

"I'm with you. In England. At a frickin' castle. How could I not enjoy myself?" Ben's smile turned mischievous. "On second thought, I can think of some other things I'd really enjoy."

Erik grinned. "Oh, I'm completely on board with that. But on our way upstairs, can we please stop at the front desk? I want to have a word with Priscilla."

"Sure. Does this have something to do with that sword?"

"Busted."

When they had checked in, Erik had been so busy with the paperwork that he hadn't taken in all of the decor. The massive wooden reception desk stood below the Mortimer family coat of arms. Dark wood-paneled wainscoting and rough stone walls set off tasteful accents—polished brass hardware, antique maps, and castle paintings done by local artists. Over the large fireplace on the other side of the lobby hung flags and crossed swords. A scattering of pumpkins, floral arrangements with autumn color, and other seasonal decorations added a low-key Halloween feel.

"Is Priscilla still around?" Erik asked the clerk on duty.

"She's in the office, just finishing up. May I say who is asking?"

"Erik Mitchell."

The clerk walked to a door and stuck her head inside, then turned back toward Erik and Ben and nodded. "She said to send you back."

Erik led the way behind the big desk, with Ben following close behind. The office was exactly what he might have imagined for Priscilla—tidy, organized, and everything of the best quality.

"To what do I owe the visit?" Priscilla asked, smiling.

"We were wondering if the Mortimer family had any connections with the Knights Templar," Erik replied. "They've come up a couple of times during our exploration in the village today, and it seemed a bit much to chalk up to chance."

Priscilla twirled a pencil, considering his words. "There have been rumors for a very long time about that. I'm impressed that you found out in less than a day."

"It's my superpower," Erik replied with a grin.

"Maybe there's something to that," Priscilla said. "The family has never been able to substantiate the stories, but they've persisted over the centuries. The castle, of course, pre-dates Protestantism, so there could have been Templar activity in Shropshire at the time of the Crusades. But they didn't tend to move openly."

"So…it's possible."

Priscilla nodded. "Theoretically. We just need proof." Her smile broadened. "As it happens, the earl left word to give you access to the family's private archives, the items not usually shared with the public. He thought that, given your interests and specialties, you might enjoy having a look."

"Very much. Please tell him thank you for me," Erik replied. "And yes, Ben and I would love to see the archive."

"What are your plans in the morning?" Priscilla asked.

Erik exchanged a look with Ben, who nodded. "We're open. What works for you?"

"Why don't you have breakfast in the dining room and meet me at ten o'clock outside the Library near the Bride's Tower?" Priscilla reached for a map of the castle grounds and circled the location. "I can take you in and show you around. We'll have two hours, and if you need more, we can arrange that on another day. I can introduce you to Mrs. Marshbanks, the Archivist. The Library and Archive are usually by-appointment-only."

"Thank you so much," Erik replied. "We really appreciate it."

"I love having an excuse to go in there," Priscilla said. "And if you could find hard evidence of a Templar connection—or the elusive Templar treasure—the earl would be absolutely thrilled."

Erik and Ben walked hand in hand back to their room. Erik had been in some of the best five-star hotels in Europe, with grand staircases and huge crystal chandeliers, modern and sleek or historic and renovated. Caynham Castle had the edge of authenticity that those other hotels didn't, nice as they were. No matter how well-traveled he was, Erik had to admit that he was just as excited as Ben at the idea of staying in a real castle.

The cold air left his cheeks and nose burning. After a long day of travel, the walk into town and back, plus a hearty dinner and some ale, was starting to get the best of Erik. One glance at Ben told him his partner was feeling the day's activities as well.

They reached their room, and Erik locked the door behind them. He pulled Ben into his arms, and let Ben flip them and push him up against the wall. Ben pressed their lips together, kissing slowly at first and then with growing hunger.

"Been looking forward to this all day," Ben murmured when he came up for air. He buried his face against Erik's neck, taking a deep inhale and then kissing his way from jaw to collarbone, something that never failed to make Erik rock hard.

"Me too," Erik confessed, baring his neck for the plunder. Ben unbuttoned Erik's shirt and pushed it off his shoulders, then tugged at the tee beneath it until he had pulled it over Erik's head. That probably left his hair a mess, but Erik didn't care. Sex hair after a night spent together was a badge of honor.

Ben tossed his sweater aside and slid calloused palms down Erik's chest, slowing to give proper attention to his nipples until they pebbled beneath his fingers. Erik was lean and narrow, compared to Ben's broad-shouldered, muscular body, a contrast that never failed to rev Erik's motor. That, and the way Erik fit just right against Ben's taller frame, slotting together perfectly.

Erik reached out to undo the buttons on Ben's shirt, but Ben batted his hands aside, doing a slow striptease while never dropping Erik's gaze. He lost the button-down and then wiggled his hips as he took off his T-shirt and tossed it to the ground.

Erik licked his lips, and Ben gave him a lascivious smile. "Like what you see?"

"You know I do," Erik said, breathy with how his heart pounded. They should be too exhausted to even think about sex after the day they'd had. Funny, but he didn't feel tired. All he wanted was Ben, naked and next to him.

Ben pushed his thigh between Erik's legs, reaching around to grab his ass and give it a good squeeze. Erik ground against him, shamelessly humping Ben's leg through their jeans, letting him feel just how hard he was, how much he needed relief.

Erik cupped Ben's face with one hand and reached down to stroke his bulge with the other, leaning in for another kiss. He let himself drink in Ben's scent, a heady mix of cedar and burnt orange that could get him hard with just a whiff. They both sported more than a day's scruff since the last time they'd shaved had been in another time zone, yesterday.

Erik loved the burn of their beards against sensitive skin. They were both a little ripe and overdue for a shower, past the promise of even an all-day deodorant, still damp from the sweat of walking back from town. All male, from the strong arms that wrapped around him to the scratch of rough body hair as their chests slid together. He shimmied his hips, riding Ben's thigh, and leaned in to lick at the spot on Ben's throat where he could see his pulse pounding.

"What do you want?" Ben's voice dropped to a sexy growl that never failed to make heat coil in Erik's belly.

"You. Don't care how. Just want us to come together, perfect end to a perfect day," he breathed.

Ben reached for Erik's belt at the same time Erik's shaking hands started to undo Ben's buckle. They managed to get jeans and boxer briefs halfway down their thighs, and then Ben's hand went around both their hard, leaking cocks, stroking and tugging, rubbing them together with the most delicious friction.

Erik wrapped his hand over Ben's, giving them both a channel to rut into, slicked by their pre-come. Ben's hips bucked, and Erik pushed against him as their breathing grew ragged. Erik arched into the sensation, loving when Ben slid his thumb over the heads of their cocks. He ran a blunt nail lightly through their slits, pressing just right just beneath the knob.

Then Ben's hand slid from his ass cheek to run his fingers down Erik's crack, lightly toying with his hole, and it was all over. Erik cried out, hips rocking, as his orgasm ripped through him, and he came over their joined hands. Ben came right behind him, painting both their chests with his release.

Ben leaned forward and sucked on the sweat-slick skin at the base of Erik's neck, where it joined his shoulder, leaving a mark. Erik loved to see proof of their lovemaking when he looked in the mirror—scratches on his back, finger-shaped bruises on his hips, or hickeys where no one else could see. From the way Ben bared his neck in the throes of passion and liked to feel Erik's hands on him when they climaxed, Erik knew he wasn't alone in wanting reminders.

Erik and Ben rested their foreheads together, still panting. Erik brought his hand up to stroke the backs of his knuckles down Ben's cheek. "How is it that you can make me come so hard even when I should be dead on my feet?"

Ben's throaty chuckle made Erik's dick twitch. "The same way you do that to me, every time." He kissed Erik, long and slow. "Love you."

"Love you too." As the endorphins slowly faded, Erik started to feel the fatigue set in.

"We should shower," Erik murmured. "We're sticky. That way we can start tomorrow with fresh sheets."

"Does this mean I should set the alarm early for breakfast?" Ben asked, mischief clear in his voice.

"Hate to waste good morning wood," Erik replied and felt Ben's dick give an obliging jump, approving of the idea even if rising to the occasion wasn't in the cards again for tonight.

They stepped apart reluctantly and let their pants and underwear slip down to their ankles, toeing off shoes and socks as well. "Go ahead, get the first shower," Erik said, kissing Ben's chin. "I haven't found a historic property in Europe yet that has room for two men in the shower."

"I'm all for getting real close," Ben joked with a leer.

"Tomorrow," Erik said. "We can give it a try. Tonight, I just want to clean up before I lie down because I'm going to be out like a light as soon as I hit the pillow."

Ben took a record-fast shower, coming out in a towel that accentuated more than it hid. "Your turn. And you're right that the shower is small. But that just makes it a challenge," he added with a cheeky grin.

"Challenge accepted—tomorrow," Erik replied, groggy enough to feel light-headed. He was in and out of the shower, lingering just long enough to wash away the sweat and come. He toweled his hair mostly dry, enjoying the huge, plush, high thread-count bath towels. The castle's brand of soap and shampoo—doubtless on sale in the gift shop —smelled of sandalwood, comforting and masculine.

When he walked into the other room, Ben had already turned down the covers and was waiting for him, naked against the sheets. "Come to bed." He held out his hand. Erik let his towel drop and went to join him, pausing only to turn off the bedside lamp.

Ben welcomed him beneath the luxurious linens and down comforter with lazy kisses. They lay facing each other in the dark, still attuned with a heightened awareness from their coupling.

"Thank you," Ben whispered. "This was a wonderful first day."

Erik gave a tired smile. "We've got a whole week. I want every day to be fantastic."

"It will be. No matter what we do." Ben twined their fingers together. "Because we're both here."

Erik turned on his side, shimmying closer until his back pressed against Ben's chest. Ben slipped an arm over Erik, splaying his hand over Erik's heart. "Go to sleep, love. We'll have new adventures in the morning."

ERIK DREAMED OF A CLANDESTINE MEETING, *long ago. A cloaked woman and two bodyguards met a small boat with two occupants on the banks of a creek, in the middle of the night, long after "decent" people were abroad. Which meant this meeting was most likely illegal, no matter that the woman's cloak and the presence of guards spoke of wealth and power.*

Erik couldn't hear what was said. A shallow boat pulled up on the rocky shore, and one of the passengers got out. The man was tall, with broad shoulders and a strong body beneath a worn. almost shabby cloak. Words were spoken, and the woman opened the clasp of her cloak, revealing an unusual silver necklace with a repeated triangle design. The boat's passenger bowed to the woman and took her hand, then knelt in fealty or gratitude. Something about the scene made Erik think the situation spoke more to politics than romance. He never saw the faces of the man and woman. But the image of that necklace burned into his mind, indelible.

Erik woke with a start, expecting to find himself crouching in the bushes by the river. It had all felt so real, and Erik needed several deep breaths to calm himself. A glance told him that he hadn't woken Ben, who was still lightly snoring.

Before the details could dim, Erik eased out of bed and found the pen and paper on the bedside table. He sketched what he had seen of the woman's necklace, leaving proof for himself for the morning.

If they had been back in Cape May, at either his apartment or Ben's, Erik would have known his way around well enough to maneuver without waking Ben. His mind raced, and he couldn't imagine being able to get back to sleep quickly. But their hotel suite was unfamiliar, and Erik didn't want to end up breaking a toe from falling over furniture in the dark. So he settled for getting up to use the restroom, pouring himself a glass of water, and taking a few minutes to collect his wits.

Erik had grown used to getting flashes of images—or full visions—from handling objects that had a strong emotional or magical resonance. Being a psychometric wasn't a common talent, but he knew another person with the same strange gift, the cousin of a friend from graduate school, and they compared notes often.

He went back over his day, trying to figure out what he might have handled to spark the dream.

The sword. That must be it. The things I saw in the dream could be from about the same time period. But what does it mean? Are we in danger? Why show me that particular image?

Erik examined his gut feeling about the dream, paying close attention to the intuition that had served him well in the past. He didn't get the feeling he and Ben were in any physical danger, although the people in his glimpse of the past might well have been, giving them good reason for their furtive meeting. A different kind of dread colored the images, something that felt more like fear of discovery, of social repercussions, of revealing a long-held secret. He didn't know what that meant, but he filed it away in his mind to think on more once the sun had risen.

He padded back to bed, glad that Ben hadn't noticed his absence. He slid back under the covers carefully, getting comfortable and hoping he could still his whirling thoughts. There had to be a reason, something that explained why here and why now. Come morning, Erik intended to figure out what was going on and what a glimpse of a night centuries past might have to do with him.

CHAPTER THREE

ERIK

When the alarm went off, Erik wondered if there had been a mistake with the setting. Ben quickly reminded him of the reason for waking early, and the happy ending of the previous night was reprised with a pleasant beginning to start the day off right. Afterward, they managed to both fit into the shower, although there wasn't room for anything aside from a handjob and washing up required coordination so that no one got an elbow in the nose.

By the time they headed down to breakfast, Erik's stomach rumbled and Ben chuckled. "Guess I'm not the only one who's ready for food."

"Yesterday was a long time ago," Erik bantered. "And I definitely need some coffee."

They headed across the open yard, taking time to appreciate the massive stone walls and impressive towers. Erik felt the same thrill that always coursed through him at museums or historic locations, the sense that history was within touching distance. His imagination filled in the people, period clothing, even the music.

"You are getting into this, aren't you?" Ben asked, smiling. "If taking you to a museum puts that look on your face, I'll take you anywhere you want to go."

Erik leaned closer and gave him a peck on his cheek. "I promise to make it worth your while."

The crisp autumn breeze raked across the courtyard, ruffling his hair and sending fallen leaves into the air.

When they entered the great hall, Ben didn't try to hide his reaction. "Wow. It's like Hogwarts without the floating candles."

Erik's architecture training served him well as he cataloged the features and described them to Ben. A hammer beam ceiling arched high above them in the English Gothic style with open timber roof trusses. Hand-cut beams arched downward at intervals, while others formed arches along the flat of the ceiling, embellished at the corners with intricate woodcutting. Wide, arched windows faced the courtyard and featured the Mortimer Crest rendered in stained glass. A fireplace large enough to roast a full ox took up most of one wall. The restaurant and lounge area were really part of the larger great hall, set apart by the arrangement of planters and decorative, moveable screens. Seating areas nearby provided space for guests to mingle and enjoy a drink together.

"Not exactly a pancake palace," Ben joked, referring to the breakfast places that were popular with the tourists back in Cape May.

"I'm sure they'd make you some if you asked nicely," Erik replied. "But if you're ever going to get a full English breakfast done right, this is the place."

Even at breakfast, the restaurant had an air of elegance, from the white tablecloths to the crystal stemware. A server in formal black and white uniform led them to their table, and within minutes their water and juice glasses were filled, coffee poured, tea offered, and orders taken.

"So what's in this English breakfast I ordered, anyhow?" Ben asked, sipping his coffee.

"Traditionally, a 'full English' is bacon, sausage, eggs, blood pudding, baked beans, tomatoes, mushrooms, and toast," Erik replied. "It's what you'll find throughout the UK."

"Hold up. What is 'blood pudding?' With real blood? And people eat it?" Ben looked a little green around the gills.

"You know how they say you shouldn't ask what's in sausage—or hot dogs?" Erik replied with an impish grin. "People have been eating it for centuries. If you hadn't heard the name of it before you tried it, you wouldn't even notice."

"Have you eaten it?"

"When in England, do as the English do," Erik replied with a shrug. "The seasoning varies by region, and I've had some I like better than others. It's usually just a small piece or a slice—not a heaping plate."

"It's just..." Ben looked like he was trying to put his reservations into words and still be polite.

"Ben, how do you order your steak?"

"Rare."

Erik raised an eyebrow. "Bloody."

"That's different."

"With the blood pudding, it's all thoroughly cooked. Not oozing on your plate." Erik shuddered. He could enjoy a good steak cooked medium, but he'd never learned to like it rare, although he had no problem with the raw fish in sushi.

"I'll try a bite," Ben said. "Since we're here. You aren't pulling my leg about this, are you?"

Erik reached for his hand. "I wouldn't do that. If I didn't care for it or I thought it was too much of an acquired taste, I'd tell you. I was surprised that it wasn't strange at all the first time I tried it. But you don't have to have any if you don't want to. This is your vacation. You don't have to impress me. I'm already impressed."

Ben smiled and gave Erik's hand a squeeze before he reached for his juice and savored a swallow. "I think I can manage a bite. What's with the beans, tomatoes, and mushrooms?"

Erik shrugged. "I've never gotten a good answer to that question. 'Because they taste good with the rest of the stuff on the plate' is the best I've heard. It's a hearty meal to keep you full for a busy day. If you decide you like it, there are restaurants that serve it back home."

Servers brought large trays laden with more food than Erik thought he could eat in a week. Ben's eyes widened as the plates were placed on the table, along with a stack of perfect toast and a plate of cold, creamy butter.

"I guess it's not any weirder than having cereal for a quick dinner," Ben said, then paused as he breathed in the aromas wafting up from his plate. "It does smell good."

Erik bumped his knee under the table. "Start eating and let me know what you think."

A few bites in and a slightly pornographic moan of pleasure let Erik know Ben was adjusting to the cuisine just fine. He smiled, enjoying Ben's progression from skeptical to won over.

"I don't know that I'm going to be a big fan of the blood sausage, but the small piece wasn't too bad. And I think I could get to like the baked beans. It's all actually pretty amazing."

Erik welcomed refills on his coffee and noted that the service was as exceptional as the food. He was glad that they only had to cross the inner bailey to meet up with Priscilla because their breakfast was too large—and too good—to be rushed.

When they finally pushed away from the table, Erik swore he'd never be hungry again.

"You booked lunch for us at the tea room? I'm looking forward to it, but I don't know how much room I'll have by then," Ben said. "Although for those little cakes, I'll make the effort."

They paid their tab and headed down the hallway toward the Library. Priscilla waved to them from where she stood.

"Did you enjoy breakfast?" she asked as keys rattled in her hand to unlock the door to the Library.

"It was phenomenal," Ben answered. "I can't wait to see what dinner is like."

She grinned. "You won't be disappointed. Our food is excellent, and our chef is amazing."

They followed her inside as she turned on the lights. "I'll refer to the floors in the American fashion, although we number them differently here," Priscilla said.

"The first and second floors are for weddings—a bridal preparation room on the first floor with an entrance into the great hall and the honeymoon suite above that. The third floor has more guest rooms, and on the second floor, we have two sitting rooms recreated with period decor and furnishings that show how the family lived during the 1920s—the *Downton Abbey* period," she added.

"The fifth floor is largely untouched, although I suspect we'll make it climate-controlled storage at some point," Priscilla continued. "We're going to the Archive, which is behind the Library."

"We truly appreciate you bringing us up here and the earl for providing access," Erik said.

Priscilla smiled. "The earl loves history and art. I'm not surprised the two of you hit it off. He also has a soft spot for anyone who takes a shine to his family's history, for obvious reasons."

"I didn't think this was open to the public," Erik said, taking in the storeroom of shelves filled with carefully labeled boxes. A sturdy library table sat near one end.

"It isn't," Priscilla replied. They took off their jackets and hung them on a coat tree near the door. "But there are always researchers and biographers who want to study very specific pieces of the Mortimer history. The earl wanted to make that accessible to authorized guests, sort of like the rare book room in a library."

"That's pretty impressive," Erik said, in awe of what it must be like to have a prominent family history stretching back, unbroken, over nearly a thousand years in the same dwelling. To have not just had ancestors who witnessed the history of a kingdom, but helped to make it. A glance at his partner suggested that Ben was intrigued as well.

Priscilla gave them a quick tour, explaining why certain pieces were stored together and talking about the rare first editions in the private library.

"We do have boxed loose items," she added. "Correspondence, diaries, ledgers, and invoices. We sign those in and out, with supervised access because of how fragile they are."

"You're thinking something," Ben surmised, no doubt reading Erik's pursed lips and narrowed eyes.

"How involved were the Mortimers with the building of St. Paul's Church?" Erik asked.

Priscilla looked up. "Very. They donated a lot of money and gave several of the bequest pieces in the sanctuary. There's a pair of stained-glass windows that were donated in memory of the wife of the earl at the time the church was built."

"Do any records survive from that time?" Erik asked. "Ledgers, details about the church construction, drawings, that sort of thing?"

Priscilla nodded. "What exists is boxed in the other room. If you want to come back tomorrow, I could ask Mrs. Marshbanks to pull what we have for you to look at. You'd need to use cotton gloves and wear a mask."

"Of course." That sort of thing was standard with art preservationists. "Thank you."

"Any records that the church itself might have had would be at the county office in Shrewsbury," Priscilla continued. "But there is a framed document in the church listing the names of all the stonemasons who did the carvings and embellishments, as well as the stained-glass artists who made the windows. I don't know if that's any help or not, but if you're going near there, you might have a look."

"That's good to know. Thank you," Erik said, thinking of their appointment with Father Andrews that afternoon.

Erik thought about his dream. The figures had been cloaked, so he didn't get much to help him place the time period, but from the shoes and a few other details, the event—if real—could have been around the time of the early Crusades. The time of the Templars.

"Okay, this is going to sound odd, but do you happen to have any jewelry in the family collection? A necklace made of triangles with dots on them?" Erik felt his cheeks flush and knew Ben was looking at him, probably figuring there'd been a vision from touching an object that they hadn't discussed.

Priscilla gave him an odd look. "That's strangely specific...and happens to describe one of the oldest pieces in the collection."

Erik met Ben's gaze and then flicked to Priscilla. "I, uh, get visions sometimes. They're usually just glimpses without much context. I had one in the middle of the night," he added with an apologetic half-smile aimed at Ben. "The only real detail was the necklace."

"What did you see?" Ben asked.

Erik thought he could hear some hurt in his partner's voice, and guessed it was for not hearing about his dream first. "I saw a nighttime rendezvous along a river or creek. There were two men in a boat and a woman and two men on the shore. One of the men got out of the boat like he meant to stay. The woman was mostly covered with a cloak and hood, but I got a good look at her necklace. I'm sorry I didn't mention it earlier. You were sound asleep, and I was still chewing things over at breakfast," Erik replied, chagrined.

Ben laid a hand on his back. "I get it. And honestly, I was tired enough I'm not sure you could have woken me if you'd tried."

"Let me find someone to retrieve that from the vaults," Priscilla said and left the room. She came back after a while with a wooden case with a glass lid. Inside it, on a bed of velvet, lay the necklace Erik had seen in his vision.

Erik paled in recognition.

Ben's hand tightened on his arm. "Erik?" he said quietly, in a protective tone.

"That's it," Erik replied.

"This belonged to Sibella Mortimer, who lived in the early 1300s," Priscilla told them. "She was the daughter of the then-earl, who funded the building of St. Paul's Church. The only note we have about it is that she said she received it from an admirer when she traveled in France some years before."

Priscilla placed the wooden tray on the table, and Erik turned on his phone's light to get a better look at the details. "I've never seen this pattern before," Erik said. "Not in jewelry. But there's something familiar...I just can't put my finger on it."

"Why would you get a vision about a piece of jewelry that almost never comes out of the vault?" Priscilla asked. "Do you think there's some kind of danger?"

Erik ran a check on his intuition once more, then shook his head. He saw Ben's worried expression and felt guilty for spoiling their vacation. Then again, he didn't volunteer for the vision.

"Not danger. But a sense of urgency. Maybe something left unfinished that needs to be resolved?" That was the problem with most psychic talents, Erik thought, whether they were clairvoyance, mediumship, or any of the many other abilities. The "messages from beyond" were never as clear as in the movies. Scriptwriters always created ghosts who spoke in full sentences, visions that revealed the exact location of a missing item, or flashes of precognition specific enough for the hero to stop a disaster.

In reality, for Erik and for the other people he knew with some kind of "gift," the messages were fragmented, unclear, and vexingly light on details requiring a lot of research and intuition to put the pieces together.

"What could be urgent after seven hundred years?" Ben asked. "That's a long time to leave unfinished business."

Erik rested a hip against the table, still studying the necklace. "It's unlikely that I'm the only person with some psychic ability to visit the castle in all that time, or even recently. But maybe there's an outside influence that changed. Something that 'woke up' the ghosts."

Priscilla regarded the necklace like it was a puzzle to be solved. "But what? We aren't doing renovations that would disturb anything that Sibella would have known in her lifetime. We've recently found some hidden rooms and passageways, but they date from a period later than the necklace. And since the village has so many historic preservation covenants, nothing much ever changes except for maintenance and a coat of paint."

"I don't know," Erik replied. "But I want to find out." He immediately shot an apologetic look at Ben, who just chuckled.

"Relax. Solving a mystery on vacation makes it a one-of-a-kind trip. Just watch. We'll go back and tell our friends, and all of a sudden, they'll all want to take 'Erik's Magical Mystery Tour.'"

That made Erik chuckle, although knowing their extended network of friends, many of whom had abilities of their own, they might enjoy a trip to solve a ghostly puzzle.

"Will it damage anything if I take pictures?" he asked Priscilla.

"I don't see how it would. Fabrics and pigment are fragile, but that's pewter. A few light flashes aren't going to damage it."

Erik's work tracking art fraud required a good knowledge of art conservation, so he understood the danger light and handling could pose to old treasures. "Thank you."

He managed to get clear, close-up photos of the entire piece. "I hate to ask, but do you know if there are markings on the reverse?" he asked, feeling like he was pushing his luck.

"Turn the case over. You won't hurt anything—the necklace is pinned in place," Priscilla told him. On the back of the case was a laminated drawing of the back of the necklace. Erik snapped photos of it, too.

"Thank you," he said. "I don't know what's going on, but when we find out more, I'll let you know." Erik wasn't sure what the mystery was, but he felt certain that the necklace—and the Templars—had something to do with it.

CHAPTER FOUR

BEN

They decided to eat at Lady Neville's Tea Room at the castle and save the other tea room in town for another day. Ben and Erik settled in at their table, and Ben glanced around the room. He felt a bit like a bull in a china shop. The chairs seemed a little small for his size, scaled for the "ladies who lunch."

The tea shop was decorated in an undeniably feminine style, from the ruffled curtains at the window to the framed oil paintings of children and pampered dogs from centuries past. Ben felt like he was visiting someone's well-off maiden aunt.

"It's a little more formal than I expected for a tea room." Ben took in the white tablecloths, monogrammed china cups and saucers, and the general garden party vibe. "I feel like I should have a jacket and pleated trousers with a pair of oxfords like the men wore to lawn parties on *Downton Abbey*."

"There's no dress code. And you look fine the way you are. You always look fine." Erik bumped their feet together beneath the table.

"Yeah, that's my line for you," Ben deflected, blushing a little. "All your tweed jackets will fit right in."

"You like my tweed jackets," Erik teased.

"I like your hot nerdy professor look," Ben corrected, teasing. "The jackets are just part of it."

At his shop back in Cape May, Erik still tended to dress like the art and antiquities expert he was, and the jackets Ben liked to tease him about fit what customers expected to see. During Cape May's relatively short summer, Erik quickly shifted to neat button-down shirts. Ben lived in jeans and polo shirts, which matched the laid-back feel of his vacation rental business.

"Did you see all the cakes and tarts in that front counter?" Ben asked, looking over Erik's shoulder at the big refrigerated glass counter they had passed on their way in. A chalkboard overhead gave the day's specials and the varieties of sandwiches available with the lunch packages.

"They all looked good," Erik confessed. "And I thought after that breakfast we had; I'd never eat again."

"Can't solve mysteries on an empty stomach," Ben replied with a grin.

"Which reminds me." Erik pulled out his phone, logged into a website, and uploaded the photos of the necklace. "There's an image recognition database I've got access to—part of the old job, and it still comes in handy when customers are looking to match or replace a particular type of antique. I thought it might connect the dots with Sibella's necklace. I know I've seen that pattern before—I just don't remember where."

Ben smiled, wondering if Erik had any idea how adorable and totally fuckable he looked when he concentrated. Erik didn't seem to realize that he bit his lip when he was deep in thought and let the pink tip of his tongue peek out. Erik was smart and clever and so damn handsome, and it always amazed Ben that a guy like Erik would fall in love with a guy like him.

When they first met, after they cleared up the dating app mistake, Ben had thought Erik was sexy in a naughty professor sort of way. They'd both been reeling after professional and romantic failures, and Ben hadn't been thinking further ahead than a summer fling. At the time, he hadn't even been sure he wanted to stay in Cape May, although he knew he didn't want to go back to Newark.

They had teamed up to solve a forty-year-old mystery, only to find out that some people wanted the past to stay buried badly enough to try to bury Erik and Ben. That's when Ben had gotten to see the grit and stubborn bravery beneath Erik's academic façade. He'd fallen head over heels but never expected Erik to want a bitter ex-cop for more than a walk on the wild side. When Ben had found out that Erik wasn't scared off by his tats, scars, or attitude, he couldn't believe his good fortune. The longer they were together, the more certain Ben became that Erik was his forever guy.

"Any luck?" Ben asked, with a nod toward Erik's phone.

Erik shook his head. "It'll take a while to run matches with the database. But we've got a few hours before we're supposed to meet Father Andrews. I have to admit that I'm very curious to see what it turns up.

Their server came then and took their order. They each chose a different type of tea from the more exotic choices on the menu. Ben picked a cinnamon rooibos while Erik went for the intriguingly named Scottish "whisky" tea, which their server assured them contained no liquor. The real centerpiece of their lunch would be served on the fancy tiered china plate cake stand. The first course had small cold sandwiches—crusts removed—with fillings like chicken salad, cucumber, cream cheese, ham salad, and watercress.

The second course brought a similar tiered stand filled with bite-size petit fours, fruit tartlets, and custards. Finally, the lunch also included their choice of a full-size slice of any of the freshly-baked layer cakes in the front case. Ben chose a chocolate fudge cake with sinfully rich icing, while Erik went for the carrot cake with cream cheese frosting.

"That was amazing," Erik said as they pushed back from the table, once the teapots were empty and they had finished off everything they'd been served.

"Those little bite-sized things are deceptive," Ben replied with a glare at the empty tiered plate stand as if it were to blame for him feeling too full. "It doesn't look like much, but it adds up."

"Want to walk it off and head into town?" Erik asked. They had brought their coats and scarves, even though the tea room was close to the castle wing where their room was located.

"Sure. It's a nice day, and if we stick around, I'll just fall asleep," Ben admitted. Since they had an appointment at the church, they retraced their steps from the day before as they headed into town. "Tomorrow, I'd love to go to the earl's brewery." Ben pointed in the opposite direction from the way they were heading. "You know, immerse ourselves in local culture."

Erik chuckled. "Sounds good. We also wanted to stroll around the castle grounds if it isn't raining. And if it does rain—this is England, after all—there are fireplaces all over the sitting areas. There's one next to the restaurant, and one in the Solar near the Solarium with all the plants. It has a fireplace too—and both of them have bar service. We could curl up and read all day in front of a cozy fire...and have tea or cocktails brought out whenever we want."

"Now you've almost got me hoping it rains at least one day while we're here," Ben replied. "That sounds fantastic."

Cadwell's bookshop was the kind of place Ben, as a child, had always wanted to go and never come out. As the glimpse they'd gotten through the window promised, books filled shelves from floor to ceiling, not only along the walls but in long rows that ran the length of the building. Side rooms, as well as nooks and crannies, were also packed with all the books that would fit on shelves. In more than one corner, marked crates of books were stacked waist-high.

New books were near the front and used books toward the rear. Hand-lettered signs indicated different genres and topics. Cadwell's wasn't a coffee shop kind of bookstore, and it didn't sell anything except books. Ben bet that Erik would have also loved to have moved in when he was a kid, with a bedroll and a stash of food, and not come out for weeks.

"This is amazing," Ben said in a hushed voice as if it were a library. "I could spend the winter in here. Hibernation wouldn't be bad at all."

A short, bald fellow in a plaid shirt, sweater vest, and corduroy pants perched on a stool behind the old-fashioned register. Ben guessed he was Ptolemy Cadwell, whose name was painted on the front window next to the word *Proprietor*.

"Just let me know if I can help you fellows. There's a lot here," Cadwell called out to them.

Ben drifted toward the fantasy, comics, and manga, then decided to see what he could find on the Templars. He found himself in the history section, in front of a shelf of books and scanned the titles and authors, trying to figure out where to begin. Surely there had to be more to the organization than what he had seen in video games, and also a reason that a group that hadn't been active in more than seven hundred years had remained a legend for so long. There hadn't been enough time for him to even do a cursory internet search on the Templars, and Ben felt like that put him behind on the mystery that had fallen into their laps.

"Didn't think I'd find you here." Erik came up behind Ben and put a hand on his shoulder.

"I like to keep you on your toes." Ben teased. "Unpredictable. Wouldn't want to get boring."

Erik leaned in to give him a peck on his cheek. "Never."

"I thought it might be a good idea to fill in some basics, at least for me," Ben said. "You probably know about all of it already. Maybe it will give us ideas about what's going on with this 'treasure' people keep talking about."

Erik picked a book from the shelf and scanned the table of contents. "I was an art history major, but that also included a lot of the 'history' part. The Templars have been gone for a long time, but they left a surprising number of churches and castles across England and throughout Europe."

"That's a lot of building for guys who were soldier monks," Ben replied, picking out a couple of books and looking for chapters about the Templars in England.

"It's been a long time since my history classes, but I'll tell you what I remember," Erik said. "You're right about them being soldier monks. Originally, they were supposed to protect religious pilgrims to the 'Holy Land.' Over time, they became bankers to European nobility, and the order grew wealthy, powerful—and feared. The kings and even the pope worried because the Templars controlled more wealth than they did. The pope renounced them and burned their leaders at the stake, seized their assets, and destroyed the Order."

Ben had known that the Templars were the chainmail-clad knights who wore the white tabard with a red cross, and their iconic image became a staple in movies and video games over the years. Apparently, that was just scratching the surface.

Ben and Erik picked a couple of books on the Templars, quickly scanning the ones that caught their attention. Ben leaned against the shelf and skimmed through the material, noting dates, names, and places as if he were reading a police file.

"Find something?" Ben asked.

"Maybe," Erik replied, closing the book.

"Light reading?"

Erik chuckled. "However this mystery of ours works out, I figure I'll want to find out more about the Templars, so I might as well bring home a couple of souvenirs."

Ben's phone buzzed with a reminder. "It's about time to head over to the church," Ben said. "Don't want to be late for the priest." He froze when he realized what he had said. He and Erik hadn't been dating long, but Ben's thoughts sometimes jumped ahead to a future he hoped they might reach together. If this thing between them worked out, could they make a forever commitment? Maybe even marriage?

He couldn't read the look in Erik's eyes, but his partner didn't shy away, so if the same thoughts crossed his mind, at least he didn't bolt like a frightened horse.

"We're practically across the street, so I think we'll make it to the church on time," Erik replied. "Wasn't that a song? Let's go pay for the books and see what we find at the church."

Mr. Cadwell took note of their purchases as he rang them up. "Templars, huh? They were in this area, back in the day. All over England, to tell you the truth." He gave them a measured look. "You looking for the treasure? I didn't figure you for treasure hunters."

"We're here on vacation and heard some of the legends, thought we'd learn more," Erik replied. "I studied a lot of history in school but seemed to have skipped much about the Templars."

That seemed to appease Cadwell, who dropped his sudden wariness. "Of course, one of the legends is that the Templars were the protectors of the Holy Grail. That even made it into an Indiana Jones movie."

Ben grinned. "I liked that one. And I'd forgotten about the old knight guarding the Grail."

Cadwell nodded. "At one time or another, people have also thought the Templars guarded the Ark of the Covenant and the Shroud of Turin. Back around the time of Prohibition, people claimed that the Temperance Movement had its roots in the Templars' strict rules. And of course, there have been rumors that when the Templars' leaders were killed, the Order went underground and became a secret society. Lots of folks have tried to link them to the Freemasons."

Having a rapt audience seemed to encourage Cadwell. "There are even legends around the murder of the leaders. When Jacques de Molay was burned at the stake in 1314, he cursed Pope Clement V and King Phillip IV of France, calling down a 'calamity' on them before the year was over. The pope died a month later, and the king died within the year," he added, raising an eyebrow.

"Wow. Quite a coincidence," Erik remarked, and Ben wondered what his partner was thinking.

"Isn't it?" Cadwell replied. "The rest of the knights were rounded up and arrested. But one key player was never accounted for—Alain de Molay, Jacques's younger brother and his most devoted and trusted supporter. The stories say Alain was smuggled out of France and given asylum by a sympathizer in another country. No one's ever proved that right or wrong, but it makes a good story, doesn't it?"

He took Erik's credit card and ran their charges. "They say that the earl's relatives had a connection to the Templars, back in the day."

"Oh?" Ben asked.

Cadwell shrugged. "It's an old story, so I'm not carrying tales. I don't know that anyone ever confirmed it, but there's a bit of romance to it being unproven. The Templars became a nostalgic lost cause after their leaders were murdered. There were all kinds of fanciful stories told in the pubs over a few drinks. But I always thought the ones about a Mortimer connection seemed a bit more likely. No disrespect to the earl's family intended, of course."

"Of course not," Erik replied.

Cadwell slipped their books into a paper bag and handed it across the counter. "Enjoy your reading."

Ben and Erik headed back outside, feeling the nip in the air a bit more after the warmth of the bookshop.

"We still have a little time before the church—do you want to grab a cup of tea to go?" Ben asked as they passed the yarn shop with the tea room in the back. Erik nodded, and they ducked inside, selecting two new flavors to try and remarking over the completely different selection of sweets and sandwiches.

"Definitely want to go back there one of our other days," Ben said as they emerged, each with a steaming cup of tea.

"It looked a little more homey—less formal than the castle's version," Erik replied. "And I really liked some of the scarves and hats I saw in the yarn shop. Susan would love something like that."

Susan Hendricks was Erik's next-door neighbor, part-time helper at Trinkets, and best friend in Cape May. Ben knew Erik had wanted to find something unique to take back for her, and a cozy hand-knit item might be just the thing.

"What did you think about what Cadwell told us?" Ben asked as they settled on a bench, waiting out the time until their appointment with Father Andrews. "I realized I'd heard the bit about the Grail. And wasn't that Freemason's stuff in the movie where Nicholas Cage stole the Declaration of Independence?"

Erik chuckled and rolled his eyes. "History as taught by pop culture?"

Ben grinned at the good-natured teasing. "Don't knock it. Comes in handy."

Erik leaned back, watching the steam rise from the lid of his tea. "I think that the rumors about a Mortimer who was a supporter are likely. Especially after this." He held up his phone for Ben to see an email from a site Ben didn't recognize.

"The image recognition scan came back. That necklace of Sibella's? The pieces are part of a cipher for a Templar secret code. That's where

I'd seen the symbols before—but laid out as the code key, not as a decorative design." Erik typed in a few more instructions and brought up a document he showed to Ben.

"This is the most credible key to the Templar Code," Erik said. "It won't be quick to decode a message, but if this is accurate, we should be able to read whatever we find."

"Sibella lived at the right time," Ben observed. "Didn't Priscilla say Sibella received the necklace as a gift from an admirer in France?"

Erik nodded. "And Jacques de Molay was killed in France. There's got to be something to all the rumors. But what it means and whether or not the treasure is real...I guess we'll find out."

By the time they walked to the church, their tea had cooled enough for them to finish before entering. Father Andrews looked up when they came in from where he had been straightening the items on a literature table in the back of the sanctuary.

"Good to see you again. Are you ready for that tour?"

Erik grinned, and Ben realized how much he loved to see his partner excited by the thrill of pursuing a mystery. "We definitely are. Can we please start with that framed document you mentioned about the stone cutters who worked on building the church?"

Ben glanced at Erik, wondering what was on his mind. Father Andrews obligingly led them across the back of the narthex and down a side corridor, then pointed to an old frame and its yellowed content.

"The writing is faded and spidery, but that's the list we found of the stonemasons who oversaw the work or worked on significant areas of the church. Of course, there are nearly as many legends about stone-masons as there are about Templars...and sometimes, the legends tangle together. For example, many of the stories about what happened to the Templars after they were shut down, linked them to the Freema-sons—who began as a secret society of stonemasons."

Erik and Ben exchanged a glance since that comment aligned so perfectly with their previous conversation. Erik gave Father Andrews his most persuasive smile. "Is there any way we could take this off the wall for a better look?"

Father Andrews grinned back, looking almost boyish despite his cassock. "I actually thought you might ask that, so I checked to see if it could be lifted off the hook—and it can. We can put it on the table over here if you'll do the honors," he added, glancing at Ben, who was the tallest of the three.

"Sure." Ben walked toward the large frame and caught movement out of the corner of his eye, a flash of red and white. He turned his head but didn't see anyone in the hallway—the same corridor where he had glimpsed the ghost before.

Ben returned his attention to the frame and lifted it down carefully, not wanting to damage the extremely old document inside. He carried it over to the sturdy table at the back, moving aside pamphlets and event fliers, and laid it down flat.

"I think our ghost is back." Ben looked down the still-empty corridor.

"You saw something?" Erik glanced up worriedly.

"Just some motion. Nothing's there now," Ben replied.

Father Andrews walked around a corner and snapped a few light switches, which dispelled the dim, reverent atmosphere of the church and made it easier to see the document.

"Kind of amazing thinking about this roster being as old as the church." Erik bent over and pulling out the jeweler's loupe from his pocket. "The ink has held up well all these years. And the writing is very precise, which helps since there's still been some fading."

"What are you looking for?" Father Andrews asked, leaning in on one side of Erik as Ben did the same on the other, trying to get a good look at the parchment.

"I'm not entirely sure," Erik confessed. "I think I'll know it when I see it."

"The names don't appear to be in any order," Ben observed. "They're not alphabetic, and if they're respecting some kind of rank or seniority, there's nothing that says so."

"Just a minute," Father Andrews said and walked off toward a nook at the front of the church. He returned, carrying two large hand-held magnifying glasses. "We keep these in the robing room for choir members or lay readers who need a little help making out the small print."

Erik stuck with his loupe, which left a magnifier for Ben and the priest. They split up the long lists, with Erik taking the two center columns while Ben and Father Andrews took the columns on the side.

For a long time, no one spoke, deep in concentration. Erik stood up and blinked, trying to ease the eye strain. Ben and their new friend kept on going. Ben was nearly at the end of his column when he hesitated. He had been hearing the names in his mind as he read them, and the last one sounded familiar. Ben glanced at the name again, and his eyes widened at the pronunciation.

"Son of a...gun," he said, quickly amending his words for the benefit of the priest. "Erik, look at this name." He pointed to one line beneath the glass. Erik bent down to read it, and Ben saw a little jolt go through his partner when Erik realized what he was seeing.

"The last name is spelled differently," Erik said quietly, as if he didn't want to jinx the find.

"It's too close to be a coincidence," Ben argued. He turned to Father Andrews. "What year was the church completed?"

"Building began in 1307 and was largely finished by 1325," the priest replied as if the details were ones he had quoted often.

Ben looked at Erik. "The timing is right. Jacques died in 1314."

Father Andrews frowned. "Jacques de Molay? The last grand master of the Knights Templars?"

"Yeah. And look here," Ben's fingertip hovered just below one of the faded names.

"Alain Molai," the priest said.

"Jacque's missing, younger brother," Erik added. "It has to be him."

Ben felt a thrill of excitement as the pieces came together in his mind. "Someone must have spirited Alain out of France, knowing what was coming."

Erik raised an eyebrow. "Maybe Jacques himself, wanting to save his brother and anything of value he could send with Alain."

Ben nodded. "And suppose...that the Mortimer family was known to them as supporters of the Templars. So Alain was smuggled across the Channel to Shropshire, an unlikely place for authorities to search for the last Templar. Maybe brought him upriver in a boat," he added, tying in Erik's vision.

"Where he was met by Sibella Mortimer and her bodyguards," Erik supplied. "She brought him to Caynham-on-Ledwyche, and he lived out his life incognito...as a stonemason."

"Maybe he apprenticed before he entered holy orders," Father Andrews mused. "Not every future priest or monk went to the church as a boy. Some were grown men who had trades, even families. All that I've ever read about Jacques de Molay is that his family was well-off but not noble. That would certainly fit for a stonemason—such trades and their secrets were carefully guarded and passed from generation to generation."

"Do we know who worked on which parts of the church?" Ben asked, looking up at the beautifully carved stone embellishments and the symmetrical framing of the windows.

Father Andrews shook his head. "Not that I've seen. Although I suspect then as now, people had specialties."

Erik pulled his drawing of Sibella's necklace from his jacket pocket and held it out to Father Andrews. "Does this pattern look familiar?"

Father Andrews took the paper and studied it under bright light. "This reminds me a lot of the decorative border in the Mortimer family crypt," he said, looking up with a startled expression.

"When was the crypt built?" Erik asked.

"The church was finished by 1325, so the crypt would have been built between 1307 and that date," the priest replied.

Ben and Erik exchanged a look. "So definitely in the period when Alain might have begun to work as a stonemason," Ben said.

Erik nodded. "Would it be possible for us to go down to the crypt now?"

"I brought the keys with me." Father Andrews held them up and let the ring dangle from his finger. "Follow me."

Ben and Erik fell in behind him, and Ben realized they were heading in the same direction that he had chased the ghost on their first day.

"This is where the ghost disappeared." Ben looked at what appeared to be a solid stone wall ahead of them.

"Interesting, because this is the 'secret' entrance to the family crypt," Father Andrews said.

He pressed on a spot in the stone, and a section of wall swung forward on silent, balanced hinges, revealing a deep alcove with a steel door embellished with the Mortimer family crest.

"There is a 'public' door accessible from the lower level of the church," the priest said. "That was used for burials. This door allowed family members to visit without drawing attention to their presence. I learned of it when the earl asked me a few months ago to see if it still functioned. As you can see, it does."

"So the ghost—" Ben started.

"Would have known about it if he was one of the stonemasons who built the crypt," Erik finished for him.

Father Andrews reached to open the inner door. Ben grabbed his arm. "Have you ever been down to the crypt?"

The priest nodded. "Once or twice. There's not much reason to go. Usually, it's because a family member requests that I accompany them for some kind of memorial."

"Did you ever sense anything strange?" Ben pressed.

"You mean, like a ghost?"

Ben nodded. "Alain is a textbook case for a protective spirit. If he's still here, standing guard, he might not have bothered anyone on normal business, but he might see us as a threat."

Father Andrews eyes widened. "You've had experience with ghosts?"

"Yeah, both of us have," Ben said. "Been thrown across a room by one too. Do you happen to have any salt? And maybe something made of iron?"

Father Andrews nodded. "Those dispel spirits?"

"Not permanently, but maybe long enough to do what we need to get done."

"If Alain was a Templar, then he is also a Catholic priest. He would not be evil," Father Andrews replied.

"We don't think he's evil," Erik said. "But he might be inclined to defend his secret...enthusiastically. Someone could get hurt."

"All right. I think I've got something." Once again, the priest left them and then returned. "I borrowed a salt shaker from the fellowship kitchen and an iron poker from the fireplace in the library. Will that do?"

"That'll be perfect," Ben assured him. He took the two items, then twisted off the lid from the salt shaker and put it in his pocket. "But I'd better go first, especially if I can see him and you can't."

Father Andrews flipped a switch, and bare bulbs illuminated the way. "Electric lights were added in the 1950s," he told them. "Before that, it was lanterns—or torches. Watch your footing—they didn't build the treads for the size of people today."

Ben led them down the steep and narrow steps. He carried the salt shaker in one hand and the poker in the other. The air grew cooler as they descended until it was several degrees colder than the main section of the church.

Ben's shoulders almost brushed the sides of the stairwell, and he had less clearance for his head than he would have liked. When they reached the bottom, the lights cast a harsh glare over the small chapel-like mausoleum. Six flat ledger stones marked tombs in the floor. Ten wall crypts on both sides provided additional resting places, as well as ten in the far wall. Each was inscribed with multiple names and dates of death since they were frequently reused.

"The last interment here was in 1815," Father Andrews said. "After that, the Mortimers were buried in the new crypt beyond the castle gardens."

"Look at the border around the edge of the walls," Ben murmured. Erik looked up, and Ben saw the moment of realization in his features when he saw the running border of tiles, each with the symbols from the necklace.

"It's a message," Erik whispered, sounding awed. "Alain Molai left some kind of testament."

"What if he brought something the Templars couldn't afford to let fall into enemy hands?" Ben speculated. "It wouldn't necessarily have value to anyone else as a 'treasure,' but perhaps something of great meaning to the Order?"

"That's certainly possible," Erik said. "A relic. A grimoire—if the stories about the Templars dabbling in the dark side were true. Final words from Jacques de Molay. Or blackmail material, to secure safety for anyone who was left."

"Do you have the code key?" Father Andrews asked.

Erik nodded and pulled it up on his phone. "I think so. We'll see if it works."

The temperature abruptly plummeted, and Ben felt a tingle he had learned to associate with the presence of a spirit.

"Alain de Molay, are you here?' Ben called out, voice firm but not challenging.

"It's cold enough to see my breath," Father Andrews marveled.

"Yeah, it's a ghost thing," Erik muttered.

Ben took a step toward the center of the crypt, and a force shoved him back. "We're not here to steal from you."

The force pushed Ben hard enough to make him stagger, then did the same to Erik but left the priest untouched.

Mist gathered in the center of the crypt, gradually taking the shape of a man. Alain de Molay looked older than Ben expected, perhaps in his mid-sixties. Somehow, Ben had expected a thirty-something warrior. Instead, he saw a hunched and weary old man.

A very angry, protective old man with the training of a warrior. The ghost came at him with fire in his eyes, jaw set, mouth in a grim line. Ben rolled, then slung the salt shaker to make the contents scatter in a wide arc, driving Alain back. He swung the iron poker through the ghostly form. The spirit vanished with an eerie cry.

"How long will that last?" Father Andrews asked.

"No idea," Ben replied.

"Not long enough. Look!" Erik pointed to the far side of the crypt, where Alain's ghost took shape again.

"Father de Molay! We need to talk. Don't harm these men. We come in the name of the earl and the Mortimer family." Father Andrews spoke with authority.

That seemed to get through. Alain eyed them warily but did not attack.

"We know Sibella Mortimer managed to arrange passage for you from France when the Order was betrayed." Ben rose to his feet but stayed a cautious distance from the ghost. "The earl sent us." That might be stretching things, but then again, the earl had given Father Andrews leave to let them tour the crypt.

"Anything we find will go to the earl. It's been seven hundred years, and the world has changed a great deal. We think that retrieving what you hid might be the best way to preserve it," Ben persisted. "Please—let us read your message and safeguard what you risked so much to save."

Alain glared at him, wary and mistrustful, but he did not move closer. Just to be on the safe side, Ben laid down a thin line of salt that cut off Alain from the rest of them. He kept the iron poker handy, just in case.

"He shouldn't be able to cross that line," Ben said for the benefit of Father Andrews, who watched in fascination. "If he wants to watch, let him watch."

Erik reached into his messenger bag and handed a legal pad and a pen to Father Andrews. "Ben, would you please turn on your phone's light and hold it up to shine on the 'border'? I'm going to try to look at each symbol and translate it with the code key. Father, would you please write down what I say as I do the translation?"

The first hour passed slowly, and they moved only a few feet. At this rate, Erik thought it might take their entire vacation to translate the message.

Ben laid a hand on his shoulder. "You're doing fine. Do you know how exciting this is? No one else found this. Nobody else knows what it says. So take your time. There's nowhere else I'd rather be."

Father Andrews went back upstairs briefly to cancel his afternoon appointments and send someone out to pick up lunch for the three of them, which they ate in the crypt.

"It's going slowly, but what you've translated so far makes sense," the priest observed, looking over his notes.

Erik shrugged. "Let's hope my code key is correct. There have been plenty of incidents over the years where people thought they'd cracked a secret language and didn't get it right."

"I believe in you," Ben said, taking a bite of the steak and ale meat pie from the Boar and Knights. Erik had gotten a chicken pie, and Father Andrews had a serving of shepherd's pie.

"So do I, which is why I'm getting all this on video—for posterity," Father Andrews said with a smile. He had grabbed the video camera the church kept on hand for special events and set it up to record the slow process of decoding Alain's message.

"Just think," he added, "we are looking at the secret of the last Knight Templar. This is the most exciting thing that's ever happened at St. Paul's."

After the first section, translating went a little faster as Erik got the hang of the cipher. Still, Ben was glad they had made a late dinner reservation at the castle since it was likely to take all day to make the rest of the circuit around the crypt.

The code had been chiseled around the top of the stone walls. The symbols resembled triangles, V-shaped forms, and what Ben thought of as 'ice cream cones'—a V-shape with an odd angular cap on it. The way the symbol pointed and whether or not it had a dot in it determined which letter it stood for. Even with Ben's extra light, Erik had to fetch a step stool from the church to be able to make out the details clearly enough to pick out the individual letters.

"My neck is never going to be the same," Erik lamented, pausing to massage stiff muscles from keeping his head tipped up.

"I'd give a lot for a selfie stick right about now," Ben joked since he had given up holding his phone with his arm outstretched and taped it to a broom handle. When his battery started to die, Father Andrew found them a couple of flashlights, and the work continued.

Little by little, they made their way. In the windowless crypt, the hours ran together. Finally, when Ben's eyes were beginning to blur and his stomach rumbled for supper, Erik parsed out the last few symbols.

"And...I think that's it." Erik blew out a huff of relief. They all searched carefully to ensure no other symbols were hidden elsewhere but found nothing.

Erik, Ben, and Father Andrews sat on the crypt floor. The church staff had gone home hours ago, and Ben's phone suggested it was almost time to walk back to the castle to make their reservation.

"Does it make any sense?" Erik asked the priest.

Father Andrews nodded. "As we went, I tried to put lines between the words when they formed. Here's what I've got."

Ben glanced at Alain's ghost, who remained visible in his corner.

The spirit's expression held wariness and...hope? Ben couldn't tell for certain.

He cleared his throat and began to read. "I, Alain de Molay, brother of Grand Master Jacques de Molay, am the last of the Knights Templar. I came in exile and found a haven thanks to the Mortimer family, may their name be blessed by God forever. I carried only one thing with me, the greatest treasure of the Templars, which I have hidden safely for the ages. If any of my brother Knights escape, or if the Order rises from the ashes, you will find the treasure here."

Father Andrews looked up. "He gives a series of numbers. I think they may be longitude and latitude coordinates."

"That would make sense," Erik said, looking as gobsmacked as Ben felt at hearing the last testament of the Templar's only survivor. Erik looked from Ben to Father Andrews. "This is bigger than figuring out where that kid got his sword. If there's still something at the coordinates, this is history in the making."

Ben turned to the ghost. "Alain, thank you for your loyal service to your brother and to your Order. Finding what you hid will help ensure that their memory is not forgotten."

Alain's expression remained cautious, but Ben thought he saw sorrow and the wariness of someone eager to lay down a burden long carried. Before he could think about it much more, the spirit winked out.

"I guess he got bored," Erik quipped, although Ben knew the ghost's presence had unnerved his partner.

"How do you figure coordinates without GPS?" Ben asked, leaving thoughts of the ghost for later.

"From the stars," Father Andrews said. "The way navigators steered their ships and mapmakers created their products. It's crazy, thinking about it now with all our computers, but with just a compass, cross-staff, and astrolabe, people traveled the open sea and made it all around the world."

"Pretty damn ballsy," Ben said, still trying to imagine setting sail with no maps and hoping to get the calculations right. His cheeks colored. "Sorry, Father."

Father Andrews laughed. "No offense taken. To be honest, I was thinking much the same thing."

They climbed to their feet. Erik bent and twisted, trying to ease his lower back from a day of standing on the stone floor. Ben felt the strain in his knees. Father Andrews looked to be slightly older than both of them, but he didn't seem to be moving quite so stiffly, as if he were accustomed to the church's hard floor.

"What do you plan to do with the information now that you have the coordinates?" Father Andrews asked.

"We need to tell the earl," Erik replied. "Right after dinner. I'd like to plot out the coordinates Alain left us and see if the map the boy with the sword drew comes close to the same spot. After that, I guess it's up to the earl."

"When you find out...whatever you learn, please let me know. I would hate not to get the end of the story!"

Ben and Erik promised to keep Father Andrews in the loop and then headed back to the castle. Erik had the transcript of the translation in his messenger bag and had taken a photo with his phone for safekeeping.

They walked hand-in-hand. Ben felt too excited by their discovery to mind the cold. His thoughts bounced from cne possibility to another of what Alain might have found important enough to carry with him. He hadn't noticed that they weren't chatting until Erik broke the silence.

"So do I know how to show a guy a good time, or what?" Erik joked, but Ben heard the undercurrent of self-consciousness beneath the humor. "Spend all day in a mausoleum."

Ben took both of Erik's hands in his and turned toward him. "Are you kidding? That was like something on *The History Channel: Legends of the Last Templar*. Dude, anyone can go to dinner and a movie. We might have made history!"

He saw Erik's tension ease and read love, lust, and gratitude in his eyes. "I'd say that calls for a celebration, don't you?"

Ben leaned closer. "Food first, then fucking. My dick won't work on an empty stomach."

CHAPTER FIVE

ERIK

They bustled into the castle's dining room with only minutes to spare, both of them red-cheeked from the brisk walk and nippy temperature. Although they hadn't expected to be gone all day, they had dressed well enough to not offend the sensibilities of the other diners.

"This place is magnificent," Ben said, taking in more of the castle's details on their second visit. "I can't imagine actually living here, even before it opened to tourists. Or now, to tell the truth. But especially back when this was someone's home."

Erik nodded. "I always feel that way, whether it's a castle or a mansion. Can you imagine getting up in the middle of the night to get a drink of water? You might not make it back by morning."

"I imagine you'd just ring a bell, and some other poor slob would have to fetch it for you," Ben replied. "But I get what you're saying. And if they had pets, what kept them from just wandering off and never being found again? My grandmother lost track of her cat in a two-bedroom house."

"Maybe there was a royal cat-herder and dog-wrangler, whose job it was to know where the pets were or retrieve them if they went walk-about," Erik joked.

"Wouldn't surprise me. There's actually a Knight of the Garter. And back in the day, rich people just stood there, and servants put their clothes on for them," Ben said. "I saw that on a TV show. Some poor bastard's whole job was buttoning the king's fly."

By mutual agreement, they didn't talk about the Templars or their find, not wanting to be overheard. Erik knew they also needed some breathing space to step away from the mystery and just be on vacation. Still, he had to rein in his restless thoughts several times, and he could tell Ben had the same struggle.

Game meats were a specialty of the chef, and since that was something neither of them usually had available in Cape May, they decided to be adventurous. Ben ordered roasted venison topped with a cherry-apple reduction with a baked potato and mashed peas. Erik chose pheasant with wild mushroom potato gratin and cider-braised Brussels sprouts with bacon and apple. Both of them ordered single-malt Scotch to go with the meal.

"I kinda want to try all the desserts we saw them make on that baking show," Ben said, admitting to one of his favorite guilty pleasures.

Erik couldn't imagine either of them working up the nerve to make the most complicated treats, but some of the simpler sweets looked manageable. He had considered stocking up on ingredients one weekend and seeing what mayhem they could create, knowing that whatever disasters happened in the kitchen, they were assured a very happy ending in the bedroom.

"I suspect between here and the two tea shops, we can make that happen."

"Everything looks so good; I don't know how to choose," Ben confessed.

"I believe they call it 'spoilt for choice,'" Erik replied with a laugh.

In the end, they took the server's recommendation. Ben chose a chocolate fudge cake that their waiter confided was "better than the ones on that show." Erik picked an autumn trifle made with roasted pears and apples and topped with pumpkin caramel sauce.

"I may fall asleep before we can give Priscilla the big story," Ben said when they settled their bill and headed out.

Erik still felt buzzed with adrenaline from their amazing discovery, but the Scotch and excellent meal mellowed that energy to a warm glow. *I'm on vacation with the love of my life and solving a mystery that might make the history books. Best trip ever.*

Erik knew that his relationship with Ben was still new, but that didn't change how he felt. He had thought he was in love before, and he had certainly felt deep affection for his past boyfriends, even when undeserved. Nothing compared to what he felt for Ben, and sometimes that shook Erik to his core. The stakes were so much higher now, not to fuck this up.

They both had emotional scars and baggage—he figured everyone did by their mid-thirties. All the more reason to move slowly, take their time, and build a solid foundation. But their first case together almost became their last when Erik had been kidnapped and nearly killed, which had reinforced the importance of not putting off things that were important.

Taking a vacation together had been a step forward, a slightly deeper commitment. He hadn't doubted they would get along well, but travel had its own stresses and close quarters, and it provided a good test—one they seemed to be passing. *Maybe when we get back, it's time to level up and tell him I'm ready to buy that house together that we've been looking at.*

"We're showing up rather late again to meet with Priscilla," Ben said, jolting Erik out of his pleasant buzz.

"This time, I texted her to let her know we wanted to stop by after our dinner and that we had big news," Erik replied. "I wouldn't be surprised if the earl happened to drop in."

When they arrived at Priscilla's office, a man about Erik's age stood in the corner closest to the desk, chatting amicably with her. Erik recognized the man immediately.

Clarence Edward Arthur Mortimer, the fifteenth Earl of Caynham and CEO of Caynham Castle Enterprises, was tall and broad-shouldered. Blue eyes, black hair, and perfect teeth softened what would otherwise be somewhat hawkish and harsh features. The tan suggested that he had spent some time outside.

"Erik!" The earl strode forward, hand outstretched, and shook

Erik's hand heartily, then clapped him on the shoulder. "It's been a while. You look like things are going well."

The man's accent was prep school and old money, but the callouses on his palms reminded Erik that this earl was also a working man, who had to be clever and industrious to keep the legacy he inherited.

"They are," Erik replied with a nod. "Very well." He glanced at Ben, who was standing a step behind him, uncharacteristically quiet.

"I'd like to present Ben Nolan, my partner."

Ben looked like he was frozen between trying to bow or shake hands. He was a fraction of a second slow when the earl extended his hand and let the other man do the shaking. "A pleasure to meet you, my lord."

The earl chuckled and looked to Erik. "You didn't tell him?"

Erik shrugged. "I tried."

"Please, call me Ward," the earl said. "The 'lord' stuff is for all those dead guys in the oil paintings."

"Of course," Ben replied, still a bit stunned.

Ward ushered them down a hallway, through a door, and into a large, elaborately appointed office. A huge wooden desk with a tufted leather chair sat on one side of the room in front of dark wooden book-shelves.

Erik, Ben, and Priscilla followed him to a small seating area with a couch and wing chairs in front of a large stone fireplace on one wall. Above the mantle hung a formal oil portrait of someone Erik guessed was Ward's father. The family resemblance bred true.

"Have a seat, please, and fill me in. Priscilla says you have exciting news."

Erik cleared his throat. "We didn't come expecting to solve a mystery or go looking for a treasure. It was supposed to be time to kick back and enjoy the sights."

Ward laughed, a deep, rich sound. "I've seen you in action, Erik. Adventure seems to find you, regardless. Have you truly found a link to the Templars?"

"To Alain de Molay, the brother of the last grand master, and to the coordinates of where he hid the treasure of the Order."

Ward's eyes widened. "Really?"

Erik nodded. "Really. It's all been a little…amazing." He recounted the whole story, not omitting his vision or Ben's ability to see ghosts. Ward and Priscilla listened without interruption, and it seemed to Erik that Ward was on the edge of his seat.

"I seem to uncover secrets about my ancestors every time one of Sorren's friends visits," Ward said when Erik finished. "Then again, this Halloween, the spirits are digging up all sorts of mischief."

Sorren was a mutual friend of Erik's and Teag's. He coordinated an alliance of mortals and immortals that helped save the world from supernatural threats. He also happened to be a nearly six-hundred-year-old vampire. More recently, Sorren had paid Erik a visit at Trinkets, explaining the part that the store and its former owner played in that alliance—and offering Erik the chance to continue the role as a protector. Of course, Erik had agreed.

"Um, glad to be of service?" Erik replied. "I have no idea what we'll find when we check out the coordinates. Seven hundred years is a long time. Floods, subsidence, rising water table—there might be nothing left."

"But that boy told you he found the sword in a hole," Ward said.

"He also said the hole had closed up," Erik reminded his patron. "And I haven't checked to match Alain's coordinates with the 'pirate' map, although I feel fairly certain they'll be one and the same."

Ward glanced toward the mullioned window with an expression of frustration. "It's too dark to go tonight. Might I suggest a treasure-hunting expedition first thing in the morning?" He glanced at Priscilla and then to Erik and Ben.

"Breakfast at eight—my treat. You can tell me more about what you're doing now, Erik, since you've left working with the authorities. I'd love to learn more about you as well, Ben," Ward said with the sincere enthusiasm Erik remembered from their projects together.

"Then I'll get a couple of the groundskeepers to go with us in case we have to dig the spot open," Ward continued. "Worst case, we have a nice breakfast and an outing we can tell stories about over cocktails for years."

Erik glanced at Ben, who nodded with a slightly glazed look. "That sounds fantastic," Erik replied. "Thank you very much."

Ward leaned forward with that intense look Erik had forgotten, the one with laser-like focus. *"Thank you.* You may have made a significant historic find, uncovered a new piece of Templar history, and added a valuable piece to the Mortimer family story. I am, once again, in your debt."

They shook hands again and slapped shoulders, and then Erik and Ben headed out into the chilly autumn night. They hadn't gone far before Erik pulled Ben into his arms and kissed him, then pointed upward to another of the gargoyles.

"Before we leave, I want to kiss you under all of them," Erik told him. "So that we're sure to get the one from the legend."

"I'm up for that," Ben replied, bumping hips so that Erik would notice just how "up" he was for the suggestion.

The bright moon set the castle yard in sharp shadows. In the moonlight, anything seemed possible, like discovering they were suddenly transported to a different time period, an age of kings and knights and Templars.

By the time they reached their room, Erik had to admit that the jet lag and excitement of the last few days were catching up to him. Ben looked equally exhausted, but that didn't keep him from falling to his knees as soon as the door locked behind them.

"Wait," Erik said, tugging gently at Ben's dark hair. "How about if we do this together…on the bed."

Ben's smile made it clear that he was on board. Since they were in slacks and button-downs instead of jeans and tees, they took a few extra moments to lay their clothes over a chair rather than tossing the pieces onto the floor, but in moments, they were both naked and sprawled on the luxurious bed with the covers pulled down.

Erik wiggled around until he had Ben's cock against his lips, and he could feel Ben's mouth against his own prick. As tired as he'd been, a few flicks of Ben's tongue woke him up and stirred his dick to harden as well. He felt rather proud of himself. Thirty-five wasn't the same as eighteen when his cock could—and did—continue without him in his sleep.

He swiped his tongue over Ben's thick cock, tasting his pre-come, inhaling a scent of soap and sweat and something uniquely *Ben*. Erik toyed with the swollen knob, flicking over the head, sliding the tip into the slit, pressing just right into the sensitive spot just under the flare.

Erik moaned as Ben palmed one of his ass cheeks and pulled him closer. Ben positioned Erik's leg to be bent and upright, giving him better access to suck at his balls and tongue his taint. When Erik tried to buck into Ben's mouth, his partner stiff-armed him, making it clear that Ben controlled the pace.

Erik thrust two of his fingers into his mouth, getting them spit-slick, and then took the head of Ben's cock between his lips. He closed one hand around the root of Ben's dick, then began to slide up and down, lips slick and tongue constantly in motion with a just-barely-there scrape of teeth now and again to keep it interesting. Erik felt a tremor run through Ben, and he shifted his other hand to slide down his lover's crack, finding his furl.

He slid one finger inside Ben without much resistance since they had made love that morning, and so he added a second digit, matching the thrusts of his fingers to the motion of his mouth until Ben's hips jerked, and he forced a delicious groan from his partner.

Ben seemed equally intent on hijacking all of Erik's thought processes and re-routing all blood to his cock. He sucked and hummed, tracing the sensitive veins with his tongue, getting nearly all of Erik into his mouth despite the slightly awkward angle.

Erik knew he wouldn't last long. From the way Ben shuddered and jerked, he figured it wouldn't be a marathon for either of them.

Ben slid a finger into Erik's ass and stroked over his prostate at nearly the same time Erik did the same to him, and that was all it took to send both of them over the edge. Erik shot his load down Ben's throat, and Ben swallowed over and over, then sucked lightly at the oversensitive flesh to get the last few drops.

Ben came in Erik's mouth, and Erik did his best to keep up, feeling some of Ben's release trickling from his lips. He coaxed Ben to keep thrusting until Erik had taken all he had to give, then he drew back and kissed the head of Ben's cock.

They rolled apart, sticky, sweaty, and sated. Ben shimmied around to be face to face and pulled Erik into his arms. Slow, languorous kisses let them taste themselves on each other's tongues.

"I love you," Erik murmured, suddenly almost incoherently tired, as if the last of his energy shot from his body along with his orgasm.

"Love you too," Ben replied, sounding equally sleep-drunk.

"We should shower," Erik said, more because he felt like he had to than because he wanted to.

"Ugh. Not now. We can shower in the morning," Ben protested. "We're having breakfast with a frickin' *earl*. Need to have clean hair and not smell like sex."

"I like it when you smell like sex," Erik teased, nuzzling at the sensitive spot behind Ben's ear.

"I doubt the earl would be amused. No matter how much I like it too." Ben carded his fingers through Erik's blond hair while Erik lazily traced Ben's tattoos with his fingers. He knew how much Ben enjoyed that, and tired as they were, he saw his lover tremble in response.

"You're probably right," Erik replied with an overdramatic sigh. "Then pull up the covers, and I'll set the alarm. Convenient that we're already naked." He rolled over to grab his phone from the messenger bag that sat next to the nightstand and set two alarms just to be safe.

"Conveniently naked. I like that," Ben smirked, adorably groggy.

"Sleep tight," Erik murmured. "We've got a big day ahead of us."

BEN MUST HAVE BEEN nervous because he was up and in the shower before Erik's alarms went off. He lay in bed, listening to the water run, thinking about Ben's reactions to Ward and the vacation. For as well as he thought he knew his partner, some of his responses had taken him by surprise.

Funny, it's not that I ever "forgot" that Ward is an earl, because it's not like that's possible. I've known people who demanded a lot more attention for a lot less reason. Maybe it was just part of being in the art and antiquities world, but all our clients had more money than I did.

I had the credentials—and later, the specialty law enforcement authority— to be treated like an equal. Or, more to the point, I had something they wanted. Not with Ward—he's just a decent human being who happened to get born rich and turned out okay anyhow.

I guess I understand where Ben's coming from, though. He wasn't mixing with the hoi polloi as a Newark cop, and private investigators don't run with the jet setters. Probably busted more than a few of them, though. So I rubbed elbows enough to get over being star-struck, while he got to see their dirty laundry.

All in all, he's taken it pretty much in stride. I know he worries that he's not "fancy" enough for me. I don't want fancy. Josh was fancy, and he broke my heart. Ben is real and loyal and protective and loving. What you see is what you get. God, he doesn't realize how rare that is in the world I left, where everything was image and PR and fronting. He's also gorgeous and sexy, and oh, my God, those tats!

He's everything I've ever wanted, and that scares the crap out of me. I want him forever. I need to take this one step at a time. I can't afford to fuck this up.

The shower turned off, and Ben stuck his head out. "All yours," he announced, looking delectable in just a towel. Erik made sure Ben noticed being noticed, which brought a slow smile to Ben's lips.

"You can look all you want, but if we're going to make it to breakfast on time, better not touch until later."

Erik could see the way Ben's hard-on tented his bath sheet, and just to be a tease, Ben turned around, dropped his towel, and wiggled that perfect ass. Erik hopped out of bed and smacked one ass cheek, then pulled Ben in for a sloppy kiss.

"No matter what we find or don't find today, I want to have celebration sex with you tonight."

Ben raised an eyebrow. "What's 'celebration' sex?"

"Fireworks and happy endings," Erik replied.

"Don't we always?"

Erik pulled back to look in Ben's beautiful green eyes. "Yes. And that's worth celebrating too."

He ducked in for a quick kiss on the lips, then swaggered off to get a shower before Ben made him forget that they were meeting others for breakfast. For once, he ignored his morning wood, knowing that he and Ben would make up for it that night. By the time he finished a fast shower and shave, Ben was getting dressed.

"Is this okay? I figure if we're going to be tramping around a field or out in the woods, I should stick with jeans and sneakers. Although I guess if the earl...Ward...is bringing groundskeepers, we won't be doing the digging ourselves."

"I thought we might ask Priscilla about taking some salt and iron with us—just in case Alain haunts more than one location," Erik replied. "And yes, what you're wearing is fine. Don't be surprised to see Ward in jeans and wellingtons. He's a down-to-earth guy who works extremely hard."

"He didn't seem stuffy," Ben said. "Gotta understand—I'm used to the New York City nouveau riche. New money, big attitude and ego, no substance."

"I figured as much. And Ward's not typical—I worked with a lot of folks at that level who took themselves far too seriously," Erik responded. "But he's one of the good ones."

Ben sauntered over and cupped his face with one hand. "I'm not freaking out, honest. I just keep reminding myself that for some crazy reason, you picked me when you could have had those James Bond types at Interpol."

Erik groaned. "God, no! There was nothing romantic about what we did. The agents were cold and ruthless—and arrogant. Our whole purpose was to fuck up deals by cartels and the Russian Mob and recover the goods. I can't think of a more dick-wilting day job."

Ben kissed him lightly but with fervor and intent. "Good. I want you to realize that you're right where you belong."

Erik kissed him back. "Oh, I think I'm catching on."

Breakfast passed pleasantly, with an unacknowledged thrum of excitement beneath it all. True to Erik's prediction, both Ward and Priscilla turned out in sweaters, jeans, and wellies. Ward enquired about Erik's shop, Trinkets, and his blog, *Treasure Trail*, and asked incisive business questions of Ben about the vacation rental business.

"We've honestly been considering side ventures in both directions for Caynham Castle Enterprises," Ward admitted. "Not that I'm looking to sell off granny's hat pins or rent out the garden shed, but high-end antiques and vacation rentals are both ideas that align with the main goal of keeping the castle self-supporting and bolstering the local economy. So thank you. You've given me a lot to think about."

A mischievous glint came to his eyes. "Anyone ready to go on a scavenger hunt?"

Priscilla brought a canister of salt and a fireplace poker to breakfast without needing to be asked. She chuckled at Erik's surprise. "We faced down a very angry Mortimer ghostly great aunt when Teag and Anthony visited. They taught us well!"

Two men in garden overalls and canvas work jackets joined them outside the lobby with one of the castle's fleet of Land Rovers. Ward drove, with Erik in the front seat to navigate. He had translated the coordinates into directions and also verified that they roughly matched the boy's "pirate" map.

The day had turned colder, with gray skies that warned of rain—or snow. Erik was grateful for his heavy coat and gloves. Ben looked equally glad he had bundled up, and even Priscilla had a woolen coat and soft knitted scarf that looked like it had come from the yarn shop in town.

"I checked the coordinates last night," Ward said as he drove. "It's on Mortimer land. So we don't have to worry about permission to go there or wrangle ownership of anything that might still be inside." He frowned. "It's also an area where we've had flooding and some subsidence where the water table has changed, so watch your footing."

They parked on the side of a road as close as they could get to the site, which was in the middle of a clearing. Erik was glad they had coordinates because there were no landmarks to guide them.

"Here." He pointed a few feet ahead to a depression in the ground. The two workmen moved forward cautiously, testing the stability of the ground. They cleared away the dead grass and found what looked like fairly recent crumbled dirt. Then they began to dig.

"It doesn't look like too much caved in," one of the men said. "Enough to close the hole, but not plug it up. Looks more like a mudslide than a collapse. There are caves all through this area. Used to play in them when I was a lad."

An hour of digging revealed an opening somewhat larger than a manhole cover. Getting in and out wasn't going to be neat.

"There are coveralls in the back of the Land Rover," Ward said. "We can pull them on over our clothes—at least for those who want to go in."

All four of them went to suit up—and also found hard hats and flashlights for everyone. Ward asked the groundskeepers to stay outside so someone would be able to mount a rescue if necessary.

Erik wasn't surprised when Ward insisted on going first.

Ben raised an eyebrow when the earl dropped flat on the ground and slithered into the muddy hole on his belly. Priscilla followed him.

"Cowabunga!" Ben said and went next, with Erik bringing up the rear.

"Holy shit," Erik murmured when he got to his feet and looked around. What had begun as a natural cave had been carved into an elaborate temple with columns, niches, arches, and bas-relief murals along the wall.

"It's like the Caynton Caves," Ward said, and Erik thought he remembered reading about a similar structure found elsewhere in England—also rumored to be a Templar hiding place.

"Alain could have done this," Ben murmured. "Stonemason and all."

As he spoke, the chill in the air grew even colder. Mist coalesced and shimmered. Alain's ghost stood before them, blocking their entrance and, presumably, guarding his treasure. From their gasps, Erik realized that Ward and Priscilla could also see the ghost.

Ward stepped forward. "Alain de Molay, I presume. Allow me to introduce myself. I am the fifteenth Earl of Caynham, the many-times great-nephew of Sibella Mortimer, your patron."

The ghost remained unmoved. Ward and Priscilla exchanged a glance. Priscilla moved up to stand beside Ward and unzipped her muddy coverall partway, then moved her scarf aside to reveal the Templar code-key necklace that had belonged to Sibella.

Erik never thought he'd see a ghost look startled, but Alain's spirit retained enough sentience to understand the significance of what he'd been shown. Alain took one last look around the cave temple, then made a low bow to Ward and vanished into mist.

Behind where he had stood was an ancient-looking trunk. Ward took a step, but Erik's voice stopped him in his tracks.

"Document everything," Erik said. "As you noted this morning, this is historic. Let's make sure we get it all for posterity."

They all dutifully whipped out their cell phones and began to videotape the cave, the carved features, and then the trunk from every angle. Erik figured that duplicating footage was better than finding out someone's camera didn't work and missing a crucial shot. He caught Ben looking into the darkness that extended behind the trunk and shook his head.

"Leave it to the spelunkers," Erik said quietly. "I don't want to lose you down a bottomless pit."

Ben hurried backward, and the four of them stood around the trunk.

"Either the hole did get smaller over time, or Alain assembled the trunk inside the cave," Ward said. "We aren't going to be able to get it out through the opening we came in."

Erik looked down at the cave floor, which was wet, like after a rain. "You said the groundwater levels changed?"

Ward nodded, taking in the same details. "Yes. It couldn't have been this wet when Alain left the trunk, or there'd be nothing left. So the only way to preserve it is to get it out of here."

He went back to the opening and called out to the groundskeepers. "Bring over the tarps that are in the back of the Land Rover. And be ready to help us lift some things out of here."

Ward crossed back to the trunk and squatted down beside it. He tugged at the lid, but it remained stuck or locked—perhaps both.

Erik raised an eyebrow when Ward produced a set of lock picks from beneath his coveralls. He noticed Erik's expression and chuckled. "Comes in handy. Ancestors don't always leave keys lying around."

It took a lot of fiddling and coaxing to pick the lock open and pry up the lid. Erik held his breath as Ward did the honors. They all shone their flashlights into the chest, and Erik didn't know what to expect. Would they see the glint of gold? Find tarnished chain mail?

"It's a folio." Ward's voice echoed the let-down the rest of them felt. "We should look at it somewhere safe and dry, but...that appears to be all that's in here."

"I thought we'd find armor," Ben said. "Since the kid found that sword."

"We might find what's left of armor, if we come back with more powerful lights," Erik said. "But it's gotten wet enough here that it doesn't bode well for anything Alain left behind. We're lucky the trunk appears to be made of some kind of oiled leather."

Priscilla and Ward removed the folio and wrapped it carefully in a tarp to protect it on the messy exodus from the cave.

Erik let his flashlight play across the walls, admiring the craftsmanship. "Did Alain do this to keep himself occupied? I don't imagine he expected visitors. Then again, after he finished the crypt, I wonder what else he did."

"He was in his mid-sixties when he helped build the crypt, so I wonder how long he lived," Ben mused.

"Since he was at odds with the Church and in exile, I doubt there's a record," Ward said. "I honestly wouldn't be surprised if we found his bones in here. His very own crypt. If that's the case, I'll ask Father Andrews to give him Last Rites."

Erik felt a chill down his spine. He traded glances with Ben and knew they both thought Ward was correct. Alain was likely to have made this cave his tomb so that his spirit could stand guard over whatever treasure the folio contained.

"Not a bad morning's adventure," Ward said in a jaunty tone as they wriggled through the muddy opening after carefully handing out the precious bundle to the groundsmen. Once he got to his feet, he turned to the two men.

"James and Robert—Stay here and guard the cave. I'll send castle security out to relieve you and put up some fencing," Ward said. "Got a bit of history to protect!"

They drove back to the castle, and Erik felt too excited to sit still, like a kid at Christmas. Ben grinned. "Like I said, best vacation ever," he told Erik.

They had peeled off their muddy coveralls before getting into the Land Rover and left them in the back. When they reached the castle, their shoes and boots stayed in the vestibule, and they made their way, sock-footed to Ward's office.

"Wait!" Priscilla said as Ward began to unwrap the folio. "Cameras out!"

The three of them got video from different angles as Ward carefully folded back the tarp and laid the folio on his desk.

"Can you believe it? My hands are shaking," Ward said. He untied the waxed leather strap that closed the top of the folio, and then took a pair of cotton archival gloves from a desk drawer and pulled them on before reaching inside and gentling out the contents.

Priscilla, Ben, and Erik crowded closer. Erik felt his heart in his throat.

"Ledgers?" Ben put their thoughts into words. "The treasure of the Templars was a bunch of spreadsheets?"

Erik smacked his palm against his forehead. "Oh my God. Of course it was. Alain was speaking very literally."

The others turned to stare at him. Erik felt his stomach drop in disappointment even as his mind searched through everything he recalled about the Order.

"The Templars were the bankers for the Vatican and the Kings of Europe. They held the wealth of kings in trust while the monarchs went off to the Crusades. They amassed more wealth than all of the monarchies and the Vatican together, which is why the king of France and the pope ganged up on Jacques de Molay, killed the Knights, and seized their assets. But this," he said, pointing at the folio, "this means they didn't get the real prize. Don't you see? Jacques won, because Alain got away with all of the IOUs."

Ward stared at him, stunned. "You think that's what this is?"

Erik grinned from ear to ear. "I'm sure it is. The biggest heist in medieval history. Alain smoked them all. This meant that the kings and the pope basically had to steal their own money back from the Templars—they couldn't reclaim their IOUs. He totally owned them."

Ward threw back his head and laughed, a deep, full-bodied sound. "That is magnificent." He walked to a cabinet and opened the doors, pulling out a bottle of Scotch and four crystal glasses on a tray.

He set the folio and its precious contents aside reverently and put the tray on the table. Erik recognized the label on the Scotch, a small-batch artisanal distillery on the coast of Scotland that turned out exceptional special edition, limited quantity, releases for connoisseurs. He figured this was likely to be the best Scotch he had ever sipped in his life.

"To Alain," Ward said, pouring a couple of fingers into each glass and distributing the glasses. They raised a toast.

"To Alain," they all repeated reverently before sampling the amber liquor. Ben's eyes widened, and his eyebrows rose as he registered the taste of the dark, smooth whiskey. Erik intended to savor his because he didn't want to think what the cask-strength, subscription-quality liquor cost.

To his surprise, Ward turned toward them and raised his glass once again. "To Erik and Ben, who solved a seven-hundred-year-old mystery in three days. Huzzah!"

Priscilla echoed his cheer, while Erik felt his cheeks color, and Ben had that poleaxed expression again. Erik slipped an arm around Ben's waist, drawing him close.

Best vacation *ever*—and the Halloween gala and Guy Fawke's bonfire were yet to come.

CHAPTER SIX

BEN

I still don't know how I let you talk me into this," Erik mock-grumbled as they dressed in their costumes for the Halloween gala.

Ben had been floored when he first found out about the event, but now that he had spent some time around the earl...Ward...the party no longer seemed as intimidating as it had at first. Not to mention that he saw how well Erik and Ward worked together, and how obvious it was that they trusted and respected each other. He really needed to ask Erik what kinds of cases they had worked on and wondered whether his partner was allowed to tell him.

And the fact that the ticket sales all benefited charity—specifically, the Piers Pedley Foundation and the local food banks, made Ben feel much more at ease.

"The website said the theme was *Roaring Twenties*," Ben said. "Everyone is going to do *The Great Gatsby*, and *Brideshead Revisited* was a bit too much."

"I had suggested alternatives," Erik replied as he pulled a sweater over his button-down shirt over jeans. "Lord Peter Whimsey and Charles Parker or Hercule Poirot and Inspector Japp would have been perfectly suitable—especially since we did just solve a mystery."

Ben shook his head and rolled his eyes, reaching for his sweater. "I don't even know who the first two are."

Erik gasped in mock horror. "Surely not! Renounce your Brit Box membership right now!"

"And neither of us look anything like Poirot or Japp," Ben continued as if Erik hadn't said anything. "We're too tall, too thin, and too young. Not to mention the mustache."

"You're just lucky *The Hardy Boys* were published in the 1920s," Erik replied.

"It's perfect. Frank has dark hair; Joe is blond. One of them is bookish, and the other is the action guy."

Erik raised an eyebrow. "Oh? And who's who?"

Ben grinned. "You're the one with the Ph.D."

"Did I mention they're brothers?" Erik muttered. "I'm going to feel squicky putting my arm around you and kinda pervy slow dancing."

"You're just now thinking about this?" Ben demanded. "If I'd have known you were going to be worried about it, we could have been Holmes and Watson."

"They weren't—" Erik began, then shut his mouth.

"Maybe not in canon, but a whole lot of fans think otherwise."

"I give up."

The costumes were simple enough, a requirement given airline luggage restrictions. Plaid button-down shirts, cable-knit sweaters— one red, one blue like on the book covers, jeans, and loafers. They kept the props minimal—a magnifying glass and a flashlight.

Ben walked over and looked Erik up and down with a surge of affection. "Thank you for indulging me," he said, kissing Erik lightly on the lips. "I loved the Hardy Boy books when I was a kid. I got all the hand-me-downs from my older brothers and cousins, and the library always had the ones we didn't. I honestly think they're part of what made me want to be a cop."

Erik sighed. "See, I'm pretty sure I went into art fraud detection thanks to *The Thomas Crown Affair* and my grandmother's re-runs of *To Catch a Thief*. The main characters were so dashing and always had reasons to run around in tuxedos." He frowned. "That may also have been how I figured out I was gay."

"You can rest assured, *The Hardy Boys* did not contribute to that part of my enlightenment," Ben replied with a laugh. "That was more James Bond and Brad Pitt."

"You know, the whole mystery with the Templars is kinda perfect for Halloween," Erik mused, pulling Ben in for a kiss. "Sibella probably had to hide her support of the Templars after they were disgraced. Alain had to live under a false identity after he was smuggled out of France. And one of our biggest clues came from watching those boys pretending to be pirates."

"Is anyone ever going to tell that kid's parents he's swashbuckling with a piece of history?" Ben asked between kisses.

Erik shrugged. "They'll probably figure it out eventually—especially after Ward goes public with the story."

Since the discovery, their vacation had taken a more leisurely turn. They spent a whole day exploring Caynham Castle. Erik led them on a "treasure hunt," looking for gargoyles—and kissing under every one. They had toured the two period-authentic sitting rooms on display, meandered down to the garden folly with its romantic statue, and followed the self-guided tour around the grounds.

Ben hadn't been sure how he was going to feel about being in England for Halloween. So he had been thrilled to see carved pumpkins here, glowing with electric candles inside. Over the last couple of days, they had seen new decorations go up around the castle. Priscilla confided it was because Ward's fiancée was American and loved Halloween. Still, the decorations were restrained, even by Cape May standards. Fewer skeletons and nothing gruesome, with more emphasis on scarecrows, corn shocks, and pumpkins. Then again, the castle had several real ghosts, so adding fake ones seemed a little silly.

Then they walked into the Great Hall and stopped in their tracks.

"Whoa," Ben murmured, eyes wide. "That's...impressive."

Animated scenes played out over the walls of the large room, shifting every few minutes. A haunted house with ghosts morphed into a castle dungeon with a chain-rattling spirit, and then an Egyptian tomb complete with wandering mummy. A DJ on a stage in front of the huge fireplace played an upbeat selection of songs from a range of decades, including many that had a spooky vibe. Disco lights in red, green, and blue played over a temporary dance floor in front of the stage.

Around the walls were several different food stations with fruit, cheese, and charcuterie, pasta and sauces, a wide variety of different hot bites, and a sumptuous spread of desserts. Servers in tuxes passed trays of hors d'oeuvres. Three bars stationed at intervals around the room were doing a brisk business. Another group of servers came by with trays of goblets filled with an intriguing blood-red punch.

Ward and his fiancée were making their way around the room. Ward looked dashing in a classic Bela Lugosi-style Dracula costume, complete with slicked-back hair, while his bride-to-be seemed to be going for a "woman-in-white" ghostly appearance.

"This is quite the shindig," Ben murmured. "I'm still trying to figure out how they've done the scenes on the wall. It's a lot more advanced than the spinning snowflakes my neighbor in Newark used to show on his garage doors at Christmas."

Erik laughed and grabbed two of the blood punch goblets from a passing waiter. He handed one to Ben and took a sip of his own. "This is pretty good." He watched as the animation changed scenes again.

"I don't know all the details, but I watched a show about it on TV. It's like what they show on the Disney World castle. It's called 'projection mapping,' and it's tailored to the exact dimensions of the structure that becomes the 'canvas,'" Erik replied. "There's a whole new event company specialty doing it. So you get a very impressive backdrop, and no cleanup after the guests leave."

Ben and Erik made their way to the food stations, filling plates. High-top tables without chairs gave guests a way to balance food and drink without encouraging groups to congregate for long. For those who actually did want to talk more than dance, the lounge area on the restaurant side had been expanded with more seating groups.

"Erik! Ben!" Ward's voice carried across the music. A woman with honey-blond hair walked beside him, arms linked.

"I'd like you to meet my fiancée, Dr. Denby Alden," Ward said. "Bee, this is Dr. Erik Mitchell and his partner, Ben Nolan. They're the ones who cracked the Templar mystery."

Bee shook hands with both men, and Ben could see why Ward

would fall for someone so vivacious. "Ward's told me so much about both of you. I'm glad to have a chance to meet you. You've certainly had a memorable vacation."

"Priscilla told us that you're a great fan of Halloween," Erik replied.

Bee laughed. "Oh, it's my favorite holiday next to Christmas. I know most people celebrate a bit differently here, but I warned Ward that I was resolved to bring some of my favorite traditions with me."

Ward eyed the two of them, looking up and down. "Interesting costumes. Obviously detectives of some sort—very fitting. No deer-stalker hat, so Sherlock is out. Too informal to be Poirot and Japp. I've got it—Lord Peter Whimsey and Charles Parker?"

Erik elbowed Ben, who just sighed and smiled. "Erik had suggested that, but we went with the Hardy Boys. From the book series?"

"Ah," Ward replied, clearly not having any idea.

"I loved those books!" Bee exclaimed. "Of course that's what you are! You know, I wanted to grow up to be Nancy Drew," she added conspiratorially, then looked warmly at Ward, who returned an adoring expression. "Then again, we did get to solve our own little mystery at Christmas, didn't we?"

"Thank you so much," Erik said. "This is an amazing party."

"I hope so," Bee exclaimed. "We want everyone to have a great time."

She and Ward moved on, stopping to greet each cluster of guests. Ben didn't doubt that the couple made every party-goer feel like they had their complete focus and attention.

"You know, we've still got almost a whole week left of vacation," Erik reminded Ben. "We can be as lazy or as touristy as you want. And on the fifth of November, there's Bonfire Night."

"Gunpowder, treason, and plot?" Ben asked as part of the rhyme surfaced in his memory.

"They've shifted the Guy Fawke's part lately, discouraging private fireworks and burning effigies," Erik replied. "It is rather odd to have a national holiday celebrating a failed plot to blow up Parliament."

Ben shrugged. "We celebrate some strange things, too. Don't knock anything that gets you a bonfire and holiday treats."

The castle's party food was as good as it looked and smelled, and the quantities appeared to be inexhaustible. Whatever was in the red punch gave Ben a pleasantly light buzz, making him truly feel like he was on vacation.

When they had eaten their fill and raided the dessert table, Erik took Ben's hand. "Wanna dance?"

"With the handsomest guy in the room? Always," Ben said, hoping Erik could read his feelings in his eyes.

They set their empty drinks aside and found their way to the dance floor. The tempo was right for a slow dance, and Erik slipped his arms around Ben's neck.

"You know, trick-or-treat was huge in Newark when I was a kid," Ben recalled with a smile. "Big Irish family—I always had my brothers, cousins, and friends to go out with. Picking a costume was a major ordeal. We'd agonize over it for weeks. And man, scoring the mother lode of candy was almost as good as Christmas. Even when I was a cop and Halloween meant breaking up bar fights and busting DUIs, it never took the magic away."

"Trick-or-treat was a more sedate affair in the Columbia suburbs. I usually went with friends, because...otherwise Halloween sucked," Erik replied. "The fun for me was researching and making my costume. There were neighbors who told me they looked for me every year because they wanted to see what I'd come up with."

Ben laughed. "I can imagine that. Leave it to you to be original." He pressed a kiss to Erik's temple. "Wouldn't have it any other way."

Erik drew back just enough that Ben could see a tempest in his eyes. He had something on his mind, but Ben couldn't imagine what.

"Let's buy that house we looked at when we get back. Together," Erik blurted, eyes widening as if he hadn't meant to say that out loud yet. "Please? At least think about it."

"Yes," Ben replied, as his heart sped up. Erik looked surprised and cautious. "Yes...you'll think about it? Or yes—"

"Yes," Ben replied, grinning broadly. "Definitely, yes."

"Really? Okay. Well. That officially makes this the best Halloween, ever," Erik replied, looking a bit dazed as if he hadn't let himself expect Ben to agree.

"Hmm…it's not over yet. I have some ideas of how to end tonight on a sweet note when we get back to the room," Ben murmured with a wicked wink. "All treat, no tricks."

"Sounds like a great idea to me," Erik said, leaning in to kiss Ben. "I can't wait to unwrap you."

MEMORY AND MALICE
A BADLANDS NOVELLA

By Morgan Brice

CHAPTER ONE

VIC

Y ou're like a kid who's had too much candy," Simon Kincaide shook his head with a smile, and his voice had a fond tone as he watched his fiancé, Vic D'Amato, fidget in his seat on the train.

"Gimme a break. There's so much to see, I don't know where to look next," Vic replied as the reality hit him that they were really, finally, in London. "I've seen so many movies set here and read so many books—it's hard to believe it's real and not just some big, elaborate movie set."

Simon reached over and took Vic's hand. "I'm excited watching you see it for the first time. And I'm looking forward to everything we've planned. When I came before, I would sneak in a little sightseeing around the edges, but I was always here for work or a conference."

Homicide Detective Vic D'Amato was far outside his jurisdiction and very happy about that fact. *Two weeks where stopping the bad guys isn't my problem. No paperwork, no overtime, and hopefully no unexpected complications.*

"When my grandparents had their fiftieth wedding anniversary, it was a big deal for everyone to go back to the village they came from in Italy," Vic mused, still staring out the window of the train. "We met great-aunts and uncles and cousins that we never knew existed. So much fun—and so much food!"

"You've been back to Italy a couple of times, haven't you? Maybe sometime we can go together. I've always wanted to see Rome," Simon replied.

"Yeah, we did a couple of family trips but only once with the whole D'Amato clan," Vic replied. "On that trip, I swear we took up half of the jet on the way over and back. And yes, I'd love to go with you. We didn't do a lot of sightseeing, so that's definitely on my bucket list."

As a detective in Myrtle Beach, South Carolina, Vic wasn't wealthy by any means. But Simon's Grand Strand Ghost Tours shop was doing well, and when they put their heads together and cut a few corners, they figured out how to take some bigger trips and still be comfortable, if not indulgent.

"I want to take you to my favorites and explore some new places," Simon said. Vic could tell his partner was equally excited about their trip. "And I promise not to drag you to endless museums and libraries—although that's where I spent most of my time when I was here before."

Vic knew that Simon had been a college professor of folklore and mythology before a student's fundamentalist father caused problems and got Simon dismissed from his position. Simon had gone to the beach to lick his wounds and then decided to reinvent himself with the shop. He used his knowledge to write several books about local hauntings and put his abilities as a psychic and a medium to work doing personal readings and séances.

Accepting that Simon's gifts were real hadn't initially been easy for Vic—and his early skepticism had nearly gotten Simon killed. Since that first case, the police department now recognized Simon as an official consultant, and the two of them worked together on murder cases with a supernatural element. They made a good team—personally and professionally.

"I like museums," Vic defended. "I want to go see the British Museum. It's been in a lot of movies, and they have mummies."

Simon grimaced. "Yeah. The British Museum has a huge collection of mummies, and the discussion over how they got there and where they really belong gets heated enough to make academics start throwing punches. It's a valid and overdue debate. But while we're there, I'm just going to be a Brendan Fraser and Indiana Jones fanboy and enjoy the moment."

They checked into their hotel just off Trafalgar Square, and Simon took Vic to a Sherlock Holmes-themed pub nearby.

"I feel like we got dropped into a movie." Vic couldn't help looking all around them at the decor—movie stills of the many actors who played the famous detective, book covers, and other memorabilia.

"Don't forget to eat—the food is good here, and they've got plenty of local ale choices," Simon told him.

Vic was surprised to discover just how tasty the traditional bangers and mash were, and washing it down with a dark stout made the meal even better.

"I could get used to this."

Simon chuckled. "Wait until we go to my favorite Indian place. The best curry I've ever eaten has been in the UK."

"That's not something we get a lot of back in Myrtle Beach." Vic loved the Grand Strand, and even though a bad situation at his former precinct in Pittsburgh had led to the move to Myrtle Beach, meeting Simon had made everything worthwhile.

"We'll have to try a 'full English' breakfast at least once," Simon told him. "Complete with baked beans, tomatoes, mushrooms—and blood pudding."

Vic gave Simon a skeptical look. "Please tell me you're kidding about that."

"Nope. It's definitely a thing here. And it's pretty good."

"You've had it?" Vic wrinkled his nose.

Simon shrugged. "When in Rome…"

They spent the afternoon walking through the parks, taking a boat ride on the Thames, and strolling past famous monuments and old Roman walls. That night, Simon was pleased to find his favorite Indian restaurant still in business, and they enjoyed an exceptional meal.

They strolled back together hand-in-hand. "This has been a wonderful introduction to the city," Vic said, loving every minute of being an unabashed tourist. "It's even more beautiful than I expected

—especially with all the Christmas decorations—and it was nice not to have to be anywhere at a certain time."

Simon kissed him as they walked along the river. "I'm glad. It's been a great night—and it's still early." He tucked a strand of his shoulder-length, wavy chestnut hair behind one ear. Simon often wore it in a bun, but Vic loved it when Simon let the hair fall loose around his shoulders, and tangling his fingers in it when they made love had become a personal fixation. In the dim light, Simon's eyes looked hazel, although in the sun, Vic often thought they were green.

Both men were in their early thirties, old enough to have been around the proverbial block a few times and know when they found a good thing.

Vic liked the contrast between them. At six-foot-two inches, he stood taller than Simon's five-ten. With his hair up and wearing his glasses, Simon looked every bit the professor he had been. Vic rocked more of a bad boy vibe despite his badge with dark eyes, short black hair, perpetual stubble, and olive skin. Where Simon was lean, Vic had more muscles. Vic's tattoos held a real fascination for Simon, a little private fetish Vic had no intention of discouraging.

Their hotel had a beautiful bar and live music, so they ordered drinks and hung out for a while. Vic knew that jet lag would be bad enough without letting their sleep schedules get completely out of whack.

"So tell me about this thing in Shropshire over Christmas and New Year's. Are we staying at a real castle? And do you actually know the earl?" He couldn't help feeling a bit starstruck over the whole thing.

"Yes to the castle. And 'sort of' for knowing the earl," Simon replied. "Erik recommended the castle as a great place to stay. He met the earl back when he was chasing down art fraud for Interpol, and they stayed in touch. That's how Erik and Ben chose Caynham Castle for their vacation. Teag and Anthony had a great time there too."

Their friend Erik Mitchell now ran an antique shop in Cape May, New Jersey. His boyfriend, Ben Nolan, was a former Newark cop. Teag Logan, another close friend, and his fiancé Anthony Benton had also recommended Caynham Castle. Thanks to Ben's ability to see ghosts, Teag's witchcraft, and Erik's psychic talents, they had all helped the earl with supernatural problems related to the castle during their stay there.

"And the big event?"

Simon leaned back and took a sip of his drink. "They're shooting an episode of *Blast from the Past* at the castle. Erik got us backstage passes."

Vic beamed. "I love that show! Everyone thinks they've inherited a priceless antique from granny. Even when stuff doesn't turn out to be valuable, some of it's just plain weird enough to be entertaining."

Blast from the Past was a "comfort" show right along with that baking competition—a feel-good distraction to watch without having to pay a lot of attention.

"We head to the castle on the twenty-third because after that, the trains pretty much shut down. That gives us a nice, quiet Christmas Eve and Christmas to enjoy the castle and two days after to explore the town. We'll get a behind-the-scenes look during the set-up and taping of the show on the twenty-eighth and twenty-ninth, and then on December thirtieth, there's a big antiques fair. On New Year's Eve, there's fireworks and bell ringing," Simon told him. "Not exactly Times Square, but I think it sounds like a lot of fun."

This time Vic leaned in for the kiss. "New Year's anywhere with you is a good time." He paused. "Is the castle haunted? I'm excited about going but a little creeped out too. You're not going to end up solving the ghosts' problems for them, are you?"

Simon chuckled. "It's a little haunted—aren't all castles? But I don't intend to go looking for ghost trouble. I'm totally planning on this being a relaxing vacation."

"Speaking of relaxing..." Vic said, with his hand under the table on Simon's thigh. "My mind can think up all sorts of things to do when we go to the room, but I'm pretty sure jet lag is going to cock block me. How early is our first tour tomorrow?"

Simon smiled and laced his fingers with Vic's. "I'm feeling the same —and totally up for taking a rain check for the morning. We don't have anything until ten."

Vic signaled for the bill and leaned into Simon. "Sounds like a great plan to me."

THE NEXT MORNING got Vic his very happy wake-up. They ordered a full English breakfast, and Vic had to admit that while the baked beans took some getting used to, they weren't as weird as he expected.

"Come on—our first tour is at St. Paul's Cathedral, and we'll need time to get there," Simon told him as they headed out.

"Can we feed the birds?" Vic felt a sharp pang of disappointment when Simon shook his head. "Dude—that was one of the best parts of *Mary Poppins!*"

"Afraid not. And we aren't having tea with the queen," Simon teased. "Although I did book us high tea at Grosvenor House, which is pretty swanky. You'd better be hungry—it's quite a spread."

"And then we have tickets for the Tower of London—aren't you worried about the ghosts?" Vic knew that Simon couldn't completely shut out his awareness of unwanted supernatural activity. "Some of the places we're going probably have some seriously vengeful spirits."

"I was worried the first time I visited, and I wouldn't want to be there alone at night. But all the tourists and electronics scatter the ghosts' energy. And then there are the ravens—protecting the crown and the tower for over five hundred years!"

Vic had originally been hesitant to plan Christmas away from home, but his family had put their emphasis on Thanksgiving instead. So he tried not to feel guilty as they walked through the lights display on Regent and Carnaby Streets and drank Irish coffee from a café.

"I love the Christmas markets," Vic said, impressed by the unique items for sale as they wandered among the many booths. "I'm going to have to buy another suitcase to get everything home!"

THE NEXT FEW days passed in a blur of unforgettable memories. Vic geeked out to his heart's content at the British Museum, marveled at the sights of the city when they rode the Eye, and wandered in awe through Westminster Abbey.

They snickered at the opulent Egyptian-themed escalators at

Harrod's, loved the Museum of Natural History, and shared a nerdgasm over Churchill's "secret" wartime bunker. Vic knew he'd picked the right person to marry when Simon brought him to London's iconic comics and fandom store and turned him loose to wander the aisles in geeky bliss.

Seeing Big Ben, riding in a carriage through Hyde Park, and taking a tour of Buckingham Palace were all high points for Vic, as were the fantastic evening meals they shared each night. He was more than willing to grab a croissant and coffee to go and a quick take-away lunch to make their suppers memorable.

"I can't believe we're leaving London already," Vic said wistfully as they stood in the train station with their luggage two days before Christmas. "It all went so fast."

Simon bumped shoulders with him and smiled. "We can come back. There's plenty more to do. Make a list, and we'll work our way through it. Don't forget—there's Wales, Scotland, and Ireland to see, too."

Simon had made their arrangements since he knew how the trains worked. They had reserved seats, and given how heavy the crowd was, Vic was glad they had splurged a bit for the convenience.

"I've never seen it this crowded," Simon told him as they waited to get on. "I know it's the Christmas season, but I wouldn't be surprised if they overbooked."

That turned out to be the case, and Vic felt happier than ever that they had reserved seats since some people ended up sitting on their luggage in the aisles.

"If we were in the States, there'd have been more than a few fist-fights by now," Vic said quietly, astounded as their fellow passengers took the inconvenience in stride, eating the boxed lunches they packed and, in some cases, popping open bottles of wine to share on the trip.

"That's one of the things I love about visiting here," Simon replied with a grin. "It's different from home in all the right ways."

By train, it would take around three hours to get to Shropshire, where a cab would get them the rest of the way to Caynham Castle. Vic stared out the window while Simon read a book.

"I never knew there were so many sheep," he murmured, prompting a laugh.

"Probably more sheep than people," Simon replied. "You know, I could use a cup of tea and a chance to stretch my legs. Do you want something from the commissary car?" Simon asked.

Vic nodded. "Sure. Tea and some kind of cookie. Surprise me. We don't have dinner reservations until pretty late."

Simon eyed the crowded aisles. "It might take me a while. Don't sell my seat to a handsome stranger," he joked, giving Vic a heated glance.

"My fiancé would never forgive me," Vic replied, dropping his voice to the sexy growl that always made Simon shiver.

Simon squeezed his hand and then wove his way through the crowd to go back a few cars to the snack shop. Vic resigned himself to counting sheep on the hillside when his book failed to keep his attention.

When Simon returned, he looked distracted. "Problems?" Vic asked. "It's okay if the tea isn't super hot. I kinda figured it wouldn't be, with the wait and all."

Simon shook his head. "I got really bad juju from someone, but I'm not sure why. I think he's got a seriously haunted object with him. The guy slipped past me, but I couldn't find him again, and it's too crowded to go looking."

"Do you remember what he looks like? If he's on the train, he's probably going to the *Blast from the Past* taping. We can look for him at the castle. With the backstage passes Erik finagled, we should have really good access," Vic said.

"Yeah, that sounds like a plan. Whatever the guy had wasn't just haunted—it was malicious and powerful. I'm surprised other people didn't cringe away from him. If he's taking a haunted object to be on the show, that could be really dangerous."

"Text Erik. Maybe he can warn the duke."

"Earl."

"Whatever." Vic jostled Simon's leg and put a hand on his knee under the table. "For now, don't worry about it. Since the onboard Wi-

Fi sucks, you can help me name the sheep." He pointed toward a puffy gray one. "I think she's totally a Maxine."

The sheep turned around, and Simon nearly snorted his tea. "Actually, I'd say *he's* more of a Max from the rear."

"Spoilsport," Vic teased. They joked while they ate their snack and drank their tea. The conversation that buzzed around them was all about the appraisal show taping and the antiques fair afterward. Vic couldn't help being excited about getting a behind-the-scenes look at a show he enjoyed watching on television.

"Hey, relax," he said as he nudged Simon. "We'll find the guy and alert the proper authorities. We know from Erik and Teag that the earl believes in your kind of stuff, so we'll head off any problems and go on our merry way."

"Maybe," Simon replied, with a thoughtful look that Vic should have known promised trouble.

CHAPTER TWO

SIMON

B y the time they reached the Caynham-on-Ledwyche train station, the mid-afternoon sun lengthened across the rolling hills. The view was vastly different from either Myrtle Beach or Columbia, South Carolina, where Simon grew up, with green pastures and stone fences that looked like something out of a painting.

"The landscape reminds me a lot of the area around Pittsburgh," Vic said as they edged out of the crowded train cars. "Fewer sheep, of course. But the hills and valleys—I can see why so many people from England settled there."

Simon knew that before Vic moved to Myrtle Beach, he had been a cop in Pittsburgh, a family tradition going back generations. His father and brothers were still on the force. Vic had witnessed something supernatural and made the mistake of admitting it during an inquest, which nearly got him fired and led to him making a move to Myrtle Beach.

Simon's attention stayed on the crowd as they got off the train, scanning the other passengers and the platform. "There!"

He pointed toward a dark-haired man some distance ahead of them. Simon and Vic maneuvered their luggage as quickly as they could in the crush of people and roller bags, but the man was gone before they could catch up to him.

Vic placed a hand on his arm. "If he's going to the show, we'll probably run into him at the castle or at least in town."

Simon took a deep breath and nodded. "I know. The haunting was just so strong—I don't want anyone to get hurt."

A man in a cabbie uniform held up a sign that read, *Kincaide/D'Amato.* Simon made a bee-line. "You must be Henry."

"Sure am! And you must be the friends of those other American fellows who came here. Good to meet you!"

"I'm Simon, and this is Vic, my fiancé," Simon told him. Teag had already assured them that Henry and the castle staff wouldn't react negatively to them being a couple.

"Welcome, and congratulations whenever the happy day is," Henry said, leading them out to his cab. He gestured for them to get in while he tucked their suitcases into the trunk. *Boot,* Simon reminded himself, aware that British and American English were similar only to a point.

On the way to the castle, Henry kept up a good-natured conversation, playing unofficial tour guide. He recommended places to eat, gave them the insider's guide to the shops, and told them when the pubs and distillery were least likely to be crowded. Their driver was also exceptionally well-versed in the history of both the castle and the town, which Simon enjoyed.

"And here we are," Henry said as they drove through the first gate. Vic leaned forward to get a better look through the windshield.

"Wow. It's a real castle."

Henry laughed. "You were expecting a Hollywood set? We have enough castles over here that we practically trip over them. You're going to have a wonderful time! And—there's Patrick." He nodded toward a young man with a golf card who pulled up next to where Henry had parked. "Once you get checked in, he'll take your bags to your room."

They thanked Henry and tipped generously. "If you need to go somewhere farther than walking distance, just ask for me at the front desk, and they'll ring me up. If I'm not working a shift, I'm available for hire," he told them.

Patrick loaded their bags into a golf cart and waved for them to take their seats. "It's a bit of a hike up to the Reception area," he told them. "I'll drive you to the right place, and you can check in, then I'll take your bags to your room." Simon figured that Patrick was in his late teens and remembered Teag saying that he was related to someone on staff.

Behind the dark wood of the reception counter, the Mortimer family coat of arms adorned the rough stone wall along with several flags and crossed swords. Evergreen swags hung from the counter and adorned the doorways, and a large fir wreath hung over the mantle of a huge fireplace, where a cozy fire blazed.

"Welcome to Caynham Castle," the front desk clerk said when Simon and Vic entered the grand foyer. "Names?"

Simon and Vic supplied their passports, confirmation number, and credit card. "By any chance, is Priscilla Donovan here?" Simon asked. "I'm a friend of Teag Logan and Erik Mitchell."

The woman behind the counter smiled. "Oh, yes. She said to expect you. I'll ring her office as soon as I get you checked in."

Vic pivoted in place, taking in all of the medieval splendor. Simon had to admit he was in awe as well. Caynham Castle was the real deal, without the over-the-top movie touches that detracted from authenticity.

"Wow," Vic said quietly. "I was sorta expecting something like the Hogwarts ride at Universal Studios."

"Better, huh?" the desk clerk, whose badge read *Susan* said with a grin. "And I promise you that the walls here aren't made out of paper mache."

Susan made a call and spoke briefly to the person on the other end, whom Simon assumed was Priscilla.

"She's just finishing up with someone, but she'll be out as soon as she can if you'd like to wander a bit."

Simon looked over his shoulder toward the door. "We don't want to keep Patrick waiting with our bags."

"How about if I take the keys and go with Patrick to the room, and you talk with Priscilla," Vic suggested. "Once we're in, I'll come back and meet you here." He grinned. "I fully intend to hit that tea shop before we do any exploring!"

"Good choice," Susan assured him.

Simon nodded. "Okay. Don't get lost."

"Rescue me from the dungeon if I go missing," Vic teased.

"I'll do my swashbuckling best," Simon joked in return.

The door had barely closed behind Vic when a dark-haired woman in her thirties came out from one of the offices behind the desk.

"Simon Kincaide. Pleased to meet you. Erik and Teag have told us about you and Vic. Welcome to Caynham Castle." Her handshake was all business, as was her dark skirted suit.

"We're thrilled to be here and looking forward to both the show and the fair," Simon assured her. He glanced behind him as other guests came into the lobby. "May I have a word with you a bit more privately?" he asked in a low voice.

Priscilla looked at him for a moment, then nodded. "Erik told me you had some very special abilities. Is something wrong?" She led them down to the other end of the counter, away from Susan and the new guests.

"I just wanted to ask if anyone is checking the pieces coming into the show and fair for malicious hauntings or bad magic." Simon felt self-conscious, as he always did when mentioning the supernatural to someone he didn't know. *She's used to Erik and Teag. This won't throw her for a loop.*

Priscilla frowned. "We talked about it, but we haven't had a chance to get to know the local folks who claim to have that sort of gift, and we didn't want to cause problems if there were unfounded claims."

Simon nodded. "I understand. But on the train coming here, I sensed a man with something powerfully strong in his suitcase—a truly malicious ghost. The kind that doesn't just cause trouble—it kills. Since everyone else on the train seemed to be coming here for the show and the fair, I figured he probably would be too. Which made me think that there could be other pieces that might not be as dangerous but could still cause problems if they were displayed to the public or sold."

Priscilla nodded. "Good point. We check for every other sort of provenance, but not that. And we certainly wouldn't want to pass along a problem piece. What would it take for you to know whether or not an item was haunted?"

"Most of the time, I don't even have to touch it," Simon replied. "I can probably walk down the queue of people waiting to be picked for the show or the rows of tables with the items displayed at the fair, and as long as I'm within arm's reach, I'd know whether something deserved closer inspection. My abilities are a little different from Teag's and Erik's. Teag senses magic woven into cloth. Erik can read the history and magic of an object by touch. I see and hear ghosts—I can channel them for séances too. And I get visions—sometimes past, sometimes future. So if there's a ghost attached to an object, I'll know, and I'll pick up on a curse or dark magic too."

Teag was the best friend of Simon's cousin in Charleston, South Carolina. Erik and Simon had gone to graduate school together, stayed in touch when Erik's work busting art fraud with Interpol took him around the world, then reconnected once Erik bought an antique shop in Cape May. Both Teag and Erik worked with others who had paranormal abilities to stop supernatural threats.

"Teag and Erik spoke very well of you and Vic, which counts a lot for me—and the earl," she said. "Speaking of whom—he's tied up with business today, but I'll mention your suggestion to him when I see him and give you a call back."

"Thank you," Simon replied. He hoped she could read his sincerity in not wanting anything to go wrong at the event and didn't think he was maneuvering to get more VIP access.

She smiled at them. "Go enjoy the tea room and stroll into town. I'm sure Henry told you all about the high points. Whether you decide to get dinner at the pub or come back to the castle, you won't go hungry!"

Simon thanked her then headed out to where Vic was strolling around, taking photos with his phone.

"Patrick had to go help the other people move in. He was really helpful and gave me a lot of tips on the best food and beer. Plus he reminded me of the legend of the gargoyles. If we kiss in front of the right one, then our love is fated to last forever. So I guess we'll just have to work through them one by one so we don't miss any," Vic said with a grin.

"Sounds like a plan." Simon reached out and took Vic's hand. "But first, let's see if those little tea cakes are as good as they look on TV."

As it turned out, they were. Simon didn't even tease his tough-guy homicide cop fiancé over the noises of appreciation he made over the petit-fours, crustless sandwiches, and other delights. The tea was magnificent, and for the adventurous and very hungry, the shop offered full-size slices of layer cake.

"Maybe later," Vic said, laughing when Simon offered the possibility. "Between jet lag and all that sugar, I'm going to be in a food coma before we even get to walk downtown."

Afterward, they walked over the bridge into Caynham-on-Ledwyche, the town at the bottom of the hill from the castle. From the thriving shops, quirky boutiques, and picturesque seasonal decorations, Simon was smitten at first sight.

"It's like something out of a Hallmark movie," he said.

Vic grinned. "Yeah, but better. Because we're gay and we're here."

Simon knew they'd be coming back more than once to do the shops thoroughly. "Look—there's a bookstore and a yarn store with another tea shop in the back—"

"We're duty-bound to check it out for comparison's sake," Vic swore solemnly.

"Absolutely. And a curio shop—I wonder if they'll be taking part in the antiques fair," Simon mused. "And there's the church where Erik and Ben found that crypt with the inscription and the pub that had some decorations that turned out to be more authentic than they bargained for."

Their friends had told them all about their inadvertent sleuthing while on vacation, and after spotting the man on the train, Simon wondered if he and Vic would have a similar story when they got home.

Teag had figured out a mysterious death and a long-lost legacy. Erik had deciphered an old Knights Templar code to find a treasure most people had written off as sheer legend.

"I wouldn't mind if we just vacationed," Simon told Vic. "You know that, right? I don't need a case to have a good time."

Vic stretched up to give him a peck on the cheek. "I know. But if you can stop something dangerous from happening, then there's a responsibility to do it. Not everyone has your abilities, and you don't want it on your conscience that you might have been able to prevent a tragedy. I can live with a little investigating on our vacation. After all, anyone can sightsee."

"You really are the best fiancé ever," Simon replied, giving Vic's hand a squeeze. "Now let's try that ale at the pub, and see if their shepherd's pie compares to what we had in London."

A quick look inside Cadwell's book store and the antique shop— named "Curioser and Curioser"—convinced both Simon and Vic that they needed to come back when they had more time to linger.

"Could you tell if anything in the shops was haunted?" Vic asked, and his curiosity warmed Simon's heart because of the hard-won acceptance it signaled.

"Nothing cursed, and only some really low-powered ghosts," Simon replied. "Not something that's going to follow someone home and make them run screaming into the night."

"Good to know."

The beautiful old church was open, and they walked around the sanctuary in awe of the hand-carved stonework and the beautiful stained glass. "Wow," Vic said in a hushed voice, although the church was empty. "This reminds me of some of the cathedrals in Rome—only Protestant."

Simon nodded. "Artists spent decades doing the detail work on a church like this. The whole thing is a piece of art."

When they walked back outside, the cold, damp air made Simon grateful he had worn his winter coat. Vic took the temperature in stride, thanks to his Pittsburgh roots.

"Let's get some ale, and maybe after we've warmed up, we'll be hungry for dinner," Vic suggested. "There's the pub Erik carried on about."

The Boar and Knight had been in continual use since the early Middle Ages. The pub looked its age. A fireplace across from the bar was blackened with soot. The dark wood of the tables, chair rail, and bar was worn from use, and the plank floor showed the toll of centuries of foot traffic. A sign with the names of every proprietor going back over six hundred years graced one wall.

"Back home, we slap a historic plaque on any building that's over a hundred years old," Vic marveled. "Myrtle Beach doesn't even have anything that old. Here, something built in the 1500s is the *new* section."

The Boar and Knight's dark wood and soot-greyed plaster walls gave the interior a cave-like feel. Antiques spanning centuries were displayed on shelves that ran around the top of the walls in each room, near the ceiling where the items were out of reach. The air smelled of woodsmoke and ale, with the lingering hint of pipe tobacco.

Simon ordered fish and chips while Vic got shepherd's pie. Both asked for a pint of the pub's signature dark stout. When they dug into their meals, Vic raised his head with a blissful expression.

"This is really good food."

Simon had started with his pint. "Pretty damn fine ale too."

While they ate, Simon couldn't help listening to the conversations around them. The accents intrigued him but so did the subject matter when he heard the *Blast from the Past* event come up more than once.

"...bit like that road trip show, or some such, I imagine."

"...everyone thinks their gran tucked away a priceless heirloom in the attic. Probably got it in the clearance bin at the charity store."

"...who knows? Sometimes a bit of rubbish really does turn out to be valuable."

"...at least they're not baking."

That last comment nearly had Simon snorting his stout from his nose. Vic looked at him worriedly as he choked and coughed, but Simon gestured that he was okay. "I'll tell you later," he said in a strangled voice, still chuckling to himself.

After they finished their meal and paid the tab, Simon and Vic wandered outside. Lightly falling snow glittered in the air. He and Vic had both dressed for the weather with down coats, fluffy woolen scarfs, knitted caps, and warm mittens. They walked back to the castle matching their strides, companionably bumping shoulders, watching their breath steam in the air.

"This is magical," Vic said with an ear-to-ear grin Simon rarely got to see back home, where the "real world" could weigh heavy on his partner's shoulders.

"It really is," he agreed. "I can see where all the fantasy stories got their start. And the castle! I've been to Biltmore and some of the big Gilded Age mansions, but they don't compare."

"Still wouldn't trade the blue bungalow for anything," Vic replied, reaching over to give Simon's forearm a squeeze. "It's cozy. I hate to think of the heating bill for a castle."

"Good point."

Vic led the way to their room in the Dower Apartments, inside the inner bailey.

"Wow," he said when Vic opened the door and flicked on the lights. "This is…impressive."

Simon had been willing to make do with a cramped space, figuring that would be the norm in such an old building. Instead, their suite had a living room as well as a very comfortable bedroom and bathroom.

He eyed the eclectic furniture suspiciously. Simon knew that any real heirlooms would be far too valuable and fragile to use, but even the obvious reproductions were probably old enough to qualify as antiques in their own right. He held his breath, waiting to see what his gift told him, fearing the room might be haunted. When no ghosts appeared and no supernatural resonance jangled his senses, Simon relaxed.

"Patrick told me that there haven't been any hauntings reported in this room," Vic assured him. "I asked. Pretty comfy for something medieval. Is this where the other guys stayed?"

"Not exactly, but it's on the same floor, so it's similar. Do you like it?" Simon asked, nervous because he had been the one to make the arrangements.

"Are you kidding? We're in a fuckin' castle! Speaking of which…" Vic gave him a jokingly lascivious grin.

"I thought you were jet-lagged?" Simon teased in return.

"Guess you can't keep a good man down."

Vic pulled Simon into his arms and brushed their lips together. Simon deepened the kiss, and Vic opened his mouth to him, letting them taste each other. Simon could feel Vic's hard cock against his thigh and parted his legs, angling them so they rubbed against each other.

Simon brought his hand up against Vic's chest, sliding under his shirt, tweaking his nipples. Vic began to mouth his way down Simon's neck, leaving a mark beneath his collar where it wouldn't show.

He let his head fall back, giving Vic full access, loving the way Vic's arms felt wrapped around him, the touch of his lips on his skin, the grip of his hands.

"I'm thrilled to be here with you," Vic whispered. "Everything else is extra. You know that, right? Love you, Simon Kincaide."

"Love you too—" A cry of pain cut Simon's declaration short, and he sank to the floor, dropping through Vic's arms to land in a heap at his feet.

"Simon!" Vic's panicked shout seemed distant as the vision overtook him.

He saw a man dressed like a workman from several centuries past digging in a cistern. When he brought up a shovelful of dirt, something in the mud gleamed...

The scene changed, and a nobleman gave testimony before a judge. Simon couldn't hear what was said, but he glimpsed the same workman dressed like a prisoner...

He saw the workman again, but now he appeared disheveled and haggard. All hope was gone from his expression. He followed the guards up the steps to the gallows and looked out over the crowd that had come to watch his hanging.

Simon saw the workman's spirit watch as his body was taken down from the scaffold and buried outside the stone wall that encircled the cemetery, glowering with hatred at the ones who consigned him to unhallowed ground for eternity.

The scene lurched to modern times. Simon glimpsed a man kneeling in an attic, looking through an old trunk. He found something that obviously caught his attention, a book and a bag.

When the image fuzzed out, Simon expected to see another glimpse of the past. Instead, the wavy, slightly out-of-focus image suggested he saw an uncertain future. This time, pictures flashed by like a rapid slideshow.

He glimpsed the same man — still from the back — in a place that looked like it was within Caynham Castle.

Another man came into view, but Simon only saw him from the shoulders down. A dark, vicious presence emerged, winding around the stranger like a boa constrictor, then sinking into his skin, robbing him of breath, crushing out his life —

"Simon!"

Simon came back to himself in Vic's arms, lying on the floor of their room.

"Vision?" Vic asked, and Simon could hear the effort his fiancé put into keeping his tone steady. Vic could handle grisly murders without showing any emotion, but he always struggled to remain stoic when Simon was hurt.

"Yeah," Simon gasped, gripping Vic's arms tightly and nestling against his chest until the world stopped spinning.

"Let's get you into bed—to sleep it off." Vic lifted Simon to his feet and half-carryied, half-dragged him to the bed.

"Sorry. Not how I wanted the evening to end," Simon mumbled.

"Didn't want it to end with you in pain, that's for sure."

Vic helped Simon get undressed and under the covers. Simon's phone rang, and Vic handed it to him. Simon put the call on speaker.

"Simon? This is Priscilla. Sorry to call so late, but the earl would like to meet you and Vic for breakfast to talk about your proposal. He's an early riser. Will seven-thirty work? Here at the main dining area— the earl's treat, since he's calling the meeting."

"That's perfect," Simon managed. "Thank you—and him."

"Are you alright?" Priscilla must have picked up on the pain in Simon's voice.

"Just a migraine—I'll be fine. Thanks for asking."

"Sorry to hear that," she replied. "Get a good night's sleep, and we'll see you early in the morning!"

Vic put the phone on the nightstand.

"Can you set an alarm on both our phones—in the right time zone?" Simon asked.

"Doing it right now," Vic replied. "I think we've had enough excitement for one night," he said and carded his fingers through Simon's hair. "Can I get you something to make it better?"

Simon still had his eyes closed, but he turned his face against Vic's palm. "Just ibuprofen—and you."

Vic chuckled. "I think that can be arranged."

Simon listened to Vic moving around the room, checking the locks, laying out clothing for the morning, getting ready for bed. The familiar sounds soothed and reassured, reminding Simon once again of how much he loved Vic. They might be an ocean away from Myrtle Beach, but wherever Vic was felt like home.

Vic slipped into bed with him, careful not to jostle the mattress. "I'll be right here if you need me. Get some sleep. I love you."

Simon felt for Vic's hand and gave it a squeeze. "Love you too."

THE EARLY WAKE-UP call reminded him that his jet lag wasn't completely over. Simon's headache was gone, although his memory of the vision remained clear. Vic puttered while Simon got ready, rarely more than an arm's length away.

"You're hovering," Simon called out from the bathroom.

"Am not."

"You totally are." Simon smiled. "Not that I mind, but I do feel a lot better."

Vic didn't look completely reassured. "Glad you're on the mend. You'll feel better with a good breakfast."

Simon glanced his way. "We're dining with an earl. Not sure I'll be able to eat a bite."

Vic laughed. "The earl is buying us breakfast. I intend to make the most of it." Both of them dressed up just a little without having to discuss it.

"You never said what you saw last night." Vic spoke quietly as they walked. "Bad?"

Simon nodded. "Yeah. The guy from the train was somewhere in the castle, and he had whatever the spirit is bound to with him. The ghost attacked the earl. It didn't go well for the earl."

"You didn't see the guy's face?"

Simon shook his head. "No. And I couldn't see where in the castle it happened. But we need to stop Train Guy and convince the earl that he needs protection."

"From what Teag and Erik said, I don't think he's the easily frightened type," Vic replied. "But I'll follow your lead. And I've always got your back."

The dining area was part of the castle's Great Hall. Everything was done up for Christmas, with evergreen boughs, red ribbons, fairy lights, and gold bells. A huge fir tree nearly reached the rafters.

"Wow. Look at the ceiling," Vic marveled.

"If I remember right, it's called 'hammerbeam'—an English Gothic style of open timber roof truss," Simon replied. Hand-cut beams arched downward at intervals, while still others formed arches along the flat of the timber ceiling, embellished at the corners with intricate woodcutting.

"I think I also read that the blown glass tree topper is a family heirloom that survived the Blitz," Simon added.

The maître d' had clearly been told to expect them. "The earl and Ms. Donovan have a table. I'll take you to them," he said. Simon and Vic followed him past the main section to an out-of-the-way alcove where they likely wouldn't be disturbed.

Priscilla and a man Simon guessed to be the Earl of Caynham sat at the table, and when she spotted them, Priscilla smiled and waved. Both she and the earl stood as Simon and Vic approached.

"So that's him, huh?" Vic murmured.

"Apparently so."

Clarence Edward Arthur Mortimer, the Fifteenth Earl of Caynham, was tall and broad-shouldered with black hair and a piercing gaze. His harsh, hawkish features weren't conventionally handsome, but something about the man promised strength and integrity.

Priscilla took a step forward. "Simon Kincaide, Vic D'Amato, I'd like you to meet the Earl of Caynham."

The earl extended his hand and gave theirs a hearty shake. "Please, when we're in conversation, call me Ward. It's less of a mouthful." His smile softened his stern first impression.

Ward motioned toward the table. "I hope you don't mind, but I placed a special request for us so you're sure to have a chance to try all our best fare at least once." He gave a broad, theatrical wink. "I have an 'in' with the kitchen."

Despite his initial nervousness and his concern over relaying a warning, the earl was sure to find preposterous, Simon's stomach rumbled. "That sounds wonderful, Lord Caynham."

Ward chuckled, and Priscilla hid a smile. "None of that. It makes conversations take forever. You're a friend of Erik Mitchell, and Teag Logan vouched for you. That counts for a lot in my book. Erik and I survived a few dicey investigations, so there's a foxhole bond there. Teag did us quite a favor despite a disruption to his vacation, and I was very impressed with his talent. So…just 'Ward.'"

"Alright…Ward," Simon replied. He'd met plenty of wealthy, famous, or well-regarded people but no one who was actually noble. *Don't make it weird,* he told himself.

They got settled at the table, and a server appeared to pour tea and coffee. Simon and Vic both opted for coffee, while Ward and Priscilla went with tea.

"Still a little jet-lagged," Simon said. "Although the tea here is amazing."

"Your trip over went well, I hope? We're happy you've chosen to spend your Christmas with us." Ward seemed to care about the reply.

"This place is amazing," Vic spoke up. "We've spent the last couple of Christmases with my family up in Pennsylvania, and with five siblings, spouses, children, dogs, aunts, uncles, and cousins, it's a madhouse. We'll do a video call with them tonight for Christmas Eve." He leaned forward conspiratorially.

"Can I make a confession? It'll be nice to have the holiday all to ourselves for once. But don't tell anyone," he added with a grin, dropping his voice.

"I think we can keep that promise," Ward replied, and Simon noticed that the laughter reached his eyes.

"Now that we're done with all the drama of travel, it's been nice to just relax," Simon replied. "We've been wandering around the grounds and exploring the castle—your decorations are gorgeous."

"Thank you," Priscilla replied with a laugh and a victorious glance at Ward. "I end up doing a lot of the coordination, so I'll take every compliment that comes my way!"

"The decorations were exceptionally lovely this year," Ward agreed, then sighed. "But I say that every year. And the next time, they manage to exceed my expectations yet again. Our team always finds something new to add. I am blessed to have amazing people who love Caynham Castle as much as I do. This is a very special place."

Their food came then, a full English breakfast with additional house-made pastries from the castle's own kitchen and locally-sourced bacon that Simon felt sure was the best he had ever tasted.

Servers kept their cups full and brought more of everything when the plates ran low. "This is all delicious," he said when they finally slowed down. "I don't think I can eat again for days!"

"That would be a pity," Priscilla said with a twinkle in her eye, "because I've sampled the supper menu, and it's one of the chef's best."

Once the dishes had been cleared and another round of hot drinks poured, Ward leaned forward, looking earnestly at Simon and Vic. "Priscilla says you have safety concerns around the event. Fill me in— and tell me everything, please."

Simon cleared his throat and gripped his coffee cup hard enough he feared he might crack the porcelain. Vic rested his hand on Simon's thigh beneath the table and gave him a reassuring squeeze, knocking their knees together.

"I'm a psychic medium," Simon replied. "My doctorate is in folklore and mythology, and I used to be a college professor. Now I run Grand Strand Ghost Tours in Myrtle Beach, and I'm an official consultant for the Myrtle Beach Police Department on supernatural crimes. Vic is a homicide detective, and we work together on cases."

He took a sip of his coffee. "I can sense spirits, and I can invite them to a reading or séance, but I can't summon or compel them. I'm able to channel a spirit and let it speak through me. I can't control when I see visions or what they're about. What I see in my visions happens—although I usually don't get full information."

Simon finally felt his nervousness ease. "I'm telling you all that upfront because nothing works like on TV, and every psychic is different. Just to set expectations."

Ward and Priscilla listened carefully as Simon talked about encountering the stranger on the train and his overwhelming reaction to the malicious ghostly presence. When he recounted his vision, Ward's expression darkened in concern, and a look passed between him and Priscilla that Simon didn't know how to read.

"Can you describe the man?" Ward sat back in his chair and crossed his arms, fingers drumming against his biceps.

"Not well enough for a sketch artist," Simon admitted. "When I've gotten a glimpse of him, it's always been in a crowd and not full-face, even in the visions. He has dark hair, and I'd bet he's under forty. But if I'm right about him being in town for the event and spot him, I'll do my best to get a photo."

"That would help a lot," Priscilla said. "And before I forget—" She pulled a large manila envelope out of her tote and slid it across the table to Simon.

"Those are your badges. Even before hearing what you had to tell us this morning, Ward authorized upgrading both of your passes to All-Access for both events," Priscilla added with a grin. "That means you can wander the stages and tents, and you can be in the event areas before and after-hours."

"Thank you," Simon replied. He turned to Ward. "Please take the vision seriously and add personal security. I plan on doing my best to prevent him from getting that far, but some version of what I saw is going to happen."

Ward frowned. "I hate bodyguards, but sometimes there's no getting around needing them. I want to keep their presence as low-key as possible so we don't alarm the participants or the public—or have the media sniffing around for a scoop. Do you think this ghost is a danger to anyone except me?"

Simon shrugged. "The imminent danger and malice I picked up

seems directed at you, personally. Whether or not the guy or the ghost would put others in harm's way to get to you, I don't know."

"Damn," Ward muttered under his breath. "I can see why you and Erik hit it off—neither of you mince words." He glanced at Priscilla. "Let's look over my itinerary during the events and see where and when I'm in public areas or close to the participants. Perhaps there's a way to adjust the walking routes or staging to keep more distance without being obvious about it."

"I'm already thinking of some possibilities," she replied. "And reconsidering a couple of schedule items."

Ward turned his attention back to Simon. "Thank you. You took a risk to warn me, and I appreciate it. We're going to take your information to heart. Please—if you spot the man or get other visions, let Priscilla know. We want to keep everyone safe."

Simon and Vic thanked Ward for breakfast. Priscilla made sure both of them had her direct number and said she'd try to come up with a "rogues gallery" of possible suspects who fit Simon's vague description for him to look at later.

"Now—enjoy the holiday before the event set-up gets underway. Make sure you wander down to the garden folly—the decorations are some of our best this year," Priscilla told them. "And don't forget the gargoyles," she added with a wink.

AFTER BREAKFAST, Simon and Vic took the opportunity to spend a quiet day exploring the castle grounds and lazing in front of the huge Great Room fireplace—books in hand—between meals. That night, after a phone call to Vic's family, Simon and Vic went to the bell ringing at the castle's chapel and then hurried back to the room to exchange token gifts and warm up with a Bailey's hot chocolate before going to bed and making long, slow love.

"Merry Christmas," Simon murmured as they lay close beneath the covers in a room that still smelled of sweat, sex, and cinnamon.

"Merry Christmas right back atcha," Vic returned with a smile, kissing Simon on the nose. Vacation was making him giddy, and Vic had to admit that it had been a very long time since he had shown anyone this more playful side. "Do you miss not being at home?"

Simon shook his head. "No. Because home is where you are. We talked to your family earlier—are you sorry for the way the scheduling worked out?"

"No," Vic replied and meant it. "We saw everyone at Thanksgiving and shipped the presents early. We already planned to have our friends over when we get back for a Twelfth Night party—whatever that is. We can open our other gifts for each other whenever. And the metallic silver tree isn't going to drop any needles, so we can leave it up until we're good and ready to be done with the holidays."

Simon folded him into his arms. "God, I love you," he whispered as his lips brushed Vic's ear and sent a shiver down his spine.

Christmas was equally laid back since everything in town was closed. They slept in, took their morning coffee and croissants in front of the fireplace, and went in search of more gargoyles. Simon snapped pictures of the castle's decorations and got a great selfie of the two of them at the castle folly. An afternoon nap turned into mid-day sex, followed by a hot shower and time to read, catch up online, and snuggle in bed to watch the classic holiday specials Vic had downloaded to his tablet.

TWO QUIET DAYS worked wonders for helping both Vic and Simon relax. All too quickly, Christmas was over, and Simon found himself feeling wistful.

"Hey," Vic said, seeming to pick up on his mood. "Let's go into town. It's Boxing Day, after all. There are bound to be some sales."

"What do you want to do first?" Simon asked as he and Vic strolled across the inner bailey toward the gates.

"Well, I'd like to spend a little more time in the bookstore and the curio shop," Vic replied. "Maybe have a light lunch at the other tea shop if they're open. I should pick something up for my mom at the yarn place—they had hand-knitted stuff in the window that she might like. And something for Russ that's easier to transport than a fifth of Scotch." Russ was Vic's detective partner and one of his best friends.

"I should get something for Tracey and Pete, although I've got no idea what they'd like," Simon replied, mentioning his closest friend aside from Vic and the assistant manager at his store.

Simon and Vic fell into step, close enough that their mittens brushed from time to time and their shoulders bumped. "Are you interested in the football game this afternoon?"

"Are the Steelers playing?" Vic asked. "And is it *our* football or *their* football? Because soccer isn't football."

"Technically—"

"You know what I mean," Vic said, with a good-natured roll of his eyes.

"It's the castle versus the town," Simon replied. "How about we see when we're ready to walk back, and if they're still playing, we watch or not, depending on how cold we are?"

"I like that idea. And I'm all for a hot chocolate if we can find some. I grew up with Pittsburgh winters, but this feels different," Vic agreed.

As they crossed the bridge, Vic turned to Simon. "You know that Ward isn't the only one with a bodyguard, right? I intend to watch your back. If Train Guy has some crazy ghost attack in mind, we'll deal with him together. Don't run off to be a hero."

Simon took Vic's hand and pressed it over his heart. "Agreed. And thank you. Yes, absolutely. Together."

CHAPTER THREE

SIMON

C*aynham-on-Ledwyche knows how to do the holidays right*, Simon thought. He loved the swags and decorations made from evergreen boughs, pinecones, and natural materials. Christmas lights still adorned shop windows, a mix of soft white bulbs and bright multi-colored strands. The town was still bedecked in all its finery, probably through Twelfth Night.

"That tree at the castle had to be thirty feet high, at least," Vic said as they took their time window-shopping. "I kinda like how things are more understated here—not quite as in-your-face the way the holiday can be back home."

"I was thinking the same thing. It doesn't feel as 'big business' as the over-the-top decorations sometimes do." Simon grinned. "Or course here, they might just be better at hiding it."

"Maybe in London, but I think this feels pretty genuine," Vic replied.

Simon paused when he saw St. Paul's Church. "Can we make a stop to see the priest before we start shopping?"

Vic raised an eyebrow teasingly. "Anything I ought to know? Planning to elope?"

Simon leaned in to kiss his cheek. "Tempting, but not this time. I wanted to see if the priest can do a banishment ritual."

"I don't imagine he gets requests for that every day."

Simon shrugged. "He helped Erik and Ben with the Templar ghost. Sounds like he's made of stern enough stuff."

The cut-stone walls and high tower of St. Paul's Anglican Church had been built to stand forever, and based on the inscription in the cornerstone, it had already lasted more than seven hundred years.

The old church held the scent of candle smoke and incense. Since no service was planned for this afternoon, the low-level lighting gave the sanctuary a shadowed, mysterious feel even in the daytime. Rows of time-worn pews stretched toward the chancel, which held elaborately-carved gothic-style choir stalls made of dark wood, overshadowed by an equally fancy canopy to amplify sound.

The dark oak pulpit was covered with fancy carvings, a raised octagonal booth with its own canopy. Arched stained glass windows along the walls gave the interior an otherworldly glow in hues of red, green, and blue, while a rose window above the apse shone down with magnificent colors.

Simon had been raised nominally Episcopalian. Vic was an equally lapsed Catholic, although Simon suspected that Vic's upbringing had been far more traditional than his own.

"Beautiful." Vic turned in a slow circle to admire the building and its vaulted ceiling. Simon's gaze went to the stained glass with its sun-bright, vibrant colors. As he stood puzzling out the images and stories contained in the windowpanes, he realized he and Vic weren't alone.

"Welcome. I'm Father Andrews. Can I be of service?"

Father Andrews looked to be in his fifth decade, slightly plump with graying brown hair and kind, intelligent eyes.

"We're friends of Erik Mitchell's," Simon replied. "I'm Simon Kincaide, and this is my fiancé, Vic D'Amato."

"Pleasure to meet you," Father Andrews said and grinned. "If you're looking to get hitched, just realize the official paperwork is hard to file over the holidays."

Vic chuckled and Simon felt his cheeks heat. "It's an appealing idea, but that's not why we came. Although the real reason might seem odd."

"You're friends with Erik. We saw some odd things together. Try me."

"I'm a psychic medium, and the earl asked me to have a look at the items being brought in for the *Blast from the Past* show and the antiques fair to see if there are any dangerous hauntings," Simon replied. "I believe there's at least one malicious ghost—and I had a vision that the spirit posed a hazard to the earl."

"My exorcisms are a little rusty," Father Andrews said with a chuckle.

Simon shook his head. "Not an exorcism. This is a ghost, not a demon. How are your banishment rituals?"

The priest's smile faded as he realized that Simon wasn't joking. He glanced to Vic for confirmation and sobered even further when Vic gave a confirming nod.

"You're really serious. And you've discussed this with the earl?" Father Andrews looked from one of them to the other as if he wondered whether this was all an elaborate prank.

"We spoke with him over breakfast at length. He's added a security detail—but this threat can't be shot or Tasered," Vic told the priest.

"I know you're a very busy man," Simon picked up the conversation. "But my sense of the ghost is that it's old and malicious—and dangerous. Whoever is bringing it to the show is an accomplice at the least and perhaps a collaborator. The police don't know how to handle something like this. They'll put the person in jail—maybe—but they aren't going to believe the ghost stuff. From what Ben and Erik told us about their visit here, I think you believe in supernatural things that go 'off-script' from your liturgies."

Father Andrews waved them both over to sit in the back of the church. He and Simon were in one pew, and Vic sat in front of them where he could keep an eye on the door.

"It sounds like Erik told you about our Templar ghost. Fortunately, the spirit didn't try to hurt us once he realized we weren't trying to stop his mission," the priest said. "There is a banishing ritual. It doesn't get a lot of use under normal circumstances. It's been a very long time since I've had a reason to remember it. How did you think I could help?"

"We're still working that out," Simon replied. "This whole situation came up quickly, and so there's a scramble to make sure the participants at the show and fair will be safe, as well as the onlookers and, of course, the earl."

"But you had a vision about the threat," Father Andrews pressed.

Simon nodded. "Yes. I glimpsed the person who is working with the ghost when we were on the train from London, but he got away in the crowded station before I could talk to him. I only saw the man briefly, but the impression the ghost made in just a few seconds was indelible. It's powerful, old, and dangerous."

"You don't have any idea why he would come forward to hurt the earl?" Father Andrews asked. "If the ghost died a long time ago, why wait?"

Simon turned his hands palm up and shrugged. "One more piece we don't have. My guess is that before this, either the spirit wasn't powerful enough to attack with good odds of succeeding, or that previous earls haven't made themselves as accessible as our current one."

"It could be both," Simon admitted. "And if we can catch him and stop him, we can figure out the details later. I'm worried that the ghost'll strike when the event is in full swing to do the worst possible damage."

He fought the urge to get up and pace. "I don't know how strong the ghost is or what it will take to protect the earl. Salt, aconite, iron, blessed silver—they all work to varying degrees, but our one shot to test the theory will be when there's no room for error."

"I don't like things I can't punch or shoot," Vic added. "I'm here to protect Simon while he does what he does. But having you with us would improve the odds."

"How are you going to look for the ghost?" Father Andrews seemed to be seriously considering offering his help. Simon couldn't blame him for his hesitance.

"The energy around the spirit is strong enough that I don't think his 'assistant' can hide him—not from a true medium," Simon replied.

"As 'consulting experts' with the event, Vic and I will be backstage among the participants and in the display areas. I'll be able to tell if any of the pieces are haunted, and I should have a fair sense of anything that's been cursed."

Father Andrews nodded. "Okay. But what about when you find something?"

"If it's a normal haunting, I can help the spirit move on or give him a psychic shove if he refuses," Simon answered. "The ghost I sensed on the train had strong energy and purpose. It wanted revenge."

"I've got a theory." They both turned to look at Vic. "We've been thinking that this is just a ghost. But maybe it's a ghost haunting an object. Someone sees all the hullabaloo about the *Blast from the Past* and the Caynham Castle Antiques Fair and figures they'll go clean out Granny's attic to make some cash,"

His voice took on the intensity Simon was used to hearing when Vic was on a case. "So they find some old stuff that's been boxed up for a long time and think they'll either get it appraised and win big or at least score some easy money by selling it," Vic said. "Maybe the ghost hasn't been active before now because it was 'bound' in a container, and when the new owner 'found' it, he accidentally released whatever kept it inactive."

"That's a very good theory, Detective," Simon said with a fond grin.

"All right. I'll help. I don't have any weddings, funerals, or baptisms over the next few days, and the religious part of the holiday is over for us, except for a blessing on New Year's Eve. I could get called out for an emergency, but I can arrange backup coverage. Although I'm not quite sure how to explain the situation," the priest said and sighed. "I'll figure something out."

Simon glanced at his watch. "We've taken up a lot of your time. I'll arrange for a badge to get you in and send you the schedule. Thank you for believing us."

Father Andrews shrugged. "I've learned that where the earl is involved, it's important to keep an open mind." He smiled. "Make sure you walk around the churchyard on your way out. I suspect you'll find it fascinating."

He walked them to the door and traded contact information with

Simon. "I'll wait to hear from you. Thank you for trusting me with your information."

Simon promised to call as soon as he had news, and then he and Vic bundled up to head out into the cold again.

"That went better than I expected," Vic admitted.

"Yeah, it did. I think we've earned hot chocolate. What do you think?"

"Sounds like a good plan to me," Vic agreed.

Simon led them around the side of St. Paul's. They admired the striking architecture from the outside. Thanks to his abilities, when he looked at the cemetery that surrounded the church, it twinkled with orbs, the faded spirits of long-buried ghosts. A flicker of stronger energy caught his eye. He frowned and followed it, leaving Vic staring, perplexed.

"Simon?"

He didn't answer, intent on not losing sight of the spirit. He could sense its age—easily as old as the malicious ghost from the train. Given the age of the church, that could go all the way back to the 1500s.

Simon pursued the spirit, which hovered above the sidewalk beyond the cemetery wall and grew more solid.

This ghost looked to be an impoverished young woman. Nothing could hide the anger in her eyes.

"Ask him. Ask him why we are buried outside the wall. Why they won't speak our names. Yes, Jeremiah took the coins, and I helped him. They were at the bottom of an old well. We didn't think of it as stealing. Because of the earl we lost everything. He should pay for what he did to us."

The ghost winked out. Simon stood staring at the place where the apparition had been, distantly aware that Vic was calling his name. Simon turned to answer his partner, and then blinding pain drove him to his knees before he blacked out completely.

———

"HE SAW SOMETHING—A ghost, I assume—and walked toward it," Vic was saying when Simon came around. He was back inside St. Paul's, laid out on a wooden bench in the back row.

"For a moment, he just stood there, like he was watching something he couldn't look away from, and then when he snapped out of it and turned toward me, he went down like he'd been hit with a sack of bricks," Vic recounted. His warm hand found Simon's shoulder and gave a reassuring squeeze.

"How long?" Simon murmured. Vic's hold on his shoulder tightened.

"Babe? You back with us?" Vic didn't try to hide his worry.

"Sorta."

"You were only out for a couple of minutes this time," Vic told him. "Do you remember what you saw?"

Vic helped Simon sit up. Father Andrews handed him a small bottle of orange juice and a candy bar. "Eat," the priest instructed. "We had leftovers from the blood drive last week. There's more if you want it."

They waited until Simon refueled before expecting answers, for which he was grateful. This vision wasn't as bad as the last one, but it still packed a wallop.

"Give me a minute," he said when he handed back the empty bottle and candy wrapper. Simon shut his eyes and focused on what he had seen.

"I saw a woman's ghost hovering over the sidewalk on the other side of the wall. She didn't tell me her name, but apparently a man— Jeremiah—was involved in whatever caused trouble. Something about finding coins in an old well and not thinking it was stealing. I guess the authorities didn't agree. Then she said that the earl cost them everything and should pay."

Simon spread his hands, palms up, unsure what to make of the vision without more information. "That's it."

Father Andrews began to pace, walking five paces back and forth in the dappled light of one of the stained glass panels. "You said she was over the sidewalk?"

"Yes."

The priest nodded and turned to look at Simon and Vic. "When the church was first founded, certain people were considered to be too tainted by sin to be buried inside the churchyard wall, on so-called 'hallowed ground.' Murderers, thieves, those who died without baptism, executed criminals and suicides…they were buried just outside the wall."

Simon and Vic exchanged a look. "Well, that explains why the ghost was so pissed off," Vic muttered.

Simon frowned. "We're missing something. If the woman's ghost is here, then she isn't traveling with the 'assistant' who came from London. So she's not the ghost we need to be on guard against. But she clearly had a partner who, in her opinion, made a mistake and was unjustly punished, leading to both their deaths. Maybe having that ghost return riled her spirit up."

"If you're going back five hundred years, the earl's word was the highest judgment in his lands," Father Andrews supplied. "So if she felt that the court did them wrong, then she's angry with the earl."

Simon felt the juice and chocolate kick in, grounding him to the real world and driving back the last wisps of the vision.

"If people actually believed that some dirt was more special than other dirt and it mattered to your eternal soul, then getting locked out would certainly give ghosts reason to hold a grudge, I'd imagine," Vic muttered.

Simon still felt spacey after fainting, so he was pleased that Vic had slipped into protective cop mode.

"Father, do church records say anything about who was buried outside the wall?" Vic asked. "And why?"

Father Andrews grimaced. "Well, that's going back quite a ways. But burials, weddings, and baptisms are the three things the church records the best. For quite a long while, church records were the only legal documentation in most places. That lasted in rural areas well into the mid-1900s. So the odds are good we might find something."

"I think this could be the key to figuring out why the malicious ghost I spotted wants to harm the earl," Simon told him. "I'm sorry to impose, but if you can find anything to do with a woman and a man buried outside the wall because of something related to 'coins found in a well,' that could be the lead we need to know what we're dealing with."

The priest nodded. "That's the kind of sleuthing I know how to do.

I'll get on it tonight and call you as soon as I find out what's in the records."

They thanked him again and left a second time. Simon noted that the sky had grown darker and the air colder. "Do you want to go back and rest?" Vic offered.

Simon shook his head. "No. I'm better now. And between coming in right before Christmas and now being involved in the *Blast from the Past* event and the antiques fair at the castle, we won't have many more free days to enjoy the town. Let's do this. Besides," he said with a self-conscious smile as his stomach rumbled, "I'm really hungry."

They stopped at the yarn store's tea shop. Simon remarked on all of the beautiful colors of yarn and how soft the skeins were. Vic chose several hand-knitted items for his mother's belated holiday present while Simon took care of getting them hot cocoa.

"We're definitely coming back for lunch," Simon told Vic as they left the store carrying bags.

A sidewalk chalkboard in front of the next shop read, *Ghost Tours. Get tickets here.*

Simon looked at Vic and grinned. "How about it? We can still be back in time for supper at the castle."

"You see ghosts everywhere without a guide. Hell, you give ghost tours for a living. The guide might not even be a medium, and it could all be fake."

Simon shrugged. "Well, then we've had a nice walk and had someone tell us stories for an hour."

Vic gave a dramatic, long-suffering sigh. "Go sign us up. But we visit the brewery afterward, to be fair."

Simon came back moments later with two tickets. "Our tour leaves right after lunch, so we have time to see the bookstore and that antique place before we go."

They whiled away the next couple of hours browsing through the shops. Simon found several out-of-print books and reassured himself that nothing in the curio store would cause paranormal problems. Looking for some small gifts for friends turned their shopping into a scavenger hunt, and Simon couldn't resist buying a set of linen tea towels printed with a picture of the castle for their house.

"I want to go through the castle's shop before it's all said and done," Simon told Vic. "We need to get a Christmas ornament."

"I hope they sell the tea blend we had at breakfast—that was amazing," Vic replied.

Simon kept an eye out for Train Guy as they maneuvered through the shoppers looking for Boxing Day sales. The town was busier than it had been over Christmas, and he wondered how many people were involved in some way with the television show and the fair.

Lunch at the yarn shop's tea room was fun, and the selection of cakes and sandwiches differed enough that it didn't feel like a repeat. By the time they polished off the last of the scones and washed them down with hot tea, both Simon and Vic were full and relaxed.

"I could go for taking a nap in front of a roaring fire right now," Vic confessed.

"I imagine that the Great Hall at the castle is in chaos getting ready for the show to set up tomorrow, but maybe that brewery has a fire we could watch." Simon dropped his voice. "Now the napping and the making out part probably needs to wait until we get to our room."

"Count on a raincheck," Vic assured him as they went to meet their tour.

The guide for their ghost tour was a chipper redhead. "I'm Emma, and I'm so happy that all of you were able to join me this afternoon. I'll collect tickets, and then we'll be on our way."

Simon didn't pick up any ripple of energy from Emma to suggest that she had psychic ability. He just wanted to hear stories about the various sites on the tour. Ghosts he could manage on his own.

"Our first stop is the florist shop," Emma told them. "Caynham-on-Ledwyche is a very old town, and we are fortunate to have most of our downtown buildings original to at least the 1650s, with a few older and some from the 1700s. Except for a couple of locations where a fire destroyed the previous structure, you'll find the newer buildings out on the edge of town. Maintaining the history of our town is a point of pride for all of us and something the earl is deeply committed to continuing."

She gestured toward the florist shop, which was currently closed.

Simon wondered if the staff were all up at the castle getting ready for the show.

"It's a flower shop now, but over the centuries, this building has been an apothecary, a hat shop, and a tailor's, among other things, but our ghost is said to have been a seamstress who sewed for the women of the town, in the days before off-the-rack clothing was available," Emma told them.

"According to the stories, Hannah Grant was widowed young and made her living as a seamstress to support her two young children back in the seventeen hundreds. When an outbreak of fever claimed lives in London, the people of Caynham-on-Ledwyche didn't think it would affect them because the city was so far away. But they were wrong.

"One of Hannah's regular customers returned from a stay in London and came in to commission several new gowns. Hannah was happy for the new orders and didn't think anything of it until her daughters fell sick. Sure enough, the customer had carried the fever with her, and within a week, she was dead—and so were Hannah and her children," Emma recounted.

"Her shop was sold and her belongings given to the poor. But ever since then, each owner of the store has reported hearing the sounds of children playing on the second floor where Hannah and her family lived and a woman weeping over her lost loved ones."

Simon felt a presence next to him and tried not to flinch away as Hannah's ghost sidled up. *"She always tells it wrong. I choked on a piece of meat. Didn't even have children."*

"Do you need help to move on?" Simon offered.

"What for? I like it here. Just wish she'd get my story right."

With that, the annoyed ghost vanished, leaving Simon chuckling. Vic shot him a questioning look. Simon shook his head. "I'll tell you later," he whispered.

Emma's stories had the small group listening in rapt attention, and while Simon doubted some of her facts, she certainly had talent as a storyteller.

Leading ghost tours was part of his job back in Myrtle Beach, so Simon enjoyed getting to be one of the listeners for once. Whether or not she could see spirits herself, Emma's energy and sincerity made her stories compelling. She sprinkled local history in between "haunted" stories, which even kept Vic paying close attention.

The tour made eight stops in all. At three of them, Simon couldn't pick up any ghost vibes. With the other five, the truth was a mix of what Emma shared in her stories and more mundane circumstances. Some of the spirits were repeaters—a faded energy loop that played over and over without consciousness, like a video clip. The others remembered their past selves but only wanted to be left in peace and intended no harm.

"Thank you," Simon told Emma when the tour ended. Vic passed her a generous tip. "You tell good stories."

"Did you enjoy it? I've always loved ghost tales, and it's fun to put my own spin on them. Plus, it gets visitors to slow down and learn a little about the townspeople. If I just called it a 'history' tour, no one would come, but ghosts are sexy."

Simon and Vic hailed a cab and asked to go to the Kings' Arms brewery on the edge of town. They settled into the backseat, and Vic rubbed his hands together.

"So how did she do? Did you send all the ghosts on to the other side?" Vic asked quietly, knowing that the cabbie couldn't hear them over the radio.

"I don't think she can sense the spirits, but she delivered the stories with a lot of heart," Simon replied. "That gets her points in my book right there. It's hard to make the script fresh night after night. Not every place had a ghost, and not every ghost's tale got the details right, but no harm was done. And no, I didn't un-haunt the town. Her livelihood is safe."

The brewery offered a broad variety of beer choices, so Simon and Vic settled on flights that would let them taste as many of the local options as possible.

Vic happily found them a couch near the brewery's large fireplace where they could bask in the glow of the roaring fire.

"What do you think?" Vic asked as they worked their way through their second flight.

"I've always preferred Canadian and European beer to American," Simon admitted. "More body and flavor. The darker, the better."

"I think you're gradually convincing me," Vic replied. "Although my brothers might give you a hard time if they found out. Pittsburgh has some good small-batch brewers of its own, but I really do think you're winning me over."

Dinner at the castle would be a bar food buffet, but both men felt peckish and ordered chips with vinegar to tide them over.

"I always have to remember that over here, fries are 'chips' and our chips are called 'crisps,'" Simon said as they dug in. They fell silent as they ate and then sat and watched the fire.

"I'm thinking about writing another book," Simon said after a while. "I'd like to do something linking old South Carolina families with their UK ancestors and trace the shared ghost stories and paranormal issues. Plus, I'm fascinated by intergenerational curses—I bet I could find plenty of examples."

Vic leaned back and snagged another chip. "Sounds like a winner. I'm all for coming here again. But next time, I want to go on a whiskey tour of Scotland. Can you find some ghosts to research that haunt distilleries?"

"That could be arranged. Of course, you might have to suck up to the author," Simon said with a wicked grin.

"Sacrifices must be made," Vic replied. The lust in his eyes countered the put-upon tone in his voice.

"Third flight?" the server asked as she cleared away the empties.

Simon and Vic exchanged a look. "No thanks. We need to get back for dinner. Maybe we can come another time and try the rest," Simon told her, closing out their tab.

When the cab brought them back downtown, Simon was surprised that the sidewalks were still full of people. "I guess no one is letting the temperatures bother them," Vic said as they headed back toward the bridge to the castle.

"I imagine they're used to it," Simon replied.

He caught a glimpse of a dark-haired man in the crowd going the other direction and froze. "I think that's him—Train Guy." Simon started maneuvering through the crowd, ignoring the urge to just clear people out of the way. He caught sight of the man now and again over the heads of the other people, but there were always too many in his way to close the gap.

Finally, Simon got close enough to snap a photo. He only had seconds before the crowd surged again. A pack of rowdy revelers forced their way between them, and when Simon looked for his quarry after the partiers passed, the dark-haired man was gone.

Vic was waiting by the bridge where Simon had left him. "Did you find him?" Vic asked.

Simon shook his head, but he held up his phone. "I got a picture—I think." He pulled up his photos and held it so Vic could see.

"Not as sharp as the cops are going to want, but it might be enough for them to run through their system—although I don't know what excuse the earl would give them to do that. Technically, Train Guy hasn't done anything wrong yet. He hasn't actually done anything at all," Vic said.

"Priscilla said that everyone who's part of the event had to have a picture taken for their badges," Simon reminded him. "It might be good enough to find a match and get a name or limit his access. It's a start."

"Sounds like a plan." Vic shivered. "I got overheated from sitting too close to the fireplace, and now I'm freezing."

"How about we go back to our room after dinner, and I help you find steamy ways to warm up?" Simon offered.

"I think it sounds like the perfect way to finish off the day," Vic replied with a wicked grin.

Simon emailed the picture of Train Guy to Priscilla, along with a note and warning. Then he put everything case-related out of his mind and resolved to be on vacation tonight.

They made quick work of the buffet since walking in the cold night air had made both of them hungry. Train Guy had been heading away from the castle, so Simon doubted he would show up here soon.

I need to give Vic my full attention. We'll be distracted enough with being consultants to the show. I already feel like noticing Train Guy ruined the vacation vibe.

"Hey," Vic said. "Stop feeling guilty."

"Who said I was—"

Vic gave him his best "interrogation" glare. "You're fidgeting. That usually means you're spinning the wheels in your head, blaming yourself for something."

"This is supposed to be a vacation, and I've turned it into a case."

Vic took his hand. "Babe, do you even hear yourself? We're staying in a *castle*, and we had breakfast with a friggin' *earl*. We started with behind-the-scenes passes, but now we've got all-access badges, and we'll see everything before it even goes on TV. I read the packet Priscilla sent up with our badges. We're invited to the fancy wrap party New Year's Eve. We had a beautiful Christmas Eve and Christmas, and we spent all day today being tourists. This is a fantastic vacation. It's one-of-a-kind and wonderful—because we're together."

Simon closed his grip around Vic's hand. "Really? Because the next couple of days are going to feel more like working than relaxing."

"We'll be together," Vic reassured him. "You'll be busy being brilliant, and I'll have your back. Like always—only we get to do it in *England*, in a *castle*, with an *earl*."

"With a candlestick? Sorry—it sounded like a game of *Clue* there for a minute," Simon replied with a self-conscious grin.

"God, you are such a nerd." Vic shook his head as his thumb slid over Simon's knuckles. "C'mon. Let's go back to the room before it's time to crash. I've got plans for tonight."

Vic kissed Simon in the elevator, slow and sweet.

"You know there are probably cameras," Simon murmured when he came up for air.

"If the security guy gets jealous, let him get his own fiancé," Vic joked. "It's not like anyone's on their knees—although that is a hot idea."

"My cop boyfriend fantasizes about exhibitionist sex? What is this world coming to?" Simon teased.

"No harm done as long as we don't get arrested," Vic replied. "Plenty of fodder for a little role play. We could always pretend the closet is an elevator. Or the bathroom on a plane."

"Silly boy—I came out of the closet a long time ago."

Vic rolled his eyes. "Seriously? That's the best you've got?"

Simon slipped an arm around Vic's waist and leaned in to kiss him again, sure and deep. "I'll show you the best I've got."

"I'm counting on it."

They broke apart when the bell chimed as they reached their floor, in case someone was waiting in the lobby. That gave them plausible deniability, although it wouldn't hide the mussed hair and kissed-red lips.

Simon fumbled the key as he tried to open the door. Vic pressed up against him, with his hands on Simon's hips and his hard-on wedged into the crack of Simon's ass.

"You're not helping."

"I'm providing inspiration."

Simon got the door open, and they both nearly fell inside. He locked the door behind them, and they stumbled toward the bed, discarding clothing as they went.

"Tell me how you want it," Vic rumbled as he backed Simon up until Simon's legs hit the end of the bed. They tumbled onto the mattress together and fell in a tangle of limbs, warm and naked.

"I want it slow, and I want it to last for a long time," Simon replied, nipping at Vic's neck, lightly scraping teeth over the stubble at the hinge of his jaw, and pressing kisses against his temples.

"What else?" Vic's low growl sent a thrill through Simon, going straight to his cock.

"Everything. I want everything, always and forever."

Vic pressed a kiss to Simon's chest, directly over his heart. "You already have that."

"I want to feel you inside me, filling me up. And I want to be inside you, deep as I can go." Simon's voice came out low and breathy.

"Hmm. I have some ideas of my own," Vic said right before he swallowed Simon's cock down to the base. Simon arched, but Vic's forearm across his hips kept him pinned. Simon grabbed fistfuls of the sheets, and he clamped his lips together to keep from crying out as Vic sucked him wet and sloppy.

Vic's tongue ran the length of Simon's hard prick, and his tongue swirled over the head, teasing at the slit. The tip of Vic's thumb pressed that sensitive spot just below the knob, and then Vic went back to sucking and humming, spit-slick and messy until Simon was panting.

His lover must have already hidden lube in the bedclothes before they went out because a tube of it appeared in Vic's hand. He kept up his rhythm sucking Simon's cock as the other hand popped the cap and squeezed out enough to slick Vic's fingers, which he worked into Simon's tight ass one at a time.

"Vic—I'm not gonna last." Simon could feel the pressure building at the base of his spine, knowing he was too tired and stressed to hold out for long.

Vic hummed a response without ever losing his pace, although Simon was too far gone to have any idea what Vic's answer might have been. Since he never faltered, Simon figured that Vic wasn't opposed.

"Want to come with you in me," Simon managed, although stringing words together was rapidly becoming more difficult with Vic's talented tongue going to work on his sensitive cock.

"Mm-hm," Vic replied, which Simon assumed was agreement and a promise.

Vic pulled off with a wet *pop* and crawled up between Simon's legs, pushing on his thighs until Simon was nearly folded in two. "Hold your ankles," he growled, in a voice rough from deep throating, and Simon hurried to comply.

Vic lifted Simon's hips for a better angle and then pushed inside, moving slowly despite the prep to give Simon a chance to adjust.

"Please, Vic—"

"Shh. Not going to hurry and hurt you. Just relax, and let me take care of you," Vic said, bending down to graze Simon's lips.

Vic sank in, balls deep, and Simon wrapped his legs around his lover's waist, crossing his ankles behind Vic's back, urging him to go deeper and faster with the nudge of his heel to Vic's firm ass.

"Feels so good. Don't make me wait." Between their long walk in the cold, dinner, ale, and the toll of his vision, Simon knew he wouldn't make it through a long foreplay. He suspected Vic was probably just as exhausted. *I'll probably be asleep before my dick stops twitching.*

Vic thrusts grew sharper and faster, and Simon dug his fingertips into Vic's back to hang on. Normally, he wouldn't mind spending an hour slowly teasing each other, even managing a few warm-up orgasms before they got to the main event. Now, he knew neither of them could switch and go for a second round tonight, although that gave Simon good ideas for how to wake Vic up the next morning.

"That's it, Simon. Babe, you're so beautiful like that." Vic's rhythm stuttered, and Simon knew they were both knife-edge close.

"C'mon, Simon. Give it up for me. I wanna see you come," Vic murmured as he held tight to Simon's hips to better control the angle. He pulled almost all the way out, then plunged in deep, making sure to hit Simon's sweet spot on each thrust.

"Vic!" Simon felt his climax sweep over him, and his release spilled between them.

Vic tensed seconds later, still managing a few more long, deep strokes to work himself to the end of his orgasm, before he collapsed to one side, sweaty and come-spattered.

Simon nuzzled his jaw and then kissed him, gentle and sated. "Raincheck on having it both ways? I can give you a very *good* morning."

"I think that sounds like a great idea," Vic replied. He got up and came back with a warm cloth to clean both of them. Simon appreciated Vic's gentleness after a round of sweaty sex.

"Love you," Simon murmured when Vic came back and turned out the light. They burrowed beneath the covers together, fucked sated and boneless.

"Love you too. Now, sleep," Vic mumbled. Simon was out before Vic finished talking.

CHAPTER FOUR

VIC

Simon made good on his promise when they woke, putting them both in an exceptionally good mood.

"We should pick up any gifts today that we haven't already bought because we're going to be busy with the show, and then it'll be New Year's Eve and New Year's Day, and then it's time to go home," Simon remarked as he got dressed after his shower.

"After breakfast, let's do the castle gift shop," Vic said from the bathroom, still getting ready. "We can probably send anything we buy up to the room."

"Sounds good. And I want to go to the brewery that the earl owns in town. Just so we can say we were thorough." Simon grinned. "We wouldn't want to half-ass the bar tour."

"Absolutely not," Vic agreed with mock seriousness. "Plus, we need to make sure we've kissed in front of all the gargoyles. We don't want to skip any."

Simon's phone buzzed. He answered and then mouthed "Priscilla" to Vic. "Good morning. What's up?" He listened intently, and Vic watched his fiancé's expression to get a read on whether the news was good or bad.

"We can do that," Simon said after a few moments. "I'll let Vic know. Thank you." He ended the call and looked up.

"The participants won't show up with their antiques until tomorrow, but Ward thought it would be good for us to get familiar with the layout and the main people once everything was set up. Priscilla says everything should be ready by two, which gives us until then to do whatever we want, and probably the evening afterward as well. She said she would show us around and introduce us. We're supposed to meet her at the tea room."

"That works. We can eat there for lunch—I won't complain," Vic replied with a grin.

The time passed quickly. Their finds at the gift shop finished off the last souvenirs and presents on their list, and Vic made sure no gargoyle went without witnessing a kiss.

"We can still go to the earl's brewery before dinner," Simon told him as they walked hand-in-hand from the folly toward the tea room.

"I like that idea. And I'd love to come back when everything is in bloom," Vic replied. "It's beautiful now, but I bet it's amazing in the spring and summer."

"Sounds like a plan to me," Simon agreed.

Lunch at the tea room was just as good as the first time, and they made a point to try a different selection of sandwiches and pastries, as well as new varieties of tea. By the time Priscilla showed up, they had eaten their fill and savored the hot tea to drive away the chill.

"Thank you for meeting with me," she said as they headed toward the large marquee tents in the outer bailey. Priscilla looked cool and collected, despite what had to have been a hectic morning.

"The TV crews got here early this morning to set up. We're filming some interviews with our appraisal experts that will be used for cutaway shots when the show is edited," she told them. "They've been setting up the lighting and sound and making sure all the connections work. It's like someone kicked an anthill, and the ants are all swarming —but they know exactly what to do."

Simon nodded. "I've been interviewed for museum videos and news programs. What goes on behind the camera is absolutely amazing."

Vic shrugged. "Every time I've been on camera, there's a dead body, so it's a little different."

Priscilla walked them through the big tents, narrating how everything went together. "We'll appraise the large pieces out here—furniture, paintings, that sort of thing. The smaller items like jewelry and decorative pieces will be handled in the Great Hall. That's why the dining options are so limited while the events are going on."

"So none of the antiques are here yet?" Simon asked as he looked all around. Vic knew his partner wouldn't miss a detail.

Priscilla shook her head. "No. The participants for *Blast from the Past* will bring the items with them, and we'll choose them out of the line. The antiques fair vendors will load in first thing the morning of the thirtieth and load out when the show closes. We can't take responsibility for storing and safeguarding their pieces."

Simon nodded. "Makes sense. So what's the plan for having me scan for ghosts?"

"One of my people will take you around and make sure you see everything. It will take a while for the appraisers to work through the line—or as much of it as they can—so you should have time to go up and down the queue," Priscilla said.

"The second day will work the same way. On the third day, with the antiques fair, you can have access as soon as the vendors arrive. There will be more items, but since you'll be mingling while they set up their booths, you'll see everything as it gets put out. If there's anything you want to flag to be cleansed, it can be done before the public shows up so the pieces can still be sold," she added.

Simon and Vic exchanged a glance. "And Train Guy? How are we going to know if he shows up?" Vic asked.

"The castle has security cameras—a necessity in today's world," Priscilla replied. "I'll have my people watching the feeds in real-time as the participants and the public enter, with the photo you took. They'll alert me if they spot him. You and Simon will probably want to be at the entrances to watch as the crowd comes in."

"Do the badges have photos?" Vic pressed. "Or are they linked to something with a photo?"

Priscilla shook her head. "Not for the participants, and the shoppers/audience only have tickets. The TV crew, experts, and appraisers all have photo badges, but I doubt that's where we'll find your Train Guy."

"Probably not, but we can look them over tonight if you have them available," Vic replied.

"I can make that happen."

They finished the tour of the shooting locations and display areas in plenty of time for supper. Vic was impressed with the crew's professionalism and Priscilla's no-nonsense, hyper-organized approach.

"Take the rest of the night off," Priscilla told them as they headed back toward the main gate. "The next few days will be a whirlwind, so do the tourist thing while you can. I'll call you when we've got the badge photos pulled together, and we can go over them in my office. It won't take long."

They thanked her, then headed into town as she strode back to the hive of activity in the marquee tents.

"I don't know about you." Vic took Simon's hand as they walked. "But I sure could use a good beer."

THE NEXT MORNING they woke early for their role as protective consultants for the *Blast from the Past* show setup and went downstairs to catch a quick continental breakfast and coffee before showing up for duty.

Vic and Simon munched their Danishes and croissants in a quiet alcove, watching the grips and roadies ready the areas where participants would bring their treasures for appraisal. In the outer bailey, under the big marquee tents, other preparations were being made for the fair that would happen in a few days.

"I can't get over waking up inside a real castle," Vic said, happier about their hotel than he had ever imagined. "So much history. And did I tell you that I saw a note on the website about the Knights Templar exhibit? That's got to be the stuff Erik and Ben uncovered."

"You're such a geek," Simon said with a chuckle. Vic leaned in to kiss him, catching the taste of chocolate croissant on his lips.

"And you love it," Vic whispered.

"You know I do."

Simon's phone rang, startling him and nearly making him drop his coffee. "It's Father Andrews." He put the call on speakerphone with the volume low enough that only he and Vic could hear.

"It took some digging and a wheedled favor from a friend at the historical archive, but I might have a match for your angry ghost," the priest said.

"Sadie Keene was the wife of Jeremiah Keene, who worked as a groundskeeper for the sixth Earl of Caynham back in 1690. He came across an ancient well on the earl's lands and as he was digging it out, found a number of old coins. He took them, and when the earl found out, Keene was accused and convicted of stealing. The earl confiscated the coins and fired Keene, who was hanged for theft," Father Andrews went on.

"That was the start of a run of bad luck for Sadie, who ended up impoverished and homeless. She committed suicide."

"Wow," Simon replied. "So the ghost I saw was Sadie?"

"Apparently so," Father Andrews said.

"But if Jeremiah was buried outside the churchyard wall, who is the ghost that's haunting Train Guy, and why?" Vic asked.

"I have a theory. I'm betting that Jeremiah didn't return all of the coins. The history of this area goes back a very long way. The coins he found might have been contemporary—or they might have been Roman. No one else knew how many coins there actually were," Father Andrews said.

Simon nodded. "That makes a lot of sense. Which might also explain a way Jeremiah's ghost could have come to possess Train Guy. If Jeremiah kept some of the coins, and they were stolen from his belongings after his death, Jeremiah might have hitched a ride."

"The coins get passed down through the years from one owner to another, until somehow, Train Guy happens onto them," Vic took up spinning the story. "But why in all those years didn't Jeremiah come after the earl himself? Or one of the other earls closer to that time?"

"Ghost possession isn't common. It requires a strong spirit and a relatively weak host," Simon mused. "It might have taken Jeremiah a while to gain the power to force himself on someone—or seduce them to let him in and allow him to keep control."

"The coins could have remained hidden for long periods without being near a person who could be influenced," Vic suggested. "Fifty years here, seventy years there—time flies."

Simon frowned. "So Train Guy might have entered the coins as his piece for the show—or the fair. But I guess he could just as easily put them in his pocket if he wanted to hide them."

"Something else we should tell Priscilla," Vic said and pointed at the time on Simon's watch.

"Shit—we need to get going. Sorry, Father," Simon said.

Father Andrews chuckled. "Don't worry about it. The first dozen swear words are free. Confessional special."

"Anglicans don't have Confession," Simon pointed out.

"Darn—there goes my leverage," the priest said with a laugh.

Priscilla came around the corner, clearly looking for them. She had a small zipped duffle in one hand. "There you are! Time to go."

"Great detective work, Father," Vic said. "Please keep us in the loop if you find out anything else."

Simon ended the call and pocketed his phone. "Sorry we're running a few minutes late—but you'll want to hear the reason."

"Walk with me. Time to put you to work," Priscilla said, handing off the duffle to Simon. She gave them an appraising glance. "I believe I got everything on your list," she said with a nod toward the bag. "You're both wearing your badges. Good. I passed along the photo you sent me to the earl. He shared it—unofficially—with a friend with the London police. We might have an ID on your 'Train Guy.'"

"You had me at 'police,'" Vic admitted. "What did you find out?"

They walked to the outer bailey, where preparations were well underway, and people scurried in purposeful chaos. So many people wore intense expressions and speed-walked from one point to another that it made Vic's head hurt to watch.

"London PD thinks Train Guy might be Addison Taylor," Priscilla said. "Age 31, has a history of having a hot temper and a tendency to blame others for his bad luck. He's worked a series of retail and hospitality jobs, been a lorry driver, lately a ride-share driver. Gotten fired or quit in a snit from all of them, so he's down on his luck. His great-uncle died last month, and it appears he's been helping his mother and aunt go through his great-uncle's things."

"That timing could work," Simon replied. "The great-uncle could have had the coins packed away for decades. Or maybe he didn't have the right kind of personality to be affected by them."

Vic nodded, catching on. "But Taylor sounds like a prime candidate to let a vengeful ghost with a chip on his shoulder go for a free ride."

"The only problem is, there's no 'Addison Taylor' registered as a participant or a vendor at the fair," Priscilla pointed out. "And we didn't find any badge photos that are a clear match. Then again, your picture of him wasn't the best, so that could make him harder to recognize, especially if he tried to change his appearance. Or he might come in as a shopper or part of the audience."

"And I'm guessing no one has entered 'ancient coins' as their item for appraisal or signed up for the antiques fair as a coin dealer?" Vic asked.

She shook her head. "No. Of course it couldn't be that simple. But Ward does have extra security in place…for the event and bodyguards for himself. He listened to you. That's a big deal—because he hates having guards dogging his steps."

"We know none of the crew or event staff photos match Taylor's picture," Vic said. "And we'll get a good look at the show participants when we check out the line."

Priscilla nodded. "My people are watching the cameras on the entrances, so if he comes in while you're checking the people in line, we'll hear about it. After we're done here, you're welcome to watch at the gate yourselves."

"Thank you," Simon replied. "I hope that Ward won't need the bodyguards, but I think we've spun some theories that show that a little bit of caution is advisable."

"I think you've done a remarkable job of uncovering a very real threat to the earl and the event. Now we just have to make sure it doesn't happen," Priscilla said.

She led them toward a long line of people clutching their heirlooms, hoping to have a chance for an expert appraisal. A man in his forties was waiting for them just off to one side. Vic thought the fellow had the air of an accountant—trustworthy and staid.

"This is Howard. He's one of my best folks," Priscilla introduced them to her assistant. "He helped me go through all of the participant applications for *Blast from the Past* and for the antiques fair dealers. So if you have questions about any of the items, he's the one to ask, and he can connect each item with an owner."

"Thank you," Simon replied. "I'm sure he'll take good care of us."

"Be sure you get your box lunches," she warned them. "Can't have you passing out from hunger."

"I'll make sure they both eat," Vic replied. "And I'll keep my eye on them."

Priscilla checked her watch. "I've got to go. The earl is waiting. Let me know if you find anything."

"Father Andrews is on standby," Simon reminded her. "So if we find anything that's truly dangerous or that has bad energy, he's willing to do a cleansing."

"Good to know. Keep a list, and we'll work out compensation for his time," Priscilla said. "Good luck ghost hunting!" She gave them a cheery wave and then headed off at a remarkable speed, considering the height of her heels.

Simon turned to Howard. "What's the best way to do this?"

Vic fell back, happy to let Simon make the decisions since he was the one using his gift to screen for problems. Vic knew how to play his role. He'd been part of security details as a cop and gone undercover as a bodyguard when he became a detective. Protecting Simon just came naturally.

"Unless there's a reason to do otherwise, it's probably best to begin at the front of the line and walk toward the back," Howard suggested. "That way, you won't miss anything accidentally. You can keep an eye out for the man you're looking for, and if you notice any items you think might be cursed or haunted, tell me, and I'll write it in my notebook along with the owner's name. Once you've done that, I can take you to the area where the large pieces are being reviewed."

Simon nodded to the small duffle that he handed off to Vic. "I asked Priscilla to pick up salt and iron to keep us a little safer with the ghosts around. In case we need it."

"If a ghost shows up and gets the drop on me, hurl salt directly at him—it's got to touch him to work. Swing the crowbar through him to dispel him," Simon told them.

"Works for me," Vic said.

"Just so you know, guards are stationed at intervals nearby," Howard said as they walked toward the queue. "They're supposed to be inconspicuous. Even without your suspect, it's a good idea to have security when people are bringing in potentially priceless antiques."

Vic kept his attention on the area around them, scanning for danger. Having the salt and iron made him feel better than going in bare-handed.

"Here." Simon paused next to someone carrying an unremarkable, embellished statue of a shepherdess, which looked gaudy to Vic's eye. "There's no spirit, but I'm picking up a heavy sense of despair. A cleansing would help," he said quietly. Howard obligingly wrote down the item in his notebook.

Simon strolled slowly alongside the line of eager, hopeful people, eyeing the treasures they clutched in their arms, making sure he came within the same proximity of each piece. He stopped again halfway down the queue. "The music box," he said with a nod. "There's a ghost with it. Low energy, but still present. Taking home a hitchhiker is never a good idea."

They worked their way down the line, which continued to grow minute by minute. Vic guessed that there were hundreds of items—and the queue hadn't been closed to newcomers yet.

Simon moved slowly, and Vic knew he was making sure that he didn't overlook anything. With so many objects crowded close together, it had to be taking all of Simon's concentration to hone in on an individual piece. Vic mentally made a note to offer ibuprofen as soon as they got back to the room since he figured Simon's head would be throbbing.

It was nearly noon by the time Simon made his way to the end of the line and then got a chance to check those with large items. Despite morning sex, early breakfast, and strong coffee, he looked exhausted.

"Is that everything?" Simon asked. "Is the queue closed for today?"

"Yes," Howard told him. "They're not taking any more items in the appraisal line today, but people with tickets for the audience can still come in. And we're telling people that if they notice anything that seems amiss, tell a staff member."

They moved to the main gate and watched as the audience for the taping filed in. Simon didn't see anyone who resembled Taylor, and he worried that they might have missed him.

"That should be everyone with tickets for today," Howard said when the gate rush turned to a trickle. Our folks will still keep an eye on the cameras, but it should be safe for you to get some lunch."

Howard led the way to another area set aside as a temporary quick-grab cantina. "It might not be the fanciest fare, but there's coffee, boxed lunches, and bottled water," Howard said. "Just show your badge. It's only for the event staff, so please don't take food out."

"Can you stay?" Vic invited him, but Howard shook his head.

"I'll eat later. I need to go help my team. Don't forget to check with Priscilla about the badge photos."

Simon thanked Howard and made sure to trade contact informa-tion while Vic went to get food. By the time he came back with a tray holding two coffees, two boxes, and two bottles of water, Simon had nabbed them a place at a table with enough privacy to talk.

"What did you think of the pieces?" Vic asked as he added mayo to his turkey sandwich and removed the lettuce.

"It was better than I expected," Simon replied as he picked off onions and smeared mustard onto the bread. "I thought there'd be more haunted items or ones with bad vibes. Glad I was wrong."

"We still don't know where the coins are—or even if Addison Taylor is our guy," Vic pointed out over a mouthful.

"True—but it's the best lead we've got. The stuff Father Andrews turned up is pretty wild, too. The sixth earl might have been a piece of work, but Ward seems like a decent guy. He certainly doesn't deserve to be hurt by Jeremiah's ghost for something that happened hundreds of years ago." Simon stopped to take a sip of his water.

The boxes included a bag of chips—'crisps'—an apple, and a 'bis-cuit.' Even though the fare was simple—a choice of cheese or turkey sandwiches—the bread tasted fresh baked, and Vic bet that the cookies came from the castle dining room's kitchen.

Vic tuned into the conversations around them, but no one was talking about anything except getting ready for the event. "Everything seems to be going pretty smoothly. I don't hear anyone complaining loudly—which is a plus."

Simon crunched a crisp. "The earl seems to run a tight ship with good people. And as far as I can tell, the staff like working here. More reasons to keep the ghost from punishing the wrong earl."

Vic had been hungrier than he expected, and they both made short work of their lunches. He kept his gaze sharp afterward as they walked over to meet Priscilla, but he didn't see Train Guy among the busy set-up teams, and nothing set his finely-honed "cop senses" into high alert.

Priscilla had left word at the reception desk for them to be brought back to a conference room, and they soon found themselves seated at a large table covered with copies of badge photos.

"I worked with some staffers to go through all of the crew and vendor IDs." She gestured toward the papers that littered the tabletop. "We eliminated the obvious misfits to narrow the search."

Priscilla looked to Simon. "Could your ghost jump bodies and possess a different person?"

Simon frowned. "Theoretically—but doing that wouldn't usually be easy or quick. And it would work best if the host was willing or at least predisposed to the same feelings of anger and resentment. Forcing itself on an unwilling host would take an enormous amount of energy. We're talking ghosts, not demons."

Priscilla nodded. "Okay. That's good. Then we're still looking for Addison Taylor."

Simon chewed his bottom lip as he looked over the photos, a sure tell, Vic knew, that his partner was deep in thought. "Taylor can't change his appearance too dramatically, or someone will question his badge—assuming that he's trying to get in as a vendor and not a member of the audience."

"Right," Priscilla replied. "The badge checkers are on high alert, so they'll be even more careful than usual. We have to have tight security because of the valuable antiques. But we also want people to come and watch the show be taped and shop the fair. It's a tough balance."

Vic flipped through the stack of photos. He narrowed it down to three, but none were a clear match. "Is there any way we can slow the entry on these people, just long enough to make sure they aren't Taylor?" He slid the photos toward Priscilla.

"Good eye, detective. We thought these were the most likely as well," she said.

"Are the entrances going to be handled the same way tomorrow? Vic and I could hang out after we check the queue and watch people come in; we might spot him. Same for the antiques fair, once we walk through the vendor tent," Simon said, looking to Priscilla.

"I can arrange for you to be near the gates—but that's still a lot of people going by."

Vic and Simon exchanged a glance. "I think we're out of options at this point. If Taylor comes in with the general public, he won't have as easy access to the behind-the-scenes areas where he'd assume the earl would be easier to attack."

"And we haven't publicized the changes to the earl's schedule that will make him less of a target. Except for the fake meet-and-greet—can I say again how much I don't like using Ward as bait?" Priscilla replied.

"None of us like that, and with luck, we won't need to use it, but it was his idea," Simon pointed out.

"Still doesn't mean I have to like it," she grumbled. "I don't want him to get hurt."

"Maybe we can wrap this up in a way where no one gets hurt. That's the goal," Vic assured her.

Simon shuffled through the photos, then pushed them away with a sigh. "Today is the first day shooting the show. I guess we'll see what happens—and hope all our preparations are enough."

CHAPTER FIVE

SIMON

Addison Taylor was a no-show." Vic's sharp tone gave Simon a good idea of his fiancé's level of frustration.

"We covered the entrances. I would have picked up on the ghost if Addison and his haunted coins had passed our way. And you're no slouch when it comes to recognizing faces."

"Kinda goes with the detective's badge," Vic observed dryly.

"You knew what I meant," Simon replied. "I just wish I could figure out Taylor's game. He's in town for a reason—so when is he going to make his move?"

The first day of taping for *Blast from the Past* had dawned cold and gray—not surprising for late December. That didn't deter the participants—or the members of the audience who were fortunate to obtain tickets to be in the live audience while the show was filmed.

After checking the items, Simon and Vic spent hours watching the gate for cast, crew, and participants. Two of Priscilla's people kept an eye on the entrance used by the public and the castle staff. To everyone's relief, the process went smoothly—except that meant their quarry was still in the wind.

They'd had all the right pieces in place and still not caught Taylor, Simon thought, unable to stop going over the details in his head.

"Father Andrews was standing by on speed dial with the banishment spell. The earl set us up with earpieces and comm links like we were fricking CIA, for fuck's sake. We had everything we needed to shut Taylor down—salt, iron, acacia, thyme. So why didn't he show?"

"Maybe he knows we made him and he's lying low. He could have spotted you spotting him. He knows we'll expect him to make his big move when the cameras are rolling, so he switched up the plan," Vic suggested.

"There's still tomorrow," Simon replied. "Assuming Jeremiah's spirit cares about playing for the cameras. Maybe he just wants vengeance, and he doesn't care about having an audience."

"It worries me that Taylor and Jeremiah have the ability to adapt their plans." Vic paced the parlor of their room, something Simon had seen him do when important clues eluded him.

"Low-level perps and amateurs make a plan and stick with it, no matter what. They believe in the plan, and they don't pay attention to all the surrounding details. Alter the details, and their plan falls apart, which makes them easier to catch," Vic continued.

"We don't know that they adapted," Simon pointed out. "Maybe Taylor intended all along to strike on the second day—or during the antiques fair. There will be a lot more people around for the fair instead of the restricted audience for the taping. That gives Taylor more cover—and a crowd to hide in until the moment is right."

"Maybe," Vic agreed grudgingly. "But something doesn't feel right."

"Trust your gut. Your intuition is your superpower."

They'd put in a long day, after an early start to watch the gates before taping started. While the cameras rolled, Simon and Vic stayed in the background, scanning the audience in case Taylor had managed to slip by them earlier, alert in case he had an accomplice.

Once the taping wrapped for the day and everyone who wasn't castle staff or hotel guests left the area, Simon and Vic joined Ward and Pricilla in the earl's office to debrief. Everyone was on edge, tensed to respond to a threat that didn't materialize. Afterward, Simon couldn't shake the way his mood tanked.

"I know we should be grateful nothing happened," Simon mused.

"I'm trying not to doubt myself and feel like we put everyone through all this for nothing."

Vic shook his head. "That's not how security works. It's much better to avoid having an incident rather than it is to win a fight. Scaring off a perp is better than a shootout. Not having a vengeful ghost attack Ward beats doing a very dangerous, very public banishment with cameras rolling and a live audience."

Simon sighed. "You're right. I just feel like the boy who cried wolf."

"Ward went out of his way to assure you he appreciated the warning and our efforts—and he's not letting his guard down," Vic pointed out. "So quit second-guessing yourself. You saw a threat that you were uniquely able to spot, and you raised an alarm. That's what's supposed to happen."

Dinner sat heavy in Simon's belly, even though they ate late and he had been hungry. The bar food buffet made feeding hotel guests and the production crew simpler for the castle dining staff, but after such a fraught day, the fried food wouldn't have been Simon's first choice.

I wonder what dinner would have been back in the sixth earl's day. They certainly wouldn't have had chicken wings and burgers. I wonder if we'd even recognize how things worked if we went back in time—or someone from back then came here.

"Wait a second," Simon said, as that last thought gave him an idea that might change everything. "I assumed that Taylor was calling the shots. I figured that if he wanted vengeance and to call the current earl to account for what happened to Jeremiah, he'd want to make the confrontation as public as possible. But that's modern thinking—and if *Jeremiah* is running the show, he's coming at this with seventeenth-century logic," Simon reasoned out loud.

Vic cocked his head, intrigued. "Go on."

"If Jeremiah is actually possessing Taylor, then it's his plan they're playing out. We don't know how much input Taylor has—or how much control," Simon continued. "So maybe Jeremiah *doesn't* want an audience when he attacks Ward. For him, that would mean witnesses who could testify against him."

Vic nodded. "Maybe. You could be on to something."

"If I'm right, then Taylor won't make his move tomorrow, either.

He'll do it during the antiques fair when there's a crowd he can hide in instead of having an audience. That would mean he's either planning to attack at Ward's meet and greet, or he's got something else up his sleeve—which is even more dangerous." Simon felt like he was working out a jigsaw puzzle in his head, and a couple of the pieces were still missing.

"On the bright side, everyone who owned the pieces you marked as being haunted or tainted by dark energy wanted them to be cleansed," Vic pointed out. "So that gets some dangerous things out of the world that had been around for a long time. That's a win. You don't know what damage they've done."

"I guess so," Simon replied, knowing Vic was right. "I'm just waiting for the other shoe to fall."

THE SECOND DAY of the *Blast from the Past* was equally uneventful. Simon and Vic watched the entrance to the taping area like before, but there was no sign of Taylor. By every other measure, the day's event was a complete success. The audience loved the appraisals; some of the participants discovered their heirlooms were more valuable than they expected, and a few truly unusual pieces got the spotlight they deserved.

Simon checked the items that came in with the new group of participants, then watched the audience members enter at the gates. Taylor didn't show.

Ward held another debriefing after supper. To Simon's surprise, the earl didn't seem rattled at all.

"I guess I'm not surprised that Taylor didn't make a move during the *Blast from the Past* filming," Ward admitted. "It's one thing to have witnesses—and another to have your picture on TV attempting murder. Taylor must have realized that, or Jeremiah is just naturally cautious."

"Well, we had an extremely safe taping for the show," Simon replied, trying—and failing—not to feel foolish for having predicted an attack that didn't happen.

"And I'm fine with that," Ward replied. "I take the safety of the people within my walls very seriously. But I doubt we'll be as lucky tomorrow."

"You think he's been waiting for the fair to attack?" Vic asked.

Ward nodded. "Yes. I wondered at the beginning, but it made sense to apply blanket precautions. Still, I think tomorrow is when he'll strike. He might think we'll slack off being careful because nothing's happened yet. He'd be wrong." Ward's wolfish smile said he relished the confrontation.

THE MORNING of the antiques fair, Simon and Vic got up early enough to walk the grounds and inside the wall of the outer bailey. They still had their earpieces and comm links, and Simon watched as Vic made frequent comments to security as they walked.

"You know, that's really hot. I think I've got a fetish for your earpiece," Simon told him.

Vic raised an eyebrow. "Oh?"

Simon grinned, despite the way heat pooled low in his belly. "It's from watching all those action movies. The hero always has one of those earpieces when the team is going up against the bad guys."

"I imagine Ward would let us keep one as a souvenir," Vic replied with a lusty grin. "In case you want to role-play when we get home."

That idea went right to Simon's groin despite the serious business of the day. "I like how you think," he said. "Are you going to be my secret agent?"

"I thought I was already your undercover angel," Vic answered with a wink.

"Oh, you definitely are," Simon answered, smirking.

Someone spoke over the link, and Vic was all business in a second. "They're just about to start letting people in. We need to go to the gate."

"Do you think Taylor has any idea that we suspect him?"

"I've thought about it, and I don't really know how he could," Vic replied as they strode across the lawn. "He's seen you a couple of times, and you chased him. But there's no reason for him to connect you to the castle, or the current earl or the event. If Jeremiah's ghost is possessing Taylor, is there any way for the *ghost* to know?"

Simon grimaced. "I don't think so—at least, not in my experience."

"You've let a ghost possess you?" Vic sounded upset.

"Dante certainly has when he was saving our asses." Dante was a ghostly ancestor, a water witch privateer from the Revolutionary War era whose magic had helped avert crises more than once by teaming up with Simon.

Vic looked away with his jaw set.

"Please don't tell me that you're jealous—of a ghost."

The slight pause before Vic replied told Simon everything he needed to know.

"Babe—you're alive. And Dante's my ancestor. It's not sexy."

Vic turned to him with a fierce look in his eyes. "I want to be the only one inside you."

"And you are—in the only way that matters," Simon assured him. The lawn was empty all around them, giving them privacy that would vanish in minutes when the gates opened.

Vic gave a curt nod. "I know that up here." He tapped his temples. "But sometimes I'm slow to get the message here," he added, laying a hand on his heart.

"You've got nothing to worry about," Simon replied. "Now let's catch this ghost and get back to our vacation."

The big tent for the Caynham Castle Antiques Fair was filled with vendors and their treasures when Simon did his walk-through early that morning. Rows of tables displayed the items for sale, ready for the hundreds of customers who were about to stream through the gates. Fortunately, Simon found very few problem pieces, which he reported to Howard.

After that, Simon and Vic chose places on either side of the gate where everyone who entered for the fair had to pass between them.

There are so many people. Even with both of us watching closely, we can't see everyone, Simon thought.

Hats and hoodies made it difficult to be sure of faces or hair color.

Then Simon realized he didn't need to *see* to know when Taylor and Jeremiah arrived.

I should be able to sense the ghost, like I did on the train. Even if I don't get a visual on Taylor, I can tune into the energy to find him.

It seemed obvious, and Simon couldn't believe he hadn't realized the truth before. *I didn't sense him at the* Blast from the Past *event. So I'm certain he wasn't there. Now, I need to see with my gift, not with my eyes.*

Simon closed his eyes and opened his abilities.

He heard the bustle of the passing crowd. Far in the background, he sensed the castle ghosts who belonged here and had withdrawn from the noisy strangers.

Here and there among the crowd, Simon sensed the faint touch of a haunted object—probably a piece of jewelry or a "good luck" amulet carried in a pocket. He didn't pick up any danger from the faded spirits and figured that they might be attached to heirloom pieces that the owner knew came with a ghost. Those didn't worry him.

There.

Simon felt the vengeful ghost's presence like a punch to the jaw. His eyes snapped open, and his gaze swept the crowd, searching.

Hurried along by the guards, the shoppers moved quickly, rushing toward the big event tent. They jostled for position, crowding through the gate and then fanning out across the lawn.

He's here. Where did he go?

Simon felt his heart pound. *I've got to find him. I can't let him hurt Ward—or anyone else. Jeremiah has to be stopped.*

Simon pushed his gift and felt a headache start in his temples. His senses swept over the crowd, searching.

There.

Once again, he caught a glimmer of malignant power, but this time Simon reached for it, grasping with his full psychic abilities like casting a fishing line and setting a hook.

Got him.

Simon touched his earpiece. "I'm moving. Follow me. Alert Ward and Father Andrews. Taylor's here—and Jeremiah has his energy cranked up to eleven."

He didn't look back to see if Vic was behind him, trusting his partner to follow. Simon kept his attention focused on Taylor. He watched with his gift, not his eyes, doing his best not to bowl people over in front of him.

Getting closer made the headache worse. Jeremiah was a powerful ghost, and the flashes of energy leading Simon to his quarry made him wonder whether Taylor had been fully able to give consent to the possession.

Did Jeremiah force himself onto Taylor? Did Taylor have any idea what he was allowing?

If Jeremiah drove Taylor to attack the earl, it would be Taylor who would pay the price for Jeremiah's centuries-late vengeance. *Jeremiah and his wife are already dead. Getting revenge won't change that. Taylor might not be well-adjusted or happy, but he still has a chance to start over—until he tries to kill the earl. There's no way he can explain that "it wasn't really him" to the cops.*

I thought all along that we were "stopping" Taylor—but it's Jeremiah who needs to be stopped. Taylor made a bad choice to let him in, but he doesn't deserve to die for it or spend the rest of his life in prison.

We might be able to save both Ward and Taylor if we play our cards right.

Simon followed his link, weaving through the crowd. Taylor slipped behind the tent instead of inside like the rest of the shoppers. Finally, Simon caught a glimpse of a man in a black hoodie.

"I've got eyes on Taylor," Simon told the others on his link. "He's heading for the meet-and-greet."

"Looks like he took the bait," Vic replied. "We're right behind you."

The highly-publicized opportunity to meet the Earl of Caynham was a ruse, a sham intended to provide Taylor with a chance he couldn't pass up to ambush his target in a place where he might not be seen. Drawing him away from the crowd to minimize the possibility of other people getting hurt was also part of the plan, something Ward had insisted on.

The smaller white tent was set off from the others. A sign outside advertised the chance to meet the earl with the hours Ward would be available for photo ops and autographs. Priscilla had told them that Ward wasn't a fan of either activity and that she suspected he dreaded the possibility of having to make good on the offer more than being jumped by a madman.

"Where's Ward?" Simon picked up his pace to narrow the space between himself and Taylor as the other man closed in on the tent.

"Inside, with his bodyguards," Priscilla replied.

"Tell him to keep his distance—same goes for the guards." Simon broke into a full run as soon as Taylor stepped into the tent. "I can feel the power coming off Taylor—he must have the coins on him, but—I don't think they're ordinary coins."

"What—" Vic started.

"If my hunch is right, at least some of what Jeremiah dug up were Roman 'curse coins.' People who had grudges against someone would scratch curses onto bits of metal and then toss them into a well. If even some of the people casting the curses had a bit of power, you're talking about a two-thousand-year-old whammy." Simon dropped his voice as he closed in on his target.

"We're right behind you," Vic told him. Simon glanced over his shoulder and saw Vic and Father Andrews jogging to catch up.

Dealing with a vengeful spirit was dangerous enough. Stopping an angry ghost who was possessing a living person added other complications, and if the spirit powered up with the curse coins, that meant a whole new level of crazy.

Simon and Vic had spent time the night before on a video call with Simon's cousin Cassidy Kincaide, Archibald Donnelly—a powerful necromancer and friend of Cassidy's—and Travis Dominick, a strong psychic medium like Simon. Together they figured out the best way to deal with Jeremiah.

An angry, disembodied ghost old enough to have gained strength could move furniture and throw people around. It could appear and disappear, but its range of where it could manifest was usually limited to being near wherever the spirit was anchored—a grave, house, or object. A spirit without a body could be repelled with salt or dispersed by slashing through it with iron.

Possessing a body changed the rules. A ghost in a living body could no longer vanish, and while it might make its host somewhat stronger than normal, "parlor tricks" like throwing people across the room untouched didn't work. A body gave the spirit a much larger range, especially if an anchor object could be easily carried. Salt and iron wouldn't hold the ghost back as long as it remained in its human shell.

Armed with that knowledge, Simon and the others had come up with a plan to trap Jeremiah's ghost. *Let's hope Jeremiah isn't the exception to the "rules."*

Taylor burst into the tent with Simon close behind. Taylor brandished a hunting knife with a manic expression on his face and a wild light in his eyes that made it clear to Simon that Jeremiah was in control.

"Stop right there," the lead guard ordered, blocking Taylor's path to the earl.

Ward stood at the other end of the tent, flanked by four burly guards. Since they didn't know whether Jeremiah would try to leave Taylor's body, Simon and Vic had prepared the grass and the outside cloth ceiling by sowing them liberally with salt and iron filings from the duffle bag Simon left near the back of the tent. That would stop a ghost, but not a person.

Salt lined three of the four walls of the tent, and Simon trusted Vic to close off the doorway with more when he arrived. If Jeremiah left his host, the salt would drain his power and keep him from escaping. None of those precautions, however, made an armed, crazed man any less dangerous.

Vic and Father Andrews came in behind Simon and took their places on either side of the doorway.

"Put down the knife," the security guard ordered. "No one has to get hurt."

Taylor looked from side to side, frantic, until his gaze landed on Ward. "You," he snarled. "You destroyed me, took everything I had, hanged me, and pushed my wife to suicide and all for a measly handful of coins."

Ward played the role as they had coached him, buying time for Simon and Father Andrews. "That was five hundred years ago. My ancestor who wronged you is long dead. All that can come of this is ruining another man's life, the man whose body you're possessing."

"Liar!" Taylor's lips drew back over his teeth in a feral grimace.

Simon wondered whether Taylor was aware of how his body was being used as the knife flashed in the man's hand.

The guards weren't permitted by law to be armed, so no one would be going down in a hail of bullets. But given the ghost's fury and unpredictability, odds were still good someone could get hurt—especially if Jeremiah chose to shed his host before the banishment ritual took hold.

"Jeremiah Keene. Stand down," Simon commanded. Behind him, Father Andrews began to read the banishment while Vic stepped closer—just off to one side but slightly in front of Simon, clearly protective.

"I want him to pay for what he did to me!" Taylor shouted. The ghost was riding its host hard—Simon could see broken blood vessels in the whites of Taylor's eyes and saw a drop of blood start from the man's nose. *If we can't get Jeremiah to let go of him soon, Taylor might not make it.*

The security guards formed a wall between Taylor and Ward. Vic and Simon blocked the tent exit, and as Father Andrews read the litany, Jeremiah's ghost grew more agitated.

"Stop saying that! Stop it!" he screamed, lunging as if he intended to attack the priest.

Father Andrews continued without missing a beat as Simon and Vic moved to keep Taylor from getting closer.

"Drop the knife," the lead security officer ordered. "This doesn't have to get any worse."

"You don't...he can't...I won't," Taylor looked like he was spinning out of control, turning one way and then the other like a trapped animal.

Father Andrews's calm voice and the rhythm of the banishment rite provided the counterpoint to Taylor's growing meltdown.

Taylor began to shake, and he fell to the ground, twitching and jerking. His eyes rolled back in his head like he was having a seizure. The lead security guard started to move toward him, but Vic gave a sharp shake of his head.

"Jeremiah Keene—you are no longer welcome in your host form," Simon ordered as the litany continued in the background. "Let go of

Addison Taylor's body and do no harm to anyone. Move on—and go in peace."

Taylor convulsed, and a scream tore from his throat before his body dropped back, pale and still. The only sound was Father Andrews's patient chant.

"Don't move," Simon warned, with a sharp glance toward Ward and his guards. "Stay in the salted area. He's not gone."

If Vic and Father Andrews followed the plan, they had salted the doorway and the area just outside as they entered, trapping Jeremiah's spirit inside the tent. Salting the ground inside meant that without possessing a body, his ghost couldn't grow more solid for long.

The temperature dropped until Simon could see his breath, and a rush of wind made the walls of the tent bulge as the ghost raced from side to side and then to the tent roof, trapped at every turn by the salt.

An enraged shriek tore through the air, and invisible hands grabbed Simon's shirt, lifting him off his feet. Vic charged forward, only to be thrown several feet across the tent.

Jeremiah's ghost tightened his grip on Simon, marshaling its energy to try to force its way inside his mind.

Simon fell back on training and long experience to still his thoughts and center himself in his abilities, drawing on the energy of the protective amulets he wore—the silver bracelet and spelled woven wristlet, iron and silver medallions on a chain around his neck, a polished onyx disk in the pocket of his jeans, and the loose salt tucked into his jacket. Dimly in the background, he heard Father Andrews chanting and Vic's worried shouts, but he did not dare let his concentration falter.

He felt a rush of air, and then Jeremiah let go so abruptly that Simon would have fallen if Vic hadn't been right next to him to grab his shoulder. He saw the iron crowbar in Vic's hands and realized that his fiancé had dispelled the ghost to break its hold.

"Thanks," he managed. They all looked around the tent, wondering where Jeremiah would strike next before the ghost grabbed Vic and shoved him out of the way.

"I will not channel your spirit," Simon swore. "You do not have permission to enter anyone in this tent. Let go of your grudge and move on to your rest."

Simon staggered as Jeremiah's spirit pushed him hard. Vic swung the crowbar through the air in front of Simon, and Jeremiah screamed at the touch of the iron.

"Can you hurry it up, Father?" Vic yelled to the priest, who continued at the same steady pace.

Simon turned his attention to Father Andrews and realized where he was in the litany. The priest was close to the end of the banishment rite, which probably made Jeremiah's spirit desperate to complete its mission before it was sent into the afterworld.

"What the bloody hell?" The lead security guard stared at a spot just to Simon's right where a fine mist formed, gradually taking the shape of a man.

Jeremiah Keene looked like he had spent weeks in a dungeon. His unkempt hair framed a too-thin face with crazed blue eyes and sharp cheekbones. Malice and fury glinted in his eyes, and the set of his jaw and hard line of his thin lips suggested that all the fight hadn't left him yet.

"You robbed me of my vengeance. I will take something of yours."

Jeremiah's ghost rushed forward, knocking Vic down. The ghost slammed Vic's arm to the ground to jar the crowbar out of his hand.

Vic bucked and fought as Jeremiah wrapped strong, icy hands around Vic's throat and tightened his grip.

"Get away from him!" Simon roared. Gathering his energy, Simon *pushed* Jeremiah away from Vic. Vic sucked in air and immediately rolled to retrieve his weapon. He rose in a crouch, ready to strike. At the same time, Simon envisioned a thin, strong vine wrapping itself around Jeremiah's wild ghost. He sank all of his psychic ability into that visualization to make it as real as possible.

"…in the name of Raphael and all the archangels, by the power of Michael and the sainted host, and by the authority of the Maker, Counselor, and Sustainer—you are banished, foul spirit, from this mortal realm. Journey through the vale to find the destination that awaits you. *Dominae expuere. Audi nos!*" Father Andrews finished the rite.

With a final shriek, Jeremiah's image trembled, then peeled apart, spiraling away in misty strands as if an unstoppable force sucked it into the void.

No one spoke for a moment.

"Is he gone?" Ward asked, steady but unnerved.

"Yes," Father Andrews answered. The priest looked tired but otherwise appeared unflustered.

Simon nodded. "I agree. I saw the spirit pulled away. He's moved on."

Vic rose from his crouch and scanned Simon from head to toe, looking for injuries. Simon couldn't look away from Vic's throat, where Jeremiah's grip had left red fingerprints that were already blooming into bruises. Vic met his gaze with a nod, reassuring him that despite the marks, he was okay.

Security guards closed in, and their captain handcuffed the still-unconscious Taylor.

Ward crossed to stand beside Simon, Vic, and Father Andrews. "What about him?" he asked with a nod toward Taylor.

Simon sighed. "Jeremiah's gone, so Addison Taylor is one hundred percent himself. I doubt that he could sell a jury on ghost possession, but he might get leniency from a psych eval."

Ward nodded. "That's up to the police. I'll have to press charges, but I can ask for leniency if the situation warrants. If he hadn't brought a knife…"

Simon looked down at Taylor and wished that he'd had the chance to go through the man's pockets. He doubted that the guards would allow that, and Simon didn't want to endanger the legal case.

He turned to Ward. "I believe that when the police check what Taylor's carrying on him, they'll find small medallions roughly the size of coins with scratches on them. If my hunch is correct, what Jeremiah found in that well were Roman curse coins—very potent ones. The cops may need to hold them for a while as evidence, but it would be safest if you can lay claim to the coins eventually so they can be properly secured."

In the background, the security chief had called in the assault to the police and asked for an ambulance to transport Taylor for medical and psychological evaluation.

"Do you think Jeremiah's ghost intended to kill Taylor?" Ward looked spooked and fascinated.

"I don't think Jeremiah cared, as long as he could take his revenge. So he may not have meant to injure Taylor, but the thought of it didn't deter him either," Simon replied.

"Thank you," Ward said, looking in turn from Simon to Vic to Father Andrews. "If we hadn't known about the danger and he had made his move in a more public place, a lot of people could have gotten hurt."

"Thank you for believing me," Simon replied.

"All in a day's work," Father Andrews answered. "Although I think I may pour my whiskey a bit heavy-handed tonight—purely in gratitude, you understand."

CHAPTER SIX

VIC

S ome shindig, huh?" Vic asked as he and Simon sat with Father Andrews and Priscilla at the wrap party on New Year's Eve.

"That's the goal," Priscilla replied. "The *Blast from the Past* taping went smoothly, the participants got excitement and glamor from the chance to show off their heirlooms, the antiquers had one-of-a-kind shopping, and no one got seriously hurt."

"I thought the earl, er, Ward, seemed to take it all in stride—considering," Vic replied.

Priscilla smiled. "That's Ward. He's made of pretty stern stuff."

Vic looked over to where the earl and his wife were making the rounds, stopping at each table to chat and express their thanks to the people who were involved in making the taping and fair a success.

He had been surprised that the wrap party guests appeared to be limited to the cast, crew, and off-duty hotel staff who had been involved in the logistics. Vic's cop cynicism had him figuring that Ward might leverage the event for publicity or political reasons, but Ward himself appeared to be the biggest fish in the room.

"Has there been any word about Addison Taylor?" Vic didn't want to ruin the party mood, but the events of the day before never strayed far from his mind.

Priscilla shook her head. "Given the holiday, I doubt he's been fully processed yet. But he's behind bars where he won't hurt anyone, thanks to the three of you."

Vic's hand started toward the marks on his throat before he forced himself not to touch. His collar hid most of the bruising on his neck, and he had summarily nixed the idea of a scarf to cover the rest.

"I am not wearing an ascot," he had told Simon.

"We're in Europe. They do things differently here. Ascots are cool," Simon had tried to convince him.

"So not."

Vic glanced over to Simon. His fiancé was talking enthusiastically with Priscilla, who seemed to be on the same wavelength for whatever they were discussing. Vic didn't need to be part of the conversation to be happy that Simon had found a new friend to geek out with.

After all the adrenaline of the last few days, Vic was content to enjoy the wine and get mellow. Although the charges against Taylor were yet to be made public, Vic suspected that the earl's involvement would ensure the case was taken seriously and handled properly.

Poor dumb bastard got more than he bargained for when he found those curse coins.

He turned to Father Andrews. "Kudos, Father, for keeping your cool while everything went down yesterday. You never even paused reading off that litany. I'm seriously impressed."

Father Andrews gave a decidedly unceremonious snort. "After nearly thirty years trying to preach over wailing babies and snoring grandfathers, not much rattles me."

Ward approached their table, accompanied by a woman with honey-blond hair. "Simon and Vic, this is Dr. Denby Alden—my better half," the earl said. "Bee, these are the friends of Erik's who kicked that ghost's arse all the way to the afterlife—with the help of Father Andrews, of course."

Dr. Alden laughed, and Vic saw how Ward could fall for such a smart, vivacious woman. After making small talk for a few minutes, Ward and Bee moved on to greet the guests at the next table.

Dinner was an elaborate buffet. A huge charcuterie offered a wide variety of local cheeses, along with crackers, spreads, olives, honey, and more. Scotch eggs, smoked salmon, and halloumi chips added more light fare.

Carving stations provided duck, pigeon, and roast beef with all the trimmings, plus mutton and rabbit kabobs. Fresh breads, crispy salads, and hot sides like new potatoes, baby beets, cauliflower cheese, and Yorkshire pudding rounded out the generous spread.

A table of desserts tempted guests with slices of cake, scrumptious trifles, apple tart, figgy pudding, and Bara Brith.

Decanters of wine and pitchers of ale from the earl's brewery were on each table, replaced by the servers who bussed the tables between courses.

Once everyone had a chance to eat, a DJ struck up music at the other end of the Great Hall, an upbeat playlist of classic songs from the fifties to the nineties that even had Vic tapping his toes.

The evening flew by, and then the earl was leading everyone outside. A huge analog clock projection on the tower counted down the minutes to midnight. Vic reached over and took Simon's hand.

"Before we leave, we still need to find the rest of the gargoyles so we're sure to kiss under the right ones," he murmured.

"You're taking this rather seriously, aren't you?" Simon asked, amused.

"I don't want to take anything for granted, ever. And if we can get a blessing from a lucky stone monster, that's fine with me," Vic told him.

He was well aware of the bruises on his throat and how that situation might have ended with one of them badly hurt—or worse. Danger was always part of Vic's detective work, and Simon dealt with a whole different level of evil. Vic had his sights set on retiring with gray hair and bad knees someday, but he knew that future wasn't guaranteed. He tried not to borrow trouble and made it a habit to focus on daily gratitude—but sometimes their work reminded him of just how fragile life and happiness could be.

Simon seemed to guess his thoughts because he gave Vic's hand a squeeze. "We're here, safe, and together. With a whole new year ahead of us."

"And some hot New Year's oh-my-God-we-didn't-die sex back in the room," Vic added with a wicked gleam in his eye.

Before Simon could respond, everyone around them called out the seconds remaining until midnight.

"Ten. Nine. Eight. Seven. Six. Five. Four. Three. Two. One. Happy New Year!"

Fireworks bloomed in the clear night sky, and the bells of the castle's chapel pealed in celebration. Simon and Vic lingered in a kiss as voices rose singing *Auld Lang Syne*.

"Let's go make some fireworks of our own," Simon murmured as he nipped at Vic's earlobe. "I've got some ideas how we can ring in the new."

FAE-TED MATES
A KINGS OF THE MOUNTAIN NOVELLA

By Morgan Brice

CHAPTER ONE
GRADY

I can't believe we're really here." Grady King pulled Dawson along by the wrist to the check-in desk. "It's a real castle!"

"It's called Caynham Castle. Not exactly a surprise—it sort of looks like one," Dawson teased fondly.

"Yeah, but 'Magic Kingdom' isn't a real kingdom," Grady retorted. "Truth in advertising is rare."

The lobby was in one of several buildings along the wall of the outer bailey. Dark wood wainscoting covered the lower half of the hewn stone wall, matching the counter. A large oil painting of a man in the opulent clothing of another century hung behind the check-in desk. Grady assumed it was one of the many Earls of Caynham whose most recent descendant still owned the castle and ran it as a hotel and event destination.

The woman behind the counter watched their banter with a bemused look. "Welcome to Caynham Castle. I'm Constance. Could I have your last names, please?"

Grady plunked their joined hands onto the counter so that the matching rings showed. "King. My *husband* and I have the honeymoon suite."

"Theatrical much?" Dawson joked. "She's seen married folks before, I'd wager."

"*We've* never been here before or been married before. Don't dim my joy." Grady knew he was being over the top, but everything about the trip had his excitement cranked up to the max. *Honeymoon. England. Castle—and our own suite. Vacation. And no monsters for two whole weeks.*

"He had a lot of coffee on the flight," Dawson told the woman in a faux-apologetic tone. His grin made it clear that he enjoyed Grady's enthusiasm.

"You have to understand," Grady confided in Constance, "we've had several friends who absolutely loved their stay here. They told us plenty about the castle. I want to find all the gargoyles."

"Let's get you checked in so you can deposit your luggage and go hunting," Constance said with a smile.

Grady's eyes widened. "I didn't mean hunting them—" He snapped his mouth shut, realizing that she hadn't meant their kind of monster hunting. Dawson subtly elbowed him in the ribs, but his unspoken message was clear.

Don't freak the mundanes.

"Grady and Dawson King." Grady tugged a bit on their joined hands, loving how the matching gold bands caught the light.

"Ah yes, here's the reservation. And it seems as if your friends have sent some welcome gifts. There's a package from Teag Logan and Anthony Benson, one from Erik Mitchell and Ben Nolan, and another from Simon Kincaide and Vic D'Amato."

Her tone shifted as she read the names, and her eyes widened. "Oh. Oh, my. Are you all in the same business?" She dropped her voice. "Do we have a ghost problem again?"

Dawson laughed. "Yes, we're all in the same 'business,' but Grady and I are off duty. This is strictly vacation," he assured her.

Grady had wondered if someone would make the connection, but he hadn't expected it to happen so quickly. Apparently their friends made an impression.

"That's good." Constance recovered her composure. "Things got rather exciting when they visited, although the earl was grateful for their help."

They finished checking in, and Constance gave them the key to their suite in the Bride's Tower. "You won't want to miss dinner in the Great Hall—the food is wonderful. If you want a snack beforehand, the Lady Neville Tea Room is a real treat. And, of course, once you're settled, you can take a stroll into Caynham-on-Ledwyche and explore the town."

They thanked her and followed the map she gave them to find their suite.

"I can't believe it looks so real," Grady said, turning his head one direction and then the other to take it all in.

"That's because it *is* real," Dawson said with a chuckle.

"Forgive me for being so American," Grady snarked. "First off, we don't have stuff this old back home. We slap a plaque on anything that lasts for a measly hundred years. And second, this actually looks like the castles in the movies. Thick stone walls. Turrets. Gargoyles," he added, pointing to one of the decorative carvings and pulling Dawson into a quick kiss.

"For luck," he said. "The legend says that if we kiss in front of the original gargoyle our love will last forever."

"Which one's the original?" Dawson looked around.

"No one knows, so we'll just have to find them all and do a lot of kissing to make sure."

Several towers and the Great Hall sat at one end of the inner bailey, with the castle's chapel off to the side.

"I can imagine what this looked like done up for the holidays with a huge Christmas tree," Dawson said. "It's beautiful right now without any special decorations."

"I picked up a map of the grounds at the desk." Grady waved the brochure. "There are a couple of rooms that have been re-done to look like they did back in the day, and outside the wall, there's a very romantic folly."

"Folly?" Dawson sounded perplexed.

"It's like a fancy gazebo with a statue," Grady told him. "Somewhere to sit and look out over the lawns. Although that would be pretty cold right now."

"Simon and Vic said there's a huge fireplace in the Great Hall and couches where we could curl up and read," Dawson said. "That sounds like it's worth the plane fare all by itself."

"Don't you want to explore? It's no colder here than back home." The mountains of North Carolina got their share of snow and winter weather.

"Of course I want to go into town," Dawson replied. "There's a pub, a brewery, a distillery, and another tea room. Plus other stuff."

Grady laughed. "You travel on your stomach." His growled just then. "I guess we're late for a meal, no matter what the local time is here."

Their suite was on the second floor. While the tower itself was centuries old, the furnishings were reproductions of the seventeen hundreds. A four-poster bed and a huge wardrobe nearly filled the bedroom, while the sitting room had a sofa with high-backed chairs on either side of the fireplace.

On a narrow table along the wall sat three ice buckets with bottles of champagne and three boxes of chocolates nearby, each with gift cards.

"We have the best friends." Grady gestured to the presents. "More thank-yous to write when we get back!"

Oil paintings of landscapes and people Grady assumed to be the earl's relatives hung on the walls. A tall bookshelf held hardback versions of classics and recent bestsellers. The large armoire hid a big-screen television, and another cabinet had a minibar and a coffee maker.

Grady loved the mix of old and new. He dove onto the bed and starfished his arms and legs. "Look! It's got bedcurtains just like in the Scrooge movie."

"You are a total goof." Dawson pounced onto the bed to join him.

"Yeah, but I'm *your* goof." Grady raised his left hand and wiggled his fingers to draw attention to his ring. "You're stuck with me now."

"I wouldn't have it any other way." Dawson leaned in to kiss him slow and deep. Grady kissed back, loving how intoxicating it felt to make out with his husband.

I've known you my whole life, been in love with you since before I understood what that really meant, and you still make me weak in the knees. I hope this lasts forever.

Grady's stomach growled again, and Dawson pulled back with a grin. "Much as I'd love to stay in bed, we might starve to death."

"If you insist," Grady huffed an exaggerated sigh. "But let's not be out too late tonight. We've got jet lag, and I want to break in this bed in proper honeymoon style."

"Oh, don't worry—I'm on board with that." Dawson stole another kiss before hopping down from the high mattress. "Let's wash up, have a look around, and maybe try out that tea room since it's a while until dinner."

"I want to eat pastries like the ones they make in that baking show." Grady sat up and headed for the bathroom to wash his face and change into a fresh shirt.

"Which we've only watched a dozen times."

"You never know. Someday I might want to bake one of those desserts for you," Grady joked. "In between hunting werewolves and ghouls."

"We're off duty, remember?" Dawson came up behind him in the bathroom and wrapped his arms around Grady. Their hips snugged together, and Grady felt Dawson's half-hard bulge against his ass, a promise of things to come.

"You know the castle's haunted, right?" Grady wiggled back against Dawson, making a promise of his own.

"Teag said the regular ghost is harmless. And since she's mentioned in the brochure, I don't think the earl would be pleased if we banished her."

"True. I'm just as happy to leave all the supernatural stuff to the British hunters. Except for that faerie thing you promised Uncle Denny," Grady said.

"You mean reaffirming our family's accords with the fae for another generation to bind the hellhounds on Cunanoon Mountain?" Dawson raised an eyebrow.

"Yeah, that."

The King family had been monster hunters by royal decree in their native Wales before the American Revolution. They received a land grant from King George III in Western North Carolina and a warrant to keep their lands and surrounding territory free from supernatural threats. An ancient family agreement with the fae provided additional protections, as well as binding the hellhounds for whom Cunanoon Mountain, the King family's home, was named.

"I've always wanted to see Wales," Grady said. "But handing off a ritual gift to seal the accords with the fae gives me the jitters. Especially after—"

"You ran into a rogue fae, and his own kind dealt with him—far more harshly, I imagine, than we would have," Dawson reassured him. "Another reason for us to stay on their good side."

Grady let his head fall back onto Dawson's shoulder. "I know," Grady replied. "I can't help that it makes me nervous to be around them. They're powerful and have bad tempers. No matter what Uncle Denny says, I'd rather steer clear of them."

Dawson pressed a kiss to Grady's neck. "How about we don't think about the trip to Wales right now? We have a castle and a village to explore, and we aren't due to go there for a couple of days. Then we'll come back and finish our honeymoon like we planned. And don't forget the Valentine Dance."

Grady believed Dawson's assurances, and he knew that Denny wouldn't have intentionally sent them on a dangerous mission. But his own experience with an evil fae left a lingering fear that had not faded in the months since the attack. *We have to present the gift, and then it will be done. I'm not going to let one afternoon ruin our honeymoon by worrying about it.*

"Okay. You're right. I've got a plan. Let's go eat, explore, and then come back and fuck like bunnies."

Dawson grinned. "I like the way you think."

Grady changed out the T-shirt he had worn on the plane for a fresh one and pulled a red sweater over the top. "Do you think the sweater is dressy enough? This is my best pair of jeans. I brought a jacket for dinner if it's required. It's just—back home a T-shirt and flannel works pretty much everywhere."

"Back home, anything that isn't camo or Carhartt is almost semi-formal. You're handsome no matter what you wear," Dawson assured him. "I'm going to grab a sweater too. I think it will be fine. I'm sure if there was a strict dress code the guys would have told us."

When Dawson and Grady weren't hunting monsters, they worked in the family auto body business. Their work and the rural area where they lived didn't require fancy clothes, so the honeymoon had been a good reason to add some upgrades.

"You clean up real well," Grady teased with an appreciative once-over. "Of course, I think you look best naked."

"You might be biased." Dawson reached over and gave Grady's ass a playful squeeze. "Come on. If we don't get going, we'll end up back in bed, and I don't know whether the castle has room service. I'm starving."

The castle's tea room was as charming as Grady had hoped. White tablecloths and linen napkins gave it a posh feel, with the castle's crest on the plates. Oil portraits and paintings of the castle hung on the walls. They ordered a selection of small sandwiches, bite-sized pastries, and two pots of steaming tea from the café's list of proprietary blends.

"I'm glad dinner is late," Grady said when the three-tiered silver and porcelain etagere arrived at the table. "They're all little, but there's still plenty to share."

"We'll walk it off going into town," Dawson promised, reaching for one of the chicken salad sandwiches, cut into a triangle with the crusts removed.

"I believe in eating dessert first." Grady took a petit-four and popped it into his mouth, savoring the taste. He licked the icing off his lips and liked the way Dawson's eyes tracked his tongue.

"Maybe we can get some of those to go." Dawson's voice dropped into a huskier tone. "I have ideas."

"Hold that thought." Grady gave a flirty smile. "You have ideas—and I have plans."

Dawson looked around at the many portraits that hung on the tea room's walls. "Are all these people the earl's relatives?"

"Actually, yes," the lady behind the counter replied. "You'll see a lot more around the castle—there have been plenty of generations and extended family in nine hundred years."

She came around to the front of the glass bakery cabinets full of cakes and cookies. "I'm Elisa. I've been working in the castle most of my life. After a while, you start to recognize the portrait people like old friends even though they've been dead for centuries."

"Any good stories?" Dawson asked.

Elisa laughed. "Oh, plenty! They might have been nobles, but they had all the same real-people problems that most folks have. The couple in that painting are Henry and Meredith. They fell in love as teenagers and remained smitten even when circumstances separated them."

"Warring families?" Grady asked.

"Actually, no. They were cousins. That wasn't the problem—it's pretty common with royalty and the nobility," Elisa replied, missing the glance that passed between Dawson and Grady. "They were pledged by their parents to marry other people for political alliances, but Henry and Meredith eloped, causing a political mess."

"I'm guessing they were forgiven since their portrait is back on family territory?" Dawson asked.

"As it turned out, the partners chosen by the parents weren't good choices. One of them turned against the crown and was hanged as a traitor, and the other lived a short, scandal-ridden life. So in the end, Henry and Meredith were forgiven and welcomed back into the family —and the tea room," Elisa said with a smile.

Dawson reached over to take Grady's hand. "Thank you for the story. Makes me feel like I know them."

"Any time! I know the backstories of most of the castle paintings. Free stories with every cup of tea." Elisa grinned.

They finished the sandwiches and pastries, then savored the two different flavors of tea before bundling up for the walk into Caynham-on-Ledwych. Overcast skies made it seem later, and the picturesque gaslight street lamps glowed in the light fog.

"We'd have fit right in with Henry and Meredith," Grady joked, "and the royals, even though we're not cousins by blood. But hey— nice to know there's precedent."

"There's plenty of precedent in North Carolina too. Not illegal, even if your dad hadn't been adopted," Dawson replied and rolled his eyes.

Grady and Dawson had been raised like cousins. Grady's father had been adopted as a child by Dawson's grandfather when his hunter parents were killed. Which explained the lack of family resemblance.

Dawson was just over six feet tall with a lean, runner's build. His dark hair and deep-set, dark eyes were a contrast to Grady, who was square-jawed, blond, and blue-eyed, and had a more muscular, compact build.

They always knew they weren't blood-related and fell in love in their teens. Their attraction survived a rocky few years when Dawson was deployed, and when he returned, they finally decided to stop fighting fate and make a permanent commitment.

"Towns that looked just like this have been in so many books and movies." Grady took in the village and bumped shoulders with Dawson as they walked. "I'm sure people here feel the same way when they go to New York City—like it's just a pretend place everyone uses in stories."

"I've really got to take you off the mountain more often," Dawson joked. "But I agree—I feel like we walked into a Hallmark movie, and it's not even Christmas."

The damp cold reinforced everything Grady had ever heard about English winters. Still, it didn't seem to bother any of the locals, whose heavy coats and knitted scarves, mittens, and hats protected them from the weather.

The town's buildings reflected a variety of ages and styles, including a few with thatched roofs. The smell of woodsmoke hung in the air and plumes rose from the chimneys. Merchants wooed shoppers looking for romantic gifts with window displays full of hearts, flowers, and candy.

A charming Valentine's-themed marketplace in the center of town caught Grady's eye. "Let's take a look," he urged, dragging Dawson toward the covered stands that sold craft items and specialty baked goods. They paused in the heated tent to drink tea and nibble cookies. After that, Dawson and Grady wandered through the rest of the market, picking up a few small handmade items to take home.

"There's the bookstore Simon mentioned," Grady said, making a beeline. Cadwell's looked like the kind of place a person would be as likely to find a real grimoire as the latest hot thriller. He paused when they walked inside to take a deep breath, redolent with the scent of paper and bookbindings.

"Are you looking for something in particular?" A short, bald fellow in a plaid shirt, sweater vest, and corduroy pants asked from behind the counter. Grady could have sworn he wasn't there a minute ago. "I'm Ptolemy Cadwell. The store is a bit of a maze, so while browsing is encouraged I can also direct you."

"Anything about the fae?" The words popped out of Grady's mouth before his brain caught up. Dawson gave him a warning glance, but Grady was on a roll. "Folklore, mythology—real stuff, not fiction."

"*Real stuff*," the man mused as Dawson pinched the bridge of his nose in exasperation. "Well now, that's not a request I get often. Any particular type of fae?" His sharp glance told Grady that the store owner knew his subject and might not chalk the tales up to fantasy.

"Welsh." Grady gave what he hoped was his best disingenuous smile. "Since we're so close to the border."

Cadwell didn't look fooled at all, but he didn't press the issue. "Follow me." He guided them into the maze of high, tightly packed bookshelves and long, narrow aisles. Dawson gave Grady a look, clearly not pleased at the choice of topic. Grady shrugged in reply, following his instinctive curiosity.

Grady glanced at the titles as they wove their way deeper into a store that seemed bigger on the inside than it looked from the street. They had left the bestsellers and self-help books behind in the front of the store, walked past the fiction and non-fiction, and came to a stretch of shelves with leather-bound volumes with yellowed pages.

A tingle slithered down Grady's spine, making him wonder just how "real" the magic might be in these books. Cadwell stopped in front of a shelf and pulled out two slim volumes although Grady had no idea what organization system let him keep track of the thousands of titles.

"These are said to be the most authoritative on the subject," the store owner said. "Mind you, I'm not vouching for their authenticity, and any actions you take are on your own heads. But you asked—and this is what we have." He peered at Grady over his reading glasses. "It pays to be wary around the Fair Folk. They aren't like you see in the movies."

"I'll take the books." Grady ignored Dawson's surprised glance. The two books were covered in worn leather with deckled page edges, and from the symbols etched into the binding, Grady felt certain these were hunter-quality lore.

He paid for his purchases, thanked the store owner, and followed Dawson out to the street. "What?" he asked defensively. "Forewarned is forearmed and all that."

"You don't think Uncle Denny told us everything we'd need to know?" Dawson looked at the plain brown paper bag like it held snakes. "I'm totally against changing up his instructions based on some used bookstore lore."

Grady sighed, eager to make peace. "I'm not trying to second-guess Denny. Of course we'll do things his way. But after what happened before, with the attack, I feel better being overprepared. I've already read all Denny's books on the subject. But he didn't have these."

"Maybe they're not solid resources," Dawson replied.

"Maybe. But we're in England, a stone's throw from Wales. Maybe they've got information here that we don't have back home. It can't hurt to look."

Dawson didn't seem to want to argue either. "Okay. Just boning up on the subject can't hurt." He gave Grady a cheesy grin. "Although I'd be *up* for a different sort of boning—"

Grady glanced around them, didn't see anyone paying attention, and gave Dawson a quick peck on the cheek. "Definitely taking a rain check on that for after dinner."

They peered into shop windows, enjoying the Valentine's Day

theme. "We need to indulge in lots of chocolate while we're here," Grady said. "Everyone says it's better than back home."

"Higher milk fat," Dawson replied. "Saw that online. I figured we'd bring some back for Uncle Denny, Colt, and Knox, plus a stash for ourselves."

The next store drew Grady like a magnet. "Curiouser and Curiouser—sounds like our kind of place." He disappeared inside, knowing Dawson would follow.

"Just don't touch anything," Dawson whispered when he caught up.

"Give me some credit—I learned my lesson. And besides, that was ages ago." Two days of only being able to speak backward thanks to a hexed object had stuck in Grady's memory, even if it had happened when they were children.

"Good evening, gentlemen. Have a look around but please don't handle the merchandise—it's very temperamental." The man at the register gave them a look that made Grady feel like he'd been X-rayed.

"Just browsing," Dawson said with a polite, slightly frozen smile.

Grady wandered off, making his way between tables stacked with Victorian indulgences and Art Deco novelties, next to Georgian trifles and a few pieces he guessed were Jacobean. *Good quality stuff—definitely not tourist knockoffs. I guess when you're in a country that's been around longer, even the antiques are older.*

In hindsight, Grady couldn't explain what drew him to the glass case atop a pedestal table deep into the store. Inside were two flat pieces of stone, each the size of his palm but half as thick, with a natural hole in the middle. Next to them were odd X-shaped stones that reminded him of the jacks game pieces he had seen in Denny's junk drawer.

"You have a discerning eye."

Grady jumped at the voice and couldn't figure out how the store manager had managed to meet him here. He saw Dawson catching up from behind, looking perplexed.

"What are they?" Something about the items captivated him.

"Faerie charms," the manager said. "The large ones are adder stones. The little pieces are staurolite. They ward off dark fae—if you believe in that sort of thing."

Grady had the definite feeling that the manager was a believer. Dawson shot him a warning glance over the man's shoulder. Grady didn't need words to know his partner was thinking, *What the hell?*

"Dark fae, or all of faerie?" Grady asked. He and Dawson had plenty of questions for Uncle Denny, who'd explained the lore and the history of their agreement. But Grady couldn't help being intrigued at the possibility of getting a second opinion.

"Dark fae...although sometimes it can be difficult to tell the difference," the manager warned. "Fair Folk don't think like mortals. Their reasoning is different. Even when they don't intend to be malicious, harm can be done because we're so...breakable."

"How much?" Dawson's voice surprised Grady. The manager named a price much lower than what Grady had supposed. "We'll take them."

Grady looked at Dawson with questions, but a slight shake of the head kept him quiet until they were back on the street. "Why?" Grady asked. "I thought for sure after the books—"

"Because you're clearly uncomfortable with this whole thing, and I want you to feel safe," Dawson admitted. "I'm sorry I have to drag you into it."

"Like hell I'd let you go alone."

"I wish you could. But we can't—so some extra precautions can't hurt," Dawson said.

"Did you see the way the store manager looked at your ring?" Grady glanced at the twisted gold and silver band on Dawson's right ring finger, a token signifying their contract with the fae.

"You think he knew what it was?" Dawson asked.

"I wouldn't be surprised if people around here are a lot closer to the folklore and legends than in the US, even if they claim to not believe," Grady suggested.

"You could be right about that." Dawson eyed the pub a few doors down. "How about we quit shopping and go get a couple of pints? Dinner is really late here compared to what we're used to."

"Sounds good," Grady replied with a grin.

The Boar and Knight Pub didn't disappoint. Grady felt like he'd walked onto a movie set with the dark wooden beams, well-worn tables, soot-blackened fireplace, and a sign on the wall tracing the tavernkeepers back in an unbroken line to the 1400s.

"I want to have dinner in the Great Hall, but I also want to eat here some nights," Grady told Dawson, taking his hand under the table. "Get the full experience."

"We can do anything we want, Gray." Dawson used his pet name for his husband. "It's our honeymoon."

The pub's signature ale was just as good as promised, and they ordered fries—chips—with malt vinegar as a snack. Grady loved listening to the conversations around them, enjoying the local accents.

"...sounds like they're at it again."

Grady's ears pricked up, curious. Local gossip was fun since he didn't know anyone and had no stake in the matter.

"...castle's haunted, no doubt about that. I say it's pixies."

"Shh! Don't mention them, you idiot!"

"Like they wouldn't know anyhow. Someone's riled them, and now they're playing tricks."

Grady squeezed Dawson's hand, a signal for him to eavesdrop. When the men at the other table got up to leave, Grady and Dawson stayed where they were.

"Pixies?" Dawson repeated in a quiet voice. "At the castle?"

Grady shrugged. "It's not impossible. All the lore says the Fair Folk can become attached to places that are very old. I'd almost expect them around a castle."

Dawson frowned. "Sounds like they're causing trouble. Or it could be another ghost—that's a lot simpler to dispel."

"I thought we were off duty." Grady knew it wasn't in Dawson's nature to let supernatural trouble go unchecked.

"If there's a ghost, we can probably do a quick banishment and be done before breakfast," Dawson replied. "Let's give it a couple of days and see what else we hear. No need to go looking for work. We can deal with it once we're back from Wales."

After they paid their tab, they headed back toward the castle. "Hey

—that's the yarn shop and tea room Teag said was so good," Grady said. "Let's get a cup of hot tea for the walk back, and maybe get a pair of matching scarves. Teag thought the knitter had some Weaver magic in her pieces."

Grady felt a sense of peace as soon as they walked in, suggesting that Teag was probably right about the magic. "The knitting is beautiful." He stroked the soft yarn of a scarf. "The blue one would bring out your eyes," he told Dawson, holding it up to his face.

"I was thinking green would look good on you."

Grady grinned. "Then let's get them. We'll have plenty of chances to wear them back home."

They went into the tea room in the back of the shop after they bought the scarves, and emerged with steaming cups of two different blends from what they'd had earlier in the day.

"It's true what they say about the British taking their tea seriously," Grady said as they walked back to the castle, cradling their hot take-away cups for warmth.

"Denny would laugh over the little cakes and us going on about tea flavors, but he's really missing out," Dawson chuckled.

"He'll laugh—but you know he'll love them just as much as we do if we bring some back for him," Grady agreed.

By the time they entered the inner bailey, they were both cold and ready for a good meal. Dawson and Grady walked side by side into the Great Hall and paused to take in the impressive architecture. A hammerbeam ceiling vaulted overhead, with English Gothic open timber roof trusses. Hand-cut beams arched downward at intervals, embellished at the corners with intricate woodcuts. The huge, ox-roaster fireplace at one end of the room had a carved firebox and ornate mantle, and was large enough for a grown man to stand upright inside.

"Those couches look amazing," Grady said with a nod toward the comfortable seating arrangement near the fire.

"We will definitely be camping out with books before too long," Dawson agreed. "But right now, whatever they're cooking smells fantastic, and I'm hungry."

"I'm all for having a good dinner and then warming up with dessert," Grady murmured, leaning in so only Dawson could hear him. "After all, I made you a promise—and I intend to keep it."

CHAPTER TWO

DAWSON

I feel like the dishes and flatware should burst into song and dance at any moment," Grady confided after they were seated at their table.

"You have watched entirely too many Disney movies," Dawson chided in a fond tone. "Newsflash—I don't think the furniture is going to talk to you, and I have it on good authority that the earl isn't a werewolf."

"Beast wasn't a werewolf," Grady corrected. "He was cursed. And misunderstood."

"Time to just let it go."

"Very funny." Grady looked around at the dining area which took up part of the massive Great Hall. "I bet this will look like something out of a fairytale once they decorate for the Valentine Dance."

"And thanks to Denny's contacts, so will we," Dawson replied. "The tuxes he rented for us should arrive two days before the ball." He reached over and took Grady's hand. "I finally get to see you all spiffed up since we just wore suits for the wedding."

"We'll make sure to get plenty of photos," Grady promised. "And if tuxes mattered to you, Daw, you should have told me. We could have sprung for them for the ceremony."

Dawson shook his head. "All that mattered to me was making it official." He let his finger run over the gold band on Grady's left hand that matched his own.

"Your soup is ready," their server said.

Despite the fanciness of the dining room, the man was friendly and approachable, quick to explain menu items that were unfamiliar to Americans.

"Potato soup might warm me up after that walk," Grady said as the ramekins were set in front of them, along with a basket of freshly baked rolls.

They were just finishing when the server brought their meals. Dawson opted for roast beef with root vegetables in a cranberry-balsamic sauce, while Grady chose venison with a shallot chutney with mashed potatoes and mushy peas.

"I'm going to be too full to move after this." Grady eyed his plate.

"Don't tell me I'll be cockblocked by venison on our honeymoon," Dawson whispered.

"I promised dessert," Grady replied. "We just need to leave more time for...foreplay."

They lingered over dinner, letting the excellent food settle as they nursed glasses of wine and then hot cups of coffee. Grady waved off dessert, promising they'd be back again another night, and Dawson agreed, doubting he could fit another bite into his stuffed stomach right now.

"Tomorrow, I want to do the castle up right," Dawson said. "Hearing you talk about it made me curious. I know you've been studying the brochure so you can play tour guide, and I'll happily follow along."

Grady gave him a lecherous wink. "I accept personal services in lieu of a tip."

"I was counting on it," Dawson joked.

After they finished their coffee, they strolled over to the fireplace and watched the flames dance.

"If it were anywhere else, you'd notice how massive it is," Dawson noted. "It's sized for this huge room." He looked at the plump-cushioned couches and eyed the people who were curled up with books and drinks, enjoying the warmth. "Definitely putting this on the to-do list for the other days."

Grady stretched like a cat. "If we stay here, I'm going to fall asleep. We need to keep walking."

Dawson turned just in time to see a server with a laden tray stumble over an invisible barrier, sending plates crashing to the floor. A co-worker came to help, and the hapless server looked up. "I swear there was something solid that tripped me. Just like when the door slammed on Briana yesterday."

The co-worker nodded as the two cleaned up the mess. "Not doubting you, mate. The place is haunted, and someone's pissed off the ghost. We need an exorcism or something."

Dawson and Grady didn't comment until they were in the lobby, but they shared a look to show they both heard the conversation.

"Ghost?" Dawson asked when they were out of earshot.

Grady frowned and looked back toward the dining room. "Maybe, but something about it doesn't sit right with me. Although I doubt they actually need an exorcism."

"Be glad—I really don't want to tangle with a demon on vacation." Dawson remembered the overheard discussion in the pub. "Do you think it could be some kind of creature? House elf gone wrong?"

Grady rolled his eyes. "Mad that he didn't get a sock? I don't know. Maybe. An old place like this probably has a bunch of supernatural squatters, the same way a suburban house has more wild animals in its backyard than the owners ever expect."

"As long as it's just breaking dishes and not hurting people, we can afford to take our time looking into it." Dawson hoped nothing serious would arise to interfere with the downtime they had planned.

Grady stopped and turned Dawson to face him. "Hey, don't worry. We are going to have an amazing honeymoon despite faeries, pixies, gargoyles, or ghosts. It's already gotten off to a good start, and the night's still young." He kissed Dawson's nose, and Dawson couldn't help laughing.

"Let's go back to the room so I can have my wicked way with you," Dawson murmured. "Some of which involves chocolate and champagne."

"You had me at 'wicked,'" Grady teased back and gave Dawson's hand a squeeze.

Their bed had been turned down and chocolates placed on each pillow. Dawson noted that the ice in the buckets had been refreshed, and champagne glasses waited next to the chocolates.

"To us." Dawson opened one of the bottles with a loud *pop*. He poured two flutes and brought one to Grady, along with a piece of chocolate from one of the boxes.

"Open your mouth." Dawson slipped the chocolate caramel inside. Grady closed his lips around Dawson's fingers and sucked on them. He met Dawson's gaze with a knowing look.

"You're wearing entirely too much clothing." Dawson shifted as his cock chubbed. "Let's fix that." Dawson set his champagne aside and sidled closer to Grady. He ran his hands over Grady's sweater and felt a shiver in response.

"Daw—"

"I'm gonna take you apart nice and slow and warm you up proper." Dawson's voice dropped to a husky whisper.

He stepped closer, backing Grady up against the wall. Dawson lifted the edge of Grady's sweater and slipped his hands underneath it and the T-shirt, moving them slowly up his lover's chest. Dawson maneuvered them so his thigh was between Grady's legs and pressed forward enough to give them friction, making them both hard.

Dawson took in the way Grady's breath caught when he slid a fingertip oh-so-gently across his nipples, a teasing brush at first, then slow circles, and finally a light pinch to now-firm nubs.

"Daw, please—"

Dawson chuckled. "What's your hurry? I'm going to make this good for you, sweetheart." He leaned forward and kissed Grady, tasting champagne and chocolate.

Grady wriggled out of his shirt and sweater, leaving them in a pile on the floor. He closed his hand around Dawson's sweater, tugging it up. "Off. Want to see you."

"Impatient brat," Dawson murmured with a smile that promised paradise. He shucked his own top layer and then reached for Grady's belt. Dawson ran the tip of his finger back and forth just at the waistband, teasing across Grady's belly. Then he dipped inside and skimmed over the head of Grady's leaking cock that peeked from the top of his boxer briefs. He reached over to cup Grady's bulge with his other hand and rocked against him with his thigh.

Grady's head fell back against the wall, baring his throat. His eyes were closed, lips parted, heart racing, breathing quickly.

"I love getting you all wound up," Dawson murmured as he licked a stripe up Grady's neck, tasting soap and sweat. He buried his nose in the hair at the nape, breathing in the scent of shampoo and something uniquely Grady. "Maybe I'll just edge you all night, see how long I can make you wait before you pop like that champagne cork."

"God, Daw, I want—"

"I'm going to give you what you want. All in good time."

Dawson sank to his knees and unbuckled Grady's belt, then shoved his pants to the floor. He mouthed at the outline of Grady's stiff cock, tasting the pre-come that had already made a dark spot. Dawson rested his hands on Grady's hips before adding underwear to the puddle of cloth around his ankles and held Grady still as he swallowed him down to the root.

"Fuck," Grady moaned, bucking forward against Dawson's grip.

Dawson sucked and licked, swirling his tongue over the tip, burying his nose in the wiry hair at the base. Grady sank his fingers into Dawson's hair but didn't try to guide him, clearly content to let Dawson set the pace.

He knew Grady was close. A few more strokes and Grady shot into his mouth. Dawson swallowed him down, then licked him clean and looked up to see Grady watching him with a flushed face and lust-blown pupils.

"You look like sin and sex on your knees like that," Grady growled.

"Just getting started," Dawson assured him. Grady kicked off his pants while Dawson stripped out of the rest of his clothing and led Grady to the big four-poster bed. They slid between the sheets, and Dawson wrapped his arms around Grady. "You're shivering."

"The castle's cold."

"I'll get you warm." Dawson leaned in to kiss him, open-mouthed and hungry, and Grady returned the kiss with equal fervor, sliding his hands up Dawson's bare back. His hips jerked against Grady's thigh, seeking relief from his almost painfully hard dick.

"I want to open you up and watch you ride my cock," Dawson whispered, drawing back from their kiss to take in how wrecked Grady already looked, hair mussed and lips kiss-swollen.

"Don't make me wait," Grady panted. He reached for Dawson's cock, but Dawson batted his hand away.

"I won't last if you jack me, and I want to come inside you." Dawson reached for the lube he had stashed under the pillow before dinner and maneuvered Grady onto his back. Grady pulled his ankles back, spreading his legs and giving Dawson full access.

Dawson licked his lips at the view. "So sexy."

He rolled Grady's soft dick in his mouth until it firmed, as one hand fondled his balls. Dawson let his tongue rove down until he found Grady's tight rim. Between his tongue and lube-slicked fingers, Dawson worked him open as Grady groaned and begged.

Dawson's cock ached, and he knew he couldn't last much longer. "Ride me." He rolled them so Grady lay on top. "I want to see you get yourself off on my dick."

Grady kissed him and then pushed back to kneel astride Dawson. He used the lube to slick both their cocks, and then lowered himself over Dawson's hard prick.

"God, you are beautiful." Dawson watched as Grady made a show of rising and falling before taking him balls-deep.

"Like that?" Grady teased. Dawson nodded, at a loss for words.

"How about this?" Grady's hips made a slow figure eight again and again.

Dawson closed his hand around Grady's cock and started to jack him, and Grady picked up the pace until he was riding Dawson hard, angling to hit his own sweet spot on every stroke as Dawson thrust into him.

Dawson felt his climax rushing through him and arched his back, shooting deep into Grady's tight channel. Grady came seconds later, painting Dawson's chest with his come.

Sweaty and sated, Grady lowered himself close enough to kiss

Dawson. He drew one finger up through the pooled jizz on Dawson's chest and they both licked it clean.

"Told you I'd take care of dessert." Grady fell to one side and let Dawson's cock slip free.

"So good," Dawson murmured, taking a moment to catch his breath. He finally got up and went to the bathroom, returning with a warm cloth to clean them both.

"Round two, I want you inside me." Grady teased his nipples and then ran his finger down Dawson's dark happy trail.

"I will never turn that down," Dawson said. "But first, let's finish that bottle of bubbly and eat some more chocolate—gotta keep up our strength."

"ROUND TWO" waited for morning, but Dawson wasn't about to complain. When they finally got out of bed they stopped in the Great Hall for a breakfast of coffee and pastries to sustain them on their adventuring.

"I like the statue of the lovers, and the folly is as pretty as I thought it would be," Grady said as they meandered.

"I thought the rooms that were done up like they would have been in the past were interesting," Dawson agreed. "It blows my mind that all the furniture is original. They must have a gigantic storage area to keep stuff for so many hundreds of years! Uncle Denny's garage is full, and he's only been a packrat for a few decades."

"I'll tell him you said that," Grady joked.

"I tell him that every time he wants us to clean out the shed." Dawson shrugged.

On their way back to the main castle they took a detour through the chapel to check a few more gargoyles—and kisses—off Grady's list, then made a stop at the gift shop.

"We have to take something back for Denny, Colt, and Knox." Grady named their uncle, Dawson's best friend, and Grady's brother. "Preferably not anything haunted, and definitely something small enough to fit in the luggage."

"That rules out the curio shop," Dawson replied. "But the gift shop's probably safe."

They browsed the upscale souvenirs commemorating Caynham Castle. Grady picked out a Christmas ornament for Denny and a coaster set for Colt and Knox. Dawson chose a different ornament and a wine stopper for their own mementos. By the time they finished it was time for lunch, and they happily returned to the castle tea shop for more sandwiches and small cakes.

"I'm glad we're walking so much," Dawson said when they finished. "That way I can eat all the sweets I want guilt-free."

Grady gave him a lecherous smile. "I'm sure I'll want dessert again later tonight."

"Still got plenty of champagne and chocolate." Dawson bumped their knees together beneath the table.

"Did you have a nice day exploring the town?" Elisa asked when she brought their check.

"There's still a lot left to see," Grady told her.

"We're having supper at the pub, and then I want to try out the brewery and the distillery—but not on the same evening!" Dawson added.

"Those are all good choices. Be sure to poke your head in the church as well—the architecture is lovely," Elisa told them.

Dawson looked up at Elisa. "You said you've been with the castle for a long time. We've heard about the Lady's ghost, but are there any legends about faeries of any sort?"

Elisa's smile didn't waver, but her eyes shuttered. "Faeries? This is England. We've got faerie stories everywhere."

"Anything here in the castle itself?"

Elisa cast a glance over her shoulder, but the helpers behind the counter were busy with other customers. "Be careful what you say and who you talk to about the Fair Folk." She dropped her voice. "They are helpful friends, but you don't want to hurt their feelings."

"We couldn't help noticing there were some strange things happening." Grady used his most persuasive smile. "Which made us wonder if there was a restless ghost—or something else."

"I really shouldn't have said anything," Elisa replied. "Please don't quote me. Pretty much every old building here has its tales, but that doesn't mean they're true."

She took their check and stepped back. "Be sure you stop in tomorrow—we'll have some specialties on the menu for Valentine's each day until the end of the week."

They left the tea shop and headed into town. Overcast skies didn't completely dim the sun, although a cold wind reminded them that February was still mid-winter here, no matter how early spring came to North Carolina.

"Did you see how nervous Elisa got?" Dawson asked.

"Yeah, she really didn't want to say anything," Grady replied. "And I didn't get the impression she was worried about what the Earl would think or even about being quoted. She didn't want to anger... *them*," he said, clearly meaning the fae.

"Which makes me think the run of bad luck might be tied to an unhappy faerie instead of a ghost," Dawson mused. "Interesting."

"Speaking of which, I saw a sign for ghost tours. Interested?" Grady offered.

"Don't you remember what Simon told us? He said that the tour guide was a very good storyteller, but her stories were made up. The ghosts kept whispering to him about what *really* happened the whole time." Their friend Simon Kincaide was a gifted psychic medium as well as knowledgeable about lore.

"I think I'm happy with not being able to talk to ghosts," Grady said. "Okay—we can pass on the ghost tour."

"I thought we could have dinner at the pub and then sit by the fireplace in the Great Hall for a while," Dawson said. "Since we're going to Wales tomorrow, we have a little preparation to do tonight, and we'll want to get to bed a bit earlier—factoring in dessert, of course," he added with a rakish smile.

"Always leave room for dessert," Grady agreed.

"That leaves the brewery and distillery to explore after we get back, and I hear there's a bar at the top of one of the castle towers with a great view we could check out too."

"We still have gargoyles to find," Grady reminded him. "There's a candlelight concert at the chapel one of the nights and the Valentine Dance. So there's a lot of good stuff coming up."

"You know I don't care about anything except being with you." Dawson took his hand.

"I feel the same way, but a change of scenery is nice too," Grady agreed. "For example, I think the view in our room is awesome." His tone and the gaze he raked over his husband's body made it clear that he was talking about Dawson and not the landscape.

"I rather like the view myself," Dawson flirted back.

The Boar and Knight was busy when they arrived, but Dawson and Grady found a table in the back. They commented on the array of antique items displayed on a high shelf on the walls, and Dawson enjoyed the babble of voices and the melodic accents, so different from those of their home state.

"I'm going to have real fish and chips," Grady said. "I'd expect theirs to be good."

"I'm having the shepherd's pie." Dawson took another drink of the house's signature ale. "I've always wanted to try it."

Both dishes were even better than expected, hot and filling on a cold winter night. They each did a flight of the pub's different ales and bantered over which they liked best. By the time they were finished, they were warm and full, slightly buzzed, and thoroughly happy.

They joked the whole way back to the castle. The warmth of the huge fireplace in the great room melted away the chill from outside. One of the large couches was unclaimed, so they curled up to read for a while. Dawson had his e-reader in his messenger bag, while Grady had the two books he had bought in town.

"Not exactly light reading," Dawson chided.

"If we're going to meet with them tomorrow, it does the most good to read this now, not later," Grady replied without looking up.

"Anything useful?" Dawson asked after a while.

Grady frowned. "I'm not sure. But we might find clues to what kind of creature is troubling Caynham Castle. There's also a section in here about protections. We can make sure we've got what we need to be safe tomorrow."

"We don't want to show bad faith by looking like we expect to be betrayed," Dawson warned.

Grady met his gaze, and Dawson could see that the meeting worried him. "We also shouldn't be too trusting. I'd like to believe that the folk will uphold their part of the old accords and acknowledge you as Denny's proxy—and eventual successor. I *want* to believe that…but I think caution would be wise."

Dawson thought through what Grady said and then nodded reluctantly. "All right. That makes sense. Let's just keep it subtle."

Before they could get too warm and sleepy, they headed back to their suite. Dawson opened another bottle of champagne and a second box of chocolates while Grady changed into a long-sleeved T-shirt and sleep pants.

"I thought we should check over Denny's instructions again and the supplies his hunter friend gathered for us," Dawson said, putting on warm, loose clothing until they were ready for bed.

Since weapons and some of the materials they relied on would have caused a stir with airport security, Denny made arrangements for a British hunter friend to meet them at Heathrow and drive them to Caynham Castle. He had a box of everything they might need but couldn't carry onto the plane, including borrowed knives and an array of crystals and powders useful for dealing with the fae.

Dawson's phone buzzed, and he glanced at the screen. "I've got an email from Denny. It's five hours earlier for him."

Grady poured himself another glass of champagne and swiped a piece of chocolate while Dawson checked mail.

"Denny said he hopes we're enjoying our honeymoon, and he apologized for needing us to make the trip to Wales. He reminded us to follow the instructions exactly, be courteous but watch our backs, and use the protections we brought with us as well as some new things in the box he sent."

"See—I'm not the only one who believes in 'trust but verify,'" Grady joked.

"I never said I didn't think we should be careful," Dawson countered. "But we can't go in there acting like the fae are our enemy and then expect to recommit to the accords."

"Then we're both right." Grady handed Dawson a flute of champagne. "Come on—drink up! We have another bottle to finish and plenty of chocolate—and then I promised you dessert."

CHAPTER THREE
GRADY

The scenery here is so beautiful," Grady said as he and Dawson watched the landscape through the train's windows. "This doesn't have to be our only trip to the UK. We can always come back."

"There's so much to see—so many castles and museums. I'd love to visit again," Grady replied. "And honestly, traveling by rail is one of my favorite things about this trip. I've only ever been on Tweetsie's train that goes around the park. Nothing like a real railroad trip."

They bought tea and cold sandwiches from the commissary, and Grady had brought along some of the chocolates from their room. While they ate, they looked at the farms and the sheep on the hillside as they passed small towns and rural stretches.

Once in Cardiff, Dawson and Grady changed trains to take another line into the countryside. As promised, a car and driver waited to take them to the meeting spot Denny had arranged with their fae contact.

Grady's nerves made his stomach tight, and he could tell Dawson was uneasy. The driver didn't speak after he confirmed their identities and answered questions with single-word responses until they reached their destination.

"When your business is through, come back here," the driver said when he let them out at a trail that opened from the side road. "I'll take you back to the station."

They thanked him and headed into the woods. Both men wore bracelets of red string and carried the staurolite and adder stones with them for protection, along with little bags filled with egg shells, salt, and iron filings. The woods were eerily silent, and Grady wondered if the animals sensed the fae and made themselves scarce.

"Denny said that there was a big tree by itself, and that's where we should make the offering," Dawson said as they hiked. They had dressed for the weather in heavy coats, boots, scarves, mittens, and hats, and still, Grady felt a chill.

"Are we actually going to meet someone, or just make the offering and leave?" Grady knew which option he preferred, but Denny's email had been vague on that point.

"Making the right offering in the appropriate place is the key thing." Dawson kept a brisk pace, and Grady guessed his partner wanted to be finished with their task as fast as possible. "We have the name of our contact," he added, carefully not speaking the name aloud, "and I guess he'll show up if he wants to. We'll have done our duty."

"How do we know if the offering is accepted? I'd hate to come all this way and freeze our nuts off only to find that it didn't 'take' because we put the bowl a foot too far to the left or something stupid like that." Grady knew that when it came to magic—and especially the fae—details mattered.

"I guess our guy will either show up and bless us, or the liquid in the bowl will disappear." Dawson shrugged. "Denny did the ritual thirty years ago with Grandpa King. He didn't know if it would work the same way for us, or if there could be some variation. Apparently the lore was hazy about that. It might be up to our contact."

"Someone different from the one we met back home?" Grady shivered at the memory. He had been taken captive by a witch and a rogue fae who schemed to open the mounds and unleash horrors on the world. An elder fae had taken the rogue into custody and removed him from the mortal realm.

"I got the feeling they have territories—kingdoms—but what that actually means, I don't know. There are lots of stories, but very few first-person accounts." Dawson stopped and turned in a slow circle, taking in their surroundings.

"Want to bet that's the tree?" He pointed to a large oak that stood alone in a small clearing. It looked ancient. Some of its limbs bent fairly low to the ground, while others soared to the sky. The leaves had fallen, leaving bare branches against the overcast sky.

"According to Denny, this whole ritual is part of showing honor and respect." Dawson unpacked the bag he had brought with them. He took out a dozen brightly colored strips of cloth and handed some to Grady.

"Help me tie these on the lower branches. Denny called them 'clooties.' They're like prayer flags."

The cloth fluttered on the breeze, and Dawson pulled a silver wind chime from his bag, which he also hung from the tree. "Time to make the offering."

Grady watched as Dawson took out a pottery bowl. He added cream, meadowsweet, whiskey, and vanilla paste. "They like all these." Dawson stirred the mixture. "And it's a sign of goodwill."

Something growled nearby, low and deep.

"Daw—something's coming," Grady warned. He pulled his knife and stood where he could protect Dawson, who knelt beside the tree, completing the offering. Dawson couldn't stop mid-ritual, and Grady had no idea what the penalty might be for interrupting the spell.

Heavy footfalls and the sound of breaking branches gave Grady a heartbeat's warning before a huge, misshapen creature broke through the underbrush, barreling toward them.

Grady had only seconds to respond. He wished he had his gun or at least a sword. The black shuck was as large as a Saint Bernard, with matted, filthy fur and malevolent red eyes. Long fangs and sharp claws seemed more than a match for his knife, but Grady had no intention of letting it get to Dawson.

The shuck lunged, and Grady stepped into the attack, landing a vicious slash that caught the beast across the chest, spilling dark blood onto the trampled grass. Dawson kept chanting, although Grady heard the fear in his partner's voice.

Still bleeding, the shuck leapt at Grady, taking them both to the ground with a snarl and the flash of teeth. Grady bucked, trying to throw the shuck off and realizing the beast equaled his weight. He twisted away from snapping fangs and the breath that stank of sulfur and carrion.

Grady sank his knife hilt-deep between the shuck's ribs, and the creature shrieked in pain. Hot blood poured over Grady like acid on his skin, and one massive paw slashed talons across his shoulder and chest, opening deep furrows.

Dawson finished the incantation with a hoarse shout and, in the next breath, threw himself onto the shuck's back, swinging his blade to sever its head and then kicking the body away from Grady.

"Gray!" Dawson fell to his knees beside him. His panicked gaze swept over Grady, taking in the gashes and all the blood. "We've got to get you to a hospital."

"The offering—"

"Fuck the offering. I did the ritual. We were supposed to be safe. Something's gone really wrong. We need to get out of here." Dawson frantically wadded up the torn remains of Grady's shirt and pressed the cloth against the gashes. He hoped to stanch the blood, but more seeped out beneath the soaked shirt.

A brilliant light flashed, revealing an impossibly handsome, fine-featured man in a tailored white suit standing in the bloody clearing.

Dawson rose, putting himself between the stranger and Grady, knife raised. "We came to renew the accords. We have honored the agreement. Why did you betray us?"

The man held up both hands in a gesture of truce. "I didn't betray you. The shuck was sent by my enemies to strike during the ritual when I could not cross the boundary."

Grady stared at the newcomer and, in the light-headed haze of blood loss, thought he was as beautiful as an angel. Grady's wounds ached with every breath, and fever burned through him although he lay on frozen ground.

"There's poison on the hellhound's claws," the fae said. "I can take you to safety where we can heal your partner. But we must go now before we're attacked again."

"You want us to go into faerie with you?" Dawson challenged, worry clear in his voice. "It would alter the agreement. We might never leave."

"Your partner's wound cannot be healed by mortal medicine," the man said. "Trust me, or bury him."

Grady struggled to hold on, but he knew he was fading fast. He saw the conflict in Dawson's eyes, but he couldn't find the breath to speak.

"Save him. Whatever it takes."

No. Don't break the agreement for me.

Light flashed, and Grady's head swam. Everything around them changed as he fought to focus and stay awake.

Instead of the winter glade they left behind, here the plants and trees bloomed with spring flowers and bright green leaves. A soft, warm wind stirred his hair, and he lay on fresh grass that made winter a distant memory. On the other side of the clearing, beyond a small pond, sat a white cottage with high arches and large windows like something from a fairytale painting.

Dawson gripped Grady's hand so tight it hurt. "Hang on, Gray. I love you. We'll make this right."

Grady tried to reply, but words wouldn't come. He gave a weak squeeze of his hand as consciousness faded with one thought clear in his mind.

We've left the mortal world. We're in faerie. Dawson, what have you done?

CHAPTER FOUR

DAWSON

When Dawson's vision cleared, he knelt in a spring garden with Grady's bloody body clutched in his arms.

"Help him," Dawson pleaded with their host—or captor. Right now, Dawson didn't care so long as Grady stopped bleeding and woke up.

"My name is Cyfrin. I will heal him."

Dawson insisted on carrying Grady, even though he suspected the fae could lift a grown man effortlessly despite his slight appearance. He'd read enough fantasy to know that faeries and elves were more than they appeared and often not nearly as beneficent as they wished to seem.

Cyfrin led Dawson to one of the cottage bedrooms.

Dawson laid Grady down as gently as he could, alarmed that the gashes still oozed blood. Grady's pallor stood out against the bedding, and he was far too still.

"Please. If this alters our family's bargain, I will stay behind to pay the debt. But fix what's wrong, I beg you."

"Don't you know never to indebt yourself to one of my kind?" Cyfrin's face was unreadable.

"The rules don't apply when it's Grady."

Cyfrin knelt beside Grady's bed, and Dawson stepped back to give him space to work. The fae gestured, and the remnants of Grady's tattered shirt disappeared. Another motion and the blood that streaked Grady's skin also vanished, leaving the wounds raw but clean.

Dawson gritted his teeth and clenched his fists. Grady seemed to be slipping away, and nothing Dawson could control would help. He hated having Grady's life depend on this stranger, someone he knew he should not trust.

Whatever bargain the fae made with our family was for their benefit more than ours. Faeries are tricky and amoral. Their ways are too different for us to understand. I've probably broken every rule and sold my soul, but if he can heal Grady, if he keeps him alive and sends him home, I'll accept the price.

The sun moved across the sky as Dawson watched Cyfrin tend Grady's wounds. He cleaned the deep gashes and stanched the flow with a styptic compress of leaves and powders. Their host closed the ragged gashes without scarring, leaving the skin smooth and unblemished. Then he mixed an elixir to drip into Grady's mouth and a poultice to spread across his chest.

Through it all, Grady never woke. He lay still, chest barely rising and falling, far too pale.

Late into the night, Cyfrin finally stood. "The poultice will draw out the poison of the shuck's claws. The elixir sustains his body without food or drink and aids healing."

"Why hasn't he woken?" Dawson felt his heart in his throat as he looked at Grady's still figure.

"The shuck was meant for me. My enemy must have known the timing of our meeting and that I would be vulnerable moving between realms. He meant to violate the sanctity of my lands, kill those under my protection, and then kill me when I crossed over. It was a coward's strike, the plan of someone who knows he cannot challenge me directly and win."

Cyfrin managed a wan smile. "He did not anticipate having his shuck killed by two mortals before it had the chance to injure me. But since I was the target, the poison on the shuck's claws was for one of my kind, far too strong to be withstood by a mortal."

"It happened so fast." Dawson struggled to understand. "How did it get so bad so quickly?"

"That is the nature of the poison. The claws dug in deep. Had we delayed longer, your partner would have been beyond my ability to heal."

Dawson swallowed hard, doing his best not to imagine that outcome. "What about now? Will he wake up?"

"I don't know. I have no experience healing a mortal from this poison. For one of my people, a small dose incapacitates, and a large dose kills."

Dawson knew he needed time to digest the information Cyfrin shared. *Maybe all I need to understand is that the poison went hard on Grady, and we don't know if he'll wake up.*

"I'll stay with him." Dawson sat next to the bed where he could hold Grady's hand. "You can go do whatever you need to do."

Cyfrin looked from Dawson to Grady and then nodded. "I'll check on you."

Dawson didn't watch him leave, turning his full attention to Grady. He twined their fingers together and rubbed his other hand up and down Grady's arm. "I'm here, Gray. Watching over you. I'm not going to leave. No matter how long it takes."

Dawson's stomach rumbled. The elixir would meet Grady's need for sustenance, but Dawson would have to make a choice about whether to accept food from the fae. Every piece of lore warned that eating or drinking in the faerie realm meant being trapped for eternity.

That might be the sacrifice Dawson needed to make to ensure Grady's safety, but he didn't intend to accept that fate any sooner than necessary.

"We'll get out of this one, you'll see," Dawson kept up the conversation. "We always do. There'll be a way. Somehow."

Grady didn't respond. He looked peacefully at rest, but Dawson noted the shallow rise and fall of his partner's chest. Despite the medications Cyfrin had given him, Grady still looked too pale.

"Do you remember the time we took Uncle Denny's boat out on the lake without asking?" Dawson felt desperate to keep talking. He hoped his voice provided a lifeline for Grady to follow back to consciousness, and he needed to fill the silence to keep himself sane.

"We hit that tree root, sank the boat, woke a lake monster, did just about everything wrong fighting it, and still managed to win," Dawson recounted. "You figured out how to kill the monster. Denny was so mad at us, but he was also proud that we didn't die. We had extra chores all summer."

Dawson couldn't hold back a chuckle at the memory. "God, Grady, we were hellions. You and me, Knox and Colt—I can't believe it took us so long to figure things out. Denny will kick my ass for letting you get hurt. So will Colt and Knox. You don't want me to get my ass handed to me, do you? You need to wake up and save me a whupping."

He grew silent for a few minutes, feeling remorse rise. "I'm sorry, Grady, about running away when I went into the Army. I told myself I was giving you time to grow up, that I wanted to make sure our feelings for each other were real. But I was afraid that you'd outgrow your crush on me, and I don't think I would have survived that."

Dawson had joined the Army and left Cunanoon Mountain for four years, breaking both their hearts. They'd still managed to find their way back to each other, but in hindsight, Dawson realized that the suffering had been unnecessary.

"You know, Denny's going to tan our asses for making a mess of this," Dawson kept talking, swallowing hard against the catch in his voice. "He'll never send us as ambassadors again. But you were badass against that shuck. I'm sorry I couldn't finish the ritual faster. You protected me, and I let you down."

A tear rolled down Dawson's cheek, and he lifted their joined hands, pressing a kiss to Grady's knuckles. "We're supposed to protect each other, and you held up your end, but I let you get hurt. I saw that monster on top of you, trying to bite your throat, and I saw red. Denny'd have my hide. I forgot my training. All I knew was that it was trying to kill you, and I had to stop it, whatever it took."

He held their hands against his cheek. "Don't hate me for letting Cyfrin bring you here. You were going to die, and I didn't have a choice. Don't be angry. I couldn't...I just couldn't let that happen if I had any way to stop it. I wouldn't be able to live with myself."

He lowered their joined hands, and his thumb stroked circles over Grady's skin. "Those four years away from you, I was never fully me without you nearby. I functioned, but I was empty. Nothing mattered except getting home to you, making things right."

Dawson gently rotated Grady's wedding band. "We made it. We worked everything out, and we're together. So you have to wake up. You've got to come back to me. I'll wait forever if I need to, but I won't go back without you, so you have to go with me."

He didn't know how time moved here, but by his reckoning, many hours must have passed. His cell phone had no signal—no surprise. Denny would want to know how the ritual went and grow increasingly worried when he couldn't get an answer by text or email. Their belongings would be fine at the castle for the length of their stay, but if they never returned...if that happened, they'd have bigger problems than their luggage.

Dawson's stomach rumbled, and he resolutely ignored it. He'd thrown protein bars and bottles of water into his gear bag, but Cyfrin hadn't brought the bag across with them, and in the desperation of the moment, Dawson hadn't had the presence of mind to insist. They'd left their regular messenger bags back in the room at the castle, so he didn't have his e-reader. *Maybe Cifryn has a library that has books in English that he'd let me borrow. I hope I don't need to. Come on, Gray! Wake up!*

At some point, Dawson fell asleep with his head pillowed on his arm on the edge of Grady's bed, hands still entwined. When he woke, he yawned and stretched his neck, sore from the awkward position. He could just make out the first glimmer of dawn on the horizon. Once he blinked the sleep out of his eyes, he looked to Grady, hoping for signs of recovery, but nothing seemed to have changed.

I'm counting on you, Gray. Don't let me down.

"You said he would recover." Dawson knew he was being reckless, even suicidal, challenging an immortal, powerful being. "Why isn't he getting better?"

Time moved differently here, but Dawson's old-school wind-up watch still worked. By its measure, he had sat at Grady's bedside for three days and nights. Grady still barely breathed, his heartbeat almost undetectable. Dawson despaired that he would be a widower before he'd barely had the chance to be a groom.

"He's not getting worse," Cyfrin replied. "I can keep him stable—for now. I'm still trying to figure out the precise poison used on the hound's claws. Whatever toxin was chosen would have been picked to be fatal to me. Its effects on a human would be unpredictable."

Dawson glanced over his shoulder and looked through the open window to where Grady lay, then back to Cyfrin. "Why do your people want you dead?"

"It's a long story."

"I'm not going anywhere."

Cyfrin moved to sit on a marble bench beneath a flowering tree and gestured for Dawson to join him, but Dawson shook his head.

"No thanks. I want to be able to see Grady."

Cyfrin nodded, seemingly unsurprised. "You've refused food and drink. Before long, I'll have two patients."

"I'm not a fool. If I consume anything here, I'll be trapped forever."

Cyfrin smiled sadly. "If you stumbled into our realm uninvited or were tricked into entering, that would be true."

"Were we tricked?" Dawson raised his head to meet Cyfrin's gaze, angry and terrified for Grady.

"Not by me. I swear on every relic and holy sigil," Cyfrin replied. "As I told you—the attack was meant for me."

"I don't care about your faerie politics," Dawson snapped. "A rogue fae nearly killed Grady in North Carolina. But back home, with the accords, the hellhounds protect us. The hound refused to do the rogue's bidding." *That was one of the stipulations of our agreement.*

Cyfrin sighed, although Dawson wasn't even certain the fae needed to breathe. "Shucks are different from hellhounds—a technicality that matters. Striking down someone under my protection, on my territory, in breach of a long-standing accord was intended to harm me, challenge my authority, and enable the rogues to mount an insurrection."

"You're telling me that Grady was just collateral damage?" Dawson grated. He clenched his fists, knowing that here in the other realm, none of the amulets he carried held enough power to protect either of them.

"Unfortunately, from the perspective of my enemies—yes," Cyfrin replied. "I don't consider it like that, which is why they oppose me."

"The attack on us was about politics?"

Cyfrin nodded. "Yes, and the situation has ensnared you and your partner, so here we are. You have a right to be angry, but right now, my enemies are your enemies."

"Is this going to spill over to Cunanoon Mountain back home? Is Uncle Denny in danger?" Dawson cast another worried look at Grady, willing him to wake up and be well.

"Not unless I lose."

"Will they attack again?"

Cyfrin shook his head. "Not here. I'm at full strength in my realm. That's why they had to strike me in the forest and why the rogue attacked you back in your home state. I can protect you here."

"But not when we leave."

"This never should have come to your attention," Cyfrin said. "Let's heal your mate. I will deal with the rogues."

Dawson wanted to scream, throw a punch, or shoot something. But he was stuck in the faerie realm and at the mercy of his host. He took several deep breaths and tried to cool his temper.

"Your politics was none of my business until it nearly killed the man I love and threatened my home. So—what do the rogues want, and why do they hate you?"

Cyfrin looked away. "It's complicated."

"I've got nothing but time."

Cyfrin studied Dawson, and a wan smile twitched the corners of his lips. "You are indeed a King. This insolence, this stubbornness, is why we extended our grace to you."

"Grace?"

"Your line are the Lords of the Hunt. Or did you forget that we began the Wild Hunt?"

Dawson knew the legends. The Wild Hunt roared through the night during the winter collecting souls. The stories differed about the details. Sometimes they rode red-eyed warhorses or spectral stags. Many figures were said to lead the hunt, including the Norse god Odin, the archangel Gabriel, or the souls of the dead.

"The true leader of the Wild Hunt is Gwynn Ap Nudd, a Welsh psychopomp," Cyfrin told him.

"Psychopomp—someone who escorts the spirits of the dead to the afterlife." Denny had made sure that the King boys knew their lore.

Cyfrin inclined his head in acknowledgment. "Very good."

"It's what we Kings do." Dawson knew his anger sprang from the terror that gripped him over Grady's condition. He feared for the safety of Denny, his best friend Colt, and Grady's brother Knox back home. He took the challenge to their fae patron as personally as a challenge to the King family and its legacy.

"The rogue fae wants to depose Gwynn. Whoever controls the Hunt has power over the souls of the dead."

"What do the rogues hope to get from that?" Despite himself, Dawson couldn't help his curiosity. He'd only just learned about his family's long-standing mutual obligation to the fae. Now he found himself caught up in its otherworldly politics, with the life of his lover hanging in the balance.

"Souls are powerful energy. True psychopomps don't try to use them for their own ends. They not only escort souls to the final rest— they are warrior guardians who protect them on their last journey from those who would seek to enslave them."

"Enslave?" Dawson asked sharply.

Cyfrin nodded. "Surely you've heard stories of armies of the dead or ghost legions? All stories are rooted in fact, sometimes too lost in time for mortals to recall."

Dawson shook his head. "It's none of my business. Way above my pay grade. Grady and I came here to make a gift and renew our agreement. And now—we're apparently in the middle of a war."

"Only because I chose to become the fae protector of the Kings,"

Cyfrin said. "You are proxies who were harmed to wound me. I will deal with the issue directly, and your involvement with the matter will end."

"I'm going to sit with Gray," Dawson said, trying his best to deal with his fear and overwhelm. "If anything changes that I can do something about, you know where to find me."

When he went back inside, he found that Grady's bed had doubled in size, more than large enough for two men. The chair Dawson had been using was pulled back, and a small table sat beside it. An enticing plate of cheese, fruit, honey, and small cakes sat next to a pot of tea and a porcelain cup and saucer. On the seat of the chair lay two leather-bound books.

"You need to rest, which you cannot do sleeping in that chair," Cyfrin said from the doorway. "And without food, you will collapse, I will have two patients, and you will accomplish nothing. I swear to you that no harm or obligation will be caused by eating and drinking, and I will stand guard over both of you while you rest."

"Thank you," Dawson replied, too heartsick, hungry, and exhausted to argue.

We're at his mercy, so he doesn't have anything to gain from poisoning me. Time may move differently here, but I can't go much longer without eating. If he means to trap us, we're already snared. At least with a night's sleep and some food, I can put up a decent fight if it comes to that.

"I'll be back in a bit to care for Grady," Cyfrin told him. "I thought you might like something to read. Those are epic tales that are quite popular among my kind. I hope you enjoy them."

"Fae fiction?" Dawson couldn't help a smile. "I'm looking forward to that."

Cyfrin inclined his head in acknowledgment and left Dawson and Grady alone. Dawson found the food to be more delicious than anything he could remember eating back home, everything at the peak of ripeness. The fragrant tea soothed his cramped muscles and eased his tension headache.

Even though he could barely keep his eyes open, Dawson couldn't help being curious about the books. By their binding and the type of paper, they appeared to be ancient. He wondered how he could possibly read books written in the language of the fae, only to find that the pages changed to English as he looked at them.

This is faerie. Of course magical translation is a thing.

"Denny is never going to believe this," he murmured, shutting the book and setting it aside until he was rested enough to stay awake while reading.

He felt a pang, wondering if he would ever return to the mortal world to see Denny and the others. *As long as Gray is alive, it'll be okay. No matter what it costs.*

Dawson climbed into bed next to Grady, touching but trying not to jostle. "I'm right here," he whispered. "I'm not going anywhere. Just come back to me. I love you, and I need you. So wake up, please."

He fell asleep almost as soon as he settled into the amazing cozy bedding. The comforter was warm but feather-light, the pillows perfectly plump, sheets unbelievably soft. Even the luxury of their room at the castle paled in comparison.

Music drew Dawson back to wakefulness hours later, stunned he had slept so hard and dreamlessly given the circumstances. When he opened his eyes, he saw Cyfrin standing by the window playing a silver flute.

The song washed over Dawson like a balm. Melody transcended mere beauty, and Dawson wondered if the notes carried magic beyond the soothing tune.

"Music is considered a form of healing, if you were wondering," Cyfrin said when he finished the song and lowered his flute. "I believe your realm also understands its ability to heal, but here we have the addition of magic."

"That was a pretty melody. You play well." Dawson shook himself awake and sat up. His heart plummeted when he realized Grady had not even shifted.

"Immortality provides time to learn skills," Cyfrin replied. "We are an ancient culture with a wealth of art when we have not wasted our energy on petty squabbles."

Dawson had the impression that last comment was not really directed at him or that he was expected to understand.

"I know you are loathe to let Grady out of your sight, but you will feel better with fresh clothing and a chance to get clean. Just beyond the garden, there is a hot spring and a cooling pool. They have healing minerals and are purer than any water you have known."

Cyfrin gave a wan smile. "I promise I will take care of Grady while you are gone. I must change his poultice, check his healing, and give him an elixir. Then I'll play a bit longer. I believe the music benefits both of you."

Dawson wanted to protest. He felt certain that Cyfrin could snap his fingers to clean Dawson's body and poof him into fresh clothing. But the idea of a short soak in hot water was a powerful temptation. Letting his guard down was probably a mistake, but Cyfrin had made no hostile moves since their arrival, and Dawson knew that if the fae meant them harm, it wouldn't matter whether he'd gone to the hot spring or stayed in the cottage.

"Thank you." Dawson wondered if their host could read his mind or just guess the direction of his thoughts. "I'll take you up on that offer. And the food was delicious." He figured that if he might be Cyfrin's "guest" indefinitely, he could use better manners.

Dawson forced himself to walk out of the cottage, and when he crossed the garden, he saw the two pools just as Cyfrin said. A thick towel and a stack of fresh clothing sat, neatly folded, on the flat rocks at the edge of the water.

He stripped off his clothing and slipped into the hot water, letting it ease his mind and body. The vapors from the steam smelled of minerals and healing herbs. Dawson wondered if anything they saw was actually real or just a construct of the fae's will.

If it's real to me, then does it matter?

But are we trapped or finding refuge? Can it be both?

Dawson couldn't fully relax with Grady out of sight. *Not that I could stop Cyfrin from attacking him. But I could throw myself in front, and we would go together.*

Despite the beauty of the grotto and the soothing hot spring, Dawson's heart ached. He believed Cyfrin's efforts to heal Grady were sincere, but as the days passed, Dawson feared they were also unlikely to succeed. Cyfrin was their best chance, their only hope. Nothing in Denny's lore was likely to present an antidote.

They had friends who were steeped in magic and witchcraft, some with great power.

If he doesn't wake up...if I took him back to the mortal realm...maybe one of them would find a cure.

Could he survive long enough for them to find an answer?

And if not, could I survive without him?

Dawson had heard whispers of desperate measures. A necromancer could tether soul to body. Powerful witches could dull pain, slow injury, cheat death. Neither would restore Grady to life and health.

Bargaining with the divine or the infernal required both faith and the certainty that someone was listening, neither of which Dawson possessed.

I would sell my soul, if such a thing were possible, to save him. I've loved him all my life. We just made our vows. What's left for me if he's gone?

Dawson rose from the pool with a heavy heart. He dried off and dressed quickly, hurrying along the path back to the cottage, needing to confirm that Grady still lived.

He ran the last portion, suddenly taken by the fear that something terrible had happened.

Dawson burst into the cottage, breathing hard. Cyfrin looked up from playing his flute. Grady lay unchanged on the bed.

"Anything?"

Cyfrin lowered his flute and shook his head. He gestured for Dawson to go outside with him. With a worried glance at Grady, Dawson followed Cyfrin to the courtyard.

"His body and mind have been cleansed of the poison."

"That's good, right? He should wake up soon."

Cyfrin's silence took Dawson's breath. "Unfortunately, a portion of his soul is damaged beyond my ability to repair or for him to regenerate," Cyfrin said after a long pause.

"His soul?"

Cyfrin looked away. "The poison was meant for me. We—the fae—don't have human souls. It would have attacked my core essence, the source of my power. It might have destroyed me, or weakened me indefinitely. But since a mortal is made differently, it attacked his soul."

Dawson felt the air go out of his lungs. His head spun, and his heart broke. *His soul?*

"So that's it? There's nothing we can do?" The words tasted like ash in Dawson's mouth, and he felt the cold numbness of grief steal over him.

"It depends."

Dawson's head snapped up. "Say what you mean."

Cyfrin regarded him with a look Dawson couldn't decipher. "There is a way—"

"What?"

"You could share enough of your soul to heal him. It would bind you together—soul bound—but it would sustain both of you."

"What's the catch?"

"You would be entwined at the soul level for eternity," Cyfrin replied.

Dawson reeled at the thought and leaned against one of the decorative pillars, staggered at the implications. "Would it bring him back? Would he be alive and healthy? Normal?"

"Yes. It would not be a significant drain on your soul. You would both be, for all human purposes, fine."

"For all human purposes?" Dawson's head spun. *I'm in over my head. Is this one of those inscrutable fae bargains that never turn out well? Is there a hidden gotcha? Would Grady forgive me?*

"Your life essences would be intermingled. It's what you promised in your wedding vows, made real. Soulmates rarely survive one another for long. When one of you dies, the other will follow. You will be emotionally bonded on a deep level. And while the soul bond doesn't make you telepathic, you will be uncommonly attuned. I believe your world's terms might be 'co-dependent' and 'enmeshed.' More tangled up in each other than you are now. But alive."

"And we could leave this realm, go home?"

Cyfrin nodded. "The bond would remain in this realm or yours."

"And after we die?"

"The bond is permanent—in this life and afterward. You would truly be together forever, at the deepest level possible."

If I agree, Grady won't die. We'd be altered, different. He promised to be my husband. We swore to love each other until death. Isn't this the same?

Dawson knew in his heart that it wasn't. He swallowed hard, and it felt like gargling glass. "I want to. I'm willing. I'd do worse to save him. But he can't consent. And I can't make that decision for him."

I've just doomed Gray. But I can't make that commitment for him. God help me, I don't want to lose him! But I won't bind him to me like that without knowing it's what he wants too.

"There is a middle way." Cyfrin gave Dawson that assessing look again as if he was taking his measure. "I may be able to briefly link your minds."

"What do you mean?" Dawson's heart clutched at hope, however fragile.

"I may be able to temporarily allow you into his thoughts," Cyfrin said. "It would enable you to explain and gain his permission."

"And if he refused?" Dawson held his breath.

"Eventually, his spark will extinguish."

"He'll die."

Cyfrin nodded.

Dawson wanted to punch something, scream, throw up, or cry—all at once. *It's no decision at all for me. I'm willing. But I can't choose for him.*

"Then send me in, and we'll let Grady decide," Dawson said, heart in his throat. "Whatever he chooses, I'll abide by it."

And wherever that leads him, I'll follow.

CHAPTER FIVE

GRADY

Grady roamed through a beautiful garden. Everything bloomed, perfuming the warm breeze. He leaned on the railing of an arched bridge, watching koi swim in the stream below. Rabbits, squirrels, and birds peeked from the foliage.

He didn't know how he'd gotten to the garden or where it was. Grady tried to remember what he had been doing before he woke up here, but the details eluded him.

Now that he thought about it, these weren't his clothes. Grady couldn't recall exactly what he'd been wearing, but he felt certain that the loose white top and pants weren't his norm. One hand went reflexively to his chest and left shoulder. They ached with a dull pain, and when Grady pushed the neckline of his shirt to the side, he saw light pink, fading scars.

Those are new. But how did I get them? Where am I, and why am I here? He looked down at his hands on the rail and saw the gold band. *Where's Daw? Why isn't he with me?*

Panic and grief flashed through him. *We were on our honeymoon.* The memories slowly returned. *Not hunting. We had to deliver a gift. Then the black shuck attacked. I don't remember anything after that.*

Oh, God. Am I dead? Daw and I just got married. I can't leave him so soon. We were supposed to have the rest of our lives together. No matter how it happened, he'll blame himself. I can't be dead. There's got to be a way out.

Grady wanted to run.

He shouted Dawson's name, making enough noise to frighten the birds, but no answer came. The peacefulness now seemed ominously quiet, and the garden felt eerily empty.

If I'm dead, can I haunt Daw, see him again to say goodbye? Maybe I can badger a medium into giving him a message.

Facing that possibility put a lump in Grady's throat and made him teary. *I don't know how to fight...death. I can banish a ghost, but how do I become one? How do spirits find mediums? Would it be easier to look for an Ouija board?*

Am I going to be stuck here, alone, forever? Will Daw join me when his time comes?

How did I fuck up our honeymoon so badly?

Grady had no idea how much time had passed since the attack in the forest. *Maybe I've only been dead for hours. What if it's been years, decades? Would I be able to tell?*

A sobering thought struck. *Did Daw get my body home? I don't want to be buried so far from everyone. What an awful burden for him. We were so happy. I can't believe it ended so soon.*

In other circumstances, Grady's curiosity would have led him to explore the garden, looking for hidden paths and pretty grottos. But now, gutted by his realization, Grady sank onto a marble bench and put his head in his hands.

I want Daw to live a long and happy life. But I don't want to be without him. What am I supposed to do?

The ache in his chest where he'd been injured gradually faded, a signal that time passed. Grady didn't feel hungry or thirsty, and he hadn't needed to sleep. He wondered whether he was safe in the garden.

Hard to kill a dead guy. Guess I don't have to worry.

Grady figured he should find shelter in case the weather changed. He wandered the pathways, and despite his sorrow, he couldn't help admiring the beautiful flowers and plantings.

Is all of this created from my memories? Could this be heaven?

Eventually he found a small pavilion with a roof and heavy curtains for walls. Inside was a daybed, a comfortable chair, and a stack of books.

At least I have shelter if it rains. Will new books show up when I've read those? Can I sleep even if I don't need to?

Given the King family's knowledge of the supernatural, Grady had always been agnostic. They saw hard evidence of evil and softer proof of goodness. He knew for a fact that powerful paranormal creatures and immortal beings existed, but had seen nothing that proved the existence of a Supreme Being. Even so, Grady tried praying, but no answer came. If anyone was watching or listening, they didn't deign to interact.

Now that he'd had some time to get over the shock of…transition… more memories returned. He remembered needing to meet with the fae to renew the agreement and their careful preparations. The plans they'd made for afterward—sightseeing, lovemaking, and the Valentine Dance, made him melancholy.

Worse were the memories of his last moments, incapacitated with pain, bleeding out in Dawson's arms. He had heard Dawson's pleas and his tearful confessions.

He shouted at someone…the fae? But if the faeries came, why did they let me die?

Now that he'd found a home base, Grady went back to exploring rather than letting his thoughts overwhelm him.

Will the seasons change? I'll need a different place to stay if it ever gets cold. Can I dream up a deck of playing cards or maybe a television that shows everything I've ever watched? Eternity could get really boring.

Am I alone? If this is the afterlife, where are my parents and everyone else I've known who died?

"Gray! Grady King!"

Dawson's voice broke the silence, and Grady sobbed with relief. "Daw! I'm over here!"

He ran toward the sound and ended up back at the pavilion. "Daw! Follow my voice!"

Grady stood just outside the pavilion, scanning the garden for movement, watching the pathway in anticipation. He realized he was holding his breath.

When Dawson came into view, Grady ran to him and threw himself into his husband's arms, sobbing. Dawson pulled him close, hugging him tight, letting Grady cry into his shoulder, not trying to hide his tears.

"You're here," Grady managed. "I've missed you so much." A sudden realization struck him, and Grady stepped back, horrified, searching Dawson's face for signs of passing time.

"How long?" he choked out. "How long have I been dead? How did you die?"

"Neither of us is dead," Dawson told him and took him by the hand. They sat side by side on the edge of the bed, pressed together from hip to knee, hands clasped tightly.

"Where am I? How did I get here?" Grady clung to Dawson's presence since nothing else made sense.

"We're in your mind. I can't stay long. You're not dead—yet. But the black shuck poisoned you, and Cyfrin—our fae contact—can't heal you completely without extra magic," Dawson told him.

"That's why I'm here. There's a way—and a price." Dawson took both Grady's hands and held them tightly. "Your soul is damaged. The only way to heal it—for you to survive—is to borrow some of mine."

Grady's eyes widened. "Borrow your soul?"

"Not all of it. Cyfrin assures me we will both be fine. You'd add a piece of my soul to what's left of yours, and I'd be okay with a little less. Kinda like giving you a kidney," Dawson said with a worried smile.

"Can he do that? How do you know it'll work? What if he's not telling you the truth?" Grady's head spun. "Will we need to stay wherever 'here' is, forever?"

"Cyfrin says he can make it work. So far, I haven't caught him in a lie, and he has nothing to gain from lying about this. Right now, you and I are in a cottage on Cyfrin's lands. He says when you're healed enough, we can go home."

"I'm dying back there," Grady said as the truth of Dawson's story settled into him. "I'm not conscious, or you wouldn't be dream walking in my mind."

"I need your consent if you want to do this," Dawson told him, and Grady saw the desperation in his husband's eyes. How Dawson kept from begging escaped him, knowing what he'd do if their situations were reversed.

"I won't force this on you. Soul binding is forever. We'd be changed, 'tangled up together,' Cyfrin said. So it has to be your choice."

"I've been wandering around this hell of a heaven thinking I'd never see you again." Grady made no effort to hide his tears. "I wouldn't dare ask you to share your soul, but if you're sure—"

"I've never been more certain of anything—except that I love you."

Grady nodded and swallowed past the lump in his throat. "Then, yes. Whatever it takes to stay together. Just don't leave me, and don't let me leave you."

Dawson leaned forward and pressed a brief, tender kiss to Grady's lips. "That's what I needed to know, Gray. I'm not sure how this will work, but Cyfrin will bring you back to me. So hang on—and when the time comes, follow the signal."

"Don't go," Grady pleaded as Dawson's figure began to fade. "I'm afraid."

"We'll get you home," Dawson promised. "I love you." His voice sounded distant, and when Grady blinked, he sat alone, hands outstretched but empty.

"Daw," he whispered. "I love you too." His heart pounded, and he blinked back fresh tears, then swiped his sleeve across his face.

Was he really here? Did I imagine everything? The fae can alter time and cheat death. They're immensely powerful. If anyone could make a soul bond happen, it would be the fae.

Grady realized that a deck of cards had materialized on the bedside table. "I sure hope you're real, Dawson, and that you've got a plan. Because I don't think I can read and play cards for eternity."

CHAPTER SIX

DAWSON

Dawson came back to himself with a gasp and jackknifed to sit up in bed. He panted for breath as if he'd run a mile, and his heart thudded in his chest. Dawson looked immediately to Grady who lay unmoving in the bed beside him.

"It worked," he managed. Cyfrin pushed a glass of water into his hand, and Dawson gulped it down.

"He agreed," Dawson said once he found his voice again. "Grady agreed to the soul binding."

"And you have not had second thoughts? Success is not guaranteed."

Dawson reached for Grady's hand. "Nothing is ever guaranteed. Even a slim chance is better than no chance at all. He's my husband. I love him. Where he goes, I'll follow. *Wherever* he goes," Dawson added, with an emphasis that made his meaning clear.

Cyfrin nodded. "Very well. I will make ready."

"Please...hurry. Grady's fading. I could feel it. He thought he was dead and in heaven. He's slipping away."

"This is complex magic, something not easily or often attempted. If we rush, you might both die."

"If we don't, Grady will die, and the rest won't matter."

Cyfrin gave Dawson a look he couldn't decipher and then turned. "Find your courage, and make your peace. I won't be long. We'll work the spell tonight and pray that luck is on our side."

Much as Dawson craved assurances, he respected Cyfrin's honesty. Dawson watched him go and turned back to Grady, clasping his left hand between both of his own.

"Thank you for trusting us to bring you back," Dawson whispered. "Thank you for agreeing to bind us together forever. It's not long now —Cyfrin is getting ready to work the spell. Just please—hang on. I'm coming for you. Wait for me. I'll bring you home."

Dawson kissed Grady's hand, then brushed their lips together. "I'm staying right here with you. One way or another, when we leave here, we'll leave together."

As they waited, Dawson filled the silence with remembered exploits and the best memories of growing up together. He talked as if Grady listened, remembering that people in comas supposedly could hear what was said to them.

He tried to will all of his love and hope for the future through their joined hands. "You know when we get home, maybe we'd better not tell Uncle Denny the whole story. We might be grown men and trained hunters, but I think he'd drag us by our ears to the woodshed."

Dawson forced a chuckle. "When we get back to the castle, we'll order the fanciest things on the menu and celebrate. We'll explore the rest of the town and dance all night at the big party, and take the train wherever you want to go. Assuming that we haven't done a Rip Van Winkle and everything's spaceships and flying cars."

He reached for one of the books Cyfrin had brought for him and read aloud from an epic fantasy full of love, treachery, and magic. One passage stood out to him, and he re-read it, then smiled.

"It's the least of our worries, but I think I know what's causing the problem at the castle. It's a house goblin called a 'bwa-batch.'"

"It's pronounced 'boobach,'" Cyfrin said from the doorway, not trying to hide his amusement.

"It only has one vowel," Dawson countered.

"Welsh is like that," Cyfrin replied drolly. "I'm curious...what is the issue with the castle goblin?"

Dawson put the book aside. "It's causing problems—tripping servers, breaking glassware, generally being a nuisance. We were hoping to find out how to send it away."

Cyfrin frowned. "If a boobach has a castle home, it can't be removed. I believe your goblin is probably misbehaving due to poor management."

"Goblins have HR issues?"

"Goblins and other fae see their bond to a castle or manor like a sacred vow. In exchange for their protection and help, they expect certain boons...saucers of cream, sweets, shiny objects, and always, respect and appreciation," Cyfrin told him. "If they don't believe they've been treated properly, they cause problems until the slights are addressed."

"That's a whole lot easier to fix than what I expected," Dawson replied. "Thank you."

"You really must be careful about thanking one of my kind," Cyfrin tutted. "It's a bad habit. I will not take advantage, but not all my brethren are generous."

"Is it time?" Dawson asked.

"Nearly so. I thought it best to check on both of you. We should be ready within the hour." He left them alone again, and Dawson went back to reading to Grady, hoping that his words and presence would help to reassure both of them.

Cyfrin returned carrying a tray of ritual items. "While the soul-sharing spell exists, it is not frequently performed for obvious reasons. You are still resolved to do this?"

Dawson held up their clasped hands. "Absolutely."

Cyfrin nodded. "Very well. Lie down and stay connected. Whatever happens, do not let go. I'm afraid that this will not be pleasant."

Dawson stretched out beside Grady. He turned toward his husband and smiled. "That's okay. Whatever it takes."

Their host brought Dawson a small cup of tea. "This has a sedative. It will ease the pain and help you remain calm. It will also quell your natural instinct to resist. You must be aware for the ritual."

"I'd give him my blood or a kidney. This is the same, only different." Dawson tried for a cocky grin but figured he wasn't fooling anyone.

Cyfrin lit leaves in a bowl and walked widdershins around the bed three times, then reversed directions and circled thrice more. He held the bowl up to the sky at each of the circle's quarters and lit candles.

The fae set the bowl aside and picked up a white length of braided silken chord. He wrapped it around their wrists and tied it fast. Then he took the bowl of charred protective leaves and ground them into a powder, which he sprinkled across both men's chests. Cyfrin took a small cup of indigo and painted a symbol on their foreheads between their eyebrows.

"This opens the link between mind and soul. I need you to direct all your thoughts to focus on Grady's healing. Picture him well again, waking up, going about his day. Focus on your bond, how much he means to you, your love for him. However you picture the soul bond, imagine it in as much detail as you can," Cyfrin directed. "My magic will make it happen."

He added more ingredients to the bowl and then pricked both men's thumbs to draw beads of blood, which he added to the mixture. Once again he lit the contents with a twitch of his fingers, sending a purple flame dancing above the silver container. The air smelled of rosemary, lemon balm, mint, and basil, all healing herbs.

Cyfrin held up a silver chalice and lifted it to the four quarters, then mixed some of the ashes into the water and sprinkled drops onto Dawson and Grady. He brought out a small silver plate with a white paste that smelled of lavender and fennel and used the back of a silver spoon to spread the mixture in the shape of a rune over both men's chests, just above the heart.

All the while he murmured in a strange, melodious language that Dawson assumed must be the native tongue of the fae. Then Cyfrin set down the chalice and picked up his flute.

The music skirled around them, sending a shiver through Dawson that he felt echoed by Grady even though the other had not woken. As Cyfrin played, Dawson swore he saw golden threads stretch from the flute toward the bed. One of those threads struck Dawson in the chest, while the other hit Grady.

Dawson gasped as fire bored through his bone and blood. His back arched, his free hand clutched the bedding, and he could not bite back a cry of pain.

Grady squeezed his hand painfully hard, body writhing, face twisted in agony. A scream ripped from Grady's throat, but he did not wake.

Cyfrin played on. The wild tune sounded like the fae themselves—an untamed force of nature, beautiful, powerful, and dangerous.

Dawson felt the magical strand move through his body like molten gold, constricting his chest and making his heart pound. He held tight to Grady, willing his partner to survive the ordeal and be healed.

Afterward, Dawson couldn't say how long the music and the pain lasted. It seemed to go on forever, suspending him in a place between life and death. It felt as if he were having heart surgery without anesthetic, a white-hot poker burning his chest and brain, penetrating deep into his belly.

All he could do was hold on, silently chanting Grady's name, hoping that sheer cussedness might pull them through.

He felt something rip free deep inside as the pain crested, refusing him the refuge of losing consciousness. His screams echoed, mirrored by Grady's shouts. Cyfrin never faltered, weaving the music around them in what Dawson imagined was a net of golden fog.

The song reached its crescendo, and Dawson swore he felt a powerful energy ride the golden glow to slide from his body into Grady.

Grady convulsed, shaking from head to toe. His eyes snapped wide and unseeing, his mouth opened in a soundless scream, every muscle tensed. Dawson thought Grady's grip might break his hand, but he held on, refusing to end the connection.

Just as abruptly, Grady dropped back onto the mattress. The shaking ended, his eyes and mouth closed, and only the rise and fall of his chest reassured Dawson that his husband was still alive.

As the flute's song wound to its conclusion, the golden fog thinned, then vanished altogether. After a final coda, the music ended, and Cyfrin lowered his instrument.

"Dawson?" Cyfrin asked. "Tell me what you feel."

Dawson tried to sort through the chaos of emotions—fear, worry, grief—and narrowed his focus to his body. "I felt energy leave me," he said slowly, searching for words to describe the indescribable. "It felt like something deep inside tore in half. That hurt—a lot. Now, I feel off-kilter, but the pain dulled. It's like I'm missing something."

"Severing a part of one's soul is difficult—even more so than losing a limb. But from a magical perspective, the spell did what it was supposed to do," Cyfrin said.

Dawson propped himself up on his elbows so he could look at Grady. Their hands remained tightly clasped, and he expected to have finger-shaped bruises tomorrow from the strength of the grip. "Gray? Can you hear me? C'mon—wake up!"

For a terrifying few seconds, nothing happened. Dawson's heart plummeted, and he feared that their efforts had failed.

Please come back to me.

Grady's eyes fluttered open, and he gasped for air as if he'd resurfaced from beneath the water. He flailed, panicked and disoriented.

"It's okay," Dawson soothed. "I'm here. You're back. We're safe. Deep breaths."

Grady turned to him, terrified and seeking an anchor. Dawson stroked the tips of his fingers down Grady's cheek, keeping their other hands clasped. "Just breathe. Hang on to me. We're going to be all right."

Dawson looked to Cyfrin. "Are we soul bound?"

Cyfrin raised a hand, and nearly invisible tendrils of golden fog danced in the air around first Dawson and then Grady before dissipating like smoke.

Cyfrin nodded. "Yes. The spell shared enough of your soul to compensate for what was damaged in Grady's. The poison from the shuck has been cleansed, and the wound is healed. He'll need some time to regain his strength, but the hard part is done."

Dawson opened his mouth to thank the fae, who raised an eyebrow and gave him a pointed look. Dawson's mouth snapped closed. "You know what I mean," he grumbled at the unspoken reproof.

Cyfrin looked amused. "I do. And I am relieved that the spell worked. Now—rest. You are safe and welcome for as long as Grady needs to recover."

Grady groaned and opened his eyes, turning his head immediately to search for Dawson, either out of long habit or already feeling the new connection between them.

"Daw?"

Dawson grinned, exhausted and sore but overjoyed that Grady was awake. "You're back, Cyfrin did it."

"Feel like I've been hit by a truck," Grady moaned. "Are you okay?"

"Better than okay," Dawson assured him, leaning in for a quick kiss. "When you're ready, we'll get some food into you and get you cleaned up. You've got a beard like a lumberjack, and you're overdue for a shower."

None of that mattered because Grady was no longer dying.

"The connection...did it work?" Grady still sounded a little out of it.

"You tell me," Dawson replied. "What do you feel?"

Grady shut his eyes and concentrated. "I've always been more aware of you than other people, but now it's dialed up to the max. If I focus, I think I can read your feelings...but I can't tell what you're thinking."

"That's as it should be," Cyfrin said. "You'll both feel better, calmer, when the other is very close. It's possible for you to be apart over a great distance, but the longer any separation goes on, the more uncomfortable it will become until it grows intolerable. It's not just a connection—it's a true bond."

"Gray?" Dawson asked, suddenly worried his partner might have second thoughts.

Grady opened his eyes and managed a tired smile. "That's good, Daw. It'll just...take some getting used to."

Dawson grinned. "That's fine. We've got all the time in the world now."

Cyfrin brought food and drink, then left them alone to regroup. Dawson had always appreciated how he and Grady could be silent together without it being weird—in the car or at home. Now, the heightened awareness of Grady's presence and his mood gave that comfort an off-the-charts boost.

Grady's pallor faded, and he no longer looked haggard. "How long was I out?" he asked after they had finished their meal of egg tarts, tea sandwiches, and pastries.

"In this realm? Three days. Back home? I have no idea." Dawson scratched his newly-acquired beard and realized they both could use a shave before they returned.

Let's hope Cyfrin told the truth—about everything.

After they ate, Dawson took Grady to the hot spring. It didn't surprise him that fresh outfits and towels were already waiting for them. A soak in the spring cleansed their bodies and lifted a weight from Dawson's mind. He wondered if the water—like the rest of this place—was magical.

When they finished, the two men wandered back to the pavilion hand in hand. Dawson filled Grady in on what happened while he was unconscious, and Grady told him about the dream world he had encountered.

"I know I've been sleeping for days, but I'm barely keeping my eyes open," Grady confessed when they reached the pavilion. "Do you mind if I take a nap?"

Dawson shook his head. "I think that with everything you've been through, sleeping is a great idea. We really don't have a schedule. I want to talk to Cyfrin about a couple of things, and then I'll join you. Keep the bed warm for me, okay?"

Grady grinned. "Always."

Dawson watched him go back inside their pavilion and then turned to the garden. He didn't know where to look for Cyfrin, but their host always managed to turn up when needed. It didn't surprise Dawson to find the fae wandering the pathways.

"Now that Grady's awake, how long do you think it will be until he's healed?" Dawson asked.

Cyfrin bent to study a rose and didn't look up. "A few more days. See how he does and how the bond sits with both of you."

"And after that?" Dawson had trusted Cyfrin to save Grady because he had no other choice. While he knew the fae had a long-standing agreement with the King family, his natural caution returned.

Cyfrin glanced at him with a knowing half-smile as if he had anticipated Dawson's wariness. "Then you may return to your realm without further obligation other than the original accord between your family and my people."

Dawson again struggled not to thank the fae and sighed. "It's not my fault my mother raised me right," he mumbled at Cyfrin's amused consternation.

Grady stirred when Dawson slipped into bed beside him. "Need to feel you next to me," Grady murmured.

Dawson spooned him, wrapping an arm across Grady's chest and tangling their legs together, with his hips against Grady's firm ass. "Right here. Where I'll always be."

"Sorry I fucked up our honeymoon," Grady murmured, still turned away from Dawson.

"What matters is that you're okay," Dawson assured him. "And we'll have one hell of a story to tell."

He paused. "We need to stay a little longer to make sure the bond doesn't have any...unexpected...side effects. Kinda like waiting around at the doctor's after you get a shot to make sure you won't faint, only with souls."

Grady was silent for a moment. "You're not angry." He made it a statement, not a question, reminding Dawson of the side effects of their new bond.

Dawson concentrated, listening with his heart for an indication of Grady's mood. He picked up gratitude, love, worry, and a surprisingly strong surge of lust.

"Slow down, cowboy," Dawson chuckled. "I want you too. But you just stopped being Sleeping Beauty. Maybe you should at least give it a day."

"Jizz has healing powers. I read that online somewhere," Grady teased.

"Oh, really?" Dawson played along.

"Wouldn't hurt to do more research to confirm."

Dawson let his hand slide down Grady's toned abs and followed his happy trail. He pulled the drawstring on the white pants and pushed them down, loosening his own at the same time. When he slid a hand beneath his pillow, he found a container of lube. *Chalk up another win for the host with the most.*

Grady tried to turn over, but Dawson kept him pinned. "Let me do all the work," he whispered, pressing light kisses to Grady's ear and neck, making him shiver. "Nothing too athletic this time, just taking the edge off for both of us. We'll do more later—I promise."

Grady nodded silent assent. Dawson slicked his hand and his cock. He gripped Grady's dick and pressed his own into the cleft of Grady's pert ass. The first stroke of his hand and buck of his hips sent a blast of feeling through Dawson that was so strong he was afraid they would be finished before they got started.

"Are we—?" Grady breathed.

Dawson nodded, amazed. "Yeah. I think I'm feeling what you're feeling—on top of the normal feels."

"Me too." Grady gave a dirty chuckle. "Oh, we're going to need to experiment with this."

Every stroke and thrust was exquisitely overstimulating as Dawson felt his own sensations and Grady's building desire. They both came embarrassingly quickly but with such a powerful climax that Dawson's sight whited out for a few seconds, and Grady went limp in his arms.

Grady stirred. "So those stories of 'the little death' are really true? Holy fuck," he slurred, sounding a little drunk.

"Damn. I haven't popped my cork that fast since puberty—and it hit like a freight train," Dawson murmured.

"Guess I don't have to ask if it was good for you," Grady said and snickered.

"Apparently not." Dawson found a small towel thoughtfully deposited next to the bed and used it to clean them both up. *Apparently, our host doesn't mind the sex. Then again, the fae aren't prudes.*

"Do you feel healed by the magic jizz?" Dawson joked, tugging up their pants and nestling next to Grady.

Grady pulled Dawson's hand onto his belly and overlaid it with his own. "Definitely. I'll be needing another dose soon."

"I'm more than happy to give it to you."

"You *give it* just fine."

Dawson ran his hand across Grady's nipples, and both men trembled. "Figuring this out is going to be so much fun." *But not worth the risk. I almost lost you. Nothing is worth that.*

Grady seemed to sense the shift in his mood.

Of course he did. That's the bond.

"Hey. Quit thinking about things that didn't happen," Grady said, guessing the direction Dawson's thoughts had taken. "We're here, we're alive, and it's all good. Take the gift for what it is, and don't look back."

"Sexy, handsome, *and* smart. How did I luck out?" Dawson kissed the back of Grady's neck.

"Just lucky, I guess." Grady's rush of love and affection undercut his teasing tone.

They spent the next two days exploring the garden, soaking in the mineral spring, eating the food that appeared out of nowhere in their pavilion, and having mind-blowing sex. It was a honeymoon-within-a-honeymoon, and while Dawson hated the reason that brought them to the faerie realm, he felt grateful for the bond and the rare chance to fully heal.

The night before they planned to leave, Dawson slipped out of bed to take in the beauty of the garden in the moonlight. He saw movement and then caught sight of Cyfrin walking along one of the paths parallel to where he was sitting.

Cyfrin's white suit was spattered with blood, and for just an instant, the moonlight gave Dawson a glimpse through the fae's glamour, revealing a gaunt face, thin lips, and razor-sharp teeth.

He blinked and Cyfrin looked as he always did, his suit immaculately clean.

Cyfrin appeared next to Dawson before Dawson saw him move. "Don't be afraid. You are safe. I have handled the rogue fae who set the shuck on you. Neither of us need worry about him anymore. Go back to sleep. Tomorrow, you and Grady return to your realm."

With that, he vanished.

In the morning, after Dawson and Grady dressed and tidied up the pavilion, they found Cyfrin waiting outside.

"Your healing is complete. The bond is strong. And the threat is over. I will return you to the place you left," Cyfrin said. "And I will honor our accord with the Kings in perpetuity."

Dawson gave a shallow bow. "Your hospitality will be remembered in stories told for generations." The fancy words conveyed appreciation without incurring further obligation and seemed to amuse Cyfrin, who inclined his head in acknowledgment.

"Give Denny my regards," Cyfrin replied.

The garden faded around them, and then Dawson and Grady emerged by the massive oak in the clearing. Their gear bag lay where they had left it, undisturbed, and colored flags fluttered from the tree's branches.

Only the body and blood of the black shuck were missing.

"Our beards are gone." Grady ran a hand over his now-smooth face where a week's growth had been seconds earlier. Dawson drew his hands over his cheeks and found only a shadow of dark stubble instead of his full beard. "And we're back in our own clothing—without the blood."

Dawson pulled his phone from the bag and stared at the display, dumbfounded. "According to this…we've been gone for four hours."

Not seven days.

"So we've still got almost our whole honeymoon left—and the Valentine Dance." Grady grinned. "Let's go—we have gargoyles to find."

CHAPTER SEVEN

GRADY

When they came back to Caynham Castle, nothing had changed. Grady kept looking for evidence that more time had elapsed, but every clock validated that they had only been gone several hours.

"Before we completely relax, we ought to fix their boobach problem," Dawson said, glancing at Grady as if he expected dissent.

"It shouldn't be too hard," Grady replied. "Let's go talk to Constance at check-in."

Constance looked up as they entered the lobby. "Are you enjoying the town and the castle?" she asked with a friendly smile.

"They're both fantastic," Grady replied. "Everything has been great. But do you remember what you asked when we checked in?"

Constance frowned, then looked worried. "About ghosts?" She dropped her voice to a whisper.

Grady nodded. "The problems in the kitchen and dining room—people tripping over 'nothing,' dishes breaking, odd mishaps. We know what's causing it and how to make it stop."

Constance caught her breath. "Wait right here. I need to get my boss." She walked down a hallway behind the front desk, knocked at an office door, then vanished inside. A few minutes later, she headed back with another woman behind her.

"Hi. I'm Priscilla—Constance's manager. She told me a little about your…connections. And you're right; we've had some strange things going on. What do you think is happening?"

"We think you have a disgruntled house goblin—a boobach—who has an HR issue," Grady replied, knowing how crazy his words sounded.

"Boobachs are a type of fae, and they help with things around a manor. He's probably been at the castle since it was built," Dawson jumped in. "But faeries are very big on formalities and contracts. We think that something's changed, and he isn't being thanked properly, and that's why he's acting out."

Grady waited for Priscilla to laugh or dismiss them with annoyance. Instead, she paled and her eyes widened. "Thanked properly—how?"

"The fae like cream, sweets, little baubles," Grady replied. "Have the kitchen or dining room staff changed recently? Or has the routine changed?"

Priscilla and Constance traded a look. "We just got a new kitchen manager a few weeks ago. He replaced someone who'd been here for decades and retired. The new manager is from London—very interested in the latest way to do things."

"Someone who might not be inclined to believe old legends?" Grady asked.

Both women laughed. "No. He's much more into computers."

"If you can convince your new manager to believe in the boobach and leave thank-you gifts like his predecessor probably did, we're certain the problems will stop, and the kitchen will run smoothly," Dalton said.

"I'll ring up Mr. Mays—he's the former manager—and have a chat about what he did to keep the faeries happy," Priscilla mused aloud. "Then I'll make sure to tell the earl, and he'll make it clear to Mr. James —the new manager—that he's to keep up the tradition."

"That should save you a lot of broken dishes." Grady felt surprised that Priscilla had believed them so quickly, but realized that since their friends had dealt with much more dangerous hauntings, an annoyed goblin probably didn't feel like a big stretch of imagination.

"You have no idea!" Priscilla replied. "I see the invoices for replacements. Annoying a faerie gets expensive."

Grady told Priscilla what they would need to win over the upset fae, and she wrote down every detail.

"Thank you so much." She tucked the note into her folio. "I'll bring it to the earl's attention right away."

Grady and Dawson went back to their room, and Grady breathed a sigh of relief. "Everything's just like we left it—"

"—earlier today, apparently," Dawson replied, and Grady could tell his partner shared the same sense of confusion and awe.

"Let's eat dinner, and then there's a concert in the chapel this evening," Grady said. "We could make an early night of it and see if the bond works the same way back in the real world," he added with a lecherous grin. He could tell from the way Dawson adjusted his stance that his partner felt the thirsty surge of feelings he sent behind his words.

"Might not make it through the concert if you keep that up," Dawson warned. "Foreplay isn't going to last four minutes unless we learn some brand new edging techniques."

"I'm up for the challenge," Grady replied, knowing his hunger was clear in his eyes.

"We'll both be *up* in no time if you keep doing that, and I'm hungry for food," Dawson chided. "Besides, eating and drinking after a trip to the 'other side' is supposed to ground you back in the mortal realm."

"Our lives are strange."

"Wouldn't have it any other way." Dawson pulled Grady in for a kiss.

They ate in the main castle dining room again, celebrating being alive. Dawson ordered trout with scallion potatoes, roasted carrots, and crème brûlée for dessert. Grady had a roast leg of lamb with mashed potatoes, green beans, and mint jelly, and for dessert, a mince tart. They shared a bottle of Malbec and finished with Irish coffee to warm against the chill outside.

Grady and Dawson took their spiked coffee with them to sit by the fireplace. Grady couldn't help replaying what had happened to them and knew from the tug at his heart that Dawson's feelings had turned introspective.

"Hey—no regrets," Grady said quietly, taking Dawson's hand. "I'm glad we agreed to the bond. I just can't fathom you giving up part of your soul for me."

Dawson turned their joined hands over and laced their fingers together. "I had to, Gray. It really wasn't a choice. And I'll never regret keeping you alive and close to me."

They held hands as they walked the short distance to the chapel and slipped into the back pew. The small space was lit with candles and white twinkle lights with a large arrangement of roses, anthuriums, and carnations in the front.

Grady hadn't been sure what to expect, worried that if the music leaned too formal, Dawson might be bored. As it turned out, the chamber music quartet played popular love songs both modern and ancient, keeping the mood sweet and lively.

To his surprise, Dawson's emotions swirled close to the surface, keeping his much more stoic partner close to tears. "Are you okay?" Grady asked after watching Dawson's throat bob and seeing him blink rapidly.

"Just a little overwhelmed," Dawson whispered. "Don't forget—I feel you too." He gave Grady's hand a squeeze. "I'm okay anywhere with you."

They meandered back toward the Bride's Tower and their room after the concert ended, enjoying the view of the stars in the clear night sky. Grady's phone buzzed, and he looked at the unfamiliar UK phone number, puzzled.

"Mr. King—this is Patricia from the front desk. The earl wanted me to ask if you and your husband could come to the kitchen. He says he'd feel better if we had 'fae experts' on hand when we try to make peace with the boo…goblin."

Grady glanced at Dawson, who nodded. "We'll be there. What time?"

"It's nearly eleven, and the kitchen is closed. Can you meet us there now?"

"See you in a few minutes," Grady promised.

When they arrived in the darkened great room, Priscilla led them into the kitchen, which had already been tidied for the next day. A distinguished man in his forties wearing an Aran knit sweater over pressed jeans and loafers stepped forward to greet them.

"A pleasure to meet you, Mr. and Mr. King. I'm the earl, but please call me Ward," he said, extending his hand.

That cleared up Grady's worry over whether to bow. He and Dawson shook hands and followed the earl to where two men waited near the walk-in freezer. Grady guessed that the older man was Mr. Mays, the recently retired kitchen manager, and the younger man was Mr. James, the new hire.

"I've assembled the items on your list," Priscilla told Grady. "And I took the liberty of asking Mr. Mays what he customarily offered to the…"

"Boobach," Mays said. "I don't know his name—not that a fae would ever tell it—but I always thought of him as Ollie."

James didn't say anything, but his expression made it clear he didn't believe a word of what was being said.

"If Ollie was happy and didn't cause mischief while you were managing the kitchen, then Mr. Mays here is the real fae expert for the castle's boobach," Grady said. "What did you do?"

Mays chuckled. "I always spoke to him when I first arrived, even though I couldn't see him. Just a friendly 'hello,' and thanking him for watching over the kitchen all night. If we ever had a near miss avoiding a disaster, I always told him we appreciated his help. Then at night when we were doing our final clean-up before we were ready to leave, I put a saucer of cream, a small pastry, and a little trinket by the sink," Mays recalled. "It disappeared as soon as I turned my back."

"What kind of trinket?" Dawson asked, and Grady sensed his sincere curiosity.

"A shiny pebble, a stray flower, a bit of ribbon or some such," Mays said. "Just something small. I wrote it all down in a letter I left for whoever came after me."

The earl looked to James. "And I'm guessing that you didn't hold with such things when you took over?"

James seemed to struggle hiding his frustration. "If I'd tried that in London, I'd have been laughed out of the kitchen."

"But we're not in London. And this isn't a modern building—it's an ancient castle with its own ways," the earl replied mildly, but James winced under his stare.

"You don't really believe—"

The earl's cool smile stopped James mid-sentence. "I've seen some very strange things here in the castle. I've learned to believe a lot."

"Would you mind please showing us how you set the night offering?" the Earl asked Mays. The older man nodded in acknowledgment and then went to the items Priscilla had assembled from Grady's list.

"A little extra touch I came up with—I add a pinch of sugar to the cream," Mays said as he poured some into a pretty saucer. "They have a sweet tooth." He took a small tart from a container and carried it and the saucer to the side of the sink, where he set them down. Then he took a tiny gold bow from his pocket and put it next to the bowl.

"I've missed you, Ollie," he said with quiet reverence. "It was time for me to leave. The castle folks didn't know about our agreement. But they do now, so please don't make mischief."

James looked about to comment, but a stern shake of the earl's head kept him silent. Grady and Dawson watched, on guard in case Ollie wasn't in a forgiving mood. The earl had a look of expectant wonder, and Grady decided he liked the castle's owner.

"Look," Priscilla said as the cream in the saucer stirred as if an invisible being lapped at it.

"Ollie, I know you're shy, but can you please let them see you—just this once," Mays cajoled.

The air rippled, and a small creature the size of a housecat appeared by the saucer. The sharp-featured face bore out its fae blood, while the body was essentially human with a hedgehog's rounded back and sharp spines.

Grady heard a gasp from James and a murmur of awe from Priscilla and the earl.

Ollie's long pink tongue lapped up the milk, nibbled the tart, and then licked its lips and nose. When finished with the offering, he sat up, plucked the bow, and looked at them. He rubbed his belly in thanks with a smile for Mays, then pointed and scowled at James, and blew a loud raspberry before vanishing with a loud *pop.*

"The castle appreciates you, Ollie," Mays said.

The earl turned to James and raised an eyebrow in an unspoken question.

James looked completely flummoxed. "Everyone saw that, right? That thing—"

"Ollie," Mays corrected.

James nodded, still gobsmacked. "Ollie—it just appeared and then, poof."

"Do you think you can abide by the custom Mr. Mays demonstrated to keep the kitchen safe and harmonious?" the earl asked. His mild tone didn't hide the weight of the question.

"Yes. Of course. I'm sorry—it's just, I'm not from around here and we never did it that way in London," James babbled. He stared at the sink where the boobach had vanished. "I'd like a second chance if you'll give me one, Ollie."

A bit of fancy ribbon floated down through the air in front of James, and he caught it in his palm. He looked up hopefully. "I guess this means yes?"

Mays smiled. "Let's talk over a pint, and I can tell you more about how Ollie and I worked together. Then I'll get out of your hair, and you and Ollie can take it from there." He and James gave a nod in respect to the earl and then left the kitchen.

The earl and Priscilla shared a glance, and then both grinned. "That has to be the wildest thing I've seen in a long while," the earl said. "I'd heard stories—my mother would tell us when we were little not to trouble the faeries, never to step into a mushroom circle, and not to follow the dancing lights into the woods. I'd heard the servants gossip about little items being taken and moved and debate whether it was ghosts or faeries. But I never thought I'd meet one!"

"We've learned from your friends that the castle has more ghosts than we thought," Priscilla said to Grady and Dawson. "And I've heard the staff say little blessings 'for the fae' or leave a few petals in a corner for them as a 'thank you.' I'm afraid I thought it was superstition. I guess I owe Ollie an apology."

"Are there more of them?" the earl asked, looking to Dawson and Grady.

"That's something you might want to ask the people who've worked at the castle the longest," Grady replied. "If they think you'll believe them, you'll find out. I don't know if you can add 'learn to make faerie offerings' to your HR manual, but it might save you a lot of trouble."

"There's already something about not bothering the ghosts, so I can't see why not," Priscilla replied and jotted a note on her phone.

"We're in your debt." The earl smiled, turning back to Grady and Dawson. "I hope you're planning to attend the dance on Valentine's Day?"

Grady and Dawson exchanged a glance. "We wouldn't miss it for the world."

"Good. I'll make sure your table has a VIP upgrade—a small 'thank you' for helping us solve our goblin problem," the earl said. "And I hope you enjoy the rest of your honeymoon."

Dawson and Grady walked back to their suite hand in hand. "Is it crazy that I'm more excited about meeting a real earl than meeting an elder fae?" Dawson asked.

"I don't think that's a question most normal people get to consider," Grady replied with a laugh. "But I agree, I'm a little star-struck even though our friends told us that the earl was very down-to-earth."

"I'm glad we could help solve the problem with the boobach and that it seemed to work out for all sides," Dawson agreed. "I felt a little bad for Mr. James. He looked like someone smacked him up the side of the head with a frying pan when the goblin showed up."

"He was definitely stunned, but he went along with it," Grady noted. "I'll give him credit for that."

When they opened the door to the honeymoon suite, Grady could smell freshly baked shortbread cookies. A tray on the table had a note from Priscilla, thanking them for their help, along with a bottle of wine.

"Looks like we made a good impression," Dawson quipped. "This is already better pay than we normally get back home."

Grady stepped up behind Dawson and wrapped his arms around him, pulling him close. "That's what's on your mind? Cookies?"

"I can think of lots of sweet endings," Dawson murmured, pushing Grady's hand down to cup his groin. "None of which leave crumbs in the bed."

"I like the sound of that." Grady led him to the four-poster, and they fell onto the mattress together. "I have all kinds of ideas about what to do tonight, and every one of them ends with you shouting my name."

"I DIDN'T THINK they could make the Great Hall even more beautiful, but they managed," Grady said as he and Dawson slow danced to the band. Twinkle lights festooned the exposed rafters. Fresh flowers—an extravagance in winter—adorned every table, along with red table-cloths, white candles, and heart-shaped, pink paper programs.

Ollie must have been content with their peacekeeping mission, since no one dropped or broke glasses or plates throughout the entire evening.

"You clean up well, Mr. King," Dawson said in a low rumble that was pure sex.

"You look pretty damn fine yourself, Mr. King," Grady replied, putting heat behind his words. He knew by the way Dawson trembled in his arms that the emotional resonance between them delivered his intent.

They swayed to the music, enjoying the moment. The chef had outdone his previous creations for the special dinner before the dance, with Beef Wellington with a mushroom Marsala sauce, roasted pota-toes, and carrots, and a bottle of Shiraz. For dessert, slices of a deca-dent chocolate cake accompanied by good whiskey capped off the evening.

The Earl had promised a VIP upgrade and did not disappoint. A bottle of fancy champagne and an excellent charcuterie welcomed them at their table. They also found tickets for a carriage ride for the next day as well as a certificate gifting them dinner and flights of house-brewed ales at the earl's brewery.

"So…good honeymoon?" Grady closed his eyes, soaking up the feelings he read even before Dawson spoke.

"Best ever," Dawson said with a grin. "Happy Valentine's Day, Gray."

AFTERWORD

I hope you've enjoyed visiting the world of Caynham Castle!

My fifth story, *Green Man Blues*, ties in with my Deadly Curiosities series and is MF. It will probably show up as a bonus story tied to an upcoming novel.

Thank you for reading! Please look for my characters in their own series: Badlands, Kings of the Mountain, Deadly Curiosities, and Treasure Trail.

ABOUT THE AUTHOR

Morgan Brice is the romance pen name of bestselling author Gail Z. Martin. Morgan writes urban fantasy male/male paranormal romance, with plenty of action, adventure, and supernatural thrills to go with the happily ever after.

Gail writes epic fantasy and urban fantasy, and together with co-author hubby Larry N. Martin, steampunk and comedic horror, all of which have less romance and more explosions.

On the rare occasions Morgan isn't writing, she's either reading, cooking, or spoiling two very pampered dogs.

Watch for additional new series from Morgan Brice and more books in the Witchbane, Badlands, Treasure Trail, Kings of the Mountain, Sharps & Springfield, and Fox Hollow universes coming soon!

Where to find me, and how to stay in touch

Join my Worlds of Morgan Brice Facebook Group and get in on all the behind-the-scenes fun! My free reader group is the first to see cover reveals, learn tidbits about works-in-progress, have fun with exclusive contests and giveaways, find out about in-person get-togethers, and more! It's also where I find my beta readers, ARC readers, and launch team! Come join the party! https://www.Facebook.com/groups/WorldsOfMorganBrice

Find me on the web at https://morganbrice.com.

Check out the ongoing, online convention ConTinual www.facebook.com/groups/ConTinual

Support Indie Authors

When you support independent authors, you help influence what kind of books you'll see and what types of stories will be available because the authors themselves decide what to write, not a big publishing conglomerate. Independent authors are local creators supporting their families with the books they produce. Thank you for supporting independent authors and small press fiction!

ALSO BY MORGAN BRICE

Badlands Series

Badlands

Restless Nights, a Badlands Short Story

Lucky Town, a Badlands Novella

The Rising

Cover Me, a Badlands Short Story

Loose Ends

Leap of Faith, A Badlands/Witchbane Novella

Night, a Badlands Short Story

No Surrender

Warm You Up, a Badlands Short Story

Point Blank

Memory and Malice, a Badlands Novella

Shine Tonight, a Badlands Short Story

Fox Hollow Zodiac Series

Huntsman

Again

Fox Hollow Universe

Romp

Nutty for You

Imaginary Lover

Haven

Gruff

Trash and Treasure

Kings of the Mountain Series

Kings of the Mountain

The Christmas Spirit, a Kings of the Mountain Short Story

Sins of the Fathers

Kings of the Mountain Universe

Roustabout

Sharps & Springfield Series

Peacemaker

Treasure Trail Series

Treasure Trail

Blink

Last Resort

Secrets and Ciphers, a Treasure Trail Novella

Treasure Trail Universe

Light My Way Home, a Treasure Trail Short Story

Witchbane Series

Witchbane

Burn, a Witchbane Novella

Dark Rivers

Flame and Ash

Unholy

The Devil You Know

Signs and Wonders

The Christmas Crunch, a Witchbane Short Story

Sandwiched, a Witchbane Short Story

Ambushed, A Witchbane Novella

Castle Magic: A Caynham Castle Collection

www.ingramcontent.com/pod-product-compliance
Lightning Source LLC
Chambersburg PA
CBHW020557120726
47903CB00001B/290